FOAM of the PAST

SELECTED WRITINGS OF FIONA MACLEOD

EDITED BY STEVE BLAMIRES

SKYLIGHT
PRESS

First published in Great Britain in 2014 by Skylight Press,
210 Brooklyn Road, Cheltenham, Glos GL51 8EA

Designed and typeset by Rebsie Fairholm
Publisher: Daniel Staniforth
Thistle roundel originally designed by John Duncan
Cover artwork based on a texture image by Sascha Duensing and photo of
St Columba's Bay, Iona, by Torsten Henning.

www.skylightpress.co.uk

Printed and bound in Great Britain by Lightning Source, Milton Keynes

Typeset in Arlt, a font by PampaType. Titles set in Estonia NouveauPro,
Cal Insular Miniscule and Hedgerow.

British Library Cataloguing in Publication Data:
A catalogue record for this book is available from the British Library.

ISBN 978-1-908011-73-2

Dedicated
to
J.
Mo Leannan

Fiona Macleod

CONTENTS

William Sharp

After an Etching by William Strang A.R.A.

INTRODUCTION

Fiona Macleod was a prolific writer. In a period of less than thirteen years she produced two full length novels, scores of short stories, dozens of essays, well over a hundred poems, two stage plays and regularly contributed articles to more than twenty-five magazines on both sides of the Atlantic. Her writings were immensely popular with the Victorian book-buying public, resulting in several offers of marriage and fan mail that produced over a thousand letters from her, many of which still survive today. When she died in 1905 she left behind much unpublished and unfinished material including at least one more stage play, a full length novel, as well as dozens of fragments of stories, essays and magazine articles. She was listed in the important social directory *Who's Who* for the last six years of her life and was the subject of many scholarly discourses in various literary publications. Her play *The Immortal Hour* was set to music by the English composer Rutland Boughton and still holds the record for the opera with the most continuous performances ever. All of these are remarkable feats in themselves but are made all the more remarkable by the fact that Fiona Macleod never existed.

All the writings attributed to her were penned by the art and literary critic William Sharp (1855-1905) who was a prolific writer in his own right. The strain of this double workload and double identity brought about his early death at the age of fifty. Perhaps his greatest literary creation though was the name – Fiona Macleod. The surname is common enough. As a child William had a nurse called Barbara Macleod and he befriended an old fisherman in the Hebrides by the name of Seumas Macleod. His early exposure to these Gaelic-speaking Highlanders (William's family were English-speaking Lowlanders) and listening to the old, strange tales that they told him, greatly influenced the material that he would later produce under the Fiona Macleod name.

But the personal name Fiona was his creation. It did not exist prior to 1893. He never explained where it came from or how he came up with it. His widow, Elizabeth Sharp, once commented after his death that, "The name flashed ready-made into my husband's mind." Perhaps it did – but there is an oral tradition in the area where Fiona allegedly came from that William Sharp took the name of his favourite island, Iona, and coupled it with the name of the great hero of early Celtic myth, Fionn MaCumhail, to produce 'Fiona'. The popularity of Fiona Macleod's books is shown by the fact that today in the English and Gaelic-speaking worlds the name Fiona has become very common. Victorian parents were christening their baby girls with this new and attractive name, just as parents today name their children after current film-stars, rock-musicians and authors. Other explanations of how he may have come up with this Gaelic-sounding name, and why, are dealt with at length in my biography of William Sharp, *The Little Book of the Great Enchantment* (2008).

After he died and the true identity of this secretive and alluring Highland lady was revealed, the public lost interest in her books and they soon went out of print. The name Fiona Macleod was all but forgotten. In 1911 William's widow Elizabeth published a biography of her late husband. It is a large volume but reads more like a social diary than a biography and says very little about the creation of Fiona Macleod and how William dealt with all the complications and difficulties this brought with it. Since then there has been very little else written on either writer but in the past two decades Fiona has been rediscovered by the present-day book buying public and her out of print volumes are changing hands for steadily increasing prices.

In 2008 I published my biography of William Sharp and in 2012 I followed this with *The Chronicles of the Sidhe*, being an interpretation of some of Fiona Macleod's prose, poetry and plays that deal with the popular but much misunderstood Highland and Gaelic belief in the Sidhe, or as it is given in English, the Faeries. This present volume is an anthology of some of her more important, curious and obscure pieces, annotated and explained where necessary, covering various periods of her writing and the changing subjects of those periods. As you read your way through the selection you will notice that many of them deal with dark subjects – madness, death, extreme loneliness and isolation, a constant struggle to survive especially against the ocean. Why, then, were these stories so popular with the Victorian gentleladies and gentlemen who snapped up each new volume as it was released? The answer is that in the mid to late 19th century the Scottish Highlands and Islands were to all intents and purposes a foreign country. They might as well have been in darkest Africa. They were hard to get to even with the coming of the railway and difficult to negotiate once there. The majority of the people spoke only Gaelic and had no knowledge of the English language or, indeed, English habits, customs or mores.

But Fiona Macleod was clearly a gentlelady of breeding and intellect. She could be trusted. She was almost 'one of us' – but not quite. It was this slight difference that allowed her to deal with dark and frightening characters and subjects in a way that gave them the glamour of the Celtic Otherworld in an intriguing and believable manner. She was not threatening or dangerous in herself and she opened up a whole new world of language, ancient songs, poems and proverbs that had never before been presented to the English-speaking peoples south of the Scottish Highlands. Her subjects were taboo for other writers but she dealt with them in such a matter-of-fact way they came across as completely normal and routine. This somewhat disturbing treatment gave them an edge, an excitement, which was captured in her eloquence and strong use of dialogue.

In amongst all the frequent darkness and gloom she managed to produce paragraph after paragraph, chapter after chapter, of minutely detailed and vivid descriptions of the world of nature, the 'green world' as she called it, in which her characters moved and lived. She dealt with some familiar historical personages as well such as St Columba of Iona of whom there are many legends. But she recounted tale after tale of this 6th century cleric that had never been heard before or recorded anywhere else. She managed to weave a golden thread through the extensive corpus of Celtic mythology by relating authentic sounding tales of characters, human and godly, that had never been named before but who fit comfortably with the ancient Celtic idiom, motifs and beliefs. She brought up the delicate subject of the Highlanders' easy mixing of the Christian and pre-Christian beliefs - despite the protestations of the Church - and revealed several beautiful tales of the Christ child that do not appear in the Bible or in the accepted canon.

For a brief period she got caught up in the whole fin-de-siècle 'Celtic Twilight' movement and ventured a couple of political essays dealing with the hot-topic of Irish nationalism and independence but quickly distanced herself from both when she realized that all it produced were fruitless and continuous arguments on a subject she had no real heart for. I reproduce two of these in this current anthology as examples of her non-fiction writing and as documents that reflect the fierce passions of the time, but it should be noted than none of her other writings contain any references to current events or, indeed, references to anything that gives them an identifiable date. In this way they are truly timeless.

I have not included her first two publications, *Pharais: A Romance of the Isles* (1894) and *The Mountain Lovers* (1895), as they are both full length novels and their subject matter deals with the same issues that she went on to write about at length for the next eleven years. Some years after their publication Fiona commented in a private letter dated

May 4th 1900 to the Celtic scholar Ernest Rhys, "They are books that I look sometimes at with dread... Can you understand that when *Pharais* was published I would have given anything to recall it, partly because of the too much suffering there expressed, but mainly because of that 'Cry of Women,' which nevertheless had brought so many strange and sorrowful letters, and made many unexpected friends." Like many writers and artists she was never satisfied with the finished work.

Also omitted from this anthology are her two published plays, *The House of Usna* and *The Immortal Hour*, as the first of these is a rather uninspired retelling of an old Irish tale and the second, a much more important piece, is dealt with at length in my book *The Little Book of the Great Enchantment*. Both were first published in 1900 in the magazine *Fortnightly Review*. *The House of Usna* was originally entitled *The King of Ireland's Son* but was later changed to its current name. It was produced at The Globe Theatre, London on April 29th 1900 under William Sharp's direction.

It should be noted that many of Fiona Macleod's writings first appeared in various British and American magazines and were later collected into volumes and published as independent books. Many of these versions differ slightly from their magazine originals and some were altered quite substantially by Fiona Macleod. When they were later collected together again and published by Sharp's widow in the seven volume set *The Collected Works of Fiona Macleod* (1911) they were subject to further alteration and editing according to the directions left by her late husband. The versions I give here are mainly the ones to be found in the Collected Works series as these are the most easily found today.

Steve Blamires
Beacon, NY
March 2014

Section One

EARLY DARK TALES

EARLY DARK TALES

The first two Fiona Macleod books were full length novels, *Pharais: A Romance of the Isles* and *The Mountain Lovers*, and they were to define Fiona's style and topics for the next four or five years. Most of these early tales were dark, brooding and, in a few cases, horrific. Their common themes were:

- tales often start with a paragraph or two from Fiona detailing where she was when she first heard the tale and who it was that related it to her. Alleging that the tale had been told to her by a third party was a device she used throughout her career that helped maintain the fantasy that she was a real person with a history, family, acquaintances etc. Naming all these third parties, each of whom had a strange, disturbing or frightening tale to tell, also helped maintain the mystery and slightly threatening aspect to the Scottish Highlands and Islands.

- the sea, lakes, rivers and boats frequently crop up, often in a dark and foreboding manner.

- long silences. Fiona used this device to instil a sense of the slow passing of time, the tedium and at times despair of life in the islands where many of her stories are set.

- English dialogue written in the Gaelic idiom. This device added authenticity and colour to the prose and, again, reminded her readers that her characters not only lived in a different place but also spoke a foreign language.

- Gaelic personal and place names with double meanings. Many words in the Gaelic, including personal and family names, have more than one meaning. Understanding these deliberate puns often opens up a deeper aspect to the story. I have given translations where necessary to explain these double meanings.

- a liberal sprinkling of allegedly ancient Gaelic songs, runes, proverbs and curses. These Gaelic sayings and proverbs helped remind the English-speaking reader that the Gaelic-speaking Gael is part of a separate race that sees the world and all it contains in a very different manner from the Southerners.

- the tragedy of love. Fiona wrote often of love but it was rarely happy.

- a mixing of names of people and places that exist with people and places that don't exist. This is a complex issue that I deal with in my book *The Chronicles of the Sidhe*.

⦿ many of the shorter tales are mere vignettes, glimpses at one or two incidents she learned of in her travels, and are by no means complete stories in themselves.

The first two tales in this section, *The Sin-Eater* and *The Dark Nameless One* are taken from the collection of short stories called *The Sin-Eater*, published in 1895, and the third tale, *Dalua*, is from the collection called *The Dominion of Dreams*, published in 1899.

The Sin-Eater contains all of the elements listed above and is one of her darkest stories. It reflects a folk-custom that carried on well into the 20th century – the belief that the sins of a person could be transferred to another person and thereby ensure the happiness of the deceased in the Afterlife. There were certain conditions that had to be met in order to ensure the sins transferred successfully and, more importantly, that the Sin-Eater would eventually be absolved of those sins and become free of their burden. This tale spells out clearly what can happen if those conditions are violated. The tiny island of Iona features in this opening story and is the setting for many of Fiona's tales. William Sharp was a frequent visitor to this sacred island and spent extended periods there where he composed many of Fiona Macleod's tales and poems.

The Dark Nameless One is centred on the old folk tales of the seal that was once a man and whose offspring walk the earth in human form. St Columba is introduced in this tale and, like Iona, his home, Columba is a character who appears frequently in her earlier tales. But the events of his life and the actions she describes the 6th century holy man as doing are not to be found in his hagiography or in the many commentaries on Columba's life that have been penned since the 7th century. This is just a short vignette revealing the underlying fear and danger in which the islanders lived despite the achingly beautiful environment in which they lived and worked.

The dark and menacing title character Dalua in the final tale of this section is not an ancient Celtic god despite Fiona's frequent comments that he is. He is the creation of her mind alone and will not be found in any of the enormous corpus of Celtic mythology from any of the Celtic countries. Yet she speaks of him with such conviction and consistency that you cannot help but feel he was (is?) indeed a dark god of the Celtic world that time has somehow forgotten. I deal with Dalua at length in my books *The Little Book of the Great Enchantment* and *The Chronicles of the Sidhe*.

The Sin-Eater

A wet wind out of the south mazed and moaned through the sea-mist that hung over the Ross. In all the bays and creeks was a continuous weary lapping of water. There was no other sound anywhere.

Thus was it at daybreak; it was thus at noon; thus was it now in the darkening of the day. A confused thrusting and falling of sounds through the silence betokened the hour of the setting. Curlews wailed in the mist; on the seething limpet-covered rocks the skuas and terns screamed, or uttered hoarse rasping cries. Ever and again the prolonged note of the oyster-catcher shrilled against the air, as an echo flying blindly along a blank wall of cliff. Out of weedy places, wherein the tide sobbed with long gurgling moans, came at intervals the barking of a seal.

Inland by the hamlet of Contullich[1], there is a reedy tarn called the Loch-a-chaoruinn[2]. By the shores of this mournful water a man moved. It was a slow, weary walk that of the man Neil Ross. He had come from Duninch, thirty miles to the eastward, and had not rested foot, nor eaten, nor had word of man or woman since his going west an hour after dawn.

At the bend of the loch nearest the clachan[3] he came upon an old woman carrying peat. To his reiterated question as to where he was, and if the tarn were Feur-Lochan above Fionnaphort, that is, on the strait of Iona on the west side of the Ross of Mull, she did not at first make any answer. The rain trickled down her withered brown face, over which the thin grey locks hung limply. It was only in the deep-set eyes that the flame of life still glimmered, though that dimly.

The man had used the English when first he spoke, but as though mechanically. Supposing that he had not been understood, he repeated his question in the Gaelic.

After a minute's silence the old woman answered in the native tongue, but only to put a question in return. "I am thinking it is a long time since you have been in Iona?"

The man stirred uneasily. "And why is that, mother?" he asked, in a weak voice hoarse with damp and fatigue; "how is it you will be knowing that I have been in Iona at all?"

---

1   Contullich i.e. Ceann-nan-tulaich - the end of the hillocks.
2   Loch-a-chaoruinn - the loch of the rowan-trees.
3   Clachan literally means 'stones' but refers to a small grouping of crofts or houses.

"Because I knew your kith and kin there, Neil Ross."

"I have not been hearing that name, mother, for many a long year. And as for the old face o' you, it is unbeknown to me."

"I was at the naming of you, for all that. Well do I remember the day that Silis Macallum gave you birth; and I was at the house on the croft of Ballyrona[4] when Murtagh Ross, that was your father, laughed. It was an ill laughing that."

"I am knowing it. The curse of God on him!"

"'Tis not the first, nor the last, though the grass is on his head three years agone now."

"You that know who I am will be knowing that I have no kith or kin now on Iona?"

"Ay, they are all under grey stone or running wave. Donald your brother, and Murtagh your next brother, and little Silis, and your mother Silis herself and your two brothers of your father, Angus and Ian Macallum, and your father Murtagh Ross, and his lawful childless wife Dionaid, and his sister Anna one and all they lie beneath the green wave or in the brown mould. It is said there is a curse upon all who live at Ballyrona. The owl builds now in the rafters, and it is the big sea-rat that runs across the fireless hearth."

"It is there I am going."

"The foolishness is on you, Neil Ross."

"Now it is that I am knowing who you are. It is old Sheen Macarthur I am speaking to."

"Tha mise ... it is I."

"And you will be alone now, too, I am thinking, Sheen?"

"I am alone. God took my three boys at the one fishing ten years ago, and before there was moonrise in the blackness of my heart my man went. It was after the drowning of Anndra that my croft was taken from me. Then I crossed the Sound, and shared with my widow sister, Elsie McVurie, till *she* went; and then the two cows had to go; and I had no rent; and was old."

In the silence that followed, the rain dribbled from the sodden bracken and dripping loneroid. Big tears rolled slowly down the deep lines on the face of Sheen. Once there was a sob in her throat, but she put her shaking hand to it, and it was still.

Neil Ross shifted from foot to foot. The ooze in that marshy place squelched with each restless movement he made. Beyond them a plover

---

4   Ballyrona - the village of the seals.

wheeled a blurred splatch in the mist, crying its mournful cry over and over and over.

It was a pitiful thing to hear; ah, bitter loneliness, bitter patience of poor old women. That he knew well. But he was too weary, and his heart was nigh full of its own burthen. The words could not come to his lips. But at last he spoke. "Tha mo chridhe goirt," he said with tears in his voice, as he put his hand on her bent shoulder; "my heart is sore."

She put up her old face against his. "'S tha e ruidhinit mo chridhe," she whispered — "it is touching my heart you are."

After that they walked on slowly through the dripping mist, each dumb and brooding deep.

"Where will you be staying this night?" asked Sheen suddenly, when they had traversed a wide boggy stretch of land; adding, as by an afterthought — "ah, it is asking you were if the tarn there was Feur-Lochan. No; it is Loch-a-chaoruinn, and the clachan that is near is Contullich."

"Which way?"

"Yonder; to the right."

"And you are not going there?"

"No. I am going to the steading of Andrew Blair. Maybe you are for knowing it? It is called the Baile-na-Chlais-nambuid-heag."[5]

"I do not remember. But it is remembering a Blair I am. He was Adam the son of Adam the son of Robert. He and my father did many an ill deed together."

"Ay, to the Stones be it said. Sure, now, there was even till this weary day no man or woman who had a good word for Adam Blair."

"And why that — why till this day?"

"It is not yet the third hour since he went into the silence."

Neil Ross uttered a sound like a stifled curse. For a time he trudged wearily on.

"Then I am too late," he said at last, but as though speaking to himself. "I had hoped to see him face to face again, and curse him between the eyes. It was he who made Murtagh Ross break his troth to my mother, and marry that other woman, barren at that, God be praised! And they say ill of him, do they?"

"Ay, it is evil that is upon him. This crime and that, God knows: and the shadow of murder on his brow and in his eyes. Well, well, 'tis ill to be speaking of a man in corpse, and that near by. 'Tis Himself only that knows, Neil Ross."

---

5   Baile-na-Chlais-nambuid-heag - the farm in the hollow of the yellow flowers.

"Maybe ay, and maybe no. But where is it that I can be sleeping this night, Sheen Macarthur?"

"They will not be taking a stranger at the farm this night of the nights, I am thinking. There is no place else, for seven miles yet, when there is the clachan before you will be coming to Fionnaphort. There is the warm byre, Neil my man, or if you can bide by my peats you may rest and welcome, though there is no bed for you, and no food either save some of the porridge that is over."

"And that will do well enough for me, Sheen, and Himself bless you for it."

And so it was.

After old Sheen Macarthur had given the wayfarer food — poor food at that, but welcome to one nigh starved, and for the heartsome way it was given, and because of the thanks to God that was upon it before even spoon was lifted — she told him a lie. It was the good lie of tender love.

"Sure now, after all, Neil my man," she said, "it is sleeping at the farm I ought to be, for Maisie Macdonald, the wise-woman, will be sitting by the corpse, and there will be none to keep her company. It is there I must be going, and if I am weary, there is a good bed for me just beyond the dead-board, which I am not minding at all. So if it is tired you are sitting by the peats, lie down on my bed there, and have the sleep, and God be with you."

With that she went, and soundlessly, for Neil Ross was already asleep, where he sat on an upturned *claar*[6] with his elbows on his knees and his flame-lit face in his hands. The rain had ceased; but the mist still hung over the land, though in thin veils now, and these slowly drifting seaward. Sheen stepped wearily along the stony path that led from her bothy to the farm-house. She stood still once, the fear upon her, for she saw three or four blurred yellow gleams moving beyond her eastward along the dyke. She knew what they were — the corpse-lights that on the night of death go between the bier and the place of burial. More than once she had seen them before the last hour, and by that token had known the end to be near.

Good Catholic that she was, she crossed herself and took heart. Then, muttering—

"Crois nan naoi aingeal leam
'O mhullach mo chinn

---

6   claar - traditional wooden bucket.

Gu craican mo bhonn."
The cross of the nine angels be about me,
From the top of my head
To the soles of my feet.
— she went on her way fearlessly.

When she came to the White House she entered by the milk-shed that was between the byre and the kitchen. At the end of it was a paved place, with washing-tubs. At one of these stood a girl that served in the house; an ignorant lass called Jessie McFall, out of Oban. She was ignorant, indeed, not to know that to wash clothes with a newly dead body near by was an ill thing to do. Was it not a matter for the knowing that the corpse could hear, and might rise up in the night and clothe itself in a clean white shroud? She was still speaking to the lassie when Maisie Macdonald, the deid-watcher, opened the door of the room behind the kitchen, to see who it was that was come. The two old women nodded silently. It was not till Sheen was in the closed room, midway in which something covered with a sheet lay on a board, that any word was spoken.

"Duit sìth mòr, Beann Macdonald."

"And deep peace to you, too, Sheen; and to him that is there."

"Och, ochone, mise 'n diugh; 'tis a dark hour this."

"Ay, it is bad. Will you have been hearing or seeing anything?"

"Well, as for that, I am thinking I saw lights moving betwixt here and the green place over there."

"The corpse-lights?"

"Well, it is calling them that they are."

"I *thought* they would be out. And I have been hearing the noise of the planks — the cracking of the boards, you know, that will be used for the coffin tomorrow."

A long silence followed. The old women had seated themselves by the corpse, their cloaks over their heads. The room was fireless, and was lit only by a tall wax death-candle, kept against the hour of the going. At last Sheen began swaying slowly to and fro, crooning low the while.

"I would not be for doing that, Sheen Macarthur," said the deid-watcher, in a low voice, but meaningly; adding, after a moment's pause, "*the mice have all left the house.*"

Sheen sat upright, a look half of terror, half of awe in her eyes. "God save the sinful soul that is hiding," she whispered.

Well she knew what Maisie meant. If the soul of the dead be a lost soul it knows its doom. The house of death is the house of sanctuary. But before the dawn that follows the death-night the soul must go forth, whosoever or whatsoever wait for it in the homeless, shelterless plains of air around and beyond. If it be well with the soul, it need have no fear; if it be not ill with the soul, it may fare forth with surety; but if it be ill with the soul, ill will the going be. Thus is it that the spirit of an evil man cannot stay and yet dare not go; and so it strives to hide itself in secret places anywhere, in dark channels and blind walls. And the wise creatures that live near man smell the terror, and flee. Maisie repeated the saying of Sheen; then, after a silence, added:

"Adam Blair will not lie in his grave for a year and a day, because of the sins that are upon him. And it is knowing that, they are, here. He will be the Watcher of the Dead for a year and a day."

"Ay, sure, there will be dark prints in the dawn-dew over yonder."

Once more the old women relapsed into silence. Through the night there was a sighing sound. It was not the sea, which was too far off to be heard save in a day of storm. The wind it was, that was dragging itself across the sodden moors like a wounded thing, moaning and sighing.

Out of sheer weariness, Sheen twice rocked forward from her stool, heavy with sleep. At last Maisie led her over to the niche-bed opposite, and laid her down there, and waited till the deep furrows in the face relaxed somewhat, and the thin breath laboured slow across the fallen jaw.

"Poor old woman," she muttered, heedless of her own grey hairs and greyer years; "bitter bad thing it is to be old, old and weary. 'Tis the sorrow that; God keep the pain of it."

As for herself she did not sleep at all that night, but sat between the living and the dead, with her plaid shrouding her. Once, when Sheen gave a low, terrified scream in her sleep, she rose, and in a loud voice cried "Sheeach-ad! Away with you!" And with that she lifted the shroud from the dead man, and took the pennies off the eyelids, and lifted each lid; then, staring into these filmed wells, muttered an ancient incantation that would compel the soul of Adam Blair to leave the spirit of Sheen alone, and return to the cold corpse that was its coffin till the wood was ready.

The dawn came at last. Sheen slept, and Adam Blair slept a deeper sleep, and Maisie stared out of her wan weary eyes against the red and stormy flares of light that came into the sky.

When, an hour after sunrise, Sheen Macarthur reached her bothy, she found Neil Ross, heavy with slumber, upon her bed. The fire was not out, though no flame or spark was visible, but she stooped and blew at the heart of the peats till the redness came, and once it came it grew.

Having done this, she kneeled and said a rune of the morning, and after that a prayer, and then a prayer for the poor man Neil. She could pray no more because of the tears. She rose and put the meal and water into the pot, for the porridge to be ready against his awaking. One of the hens that was there came and pecked at her ragged skirt. "Poor beastie," she said, "sure, that will just be the way I am pulling at the white robe of the Mother o' God. 'Tis a bit meal for you, cluckie, and for me a heating hand upon my tears — *O, och, ochone,* the tears, the tears!"

It was not till the third hour after sunrise of that bleak day in the winter of the winters that Neil Ross stirred and arose. He ate in silence. Once he said that he smelled the snow coming out of the north. Sheen said no word at all. After the porridge, he took his pipe, but there was no tobacco. All that Sheen had was the pipeful she kept against the gloom of the Sabbath. It was her one solace in the long weary week. She gave him this, and held a burning peat to his mouth, and hungered over the thin, rank smoke that curled upward.

It was within half an hour of noon that, after an absence, she returned. "Not between you and me, Neil Ross," she began abruptly, "but just for the asking, and what is beyond. Is it any money you are having upon you?"

"No."

"Nothing?"

"Nothing."

"Then how will you be getting across to Iona? It is seven long miles to Fionnaphort, and bitter cold at that, and you will be needing food, and then the ferry, the ferry across the Sound, you know."

"Ay, I know."

"What would you do for a silver piece, Neil my man?"

"You have none to give me, Sheen Macarthur. And if you had, it would not be taking it I would."

"Would you kiss a dead man for a crown-piece — a crown-piece of five good shillings?"

Neil Ross stared. Then he sprang to his feet. "It is Adam Blair you are meaning, woman! God curse him in death now that he is no longer in life!"

Then, shaking and trembling, he sat down again, and brooded against the dull red glow of the peats. But, when he rose, in the last quarter before noon, his face was white. "The dead are dead, Sheen Macarthur. They can know or do nothing. I will do it. It is willed. Yes, I am going up to the house there. And now I am going from here. God Himself has my thanks to you, and my blessing too. They will come back to you. It is not forgetting you I will be. Good-bye."

"Good-bye, Neil, son of the woman that was my friend. A south wind to you! Go up by the farm. In the front of the house you will see what you will be seeing. Maisie Macdonald will be there. She will tell you what's for the telling. There is no harm in it, sure: sure, the dead are dead. It is praying for you I will be, Neil Ross. Peace to you!"

"And to you, Sheen."

And with that the man went.

When Neil Ross reached the byres of the farm in the wide hollow, he saw two figures standing as though awaiting him, but each alone and unseen of the other. In front of the house was a man he knew to be Andrew Blair; behind the milk-shed was a woman he guessed to be Maisie Macdonald. It was the woman he came upon first.

"Are you the friend of Sheen Macarthur?" she asked in a whisper, as she beckoned him to the doorway.

"I am."

"I am knowing no names, or anything. And no one here will know you, I am thinking. So do the thing, and be gone."

"There is no harm to it?"

"None."

"It will be a thing often done, is it not?"

"Ay, sure."

"And the evil does not abide?"

"No. The — the — person — the person takes them away, and —"

"*Them?*"

"For sure, man! Them — the sins of the corpse. He takes them away, and are you for thinking God would let the innocent suffer for the guilty? No — the person — the Sin-Eater, you know — takes them away on himself, and one by one the air of heaven washes them away till he, the Sin-Eater, is clean and whole as before."

"But if it is a man you hate — if it is a corpse that is the corpse of one who has been a curse and a foe — if —"

"*Sst!* Be still now with your foolishness. It is only an idle saying, I am thinking. Do it, and take the money, and go. It will be hell enough for Adam Blair, miser as he was, if he is for knowing that five good shillings of his money are to go to a passing tramp, because of an old ancient silly tale."

Neil Ross laughed low at that. It was for pleasure to him.

"Hush wi' ye! Andrew Blair is waiting round there. Say that I have sent you round, as I have neither bite nor bit to give."

Turning on his heel Neil walked slowly round to the front of the house. A tall man was there, gaunt and brown with hairless face and lank brown hair, but with eyes cold and grey as the sea.

"Good day to you an' good faring. Will you be passing this way to anywhere?"

"Health to you. I am a stranger here. It is on my way to Iona I am. But I have the hunger upon me. There is not a brown bit in my pocket. I asked at the door there, near the byres. The woman told me she could give me nothing — not a penny even, worse luck — nor, for that, a drink of warm milk. 'Tis a sore land this."

"You have the Gaelic of the Isles. Is it from Iona you are?"

"It is from the Isles of the West I come."

"From Tiree? ... from Coll?"

"No."

"From the Long Island ... or from Uist ... maybe from Benbecula?"

"No."

"Oh well, sure it is no matter to me. But may I be asking your name?"

"Macallum."

"Do you know there is a death here, Macallum?"

"If I didn't, I would know it now, because of what lies yonder."

Mechanically, Andrew Blair looked round. As he knew, a rough bier was there, that was made of a dead-board laid upon three milking-stools. Beside it was a *claar*, a small tub to hold potatoes. On the bier was a corpse, covered with a canvas sheeting that looked like a sail.

"He was a worthy man, my father," began the son of the dead man, slowly; "but he had his faults, like all of us. I might even be saying that he had his sins, to the Stones be it said. You will be knowing, Macallum, what is thought among the folk — that a stranger, passing by, may take away the sins of the dead, and that too without any hurt whatever — any hurt whatever."

"Ay, sure."

"And you will be knowing what is done?"

"Ay."

"With the Bread ... and the Water ..."

"Ay."

"It is a small thing to do. It is a Christian thing. I would be doing it myself, and that gladly; but the — the — passer-by who — "

"It is talking of the Sin-Eater you are?"

"Yes, yes, for sure. The Sin-Eater as he is called — and a good Christian act it is, for all that the ministers and the priests make a frowning at it — the Sin-Eater must be a stranger. He must be a stranger, and should know nothing of the dead man, above all bear him no grudge."

At that, Neil Ross's eyes lightened for a moment. "And why that?"

"Who knows? I have heard this, and I have heard that. If the Sin-Eater was hating the dead man he could take the sins and fling them into the sea and they would be changed into demons of the air that would harry the flying soul till Judgment Day."

"And how would that thing be done?"

The man spake with flashing eyes and parted lips, the breath coming swift. Andrew Blair looked at him suspiciously, and hesitated, before in a cold voice he spoke again. "That is all folly, I am thinking, Macallum. Maybe it is all folly, the whole of it. But see here, I have no time to be talking with you. If you will take the bread and the water you shall have a good meal if you want it, and — and — yes, look you, my man, I will be giving you a shilling too, for luck."

"I will have no meal in this house, Anndra mhic Adam; nor will I do this thing unless you will be giving me two silver half-crowns. That is the sum I must have, or no other."

"Two half-crowns! Why, man, for one half-crown —"

"Then be eating the sins o' your father yourself, Andrew Blair! It is going I am."

"Stop, man! Stop, Macallum. See here: I will be giving you what you ask."

"So be it. Is the — are you ready?

"Ay, come this way."

With that the two men turned, and moved slowly toward the bier. In the doorway of the house stood a man and two women; farther in, a woman; and at the window to the left the serving-wench, Jessie McFall, and two men of the farm. Of those in the doorway, the man was Peter, the half-witted youngest brother of Andrew Blair; the taller and older woman was Catreen, the widow of Adam the second brother; and the thin slight woman, with staring eyes and drooping month, was Muireall, the wife of Andrew. The old woman, behind these, was Maisie Macdonald.

Andrew Blair stooped and took a saucer out of the *claar*. This he put upon the covered breast of the corpse. He stooped again and brought forth a thick square piece of new made bread. That also he placed upon the breast of the corpse. Then he stooped again, and with that he emptied a spoonful of salt alongside the bread.

"I must see the corpse," said Neil Ross, simply.

"It is not needful, Macallum."

"I must be seeing the corpse, I tell you and for that, too, the bread and the water should be on the naked breast."

"No, no, man, it —"

But here a voice, that of Maisie the wise-woman, came upon them, saying that the man was right, and that the eating of the sins should be done in that way and no other. With an ill grace the son of the dead man drew back the sheeting. Beneath it the corpse was in a clean white shirt, a death-gown long ago prepared, that covered him from his neck to his feet, and left only the dusky, yellowish face exposed. While Andrew Blair unfastened the shirt, and placed the saucer and the bread and the salt on the breast, the man beside him stood staring fixedly on the frozen features of the corpse. The new laird had to speak to him twice before he heard.

"I am ready. And you, now? What is it you are muttering over against the lips of the dead?"

"It is giving him a message I am. There is no harm in that, sure?"

"Keep to your own folk, Macallum. You are from the West you say, and we are from the North. There can be no messages between you and a Blair of Strathmore, no messages for *you* to be giving."

"He that lies here knows well the man to whom I am sending a message —" and at this response Andrew Blair scowled darkly. He would fain have sent the man about his business, but he feared he might get no other.

"It is thinking I am that you are not a Macallum at all. I know all of that name in Mull, Iona, Skye, and the near isles. What will the name of your naming be, and of your father, and of his place?"

Whether he really wanted an answer, or whether he sought only to divert the man from his procrastination, his question had a satisfactory result.

"Well, now, it's ready I am, Anndra mhic Adam."

With that, Andrew Blair stooped once more, and from the *claar* brought a small jug of water. From this he filled the saucer. "You know what to say and what to do, Macallum."

There was not one there who did not have a shortened breath because of the mystery that was now before them, and the fearfulness of it. Neil Ross drew himself up, erect, stiff, with white, drawn face. All who waited, save Andrew Blair, thought that the moving of his lips was because of the prayer that was slipping upon them, like the last lapsing of the ebb-tide. But Blair was watching him closely, and knew that it was no prayer which stole out against the blank air that was around the dead. Slowly Neil Ross extended his right arm. He took a pinch of the salt and put it in the saucer, then took another pinch and sprinkled it upon the bread. His hand shook for a moment as he touched the saucer. But there was no shaking as he raised it toward his lips, or when he held it before him when he spoke.

"With this water that has salt in it, and has lain on thy corpse, O Adam mhic Anndra mhic Adam Mòr, I drink away all the evil that is upon thee."

There was throbbing silence while he paused.

"... And may it be upon me, and not upon thee, if with this water it cannot flow away."

Thereupon he raised the saucer and passed it thrice round the head of the corpse sunways, and having done this, lifted it to his lips and drank as much as his mouth would hold. Thereafter he poured the remnant over his left hand, and let it trickle to the ground. Then he took the piece of bread. Thrice, too, he passed it round the head of the corpse sunways. He turned and looked at the man by his side, then at the others who watched him with beating hearts. With a loud clear voice he took the sins.

"Thoir dhomh do ciontachd, O Adam mhic Anndra mhic Adam Mòr! Give me thy sins to take away from thee! Lo, now, as I stand here, I break this bread that has lain on thee in corpse, and I am eating it, I am, and in that eating I take upon me the sins of thee, O man that was alive and is now white with the stillness!"

Thereupon Neil Ross broke the bread and ate of it, and took upon himself the sins of Adam Blair that was dead. It was a bitter swallowing, that. The remainder of the bread he crumbled in his hand, and threw it on the ground, and trod upon it. Andrew Blair gave a sigh of relief. His cold eyes lightened with malice.

"Be off with you, now, Macallum. We are wanting no tramps at the farm here, and perhaps you had better not be trying to get work this side Iona, for it is known as the Sin-Eater you will be, and that won't be for the helping, I am thinking! There: there are the two half-crowns for you ... and may they bring you no harm, you that are *Scapegoat* now!"

The Sin-Eater turned at that, and stared like a hill-bull. *Scapegoat!* Ay, that's what he was. Sin-Eater, scapegoat! Was he not, too, another Judas, to have sold for silver that which was not for the selling? No, no, for sure Maisie Macdonald could tell him the rune that would serve for

26

the easing of this burden. He would soon be quit of it. Slowly he took the money, turned it over, and put it in his pocket.

"I am going, Andrew Blair," he said quietly; "I am going, now. I will not say to him that is there in the silence, *'A chuid do Pharas da!'*[7] — nor will I say to you, *'Gu'n gleidheadh Dia thu'*[8] — nor will I say to this dwelling that is the home of thee and thine, *'Gu'n beannaicheadh Dia an tigh!'*"[9]

Here there was a pause. All listened. Andrew Blair shifted uneasily, the furtive eyes of him going this way and that like a ferret in the grass.

"But, Andrew Blair, I will say this; when you fare abroad, *Droch caoidh ort!*[10] and when you go upon the water, *Gaoth gun direadh ort!*[11] Ay, ay, Anndra mhic Adam, *Dia ad aghaidh 's ad aodann — agus bas dunach ort! Dhonas 's dholas ort, agus leat-sa!*"[12]

The bitterness of these words was like snow in June upon all there. They stood amazed. None spoke. No one moved.

Neil Ross turned upon his heel, and with a bright light in his eyes walked away from the dead and the living. He went by the byres, whence he had come. Andrew Blair remained where he was, now grooming at the corpse, now biting his nails and staring at the damp sods at his feet.

When Neil reached the end of the milk-shed he saw Maisie Macdonald there, waiting.

"These were ill sayings of yours, Neil Ross," she said in a low voice, so that she might not be overheard from the house.

"So, it is knowing me you are."

"Sheen Macarthur told me."

"I have good cause."

"That is a true word. I know it."

"Tell me this thing. What is the rune that is said for the throwing into the sea of the sins of the dead? See here, Maisie Macdonald. There is no money of that man that I would carry a mile with me. Here it is. It is yours, if you will tell me that rune."

Maisie took the money hesitatingly. Then, stooping, she said slowly the few lines of the old, old rune. "Will you be remembering that?"

---

7 'his share of heaven be his.'
8 'may God preserve you.'
9 'God's blessing on this house.'
10 Literally means 'bad moan on you' but implies 'may a fatal accident happen to you.'
11 Literally means 'wind without direction on you', but implies 'may you drift to your drowning.'
12 'God against thee and in thy face - and may a death of woe be yours. Evil and sorrow to thee and thine!'

"It is not forgetting it I will be, Maisie."

"Wait a moment. There is some warm milk here."

With that she went, and then, from within, beckoned to him to enter. "There is no one here, Neil Ross. Drink the milk."

He drank: and while he did so she drew a leather pouch from some hidden place in her dress.

"And now I have this to give you." She counted out ten pennies and two farthings. "It is all the coppers I have. You are welcome to them. Take them, friend of my friend. They will give you the food you need, and the ferry across the Sound."

"I will do that, Maisie Macdonald, and thanks to you. It is not forgetting it I will be, nor you, good woman. And now, tell me: Is it safe that I am? He called me a 'scapegoat', he, Andrew Blair! Can evil touch me between this and the sea?"

"You must go to the place where the evil was done to you and yours; and that, I know, is on the west side of Iona. Go, and God preserve you. But here, too, is a *sian*[13] that will be for the safety."

Thereupon with swift mutterings she said this charm: an old, familiar *sian* against Sudden Harm:

"Sian a chuir Moire air Mac ort,
  Sian ro' marbhadh, sian ro' lot ort,
  Sian eadar a' chlioch 's a' ghlun,
  Sian nan Tri ann an aon ort,
  O mhullach do chinn gu bonn do choi ort:
  Sian seachd eadar a h-aon ort,
  Sian seachd eadar a dha ort,
  Sian seachd eadar a tri ort,
  Sian seachd eadar a ceithir ort,
  Sian seachd eadar a coig ort,
  Sian seachd eadar a sia ort,
  Sian seachd paidir nan seach paidir dol deiseil ri diugh narach ort,
    ga do ghleidheadh bho bheud 's bho mhi-thapadh!"[14]

---

13 A magical rune or saying.
14 Protection of Mary of the Son on you,
    Protection against murder and hurt on you,
    Protection between the generations,
    Protection of the Three who are One on you,
    (may it) grow from the head to the sole of the foot:
    Protection of the seven who are one on you,
    Protection of the seven who are two on you,
    Protection of the seven who are three on you,
    Protection of the seven who are four on you,

Scarcely had she finished before she heard heavy steps approaching. "Away with you," she whispered; repeating in a loud angry tone, "Away with you! Seachad! Seachad!"

And with that Neil Ross slipped from the milk-shed and crossed the yard, and was behind the byres, before Andrew Blair, with sullen mien and swift wild eyes, strode from the house. It was with a grim smile on his face that Neil tramped down the wet heather till he reached the high road, and fared thence as through a marsh because of the rains there had been. For the first mile he thought of the angry mind of the dead man, bitter at paying of the silver. For the second mile he thought of the evil that had been wrought for him and his. For the third mile he pondered over all that he had heard, and done, and taken upon him that day. Then he sat down upon a broken granite-heap by the way, and brooded deep, till one hour went, and then another, and the third was upon him.

A man driving two calves came toward him out of the west. He did not hear or see. The man stopped, spoke again. Neil gave no answer. The drover shrugged his shoulders, hesitated, and walked slowly on, often looking back. An hour later a shepherd came by the way he himself had tramped. He was a tall, gaunt man with a squint. The small pale-blue eyes glittered out of a mass of red hair that almost covered his face. He stood still opposite Neil, and leaned on his cromak.

"Latha math leat," he said at last, "I wish you good day."

Neil glanced at him, but did not speak.

"What is your name, for I seem to know you?"

But Neil had already forgotten him. The shepherd took out his snuff-mull, helped himself, and handed the mull to the lonely wayfarer. Neil mechanically helped himself.

"Am bheil thu 'dol do Fhionphort?" cried the shepherd again, "are you going to Fionnaphort?"

"Tha mise 'dol a dh' I-challum-chille," Neil answered in a low, weary voice, and as a man a dream, "I am on my way to Iona."

"I am thinking I know now who you are. You are the man Macallum."

Neil looked, but did not speak. His eyes dreamed against what the other could not see or know. The shepherd called angrily to his dogs to keep the sheep from straying; then, with a resentful air, turned to his victim.

Protection of the seven who are five on you,
Protection of the seven who are six on you,
Protection of the seven pairs of seven pairs modestly going sun-wise into today, preserving you from harm and from misfortune.

"You are a silent man for sure, you are. I'm hoping it is not the curse upon you already."

"What curse?"

"Ah, *that* has brought the wind against the mist! I was thinking so!"

"What curse?"

"You are the man that was the Sin-Eater over there?"

"Ay."

"The man Macallum?"

"Ay."

"Strange it is, but three days ago I saw you in Tobermory, and heard you give your name as Neil Ross, to an Iona man that was there."

"Well?"

"Oh, sure, it is nothing to me. But they say the Sin-Eater should not be a man with a hidden lump in his pack."

"Why?"

"For the dead know, and are content. There is no shaking off any sins, then, for that man."

"It is a lie."

"Maybe ay, and maybe no."

"Well, have you more to be saying to me? I am obliged to you for your company, but it is not needing it I am, though no offence."

"Och, man, there's no offence between you and me. Sure, there's Iona in me, too, for the father of my father married a woman that was the granddaughter of Tomais Macdonald, who was a fisherman there. No, no, it is rather warning you I would be."

"And for what?"

"Well, well, just because of that laugh I heard about."

"What laugh?"

"The laugh of Adam Blair that is dead."

Neil Ross stared, his eyes large and wild. He leaned a little forward. No word came from him. The look that was on his face was the question.

"Yes: it was this way. Sure, the telling of it is just as I heard it. After you ate the sins of Adam Blair, the people there brought out the coffin. When they were putting him into it, he was as stiff as a sheep dead in the snow — and just like that, too, with his eyes wide open. Well, some one saw you trampling the heather down the slope that is in front of the house, and said, 'It is the Sin-Eater!' With that, Andrew Blair sneered, and said, 'Ay, 'tis the scapegoat he is!' Then, after a while, he went on: 'The Sin-Eater they call him; ay, just so; and a bitter good bargain it is, too, if all's true that's thought true!' — and with that he laughed, and then his wife that was behind him laughed, and then —"

"Well, what then?"

"Well, 'tis Himself that hears and knows if it is true! But this is the thing I was told: After that laughing there was a stillness, and a dread. For all there saw that the corpse had turned its head and was looking after you as you went down the heather. Then, Neil Ross, if that be your true name, Adam Blair that was dead put up his white face against the sky, and laughed."

At this, Ross sprang to his feet with a gasping sob. "It is a lie, that thing!" he cried, shaking his fist at the shepherd. "It is a lie!"

"It is no lie. And by the same token, Andrew Blair shrank back white and shaking, and his woman had the swoon upon her, and who knows but the corpse might have come to life again had it not been for Maisie Macdonald, the deid-watcher, who clapped a handful of salt on his eyes, and tilted the coffin so that the bottom of it slid forward and so let the whole fall flat on the ground, with Adam Blair in it sideways, and as likely as not cursing and groaning as his wont was, for the hurt both to his old bones and his old ancient dignity."

Ross glared at the man as though the madness was upon him. Fear, and horror, and fierce rage, swung him now this way and now that. "What will the name of you be, shepherd?" he stuttered huskily.

"It is Eachainn Gilleasbuig I am to ourselves, and the English of that for those who have no Gaelic is Hector Gillespie; and I am Eachainn mac Ian mac Alasdair, of Srathsheean, that is where Sutherland lies against Ross."

"Then take this thing, and that is, the curse of the Sin-Eater! And a bitter bad thing may it be upon you and yours!"

And with that Neil the Sin-Eater flung his hand up into the air, and then leaped past the shepherd, and a minute later was running through the frightened sheep, with his head low, and a white foam on his lips, and his eyes red with blood as a seal's that has the death wound on it.

On the third day of the seventh month from that day, Aulay Macneil, coming into Balliemore of Iona from the west side of the island, said to old Ronald MacCormick, that was the father of his wife, that he had seen Neil Ross again, and that he was "absent" — for though he had spoken to him, Neil would not answer, but only gloomed at him from the wet weedy rock where he sat.

The going back of the man had loosed every tongue that was in Iona. When, too, it was known that he was wrought in some terrible way, if not actually mad, the islanders whispered that it was because of the sins of Adam Blair. Seldom or never now did they speak of him by his name, but simply as "The Sin-Eater." The thing was not so rare as to cause this strangeness, nor did many (and perhaps none did) think that the sins of the dead ever might or could abide with the living who had merely done a good Christian, charitable thing. But there was a reason.

Not long after Neil Ross had come again to Iona, and had settled down in the ruined roofless house on the croft of Ballyrona, just like a fox or a wild-cat, as the saying was, he was given fishing-work to do by Aulay Macneil, who lived at Ard-an-teine, at the rocky north end of the màchar or plain that is on the west Atlantic coast of the island.

One moonlit night, either the seventh or the ninth after the earthing of Adam Blair at his own place in the Ross, Aulay Macneil saw Neil Ross steal out of the shadow of Ballyrona and make for the sea. Macneil was there, by the rocks, mending a lobster-creel. If he had gone there because of the sadness, well, when he saw the Sin-Eater he watched. Neil crept from rock to rock till he reached the last fang that churns the sea into yeast when the tide sucks the land, just opposite. Then he called out something that Aulay Macneil could not catch. With that he springs up, and throws his arms above him.

"Then," says Aulay, when he tells the tale, "it was like a ghost he was. The moonshine was on his face like the curl o' a wave. White! There is no whiteness like that of the human face. It was whiter than the foam about the skerry it was, whiter than the moonshining, whiter than — well, as white as the painted letters on the black boards of the fishing-cobles. There he stood, for all that the sea was about him, the slip-slop waves leapin' wild, and the tide making too at that. He was shaking like a sail two points off the wind. It was then that all of a sudden he called in a womany screamin' voice:

"'I am throwing the sins of Adam Blair into the midst of ye, white dogs o' the sea! Drown them, tear them, drag them away out into the black deeps! Ay, ay, ay, ye dancin' wild waves, this is the third time I am doing it; and now there is none left, no, not a sin, not a sin.

"'O-hi, O-ri, dark tide o' the sea,
I am giving the sins of a dead man to thee!
By the Stones, by the Wind, by the Fire, by the Tree,
From the dead man's sins set me free, set me free!
Adam mhic Anndra mhic Adam and me,
Set us free! Set us free!'

"Ay, sure, the Sin-Eater sang that over and over; and after the third singing he swung his arms and screamed:

"'And listen to me, black waters an' running tide,
   That rune is the good rune told me by Maisie the wise,
   And I am Neil, the son of Silis Macallum,
   By the black-hearted evil man Murtagh Ross,
   That was the friend of Adam Mac Anndra, God against him!'

"And with that he scrambled and fell into the sea. But, as I am Aulay MacLuais and no other, he was up in a moment, an' swimmin' like a seal, and then over the rocks again, an' away back to that lonely roofless place once more, laughing wild at times, an' muttering an' whispering."

It was this tale of Aulay Macneil's that stood between Neil Ross and the islefolk. There was something behind all that, they whispered one to another.

So it was always the Sin-Eater he was called at last. None sought him. The few children who came upon him, now and again, fled at his approach, or at the very sight of him. Only Aulay Macneil saw him at times, and had word of him.

After a month had gone by, all knew that the Sin-Eater was wrought to madness, because of this awful thing; the burden of Adam Blair's sins would not go from him! Night and day he could hear them laughing low, it was said. But it was the quiet madness. He went to and fro like a shadow in the grass, and almost as soundless as that, and as voiceless. More and more the name of him grew as a terror. There were few folk on that wild west coast of Iona, and these few avoided him when the word ran that he had knowledge of strange things, and converse, too, with the secrets of the sea.

One day Aulay Macneil, in his boat, but dumb with amaze and terror for him, saw him at high-tide swimming on a long rolling wave right into the hollow of the Spouting Cave. In the memory of man, no one had done this and escaped one of three things: a snatching away into oblivion, a strangled death, or madness. The islanders know that there swims into the cave at full tide a Mar-Tarbh[15], a dreadful creature of the sea that some call a kelpie; only it is not a kelpie, which is like a woman, but rather is a seabull, offspring of the cattle that are never seen. Ill indeed for any sheep or goat, ay or even dog or child, if any happens to be

---

15   Literally 'sea bull.'

leaning over the edge of the Spouting Cave when the Mar-Tarbh roars; for, of a surety, it will fall in and straightway be devoured.

With awe and trembling Aulay listened for the screaming of the doomed man. It was full tide, and the sea-beast would be there.

The minutes passed, and no sign. Only the hollow booming of the sea, as it moved like a baffled blind giant round the cavern-bases; only the rush and spray of the water flung up the narrow shaft high into the windy air above the cliff it penetrates.

At last he saw what looked like a mass of sea-weed swirled out on the surge. It was the Sin-Eater. With a leap, Aulay was at his oars. The boat swung through the sea. Just before Neil Ross was about to sink for the second time, he caught him, and dragged him into the boat. But then, as ever after, nothing was to be got out of the Sin-Eater save a single saying: *"Tha e lamhan fuar! Tha e lamhan fuar!"* — "It has a cold, cold hand!"

The telling of this and other tales left none free upon the island to look upon the "scapegoat" save as one accursed.

It was in the third month that a new phase of his madness came upon Neil Ross. The horror of the sea and the passion for the sea came over him at the same happening.

Oftentimes he would race along the shore, screaming wild names to it, now hot with hate and loathing, now as the pleading of a man with the woman of his love. And strange chants to it, too, were upon his lips. Old, old lines of forgotten runes were overheard by Aulay Macneil, and not Aulay only — lines wherein the ancient sea-name of the island, *Ioua*, that was given to it long before it was called Iona, or any other of the nine names that are said to belong to it, occurred again and again. The flowing tide it was that wrought him thus. At the ebb he would wander across the weedy slabs or among the rocks, silent, and more like a lost *duinshee*[16] than a man.

Then again after three months a change in his madness came. None knew what it was, though Aulay said that the man moaned and moaned because of the awful burden he bore. No drowning seas for the sins that could not be washed away, no grave for the live sins that would be quick till the Day of the Judgment! For weeks thereafter he disappeared. As to where he was, it is not for the knowing.

Then at last came that third day of the seventh month when, as I have said, Aulay Macneil told old Ronald MacCormick that he had seen the

---

16 Duinshee - Faery man (banshee - Faery woman)

Sin-Eater again. It was only a half-truth that he told, though. For after he had seen Neil Ross upon the rock, he had followed him when he rose and wandered back to the roofless place which he haunted now as of yore. Less wretched a shelter now it was, because of the summer that was come, though a cold wet summer at that.

"Is that you, Neil Ross?" he had asked, as he peered into the shadows among the ruins of the house.

"That's not my name," said the Sin-Eater; and he seemed as strange then and there, as though he were a castaway from a foreign ship.

"And what will it be then, you that are my friend, and sure knowing me as Aulay Mac Luais — Aulay Macneil that never grudges you bit or sup?"

"*I am Judas.*"

"And at that word," says Aulay Macneil, when he tells the tale, "at that word the pulse in my heart was like a bat in a shut room. But after a bit I took up the talk. "'Indeed,' I said, 'and I was not for knowing that. May I be so bold as to ask whose son, and of what place?'

"But all he said to me was, '*I am Judas*,'"

"Well, I said, to comfort him, 'Sure, it's not such a bad name in itself, though I am knowing some which have a more homelike sound.' But no, it was no good.

"'I am Judas. And because I sold the Son of God for five pieces of silver —' But here I interrupted him and said, 'Sure now, Neil, — I mean, Judas — it was eight times five.' Yet the simpleness of his sorrow prevailed, and I listened with the wet in my eyes.

"'I am Judas. And because I sold the Son of God for five silver shillings, He laid upon me all the nameless black sins of the world. And that is why I am bearing them till the Day of Days.'"

And this was the end of the Sin-Eater ... for I will not tell the long story of Aulay Macneil, that gets longer and longer every winter, but only the unchanging close of it.

I will tell it in the words of Aulay.

"A bitter wild day it was, that day I saw him to see him no more. It was late. The sea was red with the flamin' light that burned up the air betwixt Iona and all that is west of West. I was on the shore, looking at the sea. The big green waves came in like the chariots in the Holy Book. Well, it was on the black shoulder of one of them, just short of the ton o' foam that swept above it, that I saw a spar surgin' by.

"'What is that?' I said to myself. And the reason of my wondering was this. I saw that a smaller spar was swung across it. And while I was watching that thing another great billow came in with a roar, and hurled the double-spar back, and not so far from me but I might have gripped it. But who would have gripped that thing if he were for seeing what I saw?

"It is Himself knows that what I say is a true thing."

"On that spar was Neil Ross, the Sin-Eater. Naked he was as the day he was born. And he was lashed, too, ay, sure he was lashed to it by ropes round and round his legs and his waist and his left arm. It was the Cross he was on. I saw that thing with the fear upon me. Ah, poor drifting wreck that he was! *Judas on the Cross!* It was his *eric!*[17]

"But even as I watched, shaking in my limbs, I saw that there was life in him still. The lips were moving, and his right arm was ever for swinging this way and that. 'Twas like an oar working him off a lee shore; ay, that was what I thought.

"Then all at once he caught sight of me. Well, he knew me, poor man, that has his share of Heaven now, I am thinking!

"He waved, and called, but the hearing could not be, because of a big surge o' water that came tumbling down upon him. In the stroke of an oar he was swept close by the rocks where I was standing. In that flounderin', seethin' whirlpool I saw the white face of him for a moment, an', as he went out on the resurge like a hauled net, I heard these words fallin' against my ears:

"' An eirig m'anama!' — 'In ransom for my soul!'

"And with that I saw the double-spar turn over and slide down the back-sweep of a drowning big wave. Ay, sure, it went out to the deep sea swift enough then. It was in the big eddy that rushes between Skerry-Mòr and Skerry-Beag. I did not see it again, no, not for the quarter of an hour, I am thinking. Then I saw just the whirling top of it rising out of the flying yeast of a great black, blustering wave that was rushing northward before the current that is called the Black-Eddy.

"With that you have the end of Neil Ross: ay, sure, him that was called the Sin-Eater. And that is a true thing, and may God save us the sorrow of sorrows!

"And that is all."

---

17 A fine or punishment under the old Celtic legal system to be paid in recompense for spilt blood.

The Dark Nameless One

ONE day this summer I sailed with Padruic Macrae and Ivor McLean, boatmen of Iona, along the south-western reach of the Ross of Mull.

The whole coast of the Ross is indescribably wild and desolate. From Feenafort (Fhionnphort), opposite Balliemore of Icolmkill,[18] to the hamlet of Earraid Lighthouse, it were hardly exaggeration to say that the whole tract is uninhabited by man and unenlivened by any green thing. It is the haunt of the cormorant and the seal.

No one who has not visited this region can realise its barrenness. Its one beauty is the faint bloom which lies upon it in the sunlight — a bloom which becomes as the glow of an inner flame when the sun westers without cloud or mist. This is from the ruddy hue of the granite, of which all that wilderness is wrought. It is a land tortured by the sea, scourged by the sea-wind. A myriad lochs, fiords, inlets, passages, serrate its broken frontiers. Innumerable islets and reefs, fanged like ravenous wolves, sentinel every shallow, lurk in every strait. He must be a skilled boatman who would take the Sound of Earraid and penetrate the reaches of the Ross.

There are many days in the months of peace, as the islanders call the period from Easter till the autumnal equinox, when Earraid and the rest of Ross seem under a spell. It is the spell of beauty. Then the yellow light of the sun is upon the tumbled masses and precipitous shelves and ledges, ruddy petals or leaves of that vast Flower of Granite. Across it the cloud shadows trail their purple elongations, their scythe-sweep curves, and abrupt evanishing floodings of warm dusk. From wet boulder to boulder, from crag to shelly crag, from fissure to fissure, the sea ceaselessly weaves a girdle of foam. When the wide luminous stretch of waters beyond — green near the land, and farther out all of a living blue, interspersed with wide alleys of amethyst — is white with the sea-horses, there is such a laughter of surge and splash all the way from Slugan-dubh to the Rudha-nam-Maol-Mòra, or to the tide-swept promontory of the Sgeireig-a'-Bhochdaidh, that, looking inland, one sees through a rainbow-shimmering veil of ever-flying spray.

---

18 Icolmkill - old name for Iona. Literally 'island of the Dove of the Church' i.e. St Columba.

But the sun spell is even more fugitive upon the face of this wild land than the spell of beauty upon a woman. So runs one of our proverbs: as the falling of the wave, as the fading of the leaf, so is the beauty of a woman, unless — ah, that *unless,* and the indiscoverable fount of joy that can only be come upon by hazard once in life, and thereafter only in dreams, and the Land of the Rainbow that is never reached, and the green sea-doors of Tir-na-thonn,[19] that open now no more to any wandering wave!

It was from Ivor McLean, on that day, I heard the strange tale of his kinsman Murdoch, the tale of "The Ninth Wave" that I have told elsewhere. It was Padruic, however, who told me of the Sea-witch of Earraid.

"Yes," he said, "I have heard of the *uisge-each* (the sea-beast, sea-kelpie, or water-horse), but I have never seen it with the eyes. My father and my brother knew of it. But this thing I know, and this what we call *an-cailleach-uisge* (the siren or water-witch); the cailleach, mind you, not the maighdeann-mhàra (the mermaid), who means no harm. May she hear my saying it! The cailleach is old and clad in weeds, but her voice is young, and she always sits so that the light is in the eyes of the beholder. She seems to him young also, and fair. She has two familiars in the form of seals, one black as the grave, and the other white as the shroud that is in the grave; and these sometimes upset a boat, if the sailor laughs at the uisge-cailleach's song.

"A man netted one of those seals, more than a hundred years ago, with his herring trawl, and dragged it into the boat; but the other seal tore at the net so savagely, with its head and paws over the bows, that it was clear no net would long avail. The man heard them crying and screaming, and then talking low and muttering, like women in a frenzy. In his fear he cast the nets adrift, all but a small portion that was caught in the thwarts. Afterwards, in this portion, he found a tress of woman's hair. And that is just so: to the Stones be it said.

"The grandson of this man, Tòmais McNair, is still living, a shepherd on Eilean-Uamhain, beyond Lunga in the Cairnburg Isles. A few years ago, off Callachan Point, he saw the two seals, and heard, though he did not see, the cailleach. And that which I tell you — Christ's Cross before me — is a true thing."

All the time that Phadruic was speaking, I saw that Ivor McLean looked away: either as though he heard nothing, or did not wish to hear.

---

19 Tir na Thonn - 'land under the waves', a euphemism for the Faery world.

There was dream in his eyes; I saw that, so said nothing for a time.

"What is it, Ivor?" I asked at last, in a low voice. He started, and looked at me strangely.

"What will you be asking that for? What are you doing in my mind, that is secret?"

"I see that you are brooding over something. Will you not tell me?"

"Tell her," said Phadruic quietly.

But Ivor kept silent. There was a look in his eyes, which I understood. Thereafter we sailed on, with no word in the boat at all.

That night, a dark, rainy night it was, with an uplift wind beating high over against the hidden moon, I went to the cottage where Ivor McLean lived with his old deaf mother, deaf nigh upon twenty years, ever since the night of the nights when she heard the women whisper that Callum, her husband, was among the drowned, after a death-wind had blown.

When I entered, he was sitting before the flaming coal-fire; for on Iona now, by decree of MacCailin Mòr, there is no more peat burned.

"You will tell me now, Ivor?" was all I said.

"Yes; I will be telling you now. And the reason why I did not tell you before was because it is not a wise or a good thing to tell ancient stories about the sea while still on the running wave. Macrae should not have done that thing. It may be we shall suffer for it when next we go out with the nets. We were to go to-night; but no, not I, no no, for sure, not for all the herring in the Sound."

"Is it an ancient *sgeul*,[20] Ivor?"

"Ay. I am not for knowing the age of these things. It may be as old as the days of the Feinn for all I know. It has come down to us. Alasdair MacAlasdair of Tiree, him that used to boast of having all the stories of Colum and Brighde, it was he told it to the mother of my mother, and she to me."

"What is it called?"

"Well, this and that; but there is no harm in saying it is called the Dark Nameless One."

"The Dark Nameless One!"

"It is this way. But will you ever have been hearing of the MacOdrums of Uist?"

"Ay: the Sliochd-nan-ròn."

"That is so. God knows. The Sliochdnan-ròn ... the progeny of the Seal. ... Well, well, no man knows what moves in the shadow of life. And

---

20 Sgeul - story or tale.

now I will be telling you that old ancient tale, as it was given to me by the mother of my mother.

On a day of the days, Colum was walking alone by the sea-shore. The monks were at the hoe or the spade, and some milking the kye, and some at the fishing. They say it was on the first day of the Faoilleach Geamhraidh,[21] the day that is called Am fheill Brighde.[22]

The holy man had wandered on to where the rocks are, opposite to Soa. He was praying and praying, and it is said that whenever he prayed aloud, the barren egg in the nest would quicken, and the blighted bud unfold, and the butterfly cleave its shroud.

Of a sudden he came upon a great black seal, lying silent on the rocks, with wicked eyes.

"My blessing upon you, O Ròn," he said with the good kind courteousness that was his.

"Droch spadadh ort," answered the seal, "A bad end to you, Colum of the Gown."

"Sure, now," said Colum angrily, "I am knowing by that curse that you are no friend of Christ but of the evil pagan faith out of the north. For here I am known ever as Colum the White, or as Colum the Saint; and it is only the Picts and the wanton Normen who deride me because of the holy white robe I wear."

"Well, well," replied the seal, speaking the good Gaelic as though it were the tongue of the deep sea, as God knows it may be for all you, I, or the blind wind can say; "Well, well, let that thing be: it's a wave-way here or a wave-way there. But now if it is a Druid you are, whether of Fire or of Christ, be telling me where my woman is, and where my little daughter."

At this, Colum looked at him for a long while. Then he knew.

"It is a man you were once, O Ròn?"

"Maybe ay and maybe no."

"And with that thick Gaelic that you have, it will be out of the north isles you come?"

"That is a true thing."

"Now I am for knowing at last who and what you are. You are one of the race of Odrum the Pagan."

"Well, I am not denying it, Colum. And what is more, I am Angus

---

21 Faoilleach Geamhraidh - the storm days, being the first fortnight in spring and
    the last in winter.
22 Am fheill Brighde - the Festival of St Brigid.

MacOdrum, Aonghas mac Torcall mhic Odrum, and the name I am known by is Black Angus."

"A fitting name too," said Colum the Holy, "because of the black sin in your heart, and the black end God has in store for you."

At that Black Angus laughed.

"Why is there laughter upon you, ManSeal?"

"Well, it is because of the good company I'll be having. But, now, give me the word: Are you for having seen or heard aught of a woman called Kirsteen McVurich?"

"Kirsteen — Kirsteen — that is the good name of a nun it is, and no sea-wanton!"

"Oh, a name here or a name there is soft sand. And so you cannot be for telling me where my woman is?"

"No."

"Then a stake for your belly, and the nails through your hands, thirst on your tongue, and the corbies at your eyne!"

And, with that, Black Angus louped into the green water, and the hoarse wild laugh of him sprang into the air and fell dead against the cliff like a wind-spent mew.

Colum went slowly back to the brethren, brooding deep. "God is good," he said in a low voice, again and again; and each time that he spoke there came a fair sweet daisy into the grass, or a yellow bird rose up, with song to it for the first time wonderful and sweet to hear.

As he drew near to the House of God he met Murtagh, an old monk of the ancient old race of the isles.

"Who is Kirsteen McVurich, Murtagh?" he asked.

"She was a good servant of Christ, she was, in the south isles, O Colum, till Black Angus won her to the sea."

"And when was that?"

"Nigh upon a thousand years ago."

At that Colum stared in amaze. But Murtagh was a man of truth, nor did he speak in allegories. "Ay, Colum, my father, nigh upon a thousand years ago."

"But can mortal sin live as long as that?"

"Ay, it endureth. Long, long ago, before Oisìn sang, before Fionn, before Cuchullin was a glorious great prince, and in the days when the Tuatha-De Danànn were sole lords in all green Banba, Black Angus made the woman Kirsteen McVurich leave the place of prayer and go down to the sea-shore, and there he leaped upon her and made her his prey, and she followed him into the sea."

"And is death above her now?"

"No. She is the woman that weaves the sea-spells at the wild place out yonder that is known as Earraid: she that is called an-Cailleach-uisge, the sea-witch."

"Then why was Black Angus for the seeking her here and the seeking her there?"

"It is the Doom. It is Adam's first wife she is, that sea-witch over there, where the foam is ever in the sharp fangs of the rocks."

"And who will he be?"

"His body is the body of Angus the son of Torcall of the race of Odrum, for all that a seal he is to the seeming; but the soul of him is Judas."

"Black Judas, Murtagh?"

"Ay, Black Judas, Colum."

But with that, Ivor Macrae rose abruptly from before the fire, saying that he would speak no more that night. And truly enough there was a wild, lone, desolate cry in the wind, and a slapping of the waves one upon the other with an eerie laughing sound, and the screaming of a sea-mew that was like a human thing.

So I touched the shawl of his mother, who looked up with startled eyes and said, "God be with us"; and then I opened the door, and the salt smell of the wrack was in my nostrils, and the great drowning blackness of the night.

Dalua

I have heard you calling, Dalua,[23]
    Dalua!
I have heard you on the hill,
By the pool-side still,
Where the lapwings shrill
    Dalua ... Dalua ... Dalua!

What is it you call, Dalua,
    Dalua!
When the rains fall,
When the mists crawl,
And the curlews call
    Dalua ... Dalua ... Dalua!

I am the Fool, Dalua,
    Dalua!
When men hear me, their eyes
Darken: the shadow in the skies
Droops: and the keening-woman cries
    Dalua ... Dalua ... Dalua!

~~~~~~

Dalua, one of the names of a mysterious being in the Celtic mythology, the Amadan-Dhu, the Dark Witless One, or Fairy Fool.

~~~~~~

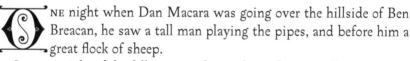 NE night when Dan Macara was going over the hillside of Ben Breacan, he saw a tall man playing the pipes, and before him a great flock of sheep.

It was a night of the falling mist that makes a thin soundless rain. But behind the blur was a rainpool of light, a pool that oozed into a wan flood; and so Macara knew that the moon was up and was riding against the drift, and would pull the rain away from the hill.

Even in slow rain, with damp moss or soaking heather, sheep do not go silently. Macara wondered if they were all young rams, that there was

---

23 Dalua - a creation of Fiona's and not, as she claimed, an ancient god of the Celtic people. He is a bringer of death and madness for no apparent reason. He features in several of Fiona's works but is conspicuous by his absence in any other Gaelic or Celtic writings. See my book *The Little Book of the Great Enchantment* for a full discussion on this curious character.

not a crying *uan* or a bleating ewe to be heard. "By the Black Stone of Iona," he muttered, "there is not even a broken *oisg*[24] among them."

True, there was a faint rising and falling méh-ing high in the darkness of the hillside; but that melancholy sound, as of lost children crying, was confused with the rustling of many leaves of ash and birch, with eddies of air through the heather and among the fronds of the bracken, and with the uncertain hum of trickling waters. No one utterance slid cleanly through the gloom, but only the voice of darkness as it speaks among the rainy hills.

As he stumbled along the path, stony and rain-gutted, but held together by the tough heather-fibres, he thought of the comfortable room he had left in the farmhouse of Pàdruig and Mary Macrae, where the very shadows were so warm, and the hot milk and whisky had been so comfortable too; and warm and comfortable both, the good friendly words of Pàdruig and Mary.

He wiped the rain from his wet lips, and smiled as he remembered Mary's words: "You, now, so tall and big, an' not ill-looking at that, for a dark Macara ... and yet with no woman to your side! ... an' you with the thirty years on you! ... for sure I would have shame in going through the Strath, with the girls knowing that!" But just then he heard the broken notes of the feadan, or "chanter," that came from the tall man playing the pipes, with the great flock of sheep before him. It was like the flight of pee-wits, all this way and that.

"What with the dark and the rain and the whisky and the good words of Mhairi Bàn, my head's like a black bog," he muttered; "and the playing of that man there is like the way o' voices in the bog."

Then he heard without the wilderness in his ears. The air came faint but clear. It angered him. It was like a mocking voice. Perhaps this was because it was like a mocking voice. Perhaps because it was the old pipe-song, "Oighean bhoidheach, slan leibh!" "Ye pretty maids, farewell!"

"Who will he be?" he wondered sullenly. "If it's Peter Macandrew Ardmore's shepherd, I'll play him a tune behind the wind that he won't like."

Then the tall man suddenly changed his chanter-music, and the wet night was full of a wild, forlorn, beautiful air.

Dan Macara had never heard that playing before, and he did not like it. Once, when he was a child, he had heard his mother tell Alan Dall, a blind piper of the Catanach, to stop an air that he was playing, because

---

24 Oisg - a yearling sheep.

it had sobs and tears in it. He moved swiftly now to overtake the man with the flock of sheep. His playing was like Alan Dall's. He wanted, too, to ask him who he was, and whose chanter-magic he had, and where he was going (and the hill way at that!) with all those sheep.

But it took him a long time to get near. He ran at last, but he got no nearer. "Gu ma h-olc dhut - ill befall thee," he cried angrily after a time; "go your own way, and may the night swallow you and your flock." And with that, Dan Macara turned to follow the burnside-way again.

But once more the tall man with the flock of sheep changed the air that he was playing. Macara stopped and listened. It was sweet to hear. Was this a sudden magic that was played upon him? Had not the rain abruptly ceased, as a breath withdrawn? He stared confusedly: for sure, there was no rain, and moonlight lay upon the fern and upon a white birch that stood solitary in that white-green waste. The sprays of the birch were like a rain of pale shimmering gold. A bird slid along a topmost branch; blue, with breast like white iris, and with wild-rose wings. Macara could see its eyes a-shine, two little starry flames. Song came from it, slow, broken, like water in a stony channel. With each note the years of Time ran laughing through ancient woods, and old age sighed across the world and sank into the earth, and the sea world moaned with the burden of all moaning and all tears. The stars moved in a jocund measure; a player sat among them and played, the moon his footstool and the sun a flaming gem above his brows. The song was Youth.

Dan Macara stood. Dreams and visions ran past him, laughing, with starry eyes. He closed his own eyes, trembling. When he opened them he saw no bird. The grey blur of the rain came through the darkness. The cold green smell of the bog-myrtle filled the night. But he was close to the shepherd now. Where had he heard that air? It was one of those old fonnsheen,[25] for sure: yes, "A Choillteach Ùrair," "The Green Woodland" ... that was it. But he had never heard it played like that.

The man did not look round as Dan Macara drew near. The pipes were shadowy black, and had long black streamers from them. The man wore a Highland bonnet, with a black plume hanging from it.

The wet slurred moonshine came out as the rain ceased. Dan looked over the shoulder of the man at the long, straggling crowd of sheep. He saw then that they were only a flock of shadows. They were of all shapes and sizes; and Macara knew, without knowing how he knew, that they were the shadows of all that the shepherd had found in his

---

25 Fonsheen - music of the Faeries.

day's wandering — from the shadows of tall pines to the shadows of daisies, from the shadows of horned cattle to the shadows of fawns and field mice, from the shadow of a woman at a well to that of a wild rose trailing on the roadside, from the shadow of a dead man in a corrie, and of a boy playing on a reed with three holes, and the shadows of flying birds and drifting clouds, and the slow, formless shadows of stones, to (as he saw with a sudden terror) the shadow of Dan Macara himself, idly decked with feather-like bracken, where he had lost it an hour ago in the darkness, when he had first heard the far-off broken lilt of the pipes.

Filled with an anger that was greater than his terror, Dan Macara ran forward, and strove to grasp the man by the shoulder; but with a crash he came against a great slab of granite, with its lichened sides wet and slippery with the hill mist. As he fell, he struck his head and screamed. Before silence and darkness closed in upon him like two waves, he heard Dalua's mocking laughter far up among the hills, and saw a great flock of curlews rise from where the shadows had been.

When he woke there was no more mist on the hill. The moonlight turned the raindrops on the bracken into infinite little wells of light. All night he wandered, looking for the curlew that was his shadow. Toward the edge of day he lay down. Sleep was on him, soft and quiet as the breastfeather of a mothering bird. His head was in a tuft of grass: above it a moist star hung, a white solitude — a silent solitude.

Dalua stood by him, brooding darkly. He was no shepherd now, but had cloudy black hair like the thin shadows of branches at dusk, and wild eyes, obscure as the brown-black tarns in the heather.

He looked at the star, smiling darkly. Then it moved against the dawn, and paled. It was no more. The man lay solitary.

It was the gloaming of the dawn. Many shadows stirred. Dalua lifted one. It was the shadow of a reed. He put it to his mouth and played upon it.

Above, in the greying waste, a bird wheeled this way and that. Then the curlew flew down, and stood quivering, with eyes wild as Dalua's. He looked at it, and played it into a shadow; and looked at the sleeping man, and played that shadow into his sleeping mind.

"There is your shadow for you," he said, and touched Dan.

At that touch Macara shivered all over. Then he woke with a laugh. He saw the dawn sliding along the tops of the pines on the east slope of Ben Breacan.

46

He rose. He threw his cromak[26] away. Then he gave three wails of the wailing cry of the curlew, and wandered idly back by the way he had come.

It was years and years after that when I saw him.

"How did this madness come upon him?" I asked; for I recalled him strong and proud.

"The Dark Fool, the Amadan-Dhu, touched him. No one knows any more than that. But that is a true thing."

He hated or feared nothing, save only shadows. These disquieted him, by the hearthside or upon the great lonely moors. He was quiet, and loved running water and the hill-wind. But at times, the wailing of curlews threw him into a frenzy.

I asked him once why he was so sad. "I have heard," he said ... and then stared idly at me; adding suddenly, as though remembering words spoken by another: — "I'm always hearing the three old ancientest cries: the cry of the curlew, an' the wind, an' the sighin' of the sea."

He was ever witless, and loved wandering among the hills. No child feared him. He had a lost love in his face. At night, on the sighing moors, or on the glen-road, his eyes were like stars in a pool, but with a light more tender.

---

26   Cromak(g) - a crooked walking stick.

Section Two

UNDER THE DARK STAR

UNDER THE DARK STAR

This section starts with three more tales from the 1895 collection *The Sin-Eater* and concludes with three tales from the 1899 collection *The Dominion of Dreams*. They feature a very dysfunctional family by the name of Achanna who, we are told, came from Galloway which is in the southern part of Scotland but moved to the Highlands and Islands because of some feuding. They live on an island called Eilanmore which, in Gaelic, means simply 'the big island' and could be anywhere. The important point is, as Fiona says, they were all 'fëy' or living partly in this world and partly in the Celtic Otherworld. The main character is one of the seven brothers who goes by the name Gloom. *Gloom* in Gaelic would be 'Dubhach' and Fiona used this name again (in its Anglicized spelling - Duvach) in the tale *Muime Chriosd* to be found in Section Four.

As in the tales contained in Section One, Fiona says that she knew these brothers and their locale, which gives them an air of authenticity and helps to reinforce the belief that Fiona Macleod was a real Highland lady who spent a highly romantic, if unconventional life, amongst the Gaelic-speaking folks of the islands, surrounded by Faeries, sea monsters and a terrible beauty. She gives out more Gaelic wisdom in the form of sayings, runes and incantations - most of which she created - but the terror and threat of death, madness and darkness is always in the background. She uses a lot of double meanings in her Gaelic names and sayings and I have explained the significance of these in the appropriate places.

The tale *The Dàn-Nan-Ròn* starts with Fiona's original introductory note and I have added my own comments by way of footnotes throughout the text.

Green Branches and *Children of the Dark Star* are Fiona's own compositions but *Green Branches* seems to borrow an important motif found in an ancient Irish legend called *Táin Bó Fraích*. I have made a footnote at the appropriate point in the text explaining this.

Children of the Dark Star does not contain any ancient Celtic motifs but Fiona may have been giving an acknowledgment to the ancient Celtic Bards, in that true Bardic poetry always started and finished with the same word or phrase. In this tale Fiona starts and finishes with the same phrase concerning blind birds. Coincidence? Perhaps.

In *Alasdair the Proud* there are several references to a tale called *Enya of the Dark Eyes* and it is described as being an old tale. This is not the case as *Enya of the Dark Eyes* is actually one of Fiona's own compositions that appeared in the same collection as *Alasdair the Proud*.

In the final tale *The Amadan* we meet again the dark god Dalua from Section One although he is not directly named as such. The rune contained within this tale, *Invocation of Peace*, is also Fiona's creation but it is in the style of the ancient Gaelic sayings or runes as can be found in Alexander Carmichael's important work *Carmina Gadelica*. William Sharp knew Carmichael and borrowed the manuscript that would later become *Carmina Gadelica* and when Fiona Macleod's books first appeared Carmichael was furious, alleging that Sharp had stolen many of the runes and sayings from his as-yet unpublished work and passed them on to Miss Macleod (Carmichael did not know Sharp and Macleod were one and the same person). As far as I have been able to determine, Fiona did not directly quote any of Carmichael's collected sayings and runes but she did use the same style and format for her own creations. Today, fragments of *Invocation of Peace* regularly appear in collections of Celtic poetry and sayings and it is often described as being "ancient Gaelic" or "9th century Irish" or some such thing. So, in a sense, at least parts of her writings have now taken on an air of the ancient and the authentic.

The Anointed Man

OF the seven Achannas — sons of Robert Achanna of Achanna in Galloway, self-exiled in the far north because of a bitter feud with his kindred — who lived upon Eilanmore in the Summer Isles, there was not one who was not, in more or less degree, or at some time or other, fëy.

Doubtless I shall have occasion to allude to one and all again, and certainly to the eldest and youngest; for they were the strangest folk I have known or met anywhere in the Celtic lands, from the sea-pastures of the Solway to the kelp-strewn beaches of the Lews. Upon James, the seventh son, the doom of his people fell last and most heavily. Some day I may tell the full story of his strange life and tragic undoing, and of his piteous end. As it happened, I knew best the eldest and youngest of the brothers, Alasdair and James. Of the others, Robert, Allan, William, Marcus, and Gloom, none save the last-named survives, if peradventure *he* does, or has been seen of man for many years past. Of Gloom (strange and unaccountable name, which used to terrify me, the more so as by the savagery of fate it was the name of all names suitable for Robert, Achanna's sixth son) I know nothing beyond the fact that ten years or more ago he was a Jesuit priest in Rome, a bird of passage, whence come and whither bound no inquiries of mine could discover. Two years ago a relative told me that Gloom was dead, that he had been slain by some Mexican noble in an old city of Hispaniola beyond the seas. Doubtless the news was founded on truth, though I have ever a vague unrest when I think of Gloom, as though he were travelling hitherward — as though his feet, on some urgent errand, were already white with the dust of the road that leads to my house.

But now I wish to speak only of Alasdair Achanna. He was a friend whom I loved, though he was a man of close on forty and I a girl less than half his years. We had much in common, and I never knew any one more companionable, for all that he was called "Silent Ally." He was tall, gaunt, loosely-built. His eyes were of that misty blue which smoke takes when it rises in the woods. I used to think them like the tarns that lay amid the canna and gale-surrounded swamps in Uist, where I was wont to dream as a child.

I had often noticed the light on his face when he smiled, a light of such serene joy as young mothers have sometimes over the cradles of their firstborn. But, for some reason, I had never wondered about it, not even when I heard and understood the half-contemptuous, half-reverent mockery with which not only Alasdair's brothers but even his father at times used towards him. Once, I remember, I was puzzled when, on a bleak day in a stormy August, I overheard Gloom say, angrily and scoffingly, "There goes the Anointed Man!" I looked; but all I could see was that, despite the dreary cold, despite the ruined harvest, despite the rotting potato-crop, Alasdair walked slowly onward, smiling, and with glad eyes brooding upon the grey lands around and beyond him.

It was nearly a year thereafter — I remember the date, because it was that of my last visit to Eilanmore — that I understood more fully. I was walking westward with Alasdair, towards sundown. The light was upon his face as though it came from within; and when I looked again, half in awe, I saw that there was no glamour out of the west, for the evening was dull and threatening rain. He was in sorrow. Three months before, his brothers, Allan and William, had been drowned; a month later, his brother Robert had sickened, and now sat in the ingle from morning till the covering of the peats, a skeleton almost, shivering, and morosely silent, with large staring eyes. On the large bed, in the room above the kitchen, old Robert Achanna lay, stricken with paralysis. It would have been unendurable for me, but for Alasdair and James, and, above all, for my loved girl-friend, Anne Gillespie, Achanna's niece and the sunshine of his gloomy household.

As I walked with Alasdair I was conscious of a well-nigh intolerable depression. The house we had left was so mournful, the bleak, sodden pastures were so mournful; so mournful was the stony place we were crossing, silent but for the thin crying of the curlews; and above all so mournful was the sound of the ocean as, unseen, it moved sobbingly round the isle — so beyond words distressing was all this to me that I stopped abruptly, meaning to go no farther, but to return to the house, where, at least, there was warmth, and where Anne would sing for me as she spun.

But when I looked up into my companion's face I saw in truth the light that shone from within. His eyes were upon a forbidding stretch of ground, where the blighted potatoes rotted among a wilderness of round skull-white stones. I remember them still, these strange far-blue eyes; lamps of quiet joy, lamps of peace, they seemed to me.

"Are you looking at Achnacarn?"[27] (as the tract was called), I asked, in what I am sure was a whisper.

---

27 Literally 'Field of Stones.'

"Yes," replied Alasdair, slowly; "I am looking. It is beautiful, beautiful; O God, how beautiful is this lovely world!"

I know not what made me act so, but I threw myself on a heathery ridge close by and broke out into convulsive sobbings. Alasdair stooped, lifted me in his strong arms, and soothed me with soft caressing touches and quieting words.

"Tell me, my fawn, what is it? What is the trouble?" he asked again and again.

"It is *you* — it is you, Alasdair," I managed to say coherently at last; "it terrifies me to hear you speak as you did a little ago. You must be fëy. Why, why, do you call that hateful, hideous field beautiful — on this dreary day — and — and after all that has happened — oh, Alasdair?"

At this, I remember, he took his plaid and put it upon the wet heather, and then drew me thither, and seated himself and me beside him, "Is it not beautiful, my fawn?" he asked, with tears in his eyes. Then, without waiting for my answer, he said quietly, "Listen, dear, and I will tell you."

He was strangely still, breathless he seemed to me, for a minute or more. Then he spoke:

"I was little more than a child, a boy just in my teens, when something happened, something that came down the Rainbow-Arches of Cathair-Sìth."[28]

He paused here, perhaps to see if I followed, which I did, familiar as I was with all fairy-lore. "I was out upon the heather, in the time when the honey oozes in the bells and cups. I had always loved the island and the sea. Perhaps I was foolish, but I was so glad with my joy that golden day that I threw myself on the ground and kissed the hot, sweet-ling, and put my hands and arms into it, sobbing the while with my vague, strange yearning. At last I lay still, nerveless, with my eyes closed.

Suddenly I was aware that two tiny hands had come up through the spires of the heather, and were pressing something soft and fragrant upon my eyelids. When I opened them, I could see nothing unfamiliar. No one was visible. But I heard a whisper: 'Arise and go away from this place at once; and this night do not venture out, lest evil befall you.' So I rose, trembling, and went home. Thereafter I was the same, and yet not the same. Never could I see, as they saw, what my father and brothers or the isle-folk looked upon as ugly or dreary.

My father was wroth with me many times, and called me a fool. Whenever my eyes fell upon those waste and desolated spots, they

---

28 Castle of the Faeries

seemed to me passing fair, radiant with lovely light. At last my father grew so bitter that, mocking me the while, he bade me go to the towns, and see there the squalor and sordid hideousness wherein men dwelled. But thus it was with me: in the places they call slums, and among the smoke of factories, and the grime of destitution, I could see all that other men saw, only as vanishing shadows. What I saw was lovely, beautiful with strange glory, and the faces of men and women were sweet and pure, and their souls were white. So, weary and bewildered with my unwilling quest, I came back to Eilanmore. And on the day of my home-coming, Morag was there - Morag of the Falls. She turned to my father, and called him blind and foolish. 'He has the white light upon his brows,' she said of me; 'I can see it, like the flicker-light in a wave when the wind's from the south in thunder-weather. He has been touched with the Fairy Ointment. The Guid Folk know him. It will be thus with him till the day of his death, if a duinshee can die, being already a man dead yet born anew. He upon whom the Fairy Ointment has been laid must see all that is ugly and hideous and dreary and bitter through a glamour of beauty. Thus it hath been since the Mhic-Alpine ruled from sea to sea, and thus is it with the man Alasdair your son.' That is all, my fawn, and that is why my brothers, when they are angry, sometimes call me the Anointed Man."

"That is all." Yes perhaps. But oh, Alasdair Achanna, how often have I thought of that most precious treasure you found in the heather, when the bells were sweet with honey-ooze! Did the wild bees know of it? Would that I could hear the soft hum of their gauzy wings! Who of us would not barter the best of all our possessions — and some there are who would surrender all — to have one touch laid upon the eyelids, one touch of the Fairy Ointment? But the place is far, and the hour is hidden. No man may seek that for which there can be no quest.

Only the wild bees know of it, but I think they must be the bees of Magh-Mell.[29] And there no man that liveth may wayfare — *yet*.

---

29   The Plain of Honey - an allusion to the World of Faery.

The Dàn-Nan-Ròn

Note To The Dàn-Nan-Ròn[30]

This story is founded upon a superstition familiar throughout the Hebrides. The legend exists also on the western coasts of Ireland; for Mr. Yeats has told me that one summer he met an old Connaught fisherman who claimed to be of the Sliochd-nan-Ròn, an ancestry, indeed, indicated in the man's name: Rooney.

As to my use of the forename "Gloom," in "Under the Dark Star" series of stories, I should explain that the designation is not a baptismal name. At the same time, I have actual warrant for its use; for I knew a Uist man who in the bitterness of his sorrow, after his wife's death in childbirth, named his son Mulad (i.e. the gloom of sorrow: grief).

HEN Anne Gillespie, that was my friend in Eilanmore, left the island after the death of her uncle, the old man Robert Achanna, it was to go far west.

Among the men of the Outer Isles who for three summers past had been at the fishing off Eilanmore there was one named Mànus MacCodrum. He was a fine lad to see, but though most of the fisher-folk of the Lews and North Uist are fair, either with reddish hair and grey eyes, or blue-eyed and yellow-haired, he was of a brown skin with dark hair and dusky brown eyes. He was, however, as unlike to the dark Celts of Arran and the Inner Hebrides as to the northmen. He came of his people, sure enough. All the MacCodrums of North Uist had been brown-skinned and brown-haired and brown-eyed: and herein may have lain the reason why, in by-gone days, this small clan of Uist was known throughout the Western Isles as the Sliochd nan Ròn, the offspring of the Seals.

Not so tall as most of the men of North Uist and the Lews, Mànus MacCodrum was of a fair height, and supple and strong. No man was a better fisherman than he, and he was well liked of his fellows, for all the morose gloom that was upon him at times. He had a voice as sweet as a woman's when he sang, and he sang often, and knew all the old runes of the islands, from the Obb of Harris to the Head of Mingulay. Often, too, he chanted the beautiful *orain spioradail*[31] of the Catholic priests and Christian Brothers of South Uist and Barra, though where he lived

---

30 There is a play on words in this title. 'Dàn' means song but also means destiny. 'Ròn' means seal. So the title could be the Song of the Seal or the Destiny of the Seal.

31 Literally 'spiritual songs' i.e. The Psalms.

in North Uist he was the sole man who adhered to the ancient faith. It may have been because Anne was a Catholic too, though, sure, the Achannas were so also, notwithstanding that their forebears and kindred in Galloway were Protestant (and this because of old Robert Achanna's love for his wife, who was of the old Faith, so it is said) — it may have been for this reason, though I think her lover's admiring eyes and soft speech and sweet singing had more to do with it, that she pledged her troth to Mànus. It was a south wind for him as the saying is; for with her rippling brown hair and soft, grey eyes and cream-white skin, there was no comelier lass in the isles.

So when Achanna was laid to his long rest, and there was none left upon Eilanmore save only his three youngest sons, Mànus MacCodrum sailed north-eastward across the Minch to take home his bride. Of the four eldest sons, Alasdair had left Eilanmore some months before his father died, and sailed westward, though no one knew whither or for what end or for how long, and no word had been brought from him nor was he ever seen again in the island which had come to be called Eilan-nan-Allmharachain, the Isle of the Strangers; Allan and William had been drowned in a wild gale in the Minch; and Robert had died of the white fever, that deadly wasting disease which is the scourge of the isles. Marcus was now "Eilanmore," and lived there with Gloom and Seumas, all three unmarried, though it was rumoured among the neighbouring islanders that each loved Marsail nic Ailpean in Eilean-Rona[32] of the Summer Isles hard by the coast of Sutherland.

When Mànus asked Anne to go with him she agreed. The three brothers were ill pleased at this, for apart from their not wishing their cousin to go so far away, they did not want to lose her, as she not only cooked for them and did all that a woman does, including spinning and weaving, but was most sweet and fair to see, and in the long winter nights sang by the hour together, while Gloom played strange wild airs upon his *feadan*, a kind of oaten pipe or flute.

She loved him, I know; but there was this reason also for her going, that she was afraid of Gloom. Often upon the moor or on the hill she turned and hastened home, because she heard the lilt and fall of that *feadan*. It was an eerie thing to her, to be going through the twilight when she thought the three men were in the house, smoking after their supper, and suddenly to hear beyond and coming toward her the shrill song of that oaten flute, playing "The Dance of the Dead," or "The Flow

---

32 Island of the Seals.

and Ebb," or "The Shadow-Reel." That, sometimes at least, he knew she was there was clear to her, because, as she stole rapidly through the tangled fern and gale, she would hear a mocking laugh follow her like a leaping thing.

Mànus was not there on the night when she told Marcus and his brothers that she was going. He was in the haven on board the *Luath*, with his two mates, he singing in the moonshine as all three sat mending their fishing gear.

After the supper was done, the three brothers sat smoking and talking over an offer that had been made about some Shetland sheep. For a time, Anne watched them in silence. They were not like brothers, she thought. Marcus, tall, broad-shouldered, with yellow hair and strangely dark blue-black eyes and black eyebrows; stern, with a weary look on his sun-brown face. The light from the peats glinted upon the tawny curve of thick hair that trailed from his upper lip for he had the *caisean-feusag*[33] of the Northmen. Gloom, slighter of build, dark of hue and hair, but with hairless face; with thin, white, long-fingered hands that had ever a nervous motion, as though they were tide-wrack. There was always a frown on the centre of his forehead, even when he smiled with his thin lips and dusky, unbetraying eyes. He looked what he was, the brain of the Achannas. Not only did he have the English as though native to that tongue, but could and did read strange unnecessary books. Moreover, he was the only son of Robert Achanna to whom the old man had imparted his store of learning for Achanna had been a schoolmaster in his youth, in Galloway, and he had intended Gloom for the priesthood. His voice, too, was low and clear, but cold as pale-green water running under ice. As for Seumas, he was more like Marcus than Gloom, though not so fair. He had the same brown hair and shadowy hazel eyes, the same pale and smooth face, with something of the same intent look which characterised the long-time missing, and probably dead, eldest brother, Alasdair. He, too, was tall and gaunt. On Seumas's face there was that indescribable, as to some of course imperceptible, look which is indicated by the phrase "the dusk of the shadow," though few there are who know what they mean by that, or, knowing, are fain to say.

Suddenly, and without any word or reason for it, Gloom turned and spoke to her. "Well, Anne, and what is it?"

"I did not speak, Gloom."

"True for you mo cailinn. But it's about to speak you were."

---

33 Curling beard.

"Well, and that is true. Marcus, and you Gloom, and you Seumas, I have that to tell which you will not be altogether glad for the hearing. 'Tis about — about — me and — and Mànus."

There was no reply at first. The three brothers sat looking at her like the kye at a stranger on the moorland. There was a deepening of the frown on Gloom's brow, but when Anne looked at him his eyes fell and dwelt in the shadow at his feet. Then Marcus spoke in a low voice: "Is it Mànus MacCodrum you will be meaning?"

"Ay, sure."

Again silence. Gloom did not lift his eyes, and Seumas was now staring at the peats. Marcus shifted uneasily.

"And what will Mànus MacCodrum be wanting?"

"Sure, Marcus, you know well what I mean. Why do you make this thing hard for me? There is but one thing he would come here wanting. And he has asked me if I will go with him; and I have said yes; and if you are not willing that he come again with the minister, or that we go across to the kirk in Berneray of Uist in the Sound of Harris, then I will not stay under this roof another night, but will go away from Eilanmore at sunrise in the *Luath*, that is now in the haven. And that is for the hearing and knowing, Marcus and Gloom and Seumas!"

Once more, silence followed her speaking. It was broken in a strange way. Gloom slipped his *feadan* into his hand and so to his mouth. The clear, cold notes of the flute filled the flame-lit room. It was as though white polar birds were drifting before the coming of snow. The notes slid in to a wild, remote air: cold moonlight on the dark o' the sea, it was. It was the Dàn-nan-Ròn.

Anne flushed, trembled, and then abruptly rose. As she leaned on her clenched right hand upon the table, the light of the peats showed that her eyes were aflame.

"Why do you play that, Gloom Achanna?"

The man finished the bar, then blew into the oaten pipe, before, just glancing at the girl, he replied: "And what harm will there be in *that*, Anna-ban?"

"You know it is harm. That is the 'Dàn-nan-Ròn'!"

"Ay, and what then, Anna-ban?"

"What then? Are you thinking I don't know what you mean by playing the 'Song o' the Seals'?"

With an abrupt gesture Gloom put the *feadan* aside. As he did so, he rose.

"See here, Anne," he began roughly, when Marcus intervened.

"That will do just now, Gloom. Anne-à-ghraidh, do you mean that you are going to do this thing?"

"Ay, sure."

"Do you know why Gloom played the 'Dàn-nan-Ròn'?"

"It was a cruel thing."

"You know what is said in the isles about ... about ... this or that man, who is under *gheasan*, who is spell-bound and ... and ... about the seals ..."

"Yes, Marcus, it is knowing it that I am: 'Tha iad a' cantuinn gur h-e daoine fo gheasan a th' anns no roin.'"

"'They say that seals,'" he repeated slowly, "'They say that seals are men under magic spells.' And have you ever pondered that thing, Anne, my cousin?"

"I am knowing well what you mean."

"Then you will know that the MacCodrums of North Uist are called the Sliochd-nan-Ròn?"

"I have heard."

"And would you be for marrying a man that is of the race of the beasts, and himself knowing what that *geas* means, and who may any day go back to his people?"

"Ah, now, Marcus, sure it is making a mock of me you are. Neither you nor any here believe that foolish thing. How can a man born of a woman be a seal, even though his sinnsear[34] were the offspring of the sea-people, which is not a saying I am believing either, though it may be; and not that it matters much, whatever, about the far-back forebears."

Marcus frowned darkly, and at first made no response. At last he answered, speaking sullenly: "You may be believing this or you may be believing that, Anna-nic-Gilleasbuig, but two things are as well known as that the east wind brings the blight and the west wind the rain. And one is this: that long ago a Seal-man wedded a woman of North Uist, and that he or his son was called Neil MacCodrum; and that the sea-fever of the seal was in the blood of his line ever after. And this is the other: that twice within the memory of living folk, a MacCodrum has taken upon himself the form of a seal, and has so met his death, once Neil MacCodrum of Ru' Tormaid, and once Anndra MacCodrum of Berneray in the Sound. There's talk of others, but these are known of us all. And you will not be forgetting now that Neil-Donn was the grandfather, and that Anndra was the brother of the father of Mànus MacCodrum?"

"I am not caring what you say, Marcus. It is all foam of the sea."

---

34 Ancestors.

"There's no foam without wind or tide, Anne, an' it's a dark tide that will be bearing you away to Uist, and a black wind that will be blowing far away behind the East, the wind that will be carrying his death-cry to your ears."

The girl shuddered. The brave spirit in her, however, did not quail. "Well, so be it. To each his fate. But, seal or no seal, I am going to wed Mànus MacCodrum, who is a man as good as any here, and a true man at that, and the man I love, and that will be my man, God willing, the praise be His!"

Again Gloom took up the *feadan*, and sent a few cold, white notes floating through the hot room, breaking, suddenly, into the wild, fantastic, opening air of the 'Dàn-nan-Ròn.' With a low cry and passionate gesture Anne sprang forward, snatched the oat-flute from his grasp, and would have thrown it in the fire. Marcus held her in an iron grip however.

"Don't you be minding Gloom, Anne," he said quietly, as he took the *feadan* from her hand and handed it to his brother: "sure he's only telling you in his way what I am telling you in mine."

She shook herself free, and moved to the other side of the table. On the opposite wall hung the dirk which had belonged to old Achanna. This she unfastened. Holding it in her right hand, she faced the three men. "On the cross of the dirk I swear I will be the woman of Mànus MacCodrum."

The brothers made no response. They looked at her fixedly.

"And by the cross of the dirk I swear that if any man come between me and Mànus, this dirk will be for his remembering in a certain hour of the day of the days."

As she spoke, she looked meaningly at Gloom, whom she feared more than Marcus or Seumas.

"And by the cross of the dirk I swear that if evil come to Mànus, this dirk will have another sheath, and that will be my milkless breast; and by that token I now throw the old sheath in the fire." As she finished, she threw the sheath on to the burning peats.

Gloom quietly lifted it, brushed off the sparks of flame as though they were dust, and put it in his pocket.

"And by the same token, Anne," he said, "your oaths will come to nought."

Rising, he made a sign to his brothers to follow. When they were outside he told Seumas to return, and to keep Anne within, by peace if possible, by force if not. Briefly they discussed their plans, and then separated. While Seumas went back, Marcus and Gloom made their way to the haven.

Their black figures were visible in the moonlight, but at first they were not noticed by the men on board the *Luath*, for Mànus was singing. When the islesman stopped abruptly, one of his companions asked him jokingly if his song had brought a seal alongside, and bid him beware lest it was a woman of the sea-people. His face darkened, but he made no reply. When the others listened they heard the wild strain of the "Dàn-nan-Ròn" stealing through the moonshine. Staring against the shore, they could discern the two brothers.

"What will be the meaning of that?" asked one of the men, uneasily.

"When a man comes instead of a woman," answered Mànus, slowly, "the young corbies are astir in the nest."

So, it meant blood. Aulay Macneil and Donull MacDonull put down their gear, rose and stood waiting for what Mànus would do. "Ho, there!" he cried.

"Ho-ro!"

"What will you be wanting, Eilanmore?"

"We are wanting a word of you, Mànus MacCodrum. Will you come ashore?"

"If you want a word of me, you can come to me."

"There is no boat here."

"I'll send the bàta-beag."[35]

When he had spoken, Mànus asked Donull, the younger of his mates, a lad of seventeen, to row to the shore.

"And bring back no more than one man," he added, "whether it be Eilanmore himself or Gloom-mhic-Achanna."

The rope of the small boat was unfastened, and Donull rowed it swiftly through the moonshine. The passing of a cloud dusked the shore, but they saw him throw a rope for the guiding of the boat alongside the ledge of the landing-place; then the sudden darkening obscured the vision. Donull must be talking, they thought, for two or three minutes elapsed without sign, but at last the boat put off again, and with two figures only. Doubtless the lad had had to argue against the coming of both Marcus and Gloom.

This, in truth, was what Donull had done. But while he was speaking Marcus was staring fixedly beyond him.

"Who is it that is there?" he asked, "there, in the stern?"

"There is no one there."

"I thought I saw the shadow of a man."

---

35 Small boat.

"Then it was my shadow, Eilanmore."

Achanna turned to his brother. "I see a man's death there in the boat."

Gloom quailed for a moment, then laughed low. "I see no death of a man sitting in the boat, Marcus, but if I did I am thinking it would dance to the air of the Dàn-nan-Ròn, which is more than the wraith of you or me would do."

"It is not a wraith I was seeing, but the death of a man."

Gloom whispered, and his brother nodded sullenly. The next moment a heavy muffler was round Donull's mouth; and before he could resist, or even guess what had happened, he was on his face on the shore, bound and gagged. A minute later the oars were taken by Gloom, and the boat moved swiftly out of the inner haven.

As it drew near Mànus stared at it intently. "That is not Donull that is rowing, Aulay!"

"No: it will be Gloom Achanna, I'm thinking."

MacCodrum started. If so, that other figure at the stern was too big for Donull. The cloud passed just as the boat came alongside. The rope was made secure, and then Marcus and Gloom sprang on board.

"Where is Donull MacDonull?" demanded Mànus sharply. Marcus made no reply, so Gloom answered for him.

"He has gone up to the house with a message to Anne-nic-Gilleasbuig."

"And what will that message be?"

"That Mànus MacCodrum has sailed away from Eilanmore, and will not see her again."

MacCodrum laughed. It was a low, ugly laugh. "Sure, Gloom Achanna, you should be taking that *feadan* of yours and playing the Codhail-nan-Pairtean,[36] for I'm thinkin' the crabs are gathering about the rocks down below us, an' laughing with their claws."

"Well, and that is a true thing," Gloom replied slowly and quietly. "Yes, for sure I might, as you say, be playing the 'Meeting of the Crabs.' Perhaps," he added, as by a sudden afterthought, "perhaps, though it is a calm night, you will be hearing the comh-thonn. The 'slapping of the waves' is a better thing to be hearing than the 'Meeting of the Crabs."

"If I hear the comh-thonn it is not in the way you will be meaning, Gloom-mhic-Achanna. 'Tis not the 'up sail and good-bye' they will be saying, but 'Home wi' the Bride.'"

Here Marcus intervened. "Let us be having no more words, Mànus MacCodrum. The girl Anne is not for you. Gloom is to be her man. So

---

36 Gathering or meeting of the crabs.

get you hence. If you will be going quiet, it is quiet we will be. If you have your feet on this thing, then you will be having that too which I saw in the boat."

"And what was it you saw in the boat, Achanna?"

"The death of a man."

"So ... And now," (this after a prolonged silence, wherein the four men stood facing each other) "is it a blood-matter if not of peace?"

"Ay. Go, if you are wise. If not, 'tis your own death you will be making."

There was a flash as of summer lightning. A bluish flame seemed to leap through the moonshine. Marcus reeled, with a gasping cry; then, leaning back, till his face blanched in the moonlight, his knees gave way. As he fell, he turned half round. The long knife which Mànus had hurled at him had not penetrated his breast more than an inch at most, but as he fell on the deck it was driven into him up to the hilt. In the blank silence that followed, the three men could hear a sound like the ebb-tide in sea-weed. It was the gurgling of the bloody froth in the lungs of the dead man. The first to speak was his brother, and then only when thin reddish-white foam-bubbles began to burst from the blue lips of Marcus.

"It is murder."

He spoke low, but it was like the surf of breakers in the ears of those who heard. "You have said one part of a true word, Gloom Achanna. It is murder — that you and he came here for!"

"The death of Marcus Achanna is on you, Mànus MacCodrum."

"So be it, as between yourself and me, or between all of your blood and me; though Aulay MacNeil as well as you can witness that though in self-defence I threw the knife at Achanna, it was his own doing that drove it into him."

"You can whisper that to the rope when it is round your neck."

"And what will you be doing now, Gloom-mhic-Achanna?"

For the first time Gloom shifted uneasily. A swift glance revealed to him the awkward fact that the boat trailed behind the *Luath*, so that he could not leap into it, while if he turned to haul it close by the rope he was at the mercy of the two men. "I will go in peace," he said quietly.

"Ay," was the answer, in an equally quiet tone, "in the white peace."

Upon this menace of death the two men stood facing each other. Achanna broke the silence at last. "You'll hear the 'Dàn-nan-Ròn' the night before you die, Mànus MacCodrum, and lest you doubt it you'll hear it again in your death-hour."

"Ma tha sìn an Dàn — if that be ordained." Mànus spoke gravely. His very quietude, however, boded ill. There was no hope of clemency; Gloom knew that.

Suddenly he laughed scornfully. Then, pointing with his right hand as if to some one behind his two adversaries, he cried out: "Put the death-hand on them, Marcus! Give them the Grave!"

Both men sprang aside, the heart of each nigh upon bursting. The death-touch of the newly slain is an awful thing to incur, for it means that the wraith can transfer all its evil to the person touched. The next moment there was a heavy splash. Mànus realised that it was no more than a ruse, and that Gloom had escaped. With feverish haste he hauled in the small boat, leaped into it, and began at once to row so as to intercept his enemy.

Achanna rose once between him and the *Luath*. MacCodrum crossed the oars in the thole-pins and seized the boat-hook. The swimmer kept straight for him. Suddenly he dived. In a flash, Mànus knew that Gloom was going to rise under the boat, seize the keel, and upset him, and thus probably be able to grip him from above. There was time and no more to leap; and, indeed, scarce had he plunged into the sea ere the boat swung right over, Achanna clambering over it the next moment.

At first Gloom could not see where his foe was. He crouched on the upturned craft, and peered eagerly into the moonlit water. All at once a black mass shot out of the shadow between him and the smack. This black mass laughed — the same low, ugly laugh that had preceded the death of Marcus.

He who was in turn the swimmer was now close. When a fathom away he leaned back and began to tread water steadily. In his right hand he grasped the boat-hook. The man in the boat knew that to stay where he was meant certain death. He gathered himself together like a crouching cat. Mànus kept treading the water slowly, but with the hook ready so that the sharp iron spike at the end of it should transfix his foe if he came at him with a leap. Now and again he laughed. Then in his low sweet voice, but brokenly at times between his deep breathings, he began to sing:

The tide was dark, an' heavy with the burden that it bore;
I heard it talkin', whisperin', upon the weedy shore;
Each wave that stirred the sea-weed was like a closing door;
'Tis closing doors they hear at last who hear no more, no more,
  My Grief,
  No more!

The tide was in the salt sea-weed, and like a knife it tore;
The wild sea-wind went moaning, sooing, moaning o'er and o'er;
The deep sea-heart was brooding deep upon its ancient lore —
I heard the sob, the sooing sob, the dying sob at its core,
    My Grief,
    Its core!

The white sea-waves were wan and grey its ashy lips before,
The yeast within its ravening mouth was red with streaming gore;
O red sea-weed, O red sea-waves, O hollow baffled roar,
Since one thou hast, O dark dim Sea, why callest thou for more,
    My Grief,
    For more!

In the quiet moonlight the chant, with its long, slow cadences, sung as no other man in the isles could sing it, sounded sweet and remote beyond words to tell. The glittering shine was upon the water of the haven, and moved in waving lines of fire along the stone ledges. Sometimes a fish rose, and spilt a ripple of pale gold; or a sea-nettle swam to the surface, and turned its blue or greenish globe of living jelly to the moon dazzle. The man in the water made a sudden stop in his treading and listened intently. Then once more the phosphorescent light gleamed about his slow-moving shoulders. In a louder chanting voice came once again:

Each wave that stirs the sea-weed is like a closing door;
'Tis closing doors they hear at last who hear no more, no more,
    My Grief,
    No more!

Yes, his quick ears had caught the inland strain of a voice he knew. Soft and white as the moonshine came Anne's singing as she passed along the corrie leading to the haven. In vain his travelling gaze sought her; she was still in the shadow, and, besides, a slow drifting cloud obscured the moonlight. When he looked back again a stifled exclamation came from his lips. There was not a sign of Gloom Achanna. He had slipped noiselessly from the boat, and was now either behind it, or had dived beneath it, or was swimming under water this way or that. If only the cloud would sail by, muttered Mànus, as he held himself in readiness for an attack from beneath or behind. As the dusk lightened, he swam slowly toward the boat, and then swiftly round it. There was no one there. He climbed on to the keel, and stood, leaning forward, as a salmon-leisterer by torchlight, with his spear-pointed boat-hook raised.

Neither below nor beyond could he discern any shape. A whispered call to Aulay MacNeil showed that he, too, saw nothing. Gloom must have swooned, and sank deep as he slipped through the water. Perhaps the dog-fish were already darting about him.

Going behind the boat Mànus guided it back to the smack. It was not long before, with MacNeil's help, he righted the punt. One oar had drifted out of sight, but as there was a sculling-hole in the stern that did not matter.

"What shall we do with it?" he muttered, as he stood at last by the corpse of Marcus. "This is a bad night for us, Aulay!"

"Bad it is; but let us be seeing it is not worse. I'm thinking we should have left the boat."

"And for why that?"

"We could say that Marcus Achanna and Gloom Achanna left us again, and that we saw no more of them nor of our boat."

MacCodrum pondered a while. The sound of voices, borne faintly across the water, decided him. Probably Anne and the lad Donull were talking. He slipped into the boat, and with a sail-knife soon ripped it here and there. It filled, and then, heavy with the weight of a great ballast-stone which Aulay had first handed to his companion, and surging with a foot-thrust from the latter, it sank. "We'll hide the — the man there ... behind the windlass, below the spare sail, till we're out at sea, Aulay. Quick, give me a hand!"

It did not take the two men long to lift the corpse, and do as Mànus had suggested. They had scarce accomplished this, when Anne's voice came hailing silver-sweet across the water.

With death-white face and shaking limbs, MacCodrum stood holding the mast, while with a loud voice, so firm and strong that Aulay MacNeil smiled below his fear, he asked if the Achannas were back yet, and if so for Donull to row out at once, and she with him if she would come.

It was nearly half an hour thereafter that Anne rowed out toward the *Luath*. She had gone at last along the shore to a creek where one of Marcus's boats was moored and returned with it. Having taken Donull on board, she made way with all speed, fearful lest Gloom or Marcus should intercept her.

It did not take long to explain how she had laughed at Seumas's vain efforts to detain her, and had come down to the haven. As she approached, she heard Mànus singing, and so had herself broken into a song she knew he loved. Then, by the water-edge she had come upon Donull lying upon his back, bound and gagged. After she had released him they waited to see what would happen, but as in the moonlight they could not see any small boat come in, bound to or from the smack, she had hailed to know if Mànus were there.

On his side he said briefly that the two Achannas had come to persuade him to leave without her. On his refusal they had departed again, uttering threats against her as well as himself. He heard their quarrelling voices as they rowed into the gloom, but could not see them at last because of the obscured moonlight.

"And now, Ann-mochree," he added, "is it coming with me you are, and just as you are? Sure, you'll never repent it, and you'll have all you want that I can give. Dear of my heart, say that you will be coming away this night of the nights! By the Black Stone on Icolmkill I swear it, and by the Sun, and by the Moon, and by Himself!"

"I am trusting you, Mànus dear. Sure it is not for me to be going back to that house after what has been done and said. I go with you, now and always, God save us."

"Well, dear lass o' my heart, it's farewell to Eilanmore it is, for by the Blood on the Cross I'll never land on it again!"

"And that will be no sorrow to me, Mànus my home!"

And this was the way that my friend Anne Gillespie left Eilanmore to go to the isles of the West.

It was a fair sailing, in the white moon-shine, with a whispering breeze astern. Anne leaned against Mànus, dreaming her dream. The lad Donull sat drowsing at the helm. Forward, Aulay MacNeil, with his face set against the moonshine to the west, brooded dark. Though no longer was land in sight, and there was peace among the deeps of the quiet stars and upon the sea, the shadow of fear was upon the face of Mànus MacCodrum.

This might well have been because of the as yet unburied dead that lay beneath the spare sail by the windlass. The dead man, however, did not affright him. What went moaning in his heart, and sighing and calling in his brain, was a faint falling echo he had heard, as the *Luath* glided slow out of the haven. Whether from the water or from the shore he could not tell, but he heard the wild, fantastic air of the "Dàn-nan-Ròn," as he had heard it that very night upon the *feadan* of Gloom Achanna.

It was his hope that his ears had played him false. When he glanced about him, and saw the sombre flame in the eyes of Aulay MacNeil, staring at him out of the dusk, he knew that which Oisìn the son of Fionn cried in his pain: "his soul swam in mist."

II

For all the evil omens, the marriage of Anne and Mànus MacCodrum
went well. He was more silent than of yore, and men avoided rather than
sought him; but he was happy with Anne, and content with his two
mates, who were now Callum MacCodrum and Ranald MacRanald. The
youth Donull had bettered himself by joining a Skye skipper who was a
kinsman, and Aulay MacNeil had surprised everyone, except Mànus, by
going away as a seaman on board one of the *Loch* line of ships which sail
for Australia from the Clyde.

Anne never knew what had happened, though it is possible she
suspected somewhat. All that was known to her was that Marcus and
Gloom Achanna had disappeared, and were supposed to have been
drowned. There was now no Achanna upon Eilanmore, for Seumas had
taken a horror of the place and his loneliness. As soon as it was commonly
admitted that his two brothers must have drifted out to sea, and been
drowned, or at best picked up by some ocean-going ship, he disposed
of the island-farm, and left Eilanmore forever. All this confirmed the
thing said among the islanders of the west, that old Robert Achanna had
brought a curse with him. Blight and disaster had visited Eilanmore over
and over in the many years he had held it, and death, sometimes tragic or
mysterious, had overtaken six of his seven sons, while the youngest bore
upon his brows the "dusk of the shadow." True, none knew for certain
that three out of the six were dead, but few for a moment believed in the
possibility that Alasdair and Marcus and Gloom were alive.

On the night when Anne had left the island with Mànus MacCodrum,
he, Seumas, had heard nothing to alarm him. Even when, an hour after she
had gone down to the haven, neither she nor his brothers had returned,
and the *Luath* had put out to sea, he was not in fear of any ill. Clearly,
Marcus and Gloom had gone away in the smack, perhaps determined to
see that the girl was duly married by priest or minister. He would have
perturbed himself little for days to come, but for a strange thing that
happened that night. He had returned to the house because of a chill
that was upon him, and convinced too that all had sailed in the *Luath*. He
was sitting brooding by the peat-fire, when he was startled by a sound at
the window at the back of the room. A few bars of a familiar air struck
painfully upon his ear, though played so low that they were just audible.
What could it be but the Dàn-nan-ròn, and who would be playing that
but Gloom? What did it mean? Perhaps, after all, it was fantasy only,

and there was no *feadan* out there in the dark. He was pondering this when, still low but louder and sharper than before, there rose and fell the strain which he hated, and Gloom never played before him, that of the Dànsa-na-mairv, the "Dance of the Dead." Swiftly and silently he rose and crossed the room. In the dark shadows cast by the byre he could see nothing, but the music ceased. He went out, and searched everywhere, but found no one. So he returned, took down the Holy Book, with awed heart, and read slowly till peace came upon him, soft and sweet as the warmth of the peat-glow.

But as for Anne, she had never even this hint that one of the supposed dead might be alive, or that, being dead, Gloom might yet touch a shadowy *feadan* into a wild remote air of the grave.

When month after month went by, and no hint of ill came to break upon their peace, Mànus grew light-hearted again. Once more his songs were heard as he came back from the fishing, or loitered ashore mending his nets. A new happiness was nigh to them, for Anne was with child. True, there was fear also, for the girl was not well at the time when her labour was near, and grew weaker daily. There came a day when Mànus had to go to Loch Boisdale in South Uist: and it was with pain and something of foreboding that he sailed away from Berneray in the Sound of Harris, where he lived. It was on the third night that he returned.

He was met by Katreen MacRanald, the wife of his mate, with the news that on the morrow after his going Anne had sent for the priest who was staying at Loch Maddy, for she had felt the coming of death. It was that very evening she died, and took the child with her.

Mànus heard as one in a dream. It seemed to him that the tide was ebbing in his heart, and a cold, sleety rain falling, falling through a mist in his brain.

Sorrow lay heavily upon him. After the earthing of her whom he loved, he went to and fro solitary: often crossing the Narrows and going to the old Pictish Tower under the shadow of Ban Breac. He would not go upon the sea, but let his kinsman Callum do as he liked with the *Luath*. Now and again Father Allan MacNeil sailed northward to see him. Each time he departed sadder. "The man is going mad, I fear," he said to Callum, the last time he saw Mànus.

The long summer nights brought peace and beauty to the isles. It was a great herring-year, and the moon-fishing was unusually good. All the Uist men who lived by the sea-harvest were in their boats whenever they could. The pollack, the dogfish, the otters, and the seals, with flocks of sea-fowl beyond number, shared in the common joy. Mànus MacCodrum alone paid no heed to herring or mackerel. He was often seen striding along the shore, and more than once had been heard laughing; sometimes, too, he was come upon at low tide by the great Reef of Berneray, singing wild strange runes and songs, or crouching upon a rock and brooding dark.

The midsummer moon found no man on Berneray except MacCodrum, the Rev. Mr. Black, the minister of the Free Kirk, and an old man named Anndra McIan. On the night before the last day of the middle month, Anndra was reproved by the minister for saying that he had seen a man rise out of one of the graves in the kirk-yard, and steal down by the stone-dykes towards Balnahunnur-sa-mona,[37] where Mànus MacCodrum lived.

"The dead do not rise and walk, Anndra."

"That may be, maighstir, but it may have been the Watcher of the Dead. Sure it is not three weeks since Padruig McAlistair was laid beneath the green mound. He'll be wearying for another to take his place."

"Hoots, man, that is an old superstition. The dead do not rise and walk, I tell you."

"It is right you may be, maighstir, but I heard of this from my father, that was old before you were young, and from his father before him. When the last-buried is weary with being the Watcher of the Dead he goes about from place to place till he sees man, woman, or child with the death-shadow in the eyes, and then he goes back to his grave and lies down in peace, for his vigil it will be over now."

The minister laughed at the folly, and went into his house to make ready for the Sacrament that was to be on the morrow. Old Anndra, however, was uneasy. After the porridge, he went down through the gloaming to Balnahunnur-sa-mona. He meant to go in and warn Mànus MacCodrum. But when he got to the west wall, and stood near the open window, he heard Mànus speaking in a loud voice, though he was alone in the room.

"B'ionganntach do ghràdh dhomhsa, a' toirt barrachd air gràdh nam ban!"[38]

This Mànus cried in a voice quivering with pain. Anndra stopped still, fearful to intrude, fearful also, perhaps, to see someone there beside MacCodrum whom eyes should not see. Then the voice rose into a cry of agony. "Aoram dhuit, ay an déigh dhomh fàs aosda!"[39]

---

37 The solitary farm on the hillside.
38 'Your love to me was wonderful, surpassing the love of women.'
39 'I shall worship thee, ay, even after I have become old.'

With that, Anndra feared to stay. As he passed the byre he started, for he thought he saw the shadow of a man. When he looked closer he could see nought, so went his way, trembling and sore troubled.

It was dusk when Mànus came out. He saw that it was to be a cloudy night; and perhaps it was this that, after a brief while, made him turn in his aimless walk and go back to the house. He was sitting before the flaming heart of the peats, brooding in his pain, when suddenly he sprang to his feet. Loud and clear, and close as though played under the very window of the room, came the cold, white notes of an oaten flute. Ah, too well he knew that wild, fantastic air. Who could it be but Gloom Achanna, playing upon his *feadan*; and what air of all airs could that be but the Dàn-nan-Ròn?

Was it the dead man, standing there unseen in the shadow of the grave? Was Marcus beside him, Marcus with the knife still thrust up to the hilt, and the lung-foam upon his lips? Can the sea give up its dead? Can there be strain of any *feadan* that ever was made of man — there in the Silence?

In vain Mànus MacCodrum tortured himself thus. Too well he knew that he had heard the Dàn-nan-Ròn and that no other than Gloom Achanna was the player.

Suddenly an excess of fury wrought him to madness. With an abrupt lilt the tune swung into the Dànsa-na-mairv, and thence, after a few seconds, and in a moment, into that mysterious and horrible Codhail-nan-Pairtean which none but Gloom played. There could be no mistake now, nor as to what was meant by the muttering, jerking air of the "gathering of the crabs." With a savage cry Mànus snatched up a long dirk from its place by the chimney, and rushed out.

There was not the shadow of a sea-gull even in front; so he sped round by the byre. Neither was anything unusual discoverable there.

"Sorrow upon me," he cried; "man or wraith, I will be putting it to the dirk!"

But there was no one; nothing; not a sound.

Then, at last, with a listless droop of his arms, MacCodrum turned and went into the house again. He remembered what Gloom Achanna had said: *"You'll hear the Dàn-nan-Ròn the night before you die, Mànus MacCodrum, and lest you doubt it, you'll hear it in your death-hour."* He did not stir from the fire for three hours; then he rose, and went over to his bed and lay down without undressing.

He did not sleep, but lay listening and watching. The peats burned low, and at last there was scarce a flicker along the floor. Outside he could hear the wind moaning upon the sea. By a strange rustling sound he knew that the tide was ebbing across the great reef that runs out from Berneray. By midnight the clouds had gone. The moon shone clear and full. When he heard the clock strike in its worm-eaten, rickety case, he sat up, and listened intently. He could hear nothing. No shadow stirred. Surely if the wraith of Gloom Achanna were waiting for him it would make some sign, now, in the dead of night.

An hour passed. Mànus rose, crossed the room on tip-toe, and soundlessly opened the door. The salt wind blew fresh against his face. The smell of the shore, of wet sea-wrack and pungent bog-myrtle, of foam and moving water, came sweet to his nostrils. He heard a skua calling from the rocky promontory. From the slopes behind, the wail of a moon-restless lapwing rose and fell mournfully.

Crouching and with slow, stealthy step, he stole round by the seaward wall. At the dyke he stopped, and scrutinised it on each side. He could see for several hundred yards, and there was not even a sheltering sheep. Then, soundlessly as ever, he crept close to the byre. He put his ear to chink after chink: but not a stir of a shadow even. As a shadow, himself, he drifted lightly to the front, past the hayrick; then, with swift glances to right and left, opened the door and entered. As he did so, he stood as though frozen. Surely, he thought that was a sound as of a step, out there by the hay-rick. A terror was at his heart. In front, the darkness of the byre, with God knows what dread thing awaiting him; behind, a mysterious walker in the night, swift to take him unawares. The trembling that came upon him was nigh overmastering. At last, with a great effort, he moved towards the ledge, where he kept a candle. With shaking hand he struck a light. The empty byre looked ghostly and fearsome in the flickering gloom. But there was no one, nothing. He was about to turn, when a rat ran along a loose hanging beam, and stared at him, or at the yellow shine. He saw its black eyes shining like peat-water in moonlight.

The creature was curious at first, then indifferent. At last, it began to squeak, and then make a swift scratching with its forepaws. Once or twice came an answering squeak; a faint rustling was audible here and there among the straw.

With a sudden spring Mànus seized the beast. Even in the second in which he raised it to his mouth and scrunched its back with his strong teeth, it bit him severely. He let his hands drop, and grope furtively in the darkness. With stooping head he shook the last breath out of the rat, holding it with his front teeth, with back-curled lips. The next moment he dropped the dead thing, trampled upon it, and burst out laughing. There was a scurrying of pattering feet, a rustling of straw. Then silence again. A draught from the door had caught the flame and extinguished it. In the silence and darkness MacCodrum stood, intent, but no longer afraid. He laughed again, because it was so easy to kill with the teeth. The noise of his laughter seemed to him to leap hither and thither like a shadowy ape. He could see it: a blackness within the darkness. Once more he laughed. It amused him to see the thing leaping about like that.

Suddenly he turned, and walked out into the moonlight. The lapwing was still circling and wailing. He mocked it, with loud shrill pee-weety, pee-weety, pee-weet. The bird swung waywardly, alarmed: its abrupt cry, and dancing flight aroused its fellows. The air was full of the lamentable crying of plovers.

A sough of the sea came inland. Mànus inhaled its breath with a sigh of delight. A passion for the running wave was upon him. He yearned to feel green water break against his breast. Thirst and hunger, too, he felt at last, though he had known neither all day. How cool and sweet, he thought, would be a silver haddock, or even a brown-backed liath, alive and gleaming, wet with the sea-water still bubbling in its gills. It would writhe, just like the rat; but then how he would throw his head back, and toss the glittering thing up into the moonlight, catch it on the downwhirl just as it neared the wave on whose crest he was, and then devour it with swift voracious gulps!

With quick, jerky steps he made his way past the landward side of the small, thatch-roofed cottage. He was about to enter, when he noticed that the door, which he had left ajar, was closed. He stole to the window and glanced in. A single, thin, wavering moonbeam flickered in the room. But the flame at the heart of the peats had worked its way through the ash, and there was now a dull glow, though that was within the "smooring"[40] and threw scarce more than a glimmer into the room. There was enough light, however, for Mànus MacCodrum to see that a man sat on the three-legged stool before the fire. His head was bent, as though he were listening. The face was away from the window. It was his own wraith, of course; of that, Mànus felt convinced. What was it doing there? Perhaps it had eaten the Holy Book, so that it was beyond his putting a *rosad* on it! At the thought he laughed loud. The shadow man leaped to his feet.

The next moment MacCodrum swung himself on to the thatched roof, and clambered from rope to rope, where these held down the big stones

---

40 The act of covering the peat-fire with crumbled peat bricks in order to hold the heat until morning.

which acted as dead-weight for thatch, against the fury of tempests. Stone after stone he tore from its fastenings, and hurled to the ground over beyond the door. Then with tearing hands he began to burrow an opening in the thatch. All the time he whined like a beast. He was glad the moon shone full upon him. When he had made a big enough hole, he would see the evil thing out of the grave that sat in his room and would stone it to death. Suddenly he became still. A cold sweat broke out upon him. The *thing*, whether his own wraith, or the spirit of his dead foe, or Gloom Achanna himself, had begun to play, low and slow, a wild air. No piercing, cold music like that of the *feadan!* Too well he knew it, and those cool, white notes that moved here and there in the darkness like snowflakes. As for the air, though he slept till Judgment Day and heard but a note of it amidst all the clamour of heaven and hell, sure he would scream because of the Dàn-nan-Ròn.

The Dàn-nan-Ròn: the Roin! the Seals! Ah, what was he doing there, on the bitter, weary land! Out there was the sea. Safe would he be in the green waves. With a leap he was on the ground. Seizing a huge stone he hurled it through the window. Then, laughing and screaming, he fled towards the Great Reef, along whose sides the ebb-tide gurgled and sobbed, with glistening white foam. He ceased screaming or laughing as he heard the Dàn-nan-Ròn behind him, faint, but following; sure, following. Bending low, he raced towards the rock-ledges from which ran the reef.

When at last he reached the extreme ledge he stopped abruptly. Out on the reef he saw from ten to twenty seals, some swimming to and fro, others clinging to the reef, one or two making a curious barking sound, with round heads lifted against the moon. In one place there was a surge and lashing of water. Two bulls were fighting to the death.

With swift, stealthy movements Mànus unclothed himself. The damp had clotted the leathern thongs of his boots, and he snarled with curled lip as he tore at them. He shone white in the moonshine, but was sheltered from the sea by the ledge behind which he crouched. "What did Gloom Achanna mean by that?" he muttered savagely, as he heard the nearing air change into the "Dance of the Dead." For a moment Mànus was a man again. He was nigh upon turning to face his foe, corpse or wraith or living body; to spring at this thing which followed him, and tear it with hands and teeth. Then, once more, the hated "Song of the Seals" stole mockingly through the night. With a shiver he slipped into the dark water. Then with quick, powerful strokes he was in the moon-flood, and swimming hard against it out by the leeside of the reef.

So intent were the seals upon the fight of the two great bulls that they did not see the swimmer, or if they did, took him for one of their own people. A savage snarling and barking and half-human crying came from them. Mànus was almost within reach of the nearest, when one of the combatants sank dead, with torn throat. The victor clambered on the reef, and leaned high, swaying its great head and shoulders to and fro. In the moonlight its white fangs were like red coral. Its blinded eyes ran with gore. There was a rush, a rapid leaping and swirling, as Mànus surged in among the seals, which were swimming round the place where the slain bull had sunk.

The laughter of this long, white seal terrified them.

When his knees struck against a rock, MacCodrum groped with his arms, and hauled himself out of the water. From rock to rock and ledge to ledge he went, with a fantastic, dancing motion, his body gleaming foam-white in the moon-shine. As he pranced and trampled along the weedy ledges, he sang snatches of an old rune — the lost rune of the MacCodrums of Uist. The seals on the rocks crouched spellbound; those slow-swimming in the water stared with brown unwinking eyes, with their small ears strained against the sound:

It is I, Mànus MacCodrum,
I am telling you that, you, Anndra of my blood,
And you, Neil my grandfather, and you, and you, and you!
Ay, ay, Mànus my name is, Mànus Mac Mànus!
It is I myself, and no other.
Your brother, O Seals of the Sea!
Give me blood of the red fish,
And a bite of the flying sgadan:
The green wave on my belly,
And the foam in my eyes!
I am your bull-brother, O Bulls of the Sea,
Bull — better than any of you, snarling bulls!
Come to me, mate, seal of the soft, furry womb,
White am I still, though red shall I be,
Red with the streaming red blood if any dispute me!
Aoh, aoh, aoh, arò, arò, ho-rò!
A man was I, a seal am I,
My fangs churn the yellow foam from my lips:
Give way to me, give way to me, Seals of the Sea;
Give way, for I am fèy of the sea

And the sea-maiden I see there,
And my name, true, is Mànus MacCodrum,
The bull-seal that was a man, Arà! Arà!

By this time he was close upon the great black seal, which was still monotonously swaying its gory head, with its sightless eyes rolling this way and that. The sea-folk seemed fascinated. None moved, even when the dancer in the moonshine trampled upon them.

When he came within arm-reach he stopped. "Are you the Ceann-Cinnidh?" he cried. "Are you the head of this clan of the sea-folk?"

The huge beast ceased its swaying. Its curled lips moved from its fangs.

"Speak, Seal, if there's no curse upon you! Maybe, now, you'll be Anndra himself, the brother of my father! Speak! H'st — are you hearing that music on the shore? 'Tis the Dàn-nan-Ròn! Death o' my soul, it's the Dàn-nan-Ròn! Aha, 'tis Gloom Achanna out of the grave. Back, beast, and let me move on!" With that, seeing the great bull did not move, he struck it full in the face with clenched fist. There was a hoarse, strangling roar, and the seal champion was upon him with lacerating fangs.

Mànus swayed this way and that. All he could hear now was the snarling and growling and choking cries of the maddened seals. As he fell, they closed in upon him. His screams wheeled through the night like mad birds. With desperate fury he struggled to free himself. The great bull pinned him to the rock; a dozen others tore at his white flesh, till his spouting blood made the rocks scarlet in the white shine of the moon. For a few seconds he still fought savagely, tearing with teeth and hands. Once, a red irrecognisable mass, he staggered to his knees. A wild cry burst from his lips, when from the shore-end of the reef came loud and clear the lilt of the rune of his fate.

The next moment he was dragged down and swept from the reef into the sea. As the torn and mangled body disappeared from sight, it was amid a seething crowd of leaping and struggling seals, their eyes wild with affright and fury, their fangs red with human gore.

And Gloom Achanna, turning upon the reef, moved swiftly inland, playing low on his *feadan* as he went.

Green Branches

I N the year that followed the death of Mànus MacCodrum, James Achanna saw nothing of his brother Gloom. He might have thought himself alone in the world, of all his people, but for a letter that came to him out of the west. True, he had never accepted the common opinion that his brothers had both been drowned on that night when Anne Gillespie left Eilanmore with Mànus. In the first place, he had nothing of that inner conviction concerning the fate of Gloom which he had concerning that of Marcus; in the next, had he not heard the sound of the *feadan*, which no one that he knew played, except Gloom; and, for further token, was not the tune that which he hated above all others — the "Dance of the Dead" — for who but Gloom would be playing that, he hating it so, and the hour being late, and no one else on Eilanmore? It was no sure thing that the dead had *not come* back; but the more he thought of it the more Achanna believed that his sixth brother was still alive. Of this, however, he said nothing to any one.

It was as a man set free that, at last, after long waiting and patient trouble with the disposal of all that was left of the Achanna heritage, he left the island. It was a grey memory for him. The bleak moorland of it, the blight that had lain so long and so often upon the crops, the rains that had swept the isle for grey days and grey weeks and grey months, the sobbing of the sea by day and its dark moan by night, its dim relinquishing sigh in the calm of dreary ebbs, its hollow, baffling roar when the storm-shadow swept up out of the sea — one and all oppressed him, even in memory. He had never loved the island, even when it lay green and fragrant in the green and white seas under white and blue skies, fresh and sweet as an Eden of the sea. He had ever been lonely and weary, tired of the mysterious shadow that lay upon his folk, caring little for any of his brothers except the eldest — long since mysteriously gone out of the ken of man — and almost hating Gloom, who had ever borne him a grudge because of his beauty, and because of his likeness to and reverent heed for Alasdair. Moreover, ever since he had come to love Katreen Macarthur, the daughter of Donald Macarthur who lived in Sleat of Skye, he had been eager to live near her; the more eager as he knew that Gloom loved the girl also, and wished for success not only for his own sake, but so as to put a slight upon his younger brother.

So, when at last he left the island, he sailed southward gladly. He was leaving Eilanmore; he was bound to a new home in Skye, and perhaps he was going to his long-delayed, long-dreamed-of happiness. True, Katreen was not pledged to him; he did not even know for sure if she loved him. He thought, hoped, dreamed, almost believed that she did; but then there was her cousin Ian, who had long wooed her, and to whom old Donald Macarthur had given his blessing. Nevertheless, his heart would have been lighter than it had been for long, but for two things. First, there was the letter. Some weeks earlier he had received it, not recognising the writing, because of the few letters he had ever seen, and, moreover, as it was in a feigned hand. With difficulty he had deciphered the manuscript, plain printed though it was. It ran thus:

"Well, Seumas, my brother, it is wondering if I am dead, you will be. Maybe ay, and maybe no. But I send you this writing to let you see that I know all you do and think of. So you are going to leave Eilanmore without an Achanna upon it? And you will be going to Sleat in Skye? Well, let me be telling you this thing. Do not go. I see blood there. And there is this, too: neither you nor any man shall take Katreen away from me. You know that; and Ian Macarthur knows it; and Katreen knows it; and that holds whether I am alive or dead. I say to you: do not go. It will be better for you, and for all. Ian Macarthur is away in the north-sea with the whaler-captain who came to us at Eilanmore, and will not be back for three months yet. It will be better for him not to come back. But if he comes back he will have to reckon with the man who says that Katreen Macarthur is his. I would rather not have two men to speak to, and one my brother. It does not matter to you where I am. I want no money just now. But put aside my portion for me. Have it ready for me against the day I call for it. I will not be patient that day; so have it ready for me. In the place that I am I am content. You will be saying: why is my brother away in a remote place (I will say this to you: that it is not further north than St. Kilda nor further south than the Mull of Cantyre!), and for what reason? That is between me and silence. But perhaps you think of Anne sometimes. Do you know that she lies under the green grass? And of Mànus MacCordrum? They say that he swam out into the sea and was drowned; and they whisper of the seal-blood, though the minister is wrath with them for that. He calls it a madness. Well, I was there at that madness, and I played to it on my feadan. And now, Seumas, can you be thinking of what the tune was that I played?

Your brother, who waits his own day,
GLOOM

"Do not be forgetting this thing: I would rather not be playing the 'Damhsa-na-mairbh.' *It was an ill hour for Mànus when he heard the 'Dàn-nan-Ròn;' it was the song of his soul, that; and yours is the 'Davsa-na-Mairv.' "*

This letter was ever in his mind: this, and what happened in the gloaming when he sailed away for Skye in the herring-smack of two men who lived at Armadale in Sleat. For, as the boat moved slowly out of the haven, one of the men asked him if he was sure that no one was left upon the island; for he thought he had seen a figure on the rocks, waving a black scarf. Achanna shook his head; but just then his companion cried that at that moment he had seen the same thing. So the smack was put about, and when she was moving slow through the haven again Achanna sculled ashore in the little coggly punt. In vain he searched here and there, calling loudly again and again. Both men could hardly have been mistaken, he thought. If there were no human creature on the island, and if their eyes had not played them false, who could it be? The wraith of Marcus, mayhap; or might it be the old man himself (his father), risen to bid farewell to his youngest son, or to warn him?

It was no use to wait longer, so, looking often behind him, he made his way to the boat again, and rowed slowly out towards the smack.

Jerk — jerk — jerk across the water came, low but only too loud for him, the opening motif of the Damhsa-na-Mairbh. A horror came upon him, and he drove the boat through the water so that the sea splashed over the bows. When he came on deck, he cried in a hoarse voice to the man next him to put up the helm, and let the smack swing to the wind.

"There is no one there, Callum Campbell," he whispered.

"And who is it that will be making that strange music?"

"What music?"

"Sure it has stopped now, but I heard it clear, and so did Anndra MacEwan. It was like the sound of a reed-pipe, and the tune was an eerie one at that."

"It was the Dance of the Dead."

"And who will be playing that?" asked the man, with fear in his eyes.

"No living man."

"No living man?"

"No. I'm thinking it will be one of my brothers who was drowned here, and by the same token that it is Gloom, for he played upon the *feadan*. But if not, then — then —"

The two men waited in breathless silence, each trembling with superstitious fear; but at last the elder made a sign to Achanna to finish.

"Then — it will be the Kelpie."

"Is there — is there one of the — the cave-women here?"

"It is said; and you know of old that the Kelpie sings or plays a strange tune to wile seamen to their death."

At that moment, the fantastic, jerking music came loud and clear across the bay. There was a horrible suggestion in it, as if dead bodies were moving along the ground with long jerks, and crying and laughing wild. It was enough; the men, Campbell and MacEwan, would not now have waited longer if Achanna had offered them all he had in the world. Nor were they, or he, out of their panic haste till the smack stood well out at sea, and not a sound could be heard from Eilanmore.

They stood watching, silent. Out of the dusky mass that lay in the seaward way to the north came a red gleam. It was like an eye staring after them with blood-red glances.

"What is that, Achanna?" asked one of the men at last.

"It looks as though a fire had been lit in the house up in the island. The door and the window must be open. The fire must be fed with wood, for no peats would give that flame; and there were none lit when I left. To my knowing, there was no wood for burning except the wood of the shelves and the bed."

"And who would be doing that?"

"I know of that no more than you do, Callum Campbell."

No more was said, and it was a relief to all when the last glimmer of the light was absorbed in the darkness.

At the end of the voyage Campbell and MacEwan were well pleased to be quit of their companion; not so much because he was moody and distraught, as because they feared that a spell was upon him — a fate in the working of which they might become involved. It needed no vow of the one to the other for them to come to the conclusion that they would never land on Eilanmore, or, if need be, only in broad daylight and never alone.

The days went well for James Achanna, where he made his home at Ranza-beag, on Ranza Water in the Sleat of Skye. The farm was small but good, and he hoped that with help and care he would soon have the place as good a farm as there was in all Skye.

Donald Macarthur did not let him see much of Katreen, but the old man was no longer opposed to him. Seumas must wait till Ian Macarthur came back again, which might be any day now. For sure, James Achanna of Ranza-beag was a very different person from the youngest of the Achanna-folk who held by on lonely Eilanmore; moreover, the old man could not but think with pleasure that it would be well to see Katreen able to walk over the whole land of Ranza from the cairn at the north of his own Ranza-Mòr to the burn at the south of Ranza-beag, and know it for her own.

But Achanna was ready to wait. Even before he had the secret word of Katreen he knew her from her beautiful dark eyes that she loved him. As the weeks went by they managed to meet often, and at last Katreen told him that she loved him too, and would have none but him; but that they must wait till Ian came back, because of the pledge given to him by her father. They were days of joy for him. Through many a hot noontide hour, through many a gloaming, he went as one in a dream. Whenever he saw a birch swaying in the wind, or a wave leaping upon Loch Liath, that was near his home, or passed a bush covered with wild roses, or saw the moonbeams lying white on the holes of the pines, he thought of Katreen — his fawn for grace, and so lithe and tall, with sun-brown face and wavy, dark mass of hair, and shadowy eyes and rowan-red lips. It is said that there is a god clothed in shadow who goes to and fro among the human kind, putting silence between lovers with his waving hands, and breathing a chill out of his cold breath, and leaving a gulf of deep water flowing between them because of the passing of his feet. That shadow never came their way. Their love grew as a flower fed by rains and warmed by sunlight.

When midsummer came, and there was no sign of Ian Macarthur, it was already too late. Katreen had been won.

During the summer months, it was the custom for Katreen and two of the farm-girls to go up Maol-Ranza, to reside at the shealing of Cnoc-an-Fhraoch:[41] and this because of the hill-pasture for the sheep. Cnoc-an-Fhraoch is a round, boulder-studded hill covered with heather, which has a precipitous corrie on each side, and in front slopes down to Lochan Fraoch, a lochlet surrounded by dark woods. Behind the hill, or great hillock rather, lay the shealing. At each week-end Katreen went down

---

41 Cnoc-an-Fhraoch means 'the hill of heather' and I believe Fiona used this common enough name by way of silent tribute to the ancient Irish legend *Táin Bó Fraoch* – The Cattle Raid of Fraoch – which contains a very similar motif of a swimmer in a loch with rowan branches in his teeth. It should be noted that Fraoch – heather – was originally a man's name because it also means 'fierce,' an appellation any Celtic warrior would have been proud of. I do not know when, or why, it changed to being a woman's name.

to Ranza-Mòr, and on every Monday morning at sunrise returned to her heather-girt eyrie. It was on one of these visits that she endured a cruel shock. Her father told her that she must marry someone else than Seumas Achanna. He had heard words about him which made a union impossible, and, indeed, he hoped that the man would leave Ranza-beag. In the end, he admitted that what he had heard was to the effect that Achanna was under a doom of some kind; that he was involved in a blood feud; and, moreover, that he was fëy. The old man would not be explicit as to the person from whom his information came, but hinted that he was a stranger of rank, probably a laird of the isles. Besides this, there was word of Ian Macarthur. He was at Thurso, in the far north, and would be in Skye before long, and he — her father — had written to him that he might wed Katreen as soon as was practicable.

"Do you see that lintie yonder, father?" was her response to this.

"Ay, lass, and what about the birdeen?"

"Well, when she mates with a hawk, so will I be mating with Ian Macarthur, but not till then."

With that she turned, and left the house, and went back to Cnoc-an-Fhraoch. On the way she met Achanna. It was that night that for the first time he swam across Lochan Fraoch to meet Katreen.

The quickest way to reach the shealing was to row across the lochlet, and then ascend by a sheep-path that wound through the hazel copses at the base of the hill. Fully half an hour was thus saved, because of the steepness of the precipitous corries to right and left. A boat was kept for this purpose, but it was fastened to a shore-boulder by a padlocked iron chain, the key of which was kept by Donald Macarthur. Latterly he had refused to let this key out of his possession. For one thing, no doubt, he believed he could thus restrain Achanna from visiting his daughter. The young man could not approach the shealing from either side without being seen.

But that night, soon after the moon was whitening slow in the dark, Katreen stole down to the hazel copse and awaited the coming of her lover. The lochan was visible from almost any point on Cnoc-an-Fhraoch, as well as from the south side. To cross it in a boat unseen, if any watcher were near, would be impossible, nor could even a swimmer hope to escape notice unless in the gloom of night, or mayhap, in the dusk. When, however, she saw, half way across the water, a spray of green branches slowly moving athwart the surface, she knew that Seumas was keeping his tryst. If, perchance, anyone else saw, he or she would never guess that those derelict rowan-branches shrouded Seumas Achanna.

It was not till the spray had drifted close to the ledge, where, hid among the bracken and the hazel undergrowth, she awaited him, that Katreen descried the face of her lover, as with one hand he parted the green sprays, and stared longingly and lovingly at the figure he could just discern in the dim, fragrant obscurity. And as it was this night so was it many of the nights that followed. Katreen spent the days as in a dream. Not even the news of her cousin Ian's return disturbed her much.

One day the inevitable meeting came. She was at Ranza-Mòr, and when a shadow came into the dairy where she was standing she looked up and saw Ian before her. She thought he appeared taller and stronger than ever, though still not so tall as Seumas, who would appear slim beside the Herculean Skye man. But as she looked at his close curling black hair and thick bull-neck and the sullen eyes in his dark wind-red face, she wondered that she had ever tolerated him at all.

He broke the ice at once. "Tell me, Katreen, are you glad to see me back again?"

"I am glad that you are home once more safe and sound."

"And will you make it my home for me by coming to live with me, as I've asked you again and again?"

"No: as I've told you again and again."

He gloomed at her angrily for a few moments before he resumed.

"I will be asking you this one thing, Katreen, daughter of my father's brother; do you love that man Achanna who lives at Ranza-beag?"

"You may ask the wind why it is from the east or the west, but it won't tell you. You're not the wind's master."

"If you think I will let this man take you away from me, you are thinking a foolish thing."

"And you saying a foolisher."

"Ay?"

"Ay, sure. What could you do, Ian Mhic Ian? At the worst, you could do no more than kill James Achanna. What then? I too would die. You cannot separate us. I would not marry you, now, though you were the last man on the world and I the last woman."

"You're a fool, Katreen Macarthur. Your father has promised you to me, and I tell you this: if you love Achanna you'll save his life only by letting him go away from here. I promise you he will not be here long."

"Ay, you promise *me*; but you will not say that thing to James Achanna's face. You are a coward."

With a muttered oath the man turned on his heel.

"Let him beware o' me, and you, too, Katreen-mo-nighean-donn. I swear it by my mother's grave and by St. Martin's Cross that you will be mine by hook or by crook."

The girl smiled scornfully. Slowly she lifted a milk-pail.

"It would be a pity to waste the good milk, Ian-gòrach, but if you don't go it is that I will be emptying the pail on you, and then you'll be as white without as your heart is within."

"So you call me witless, do you? *Ian gòrach!* Well, we shall be seeing as to that. And as for the milk, there will be more than milk spilt because of *you*, Katreen-donn."

From that day, though neither Seumas nor Katreen knew of it, a watch was set upon Achanna.

It could not be long before their secret was discovered, and it was with a savage joy overmastering his sullen rage that Ian Macarthur knew himself the discoverer, and conceived his double vengeance. He dreamed, gloatingly, on both the black thoughts that roamed like ravenous beasts through the solitudes of his heart. But he did not dream that another man was filled with hate because of Katreen's lover, another man who had sworn to make her his own, the man who, disguised, was known in Armadale as Donald McLean, and in the north isles would have been hailed as Gloom Achanna.

There had been steady rain for three days, with a cold, raw wind. On the fourth the sun shone, and set in peace. An evening of quiet beauty followed, warm, fragrant, dusky from the absence of moon or star, though the thin veils of mist promised to disperse as the night grew.

There were two men that eve in the undergrowth on the south side of the lochlet. Seumas had come earlier than his wont. Impatient for the dusk, he could scarce await the waning of the afterglow; surely, he thought, he might venture. Suddenly, his ears caught the sound of cautious footsteps. Could it be old Donald, perhaps with some inkling of the way in which his daughter saw her lover in despite of all; or, mayhap, might it be Ian Macarthur, tracking him as a hunter stalking a stag by the water-pools? He crouched, and waited. In a few minutes he saw Ian carefully picking his way. The man stooped as he descried the green branches; smiled as, with a low rustling, he raised them from the ground.

Meanwhile yet another man watched and waited, though on the farther side of the lochan, where the hazel copses were. Gloom Achanna half hoped, half feared the approach of Katreen. It would be sweet to see her again, sweet to slay her lover before her eyes, brother to him though he was. But, there was the chance that she might descry him, and, whether recognisingly or not, warn the swimmer. So it was that he had come there before sundown, and now lay crouched among the bracken underneath a projecting mossy ledge close upon the water, where it could scarce be that she or any should see him.

As the gloaming deepened, a great stillness reigned. There was no breath of wind. A scarce audible sigh prevailed among the spires of the heather. The churring of a night-jar throbbed through the darkness. Somewhere a corncrake called its monotonous *crék-craik:* the dull harsh sound emphasising the utter stillness. The pinging of the gnats hovering over and among the sedges made an incessant rumour through the warm, sultry air. There was a splash once as of a fish. Then, silence. Then a lower but more continuous splash, or rather wash of water. A slow susurrus rustled through the dark.

Where he lay among the fern Gloom Achanna slowly raised his head, stared through the shadows, and listened intently. If Katreen were waiting there she was not near.

Noiselessly he slid into the water. When he rose it was under a clump of green branches. These he had cut and secured three hours before. With his left hand he swam slowly, or kept his equipoise in the water; with his right he guided the heavy rowan-bough. In his mouth were two objects, one long and thin and dark, the other with an occasional glitter as of a dead fish.

His motion was scarce perceptible. None the less he was nigh the middle of the loch almost as soon as another clump of green branches. Doubtless the swimmer beneath it was confident that he was now safe from observation.

The two clumps of green branches drew nearer. The smaller seemed a mere spray blown down by the recent gale. But all at once the larger clump jerked awkwardly and stopped. Simultaneously a strange low strain of music came from the other.

The strain ceased. The two clumps of green branches remained motionless. Slowly, at last, the larger moved forward. It was too dark for the swimmer to see if any one lay hid behind the smaller. When he reached it he thrust aside the leaves.

It was as though a great salmon leaped. There was a splash, and a narrow, dark body shot through the gloom. At the end of it something gleamed. Then suddenly there was a savage struggle. The inanimate green branches tore this way and that, and surged and swirled. Gasping cries came from the leaves. Again and again the gleaming thing leapt. At the third leap an awful scream shrilled through the silence. The echo of it wailed thrice, with horrible distinctness, in the corrie beyond Cnoc-an-Fhraoch. Then, after a faint splashing, there was silence once more. One clump of green branches drifted slowly up the lochlet. The other moved steadily towards the place whence, a brief while before, it had stirred.

Only one thing lived in the heart of Gloom Achanna — the joy of his exultation. He had killed his brother Seumas. He had always hated him because of his beauty; of late he had hated him because he had stood between him, Gloom, and Katreen Macarthur — because he had become her lover. They were all dead now, except himself, all the Achannas. He was "Achanna." When the day came that he would go back to Galloway, there would be a magpie on the first birk, and a screaming jay on the first rowan, and a croaking raven on the first fir; ay, he would be their suffering, though they knew nothing of him meanwhile! He would be Achanna of Achanna again. Let those who would stand in his way beware. As for Katreen: perhaps he would take her there, perhaps not. He smiled.

These thoughts were the wandering fires in his brain while he slowly swam shoreward under the floating green branches, and as he disengaged himself from them, and crawled upward through the bracken. It was at this moment that a third man entered the water, from the farther shore.

Prepared as he was to come suddenly upon Katreen, Gloom was startled when, in a place of dense shadow, a hand touched his shoulder, and her voice whispered, "*Seumas, Seumas!*" The next moment she was in his arms. He could feel her heart beating against his side. "What was it, Seumas? What was that awful cry?" she whispered.

For answer, he put his lips to hers, and kissed her again and again. The girl drew back. Some vague instinct warned her. "What is it, Seumas? Why don't you speak?"

He drew her close again. "Pulse of my heart, it is I who love you, I who love you best of all; it is I, Gloom Achanna!"

With a cry, she struck him full in the face. He staggered, and in that moment she freed herself. "You coward!"

"Katreen, I —"

"Come no nearer. If you do, it will be the death of you!"

"The death o' me! Ah, bonnie fool that you are, and is it you that will be the death o' me?"

"Ay, Gloom Achanna, for I have but to scream and Seumas will be here, and he would kill you like a dog if he knew you did me harm."

"Ah, but if there were no Seumas, or any man to come between me an' my will!"

"Then there would be a woman! Ay, if you overbore me I would strangle you with my hair, or fix my teeth in your false throat!"

"I was not for knowing you were such a wild-cat: but I'll tame you yet, my lass! Aha, wild-cat!" and as he spoke he laughed low.

"It is a true word, Gloom of the black heart. I *am* a wild-cat, and like a wild-cat I am not to be seized by a fox; and that you will be finding to your cost, by the holy St. Bridget! But now, off with you, brother of my man!"

"Your man — ha! ha! —"

"Why do you laugh?"

"Sure, I am laughing at a warm, white lass like yourself having a dead man as your lover!"

"A — dead — man?"

No answer came. The girl shook with a new fear. Slowly she drew closer, till her breath fell warm against the face of the other. He spoke at last. "Ay, a dead man."

"It is a lie."

"Where would you be that you were not hearing his good-bye? I'm thinking it was loud enough!"

"It is a lie — it is a lie!"

"No, it is no lie. Seumas is cold enough now. He's low among the weeds by now. Ay, by now: down there in the lochan."

"What — you, you devil! Is it for killing your own brother you would be?"

"I killed no one. He died his own way. Maybe the cramp took him. Maybe — maybe a kelpie gripped him. I watched. I saw him beneath the green branches. He was dead before he died. I saw it in the white face o' him. Then he sank. He's dead. Seumas is dead. Look here, girl, I've always loved you. I swore the oath upon you. You're mine. Sure, you're mine now, Katreen! It is loving you I am! It will be a south wind for you from this day, *muirnean mochree!* See here, I'll show you how I —"

"Back — back — murderer!"

"Be stopping that foolishness now, Katreen Macarthur! By the Book I am tired of it. I am loving you, and it's having you for mine I am! And if you won't come to me like the dove to its mate, I'll come to you like the hawk to the dove!"

With a spring he was upon her. In vain she strove to beat him back. His arms held her as a stoat grips a rabbit. He pulled her head back, and kissed her throat till the strangulating breath sobbed, against his ear. With a last despairing effort she screamed the name of the dead man:

"Seumas! Seumas! Seumas!" The man who struggled with her laughed.

"Ay, call away! The herrin' will be coming through the bracken as soon as Seumas comes to your call! Ah, it is mine you are now, Katreen! He's dead an' cold — an' you'd best have a living man — an' —"

She fell back, her balance lost in the sudden releasing. What did it mean? Gloom still stood there, but as one frozen. Through the darkness she saw, at last, that a hand gripped his shoulder; behind him a black mass vaguely obtruded. For some moments there was absolute silence. Then a hoarse voice came out of the dark.

"You will be knowing now who it is, Gloom Achanna!"

The voice was that of Seumas, who lay dead in the lochan. The murderer shook as in a palsy. With a great effort, slowly he turned his head. He saw a white splatch, the face of the corpse; in this white splatch flamed two burning eyes, the eyes of the soul of the brother whom he had slain. He reeled, staggered as a blind man, and, free now of that awful clasp, swayed to and fro as one drunken. Slowly, Seumas raised an arm and pointed downward through the wood towards the lochan. Still pointing, he moved swiftly forward.

With a cry like a beast, Gloom Achanna swung to one side, stumbled, rose, and leaped into the darkness.

For some minutes Seumas and Katreen stood, silent, apart, listening to the crashing sound of his flight — the race of the murderer against the pursuing shadow of the Grave.

Children of the Dark Star

IT is God that builds the nest of the blind bird. I know not when or where I heard that said, if ever I heard it, but it has been near me as a breast-feather to a bird's heart since I was a child. When I ponder it, I say to myself that it is God also who guides sunrise and moonrise into obscure hearts, to build, with those winged spirits of light, a nest for the blind soul. Often and often I have thought of this saying of late, because of him who was known to me years ago as Alasdair Achanna, and of whom I have written elsewhere as "The Anointed Man": though now from the Torridons of Ross to the Rhinns of Islay he is known by one name only, "Alan Dall."

No one knows the end of those who are born under the Dark Star. It is said they are born to some strange, and certainly obscure, destiny. Some are fëy from their youth, or a melancholy of madness comes upon them later, so that they go forth from their kind, and wander outcast, haunting most the lonely and desolate regions where the voice of the hill-wind is the sole voice. Some, born to evil, become, in strange ways, ministers of light. Some, born of beauty, are plumed spirits of decay. But of one and all this is sure: that, in the end, none knows the when or how of their going.

Of these Children of the Dark Star my friend Alasdair Achanna, "Alan Dall," was one.

"Alan Dall" — blind, as the Gaelic word means: it was difficult for me to believe that darkness could be fallen, without break, upon the eyes of Alasdair Achanna. He had so loved the beauty of the world that he had forfeited all else. Yet, blind wayfarer along the levens of life as he was, I envied him — for, truly, this beautiful soul had entered into the kingdom of dreams.

When accidentally I met him once again, it was with deep surprise on both sides. He thought I had gone to a foreign land, either the English southlands or "away beyond." I, for my part, had believed him to be no longer of the living, and had more than once wondered if he had been lured away, as the saying is. We spoke much of desolate Eilanmore, and wondered if the rains and winds still made the same gloom upon the isle as when we lived there. We spoke of his kinswoman, and my dear friend, Anne Gillespie, she who went away with Mànus MacCodrum, and died so young; and of Mànus himself and his terrible end, when

Gloom his brother played death upon him, in the deep sea, where the seals were, and he hearing nothing, nothing in all the world, but the terror and horror of the Dàn-nan-Ròn. And we spoke of Gloom himself, of whom none had heard since the day he fled from the west — not after the death of Mànus, about which few knew, but after the murder of the swimmer in the loch, whom he took to be his own brother Seumas and the lover of his desire, Katreen Macarthur. I thought — perhaps it was rather I preferred to think — that Gloom was no longer among the evil forces loose in the world; but I heard from Alasdair that he was alive, and would some day come again; for the men who are without compassion, and sin because it is their life, cannot for too long remain from the place of their evil-doing.

Since then I have had reason to know how true was Alasdair's spiritual knowledge, though this is not the time for me to relate either what I then heard from " Alan Dall," or what terrible and strange revealing of Gloom Achanna there was some three years ago, when his brother, whom he was of old so wont to mock, was no longer among those who dwell visibly on earth. But naturally that which the more held me in interest was the telling by Alasdair of how he whom I had thought dead was alive, and known by another name than his own. It is a story I will tell again, that of "Alan Dall": of how his blindness came to him, and of how he quickened with the vision that is from within, and of divers strange things; but here I speak only of that which brought him to Love and Death and the Gate of Dreams.

For many weeks and months after he left Eilanmore, he told me, he wandered aimlessly abroad among the Western Isles. The melancholy of his youth had become a madness, but this was only the air that blew continually upon the loneliness of his spirit. There was a star upon his forehead, I know, for I have seen it: I saw it long ago when he revealed to me that beauty was a haunting spirit everywhere: when I looked upon him, and knew him as one anointed. In the light of that star he walked ever in a divine surety. It was the star of beauty.

He fared to and fro as one in a dream, a dream behind, a dream his quest, himself a dream. Wherever he went, the light that was his spirit shone for healing, for peace, for troubled joy. He had ever lived so solitary, so few save his own kin and a scattered folk among the inner isles knew him even by sight, that in all the long reach of the Hebrides from the Butt of the Lews to Barra Head he passed as a stranger — Gael and an islesman, it is true, because of his tongue and accent, but still a stranger. So great was the likeness he bore to one who was known throughout the

Hebrides, and in particular to every man and woman in the South Isles, so striking in everything save height was he to the priest, Father Alan M'Ian, known everywhere simply as Father Alan, that he in turn came to be called Alan Mòr.

He was in Benbecula, the isle of a thousand waters, when he met his brother Gloom, and this on the day or the next day but one following the wild end of Mànus MacCodrum. His brother, dark, slim, furtive as an otter, was moving swiftly through a place of heather-clumps and brown tangled fern. Alasdair was on the ground, and saw him as he came. There was a smile on his face that he knew was evil, for Gloom so smiled when his spirit rose within him. He stopped abruptly, a brief way off. He had not descried any other, but a yellowhammer had swung sidelong from a spire of furze, uttering a single note. Somewhere, he thought, death was on the trail of life. There was motionless stillness for a brief while. The yellowhammer hopped to the topmost spray of the bramble bush where he had alit, and his light song flirted through the air.

Then Gloom spoke. He looked sidelong, smiling furtively; yet his eyes had not rested on his brother. "Well, now, Alasdair, soon there will not be an Achanna on Eilanmore."

Alasdair — tall, gaunt, with his blue dreaming eyes underneath his grizzled tangled hair — rose, and put out his right hand in greeting; but Gloom looked beyond it. Alasdair broke the silence which ensued. "So you are here in Benbecula, brother? I, and others too, thought you had gone across the seas when you left Eilanmore."

"The nest was fouled, I am thinking, brother, or you, and Mànus too, and then I myself, would not be here and be there."

"Are you come out of the south, or going there?"

"Well, and for why that?"

"I thought you might be having news for me of Mànus. You know that Anne, who was dear to us, is under the grass now?"

"Ay, she is dead. I know that."

"And Mànus? Is he still at Balnahunnur-sa-mona? Is he the man he was?"

"No, I am not for thinking, brother, that Mànus is the man he was."

"He will be at the fishing now? I heard that more than a mile o' the sea foamed yesterday off Craiginnish Heads, with the big school of mackerel there was."

"Ay, he was ever fond o' the sea, Mànus MacCodrum: fëy o' the sea, for the matter o' that, Alasdair Achanna."

"I am on my way now to see Mànus."

"I would not be going, brother," answered Gloom, in a slow, indifferent voice.

"And for why that?"

Gloom advanced idly, and slid to the ground, lying there and looking up into the sky.

"It's a fair, sweet world, Alasdair."

Alasdair looked at him, but said nothing.

"It's a fair, sweet world. I have heard that saying on your mouth a score of times, and a score upon a score."

"Well?"

"Well? But is it not a fair, sweet world?"

"Ay, it is fair and sweet."

"Lie still, brother, and I will tell you about Mànus, who married Anne whom I loved. And I will be beginning if you please, with the night when she told us that he was to be her man, and when I played on my *feadan* the air of the Dàn-nan-Ròn. Will you be remembering that?"

"I remember."

Then, with that, Gloom, always lying idly on his back, and smiling often as he stared into the blue sky, told all that happened to Anne and Mànus, till death came to Anne; and then how Mànus heard the seal-voice that was in his blood calling to him; and how he went to his sea-folk, made mad by the secret fatal song of the *feadan*, the song that is called the Dàn-nan-Ròn; and how the pools in the rocky skerries out yonder in the sea were red still with the blood that the seals had not lapped, or that the tide had not yet lifted and spilled greying into the grey wave.

There was a silence when he had told that thing. Alasdair did not look at him. Gloom, stared into the sky, still lying on his back, smiling furtively. Alasdair was white as foam at night. At last he spoke.

"The death of Mànus is knocking at your heart, Gloom Achanna."

"I am not a seal, brother. Ask the seals."

"They know. He was of their people: not of us."

"It is a lie. He was a man, as we are. He was our friend, and the husband of Anne."

"His death is knocking at your heart, Gloom Achanna."

"Are you for knowing if our brother Seumas is still on Eilanmore?"

Alasdair looked long at him, anxious, puzzled by the abrupt change.

"And for why should he not still be on Eilanmore?"

"Have you not had hearing of anything about Seumas - and - and - about Katreena nic Airt?"

"About Katreen, daughter of Art Macarthur, in the Sleat of Skye?"

"Ay — about Seumas, and Katreen Macarthur?"

"What about them?"

"Nothing. Ah, no, for sure, nothing. But did you never hear Seumas speak of this bonnie Katreen?"

"He has the deep love for her, Gloom; the deep, true love."

"H'm!"

With that Gloom smiled again, as he stared idly into the sky from where he lay on his back amid the heather and bracken. With a swift, furtive gesture he slipped his *feadan* from his breast, and put his breath upon it. A cool, high spiral of sound, like delicate blue smoke, ascended. Then, suddenly, he began to play the Dannhsa-na-Mairbh — the Dance of Death.

Alasdair shivered but said nothing. He had his eyes on the ground. When the wild, fantastic, terrifying air filled the very spires of the heather with its dark music — its music out of the grave — he looked at his brother.

"Will you be telling me now, Gloom, what is in your heart against Seumas?"

"Is not Seumas wishful to be leaving Eilanmore?"

"Like enough. I know nothing of Eilanmore now. It is long since I have seen the white o' the waves in Catacol haven."

"I am thinking that that air I was playing will help him to be leaving soon, but not to be going where Katreen Macarthur is."

"And why not?"

"Well, because I am thinking Katreen, the daughter of Art Macarthur, is to have another man to master her than our brother Seumas. I will tell you his name, Alasdair: it is Gloom Achanna."

"It is a cruel wrong that is in your mind. You would do to Seumas what you have done to Mànus, husband of Anne, our friend and kinswoman. There is death in your heart, Gloom: the blue mould is on the corn that is your heart."

Gloom played softly. It was a little eddy of evil bitter music, swift and biting and poisonous as an adder's tongue. Alasdair's lips tightened, and a red splash came into the whiteness of his face, as though a snared bird were bleeding beneath a patch of snow.

"You have no love for the girl. By your own word to me on Eilanmore, you had the hunger on you for Anne Gillespie. Was that just because you saw that she loved Mànus? And is it so now — that you have a hawk's eye for the poor birdeen yonder in the Sleat, and that just because you know, or have heard, that Seumas loves her, and loves her true, and because she loves him?"

"I have heard no such lie, Alasdair Achanna."

"Then what is it that you have heard?"

"Oh, the east wind whispers in the grass; an' a bird swims up from the grass an' sings it in the blue fields up yonder; an' then it falls down again in a thin, thin rain; an' a drop trickles into my ear. An' that is how I am knowing what I know, Alasdair Achanna."

"And Anne — did you love Anne?"

"Anne is dead."

"It's the herring-love that is yours, Gloom. To-day it is a shadow here: to-morrow it is a shadow yonder. There is no tide for you: there is no haven for the likes o' you."

"There is one woman I want. It is Katreen Macarthur."

"If it be a true thing that I have heard, Gloom Achanna, you have brought shame and sorrow to one woman already."

For the first time Gloom stirred. He shot a swift glance at Alasdair, and a tremor was in his white, sensitive hands. He looked as a startled fox does, when, intent, its muscles quiver before flight. "And what will you have heard?" he asked in a low voice.

"That you took away from her home a girl who did not love you, but on whom you put a spell; and that she followed you to her sorrow, and was held by you to her shame; and that she was lost, or drowned herself at last, because of these things."

"And did you hear who she was?"

"No. The man who told me was Aulay MacAulay, of Carndhu in Sutherland. He said he did not know who she was, but I am thinking he did know, poor man, because his eyes wavered, and he put a fluttering hand to his beard and began to say swift, stammering words about the herrin' that had been seen off the headland that morning."

Gloom smiled, a faint fugitive smile; then, half turning where he lay, he took a letter from his pocket. "Ay, for sure, Aulay MacAulay was an old friend of yours; to be sure, yes. I am remembering he used sometimes to come to Eilanmore in his smack. But before I speak again of what you said to me just now, I will read you my letter that I have written to our brother Seumas; he is not knowing if I am living still, or am dead."

With that he opened the letter, and, smiling momently at times, he read it in a slow, deliberate voice, and as though it were the letter of another man:

Well, Seumas, my brother, it is wondering if I am dead you will be. Maybe ay, and maybe no. But I send you this writing to let you see that I know all you do and think of. So you are going to leave Eilanmore without an Achanna upon it? And you will be going to Sleat in Skye? Well, let me be telling you this thing: Do not go. I see blood there. And there is this, too: neither you nor any man shall take Katreen away from me. You know that; and Ian Macarthur knows it; and Katreen knows it: and that holds whether I am alive or dead. I say to you: Do not go. It will be better for you and for all. Ian Macarthur is away on the north-sea with the whaler-captain who came to us at Eilanmore, and will not be back for three months yet. It will be better for him not to come back. But if he comes back he will have to reckon with the man who says that Katreen Macarthur is his. I would rather not have two men to speak to, and one my brother. It does not matter to you where I am. I want no money just now. But put aside my portion for me. Have it ready for me against the day I call for it. I will not be patient that day: so have it ready for me. In the place that I am, I am content. You will be saying: Why is my brother away in a remote place (I will say this to you: That it is not further north than St. Kilda nor further south than the Mull of Cantyre!), and for what reason? That is between me and silence. But perhaps you think of Anne sometimes. Do you know that she lies under the green grass? And of Mànus MacCodrum? They say that he swam out into the sea and was drowned; and they whisper of the seal-blood, though the minister is angered with them for that. He calls it a madness. Well, I was there at that madness, and I played to it on my feadan. And now, Seumas, can you be thinking of what the tune was that I played?

Your brother, who waits his own day.

Gloom

Do not be forgetting this thing: I would rather not be playing the Dàn-nan-Ròn; it was the song of his soul, that; and yours is the Dannhsa-na-Mairbh."

When he had read the last words, Gloom looked at Alasdair. His eyes quailed instinctively at the steadfast gaze of his brother.

"I am thinking," he said lightly, though uneasily as he himself knew, "that Seumas will not now be putting his marriage-thoughts upon Katreen."

For a minute or more Alasdair was silent. Then he spoke.

"Do you remember, when you were a child, what old Morag said?"

"No."

"She said that your soul was born black, and that you were no child for all your young years; and that for all your pleasant ways, for all your smooth way and smoother tongue, you would do cruel evil to man and woman as long as you lived. She said you were born under the Dark Star."

Gloom laughed. "Ay, and you too, Alasdair. Don't be forgetting that. You too, she saw, were born so. She said we — you and I — that we two were the Children of the Dark Star."

"But she said no evil of me, Gloom, and you are knowing that well."

"Well, and what then?"

"Do not send that letter to Seumas. He has deep love for Katreen. Let the lass be. You do not love her, Gloom. It will be to her sorrow and shame if you seek her. But if you are still for sending it, I will sail to-morrow for Eilanmore. I will tell Seumas, and I will go with him to the Sleat of Skye. And I will be there to guard the girl Katreen against you, Gloom."

"No: you will do none of these things. And for why? Because to-morrow you will be hurrying far north to Stornoway. And when you are at Stornoway you may still be Alan Mòr to every one, as you are here, but to one person you will be Alasdair Achanna no other, and now and for evermore."

Alasdair stared, amazed. "What wild-goose folly is this that you would be setting me on, you whom it is my sorrow to call brother?"

"I have a letter here for you to read. I wrote it many days ago, but it is a good letter now for all that. If I give it to you now, you pass me the word that you will not read it till I am gone away from here — till you cannot have a sight of me, or of the shadow of my shadow?"

"I promise."

"Then here it is: an' good day to you, Alasdair Achanna. An' if ever we meet again, you be keeping to your way, as I will keep to my way: and in that doing there shall be no blood between brothers. But if you want to seek me you will find me across the seas, and mayhap Katreen — ah, well, yes, Katreen or some one else — by my side."

And with that, and giving no hand, or no glance of the eyes, Gloom rose, and turned upon his heel, and walked slowly but lightly across the tangled bent.

Alasdair watched him till he was a long way off. Gloom never once looked back. When he was gone a hundred yards or more, he put his *feadan* to his mouth and began to play. Two airs he played, the one ever running into the other: wild, fantastic, and, in Alasdair's ears, horrible to listen to. In the one he heard the moaning of Anne, the screams of Mànus among the seals: in the other, a terror moving stealthily against his brother Seumas, and against Katreen, and — he knew not whom. When the last faint wild spiral of sound, that seemed to be neither of the Dàn-nan-Ròn nor of the Dannhsa-na-Mairbh, but of the soul of evil that inhabited both — when this last perishing echo was no more, and only the clean cold hill-wind came down across the moors with a sighing sweetness, Alasdair rose. The letter could wait now, he muttered, till he was before the peats.

When he returned to the place where he was lodging, the crofter's wife put a bowl of porridge and some coarse rye-bread before him. "And when you've eaten, Alan Mòr," she said, as she put her plaid over her head and shoulders, and stood in the doorway, "will you be having the goodness to smoor the peats before you lie down for the sleep that I'm thinking is heavy upon you?"

"Ay, for sure," Alasdair answered gently. "But are you not to be here to-night?"

"No. The sister of my man Ranald is down with the fever, and her man away with mine at the fishing, and I am going to be with her this night; but I will be here before you wake for all that. And so good-night again, Alan Mòr."

"God's blessing, and a quiet night, good woman."

Then, after he had supped, and dreamed a while as he sat opposite the fire of glowing peats, he opened the letter that Gloom had given him. He read it slowly. It was some minutes later that he took it up again, from where it had fallen on the red sandstone of the hearth. And now he read it once more, aloud, and in a low, strained voice that had a bitter, frozen grief in it — a frozen grief that knew no thaw in tears, in a single sob.

You will remember well, Alasdair my brother, that you loved Marsail nic Ailpean, who lived in Eilan-Rona. You'll be remembering, too, that when Ailpean MacAilpean said he would never let Marsail put her hand in yours, you went away and said no more. That was because you were a fool, Alasdair my brother. And Marsail — she, too, thought you were a fool. I know you did that doing because you thought it was Marsail's wish: that is, because she did not love you. What had that to do with it? I am asking you, what had that to do with it, if you wanted Marsail? Women are for men, not men for women. And, brother, because you are a poet, let me tell you this, which is old ancient wisdom, and not mine alone, that no woman likely to be loved by a poet can be true to a poet. For women are all at heart cowards, and it takes a finer woman than any you or I have known to love a poet. For that means to take the steep brae instead of the easy lily leven. I am thinking, Alasdair, you will not find easily the woman that in her heart of hearts will leave the lily leven for the steep brae. No, not easily.

Ah yes, for sure, I am hearing you say — women bear pain better, are braver, too, than men. I have heard you say that. I have heard the whistle-fish at the coming of the tide — but a little later the tide came nearer. And are they brave, these women you who are poets speak of, but whom we who are men never meet! I will tell you this little thing, brother: they are always crying for love, but love is the one thing they fear. And in their hearts they hate poets, Alasdair, because poets say, Be true: *but that cannot be, because women can be true to their lovers, but they cannot be true to love — for love wishes sunrise and full noon everywhere, so that there be no lie anywhere, and that is why women fear love.*

And I am thinking of these things, because of Marsail whom you loved, and because of the song you made once about the bravery of woman. I have forgotten the song, but I remember that the last line of that song was 'foam o' the sea.'

And what is all this about? you will be saying when you read this. Well, for that, it is my way. If you want a woman — not that a man like you, all visions and bloodless as a skate, could ever have that want — you would go to her and say so. But my way is to play my feadan at the towers of that woman's pride and self-will, and see them crumbling, crumbling, till I walk in when I will, and play my feadan again, and go laughing out once more, and she with me.

But again you will say, Why all this? Brother, will you be remembering this: that our brother Marcus also loved Marsail. Marcus is under the wave, you will say. Yes, Marcus is under the wave. But I, Gloom Achanna, am not: and I too loved Marsail. Well, when you went away, you wrote a letter to her to say that you would never love any other woman. She did not get that letter. It is under the old black stone with the carvings on it, that is in the brown water of the bog that lies between Eilanmore farmhouse and the Grey Loch. And once, long afterward, you wrote again, and you sent that letter to Marcus, to take to her and to give to her in person. I found it on the day of his death in the pocket of a frieze coat he had worn the day before. I do not know where it is now. The gulls know. Or perhaps the crabs at the bottom of the sea do. You with your writing, brother: I with my feadan.

Well, I went to Eilan-Rona. I played my feadan there, outside the white walls of Marsail nic Ailpean. And when the walls were crumbling I entered, and I said Come, and she came.

No, no, Alasdair my brother, I do not think you would have been happy. She was ever letting tears come in the twilight, and in the darkness of the sleeping hours. I have heard her sob in full noon, brother. She was fair to see, a comely lass; but she never took to a vagrant life. She thought we were going to Coleraine to sail to America. America is a long way — it is a longer way than love for a woman who has too many tears. She said I had put a spell upon her. Tut, tut. I played my feadan to pretty Marsail. No harm in that, for sure, Alasdair aghrày?

For six months or more we wandered here and there. She had no English — so, to quiet her with silence, I went round by the cold bleak burghs and grey stony towns northward and eastward of Inverness, as far and further than

Peterhead and Fraserburgh. A cold land, a thin, bloodless folk. I would not be recommending it to you, Alasdair. And yet, for why not? It would be a good place for the 'Anointed Man.' You could be practising there nicely, brother, against cold winds and cold hearths nicely and bitter cold ways.

This is a long, long letter, the longest I have ever written. It has been for pleasure to me to write this letter, though I have written slowly, and now here, and now there. And I must be ending. But I will say this first: That I am weary of Marsail now, and that, too, for weeks past. She will be having a child soon. She is in Stornoway, at the house of Bean Marsanta MacIlleathain ('Widow M'Lean,' as they have it in that half-English place), in the street that runs behind the big street where the Courthouse is. She will be there till her time is over. It is a poor place, ill-smelling, too. But she will do well there: Bean Catreena is a good woman, if she is paid for it. And I paid good money, Alasdair. It will do for a time. Not for very long, I am thinking, but till then. Marsail has no longer her fair-to-see way with her. It is a pity that — for Marsail.

And now, brother, will you be remembering your last word to me on Eilanmore? You said, 'You shall yet eat dust, Gloom Achanna, whose way is the way of death.' And will you be remembering what I said? I said, 'Wait, for I may come later than you to that bitter eating.' And now I am thinking that it is you, and not I, who have eaten dust. — Your brother,

GLOOM

And so — his dream was over. The vision of a happiness to be, of a possible happiness — and, for long, it had not been with Alasdair a vision of reward to him, but one of a rarer happiness, which considered only the weal of Marsail, and that whether ultimately he or some other won her — this, which was, now was not: this was become as the dew on last year's grass. Not once had he wavered in his dream. By day and by night the wild-rose of his love had given him beauty and fragrance. He had come to hope little: indeed, to believe that Marsail might already be wed happily, and perhaps with a child's little hands against her breast. I am thinking he did not love as most men love.

When the truth flamed into his heart from the burning ashes of Gloom's letter, he sat a while, staring vaguely into the glow of the peats. There had been a bitter foolishness in his making, he muttered to himself: a bitter foolishness. Had he been more as other men and less a dreamer, had he shown less desire of the soul and more desire of the body, then surely Marsail would not have been so hard to win. For she had lingered with him in the valley, if she had not trod the higher slopes: that he remembered with mingled joy and grief. Surely she had loved him. And, of a truth, his wrought imaginings were not rainbow-birds. Their wings had caught the spray of those bitter waters which we call experience, the wisdom of the flesh. Great love claims the eternal stars behind the perishing stars of the beloved's eyes, and would tread "the vast of dreams" beneath a little human heart. But there are few who love thus. It was not likely that Marsail was of those strong enough to mate with the great love. The many love too well the near securities.

All night long Alasdair sat brooding by the fire. Before dawn, he rose and went to the door. The hollow infinitude of the sky was filled with the incense of a myriad smoke of stars. His gaze wandered, till held where Hesperus and the planets called The Hounds leaped, tremulously incessant, forever welling to the brim, yet never spilling their radiant liquid fires. An appalling stillness prevailed in these depths.

Beyond the heather-slope in the moor he could hear the sea grinding the shingle as the long, slow wave rose and fell. Once, for a few moments, he listened intent: invisibly overhead a tail of wild geese travelled wedgewise towards polar seas, and their forlorn honk slipped bell-like through the darkness, and as from ledge to ledge of silent air.

As though it were the dew of that silence, peace descended upon him. There was, in truth, a love deeper than that of the body. Marsail — ah, poor broken heart, poor wounded life! Was love not great enough to heal that wound; was there not balm to put a whiteness and a quietness over that troubled heart, deep calm and moonrise over drowning waters?

Mayhap she did not love him now, could never love him as he loved her, with the love that is blind to life and deaf to death: well, her he loved. It was enough. Her sorrow and her shame, at least, might be his too. Her will would be his will: and if she were too weary to will, her weariness would be his to guide into a haven of rest: and if she had no thought of rest, no dream of rest, no wish for rest, but only a blind, baffled crying for the love which had brought her to the dust, well, that too he would take as his own, and comfort her with a sweet, impossible dream, and crown her shame with honour, and put his love like cool green grass beneath her feet.

"And she will not lose all," he said, smiling gently: adding, below his breath, as he turned to make ready for his departure against the dawn, "because, for sure, it is God that builds the nest of the blind bird."

Alasdair the Proud

"THERE were crowns lying there, idle gold in the yellow sand, and no man heeded them. Why should any man heed them? And where the long grass waved, there were women's breasts, so still in the brown silence, that the flittering moths, which shake with the breaths of daisies, motionlessly poised their wings above where so many sighs once were, and where no more was any pulse of joy."

"And what was the name of the man who led the spears on that day?"

"He had the name that you have — Alasdair; Alasdair the Proud."

"What was the cause of that red trail and of the battle among the hills?"

Gloom Achanna smiled, that swift, furtive smile which won so many, and in the end men and women cursed.

"It was a dream," he said slowly.

"A dream?"

"Yes. Her name was Enya — Enya of the Dark Eyes."

Alasdair M'Ian's grey-blue eyes wandered listlessly from the man who lay beside him in the heather. Enya of the Dark Eyes! The name was like a moonbeam in his mind.

Gloom Achanna watched him, though he kept his gaze upon the dry, crackled sprays of the heather, and was himself, seemingly, idly adrift in the swimming thought that is as the uncertain wind.

How tall and strong his companion was, he meditated. Had he forgotten, Gloom wondered: had he forgotten that day, years and years ago, when he had thrust him, Gloom Achanna, aside, and had then with laughing scorn lifted him suddenly and thrown him into the Pool of Diarmid? That was in Skye, in the Sleat of Skye. It was many years ago. That did not matter, though. There are no years to remembrance; what was, either is or is not.

And now they had met again by the roadside; and if not in Skye, not far from it, for they were now in Tiree, the low surf-girt island that for miles upon miles swims like a green snake between the Southern Minch and the Hebrid seas. It was a chance meeting too, if there is any chance; and after so many years. Gloom Achanna smiled; a sudden swift shadow it was that crossed his face, smooth, comely, pale beneath his sleek, seal-like dark hair. No, it was not chance this, he whispered to himself ; no, for sure, it was not chance. When he looked suddenly at Alasdair M'Ian, with furtive, forgetting eyes, he did not smile again, but the dusky pupils expanded and contracted.

And so, his thought ran, Alasdair M'Ian was a great man in that little world over yonder, the world of the towns and big cities! He had made a name for himself by his books, his poems, and the strange music wherewith he clothed his words, whether in song or story.

H'm; for that, did not he, Gloom know many a *dàn*, many a wild *òran*; could he not tell many a *sgeul* as fine, or finer? Ay, by the Black Stone of Iona! Why, then, should this Englishman have so much fame? Well, well, if not English, he wrote and spoke and thought in that foreign tongue, and had forgotten the old speech, or had no ease with it, and no doubt was Sasunnach[42] to the core. But for all his fame, and though he was still young and strong and fair to see, had he forgotten? He, Gloom Achanna, did not ever forget. Indeed, indeed, there was no chance in that meeting. Why had he, Gloom, gone to Tiree at all? It had been a whim. But now he understood.

And Alasdair M'Ian — Alasdair the Proud? What was *he* there for? There were no idle silly folk on the long isle of Tiree to listen to English songs. Ah yes, indeed; of course he was there. Where would he be coming to, after these long seven years, but to the place where he had first met and loved Ethlenn Maclaine?

Gloom pondered a while. That was a strange love, that of Alasdair M'Ian, for a woman who was wife to another man, and he loving her and she him. She had been the flame behind all these poems and stories which had made him so famous. For seven years he had loved her, and Alasdair the Proud was not the man to love a woman for seven years unless it was out of the great love, which is as deep as the sea, and as wild and hopeless as the south wind when she climbs against the stars.

Then all that he knew, all that he had heard of fact and half fact and cloudy rumour, all that he surmised, became in Gloom's mind a clear vision. He understood now, and he remembered. Had he not heard but a brief while ago that Alasdair was fëy with his love-dream? Did he not know that the man had endured so long, and become what he was, because for all these years he had held Ethlenn's love, because he believed that she loved him as he her? Was it not by this that he lived; that he made beauty with cunning, haunting words? Was it not true that for all her marriage with the good, loving, frail son of Maclaine of Inch, she

---

42 A southerner.

was in body and mind and soul wife to the man whom, too late, she had met, and who in her had found the bitter infinite way?

Yes; now, in a myriad sudden eddies of remembrance and surmise, he knew the poor tired soul, with its great dreams and imperishable desires, of Alasdair the Proud; and like a hawk his spirit hovered over it, uttering fierce cries of a glad and terrible hate. And of one thing he thought with almost an awe of laughing joy — that, even then, he had upon him the letter which, more than a week before, he had idly taken from Uille Beag, the lad who carried the few letters in that remote place. It was, as he knew, having read it, a letter from Ethlenn to Ronald Maclaine, her husband, who was then in Tiree, and she somewhere in the Southlands, in her and his home. He loved much to play the evil, bitter seduction of his music; that strange playing upon his *feadan* which none heard without disquietude, and mayhap fear and that which is deeper than fear. But he smiled when he thought of that letter; and the unspoken words upon his lips were that he was glad he had now two *feadans*, though one was only a little sheet of paper.

For two hours they had walked the same road that day, having met by the wayside. Then, having had milk and some oat-bread from a woman who had a little croft, they had rested on the heather, and Gloom Achanna had told old tales, old tales that he knew would fill the mind of Alasdair M'Ian with ancient beauty, and with the beauty that does not perish, for that which was, being perfect, is proudly enduring with other than mortal breath. In this way he won his companion to forgetfulness.

For a time there had been a dreaming silence. A pyot called loudly; a restless plover wheeled this way and that, crying forlornly. There were no other sounds, save when a wandering air whinnied in the gorse or made a strange, faint whistling among the spires of the heather.

With a stealthy movement, Gloom Achanna drew his *feadan* from its clasps beneath his coat. He put the flute to his mouth and breathed. It was as though birds were flitting to and fro in the moonshine, and pale moths of sound fluttered above drowning pools.

Alasdair did not hear, or made no sign. After a time he closed his eyes. It was sweet to lie there, in the honey-fragrant heather, in that remote isle, there where he had first seen the woman of his love; healing-sweet to be away from the great city in the south, from the deep weariness of his life there, from the weariness of men with whom he had so little in common. He was so fevered with the bitter vanity of his love that life had come to mean nothing else to him but the passing of coloured or discoloured moments. If only he might find peace; that, for long, he had wanted more than joy, whose eyes were too sorrowful now. Out of that great love and passion he had woven beautiful things — Beauty. That was his solace; by that, in that, for that, he lived.

But now he was tired. Too great a weariness had come upon his spirit. He heard other voices than those of Ethlenn whom he loved. They whispered to him by day, and were the forlorn echoes of his dreams.

For Beauty: yes, he would live for that; for his dream, and the weaving anew of that loveliness which made his tired mind wonderful and beautiful as an autumnal glen filled with moonshine. He had strength for this, since he knew that Ethlenn loved him, and loved him with too proud and great a love to be untrue to it even in word or deed, and so far the less in thought. By this he lived.

But now he lay upon the heather, tranced, at rest. He heard the cold, delicate music float idly above the purple bloom around him. Old foonsheen, enchanted airs: these, later, Gloom Achanna played. He smiled when he saw the frown passing from Alasdair's brows, and the lines in the face grow shadowy, and rest dwell beneath the closed eyes.

Then a single, wavering note wandered fitfully across the heather; another, and another. An old, sorrowful air stole through the hush, till the sadness had a cry in it that was as the crying of a lamentation not to be home. Alasdair stirred, sighing wearily. Below the lashes of his eyes tears gathered. At that, Gloom smiled once more; but in a moment watched again, furtively, with grave, intent gaze.

The air changed, but subtly, as the lift of the wind from grass to swaying foliage. The frown came back into Alasdair's forehead.

"Achanna," he said suddenly, raising his head and leaning his chin against his hand, with his elbow deep in the heather; "that was a bitter, cruel letter you sent to your brother Alasdair, that is now Alan Dall."

Gloom ceased playing, and quietly blew the damp out of his *feadan*. Then he looked at it sidelong, and slowly put it away again.

"Yes?" he said at last.

"A bitter, cruel letter, Gloom Achanna!"

"Perhaps you will be having the goodness, Alasdair mac Alasdair, if it is not a weariness to you, to tell me how you came to know of that letter?"

"Your brother Alasdair left it in the house of the woman in Benbecula, when his heart was broken by it, and he went north to the Lews, to find that poor woman he loved, and whom you ruined. And there the good priest, Father Ian Mackellar, found it, and sent it to me, saying, 'Here is a worse thing than any told in any of your stories.'"

"Well, and what then, Alasdair, who is called Alasdair the Proud?"

"Why am I called that, Achanna?"

"Why? Oh, for why am I called Gloom of the Feadan? Because it is what people see and hear when they see me and hear me. You are proud because you are big and strong; you are proud because you have the kiss of Diarmid; you are proud because you have won great love; you are proud because you have made men and women listen to your songs and tales; you are proud because you are Alasdair M'Ian; you are proud because you dream you are beyond the crushing Hand; you are proud because you are (and not knowing that) feeble as water, and fitful as wind, and weak as a woman."

Alasdair frowned. What word he was going to say died unsaid.

"Tell me," he said at last, quietly, "what made you write these words in that letter: 'Brother, because you are a poet, let me tell you this, which is old, ancient wisdom, and not mine alone, that no woman likely to be loved by a poet can be true to a poet?'"

"Why did I write that, Alasdair MacAlasdair?"

"Yes."

"If you read that letter, you know why. I said they were cowards, these loving women whom you poets love, for they will give up all save the lies they love, the lies that save them."

"It is a lie. It means nothing, that evil lie of yours."

"It means this. They can be true to their lovers, but they cannot be true to love. They love to be loved. They love the love of a poet, for he dreams beauty into them, and they live as other women cannot, for they go clothed in rainbows and moonshine. But ... what was it that I wrote? They have to choose at last between the steep brae and the easy lily leven; and I am thinking you will not find easily the woman that in her heart of hearts will leave the lily leven for the steep brae. No, not easily."

"What do *you* know of love, Gloom Achanna — you, of whom the good Father Ian wrote to me as the most evil of all God's creatures?"

Gloom smiled across pale lips, with darkening eyes.

"Did he say that? Sure, it was a hard thing to say. I have done harm to no man that did not harm me; and as to women ... well, well, for sure, women are women."

"It was well that you were named Gloom. You put evil everywhere."

After that there was silence for a time. Once Achanna put his hand to his *feadan* again, but withdrew it.

"Shall I be telling you now that old tale of Enya of the Dark Eyes?" he said gently at last, and with soft, persuasive eyes.

Alasdair lay back wearily.

"Yes, tell me that tale."

"Well, as I was saying, there were crowns lying there, idle gold in the yellow sand, and no man heeded them. And where the long grass waved, there were women's breasts, so still in the brown silence, that the flittering moths, which shake with the breaths of daisies, motionlessly poised their wings above where so many sighs once were, and where no more was any pulse of joy ..." And therewith Gloom Achanna told the tale of Enya of the Dark Eyes, and how Aodh (whom he called Alasdair the Proud) loved her overmuch, and in the end lost both kinghood and manhood because of her wanton love that could be the same to him and to Cathba Fleetfoot. And with these words, smiling furtively, he ended the tale —

"This is the story of Alasdair the Proud, Alasdair the Poet-King, who made deathless beauty out of the beauty and love of Enya of the Dark Eyes, who sang the same song to two men."

When Gloom had come to that part of his tale where he told of what the captive woman said to the king, Alasdair slowly turned and again fixed his gaze on the man who spoke, leaning the while on his elbow as before, with his chin in his hand.

When Achanna finished, neither said any word for a time. Alasdair looked at the man beside him with intent, unwavering gaze. Gloom's eyes were lidded, and he stared into the grass beneath the heather.

"Why did you tell me that tale, Gloom Achanna?"

"Sure, I thought you loved *sgeulan* of the old, ancient days?"

"Why did you tell me that tale?"

Gloom stirred uneasily. But he did not answer, though he lifted his eyes.

"Why did you call the man who loved Enya, Alasdair? It is not a name of that day. And why do you tell me a tale little altered from one that I have already told with my pen?"

"For sure, I forgot that. And you called the man ...?"

"I called him Aodh, which was his name. It was Aodh the Proud who loved Enya of the Dark Eyes."

"Well, well, the end was the same. It was not a good end, that of ... Aodh the Proud."

"Why did you tell me that tale?"

Suddenly Achanna rose. He stood, looking down upon Alasdair.

"It is all one," he said slowly: "Aodh and Enya, or Alasdair and Ethlenn."

A deep flush came into Alasdair's face. A splatch stained his forehead.

"Ah," he muttered hoarsely: "and will you be telling me, Gloom Achanna, what you have to do with that name that you have spoken?"

"Man, you are but a fool, I am thinking, for all your wisdom. Here is a letter. Read it. It is from Ethlenn Maclaine."

"From Ethlenn Maclaine?"

"Ay, for sure. But not to you: no, nor yet to me; but to Ronald Maclaine her man."

Alasdair rose. He drew proudly back.

"I will not read the letter. The letter is not for me."

Gloom smiled.

"Then I will read it to you, Alasdair M'Ian. It is not a long letter. Oh no; but it is to Ronald Maclaine."

Alasdair looked at the man. He said a word in Gaelic that brought a swift darkening into Gloom's eyes. Then, slowly, he moved away.

"A fool is bad; a blind fool is worse," cried Achanna mockingly.

Alasdair stopped and turned. "I will neither look nor hear," he said. "What was not meant for me to see or hear, I will not see or hear."

"Is there madness upon you that you believe in a woman because she asks you to take her pledged word? Do you not know that a pressed woman always falls back upon the man's trusting her absolutely? When she will be knowing that, she can have quiet laughter because of all her shadowy vows and smiling coward lies that are worse than spoken lies. She knows, or thinks she knows, he will be blind and deaf as well as dumb. It is a fine thing that for a proud man, Alasdair M'Ian! It is a fine thing, for sure! And he is a wise man, oh yes, he is a wise man, who will put all his happiness in one scale of the balance, and his trust in another. It is easy for the woman ... oh yes, for sure. It is what I would do if I were a woman, what you would do. I would say to the man who loved me, as you love Ethlenn Maclaine, 'You must show your love by absolute unquestioning trust.' That is how women try to put a cloud about a man's mind. That is how a woman loves to play the game of love. Then, having said that, if I were a woman, I would smile; and then I would go to the other man, and I would be the same with him, and kiss him, and be all tender sweetness to him, and say the same things, and trust him to believe all. It is quite easy to say the same things to two men. I have said to you already, Alasdair M'Ian, that a woman like that is not only untrue to the men who love her, but to love. She cannot say in her heart of hearts, 'Love is the one thing.' She will say it, yes: first to one, then to the other; and perhaps both will believe. And to herself (she will be sorry for herself) she will say, 'I love one for this, and the other for that: they do not clash ...' knowing well, or perhaps persuading herself so, that this is not a subterfuge. It is the subterfuge of a coward, for she dare not live truly; she must needs be for ever making up to the one what she gives or says to the other. And you ... you are a poet, they say; and have the thing that makes you see deeper and further and surer; and so it must be you, and not Ronald Maclaine, who will be the one of the two to doubt!" Achanna ceased abruptly, and began laughing.

Alasdair stood still, staring fixedly at him.

"I wish to hear no more," he said at last quietly, though with a strange, thin, shrill voice; "I wish to hear no more. Will you go now? If not, then I will go."

"Wait now, wait now, for sure! Sure, I know the letter off by heart. It goes this way, Alasdair mac Alasdair —"

But putting his hands to his ears, Alasdair again turned aside, and made no sound save with his feet as he trod the crackling undertwigs of the heather. Gloom swiftly followed. Coming upon Alasdair suddenly and unheard, he thrust the letter before his eyes.

Gloom Achanna smiled as he saw the face of Alasdair the Proud flush deeply again, then grow white and hard, and strangely drawn.

As he did not speak, he muttered against his ears: *"And this is the story of Aodh the Proud, who made deathless beauty out of the beauty and love of Enya of the Dark Eyes, who sang the same song to two men."*

Still silence.

In a whisper he repeated: "Who sang ... the same song ... to ... two ... men."

A change had come over Alasdair. He was quiet, but his fingers restlessly intertwined. His face twitched. His eyes were strained.

"That is a lie ... a forgery ... that letter!" he exclaimed abruptly, in a hoarse voice. "She did not write it."

Achanna unfolded the letter again, and handed it to his companion, who took it, only in the belief that it was Gloom's doing. Alasdair's pulse leaped at the writing he knew so well. He started, and visibly trembled, when he saw and realised the date. The letter fluttered to the ground. When Gloom stooped to pick it up, he noticed that the veins on Alasdair's temples were purple and distended.

From his breast-pocket Alasdair drew another letter. This he unfolded and read. When he had finished, the flush was out of his white face, and was in his brow, where it lay a scarlet splatch.

He was dazed, for sure, Gloom thought, as he watched him closely; then suddenly began to play.

For a time Alasdair frowned. Then two tears rolled down his face. His mouth ceased twitching, and a blank idle look came into the dulled eyes.

Suddenly he began laughing.

Gloom Achanna ceased playing for a moment. He watched the man. Then he smiled, and played again.

He played the Dàn-nan-Ròn, which had sent Mànus MacCodrum to his death among the seals; and the Davsa-na-Mairv, to which Seumas his brother had listened in a sweat of terror; and now he played the dàn which is known as the Pibroch of the Mad. He walked slowly away, playing lightly as he went. He came to a rising ground, and passed over it, and was seen no more. Alasdair stood, intently listening. His limbs shook. Sweat poured from his face. His eyes were distended. A terror that no man can tell, a horror that is beyond words, was upon him.

When he could hear no more, he turned and looked fearfully about him. Suddenly he uttered a hoarse cry. A man stood near him, staring at him curiously. He knew the man. It was himself. He threw up his arms. Then slowly, he let them fall. It was life or death; he knew that; that he knew. Stumblingly he sank to his knees. He put out wavering hands, wet with falling tears and cried in a loud, strident voice.

There was no meaning in what he said. But that which was behind what he cried was, "*Lord, deliver me from this evil! Lord, deliver me from this evil!*"

The Amadan

I

THE fishermen laughed when they saw "The Amadan," the fool, miscalculate his leap and fall from the bow of the smack *Tonn* into the shallows. He splashed clumsily, and stared in fear, now at the laughing men, now at the shore.

Stumbling, he waded through the shallows. A gull wheeled above his head, screaming. He screamed back. The men in the *Tonn* laughed.

The Amadan was tall, and seemed prematurely bent; his hair was of a dusty white, though he had not the look of age, but of a man in the prime of life.

It was not a month since Gloom Achanna had played madness upon him. Now, none of his Southland friends would have recognised Alasdair M'Ian, Alasdair the Proud. His clothes were torn and soiled; his mien was wild and strange; but the change was from within. The spirit of the man had looked into hell. That was why Alasdair the Proud had become "The Amadan," the wandering fool.

It was a long way from Tiree to Askaig in the Lews, or the Long Island, as the Hebrideans call it. Alasdair had made Peter Macaulay laugh by saying that he had been sailing, sailing, from Tiree for a hundred years. When he stood upon the dry sand, he looked at the smack wonderingly. He waved his hand.

"Where ... where ... is Tiree?" he cried. The men laughed at the question and at his voice. Suddenly old Ewan MacEwan rose and took his pipe from his mouth.

"That will do now, men, for sure," he said quietly. "It is God that did that. We have laughed too much."

"Oh," answered Peter Macaulay, abashed, "he is only an amadan. He does not know whether we laugh or why."

"God knows."

"Ay, ay, for sure. Well, to be sure, yes, you will be right in what you say, Ewan."

With that, Macaulay made as though he would call to the man; but the old man, who was skipper, put him aside. Ewan went to the bow, and slid over by a rope. He stood for a moment in his sea-boots, with the tide-wash reaching to his knees. Then he waded to the shore and went up to the man who was a fool.

"Tell me, poor man, what is your name?"

"Enya."

"Ay, that is all you will say. But that is not a man's name. It is a woman's name that. Tell me your name, poor man."

"Enya — Enya of the Dark Eyes."

"No, no, now, for sure, you said it was Aodh."

"Yes; Aodh. Aodh the Proud."

"Ah, for sure, may God give you peace, poor soul! It is a poor pride, I am fearing." The man did not answer.

"And have you no thought now of where you will be going?"

"Yes ... no ... yes ... there is a star in the west."

"Have you any money, poor man? Well, now, see here; here is a little money. It is a shilling and two pennies. It is all I have. But I have my mind, and God is good. Will you be caring, now, to have my pipe, poor man? A good smoke is a peaceful thing; yes, now, here is my pipe. Take it, take it!"

But Alasdair M'Ian only shook his head. He took the money and looked at it. A troubled look came into his face. Suddenly there were tears in his eyes. "I remember ... I remember ... " he began, stammeringly. "It is an old saying. It is ... it is God ... that builds ... it is God that builds the nest ... of the blind bird."

Ewan MacEwan took off his blue bonnet. Then he looked up into the great, terrible silence. God heard.

Before he spoke again, a man came over the high green-laced dune which spilt into the machar beyond the shore. He was blind, and was led by a dog. Ewan gave a sigh of relief. He knew the man. It was Alan Dall. There would be help now for the Amadan, if help there could be.

He went towards the blind man, who stopped when he heard steps. "How tall and thin he was!" thought Ewan. His long, fair hair, streaked with grey, hung almost to his shoulders. His pale face was lit by the beauty of his spirit. It shone like a lamp. Blind though he was, there was a strange living light in his blue eyes.

"Who is it?" he asked, in the Gaelic, and in a voice singularly low and sweet. "Who is it? I was lying asleep in the warm sand when I heard laughter."

Ewan MacEwan went close to him, and told all he had to tell. When he was done, Alan Dall spoke. "Leave the poor man with me, Ewan my friend. I will guide him to a safe place, and mayhap Himself, to whom be praise, will build the nest that he seeks, blind bird that he is."

And so it was.

II

It was not till the third day that Alan Dall knew who the Amadan was. A heavy rain had fallen since morning. Outside the turf bothie where Alan Dall had his brief home, a ceaseless splash made a drowsy peace like the humming of bees. Through it moved in sinuous folds of sound a melancholy sighing; the breathing of the tide wearily lifting and falling among the heavy masses of wrack which clothed the rocks of the inlet above which the bothie stood.

Since he had eaten of the porridge and milk and coarse bread brought him by the old woman who came every morning to see to his fire and food, Alan Dall had sat before the peats, brooding upon many things, things of the moment, and the deep insatiable desires of the hungry spirit; but most upon the mystery of the man whom he had brought thither. He slept still, the poor Amadan. It was well; he would not arouse him. The sound of the rain had deep rest in it.

The night before, the Amadan, while staring into the red heart of the peats, had suddenly stirred.

"What is it?" Alan had asked gently.

"My name is Alasdair."

"Alasdair? I too ... I know well one who is named Alasdair."

"Is he called Alasdair the Proud?"

"No; he is not called the Proud."

"You have told me that your name is Alan?"

"Ay. I am called Alan Dall because I am blind."

"I have seen your face before, or in a dream, Alan Dall."

"And what will your father's name be, and the name of your father's fathers?"

"I do not know that name, nor the name of my clan."

Thereupon a long silence had fallen. Thrice Alan spoke, but the Amadan either did not hear, or would make no answer. An eddy of wind rose and fell. The harsh screaming cry of a heron rent the silence. Then there was silence again. The Amadan stirred restlessly.

"Who was that?" he asked in a whisper.

"It was no one, Alasdair my friend."

Alasdair rose and stealthily went to the door. He lifted the latch and looked out. The dog followed him, whimpering.

"Hush-sh, sùil!" whispered Alan Dall. The dog slipped beyond Alasdair. He put back his ears, and howled.

Alan rose and went to the Amadan, and took him by the sleeve, and so led him back to the stool before the glowing peats.

"Who did you think it was?" he asked, when the Amadan was seated again, and no longer trembled.

"Who was it, Alan Dall?"

"It was a heron."

"They say herons that cry by night are people out of the grave."

"It may be so. But there is no harm to them that hear if it is not their hour."

"It was like a man laughing."

"Who would laugh, here, in this lonely place, and at night; and for why?"

"I know a man who would laugh here, in this lonely place, and at night, and for why, too."

"Who?"

"His name is Gloom."

Alan Dall started. A quiver passed over his face, and his hand trembled.

"That is a strange name for a man, Gloom. I have heard only of one man who bore that name."

"There can be only one man. His name is Gloom Achanna."

"Gloom Achanna. Yes ... I know the man."

He would not tell the Amadan that this man was his brother; or not yet. He, too, then, poor fool, had been caught in the mesh of that evil. And now, perhaps, he would be able to see through the mystery which beset this man whom he had taken to guard and to heal.

But Alasdair M'Ian said one saying only, and would speak no more; and that saying was, "He is not a man; he is a devil." Soon after this the Amadan suddenly lapsed into a swoon of sleep, even while words were stammering upon his lips. But now Alan Dall understood better. A deeper pity, too, was in his heart. This poor man, this Amadan, was indeed his comrade, if his cruel sorrow had come to him through Gloom Achanna.

When he rose in the morning at the first sobbing of the rainy wind, and saw how profoundly the Amadan slept, he did not wake him.

Thus it was that throughout that long day Alan Dall sat, pondering and dreaming before the peats, while Alasdair the Proud lay drowned in sleep. The day darkened early, because of the dense mists which came out of the sea and floated heavily between the myriad grey reeds of the rain and the fluent green and brown which was the ground. With the dusk the Amadan stirred. Alan Dall crossed to the inset bed, and stood listening intently. Alasdair muttered strangely in his sleep; and though he had hitherto, save for a few words, spoken in the English tongue, he now used the Gaelic. The listener caught fragments only ... *an Athair Uibhreach*, the Haughty Father ... *Agus thug e aoradh dha*, and worshipped him ... *Biodh uachdaranachd aca*, let them have dominion.

"Those evil ones that go with Gloom my brother," he muttered; "those evil spirits have made their kingdom among his dreams."

"Who are they who are about you?" he whispered.

The Amadan turned, and his lips moved. But it was as though others spoke through him —

> "*Cha 'n ann do Shiol Adhamh sinn,*
> *Ach tha sinn de mhuinntir an Athar Uaibhrich.*"
> (We are not of the seed of Adam,
> But we are the offspring of the Haughty Father.)[43]

Alan Dall hesitated. One of the white prayers of Christ was on his lips, but he remembered also the old wisdom of his fathers. So he kneeled, and said a *seun*, that is strong against the bitter malice of demoniac wiles.

Thereafter he put upon him this *eolas* of healing, touching the brow and the heart as he said '*here*' and '*here*' —

> "*Deep peace I breathe into you, O weariness, here:*
> *O ache, here!*
> *Deep peace, a soft white dove to you;*
> *Deep peace, a quiet rain to you;*
> *Deep peace, an ebbing wave to you!*
> *Deep peace, red wind of the east from you;*
> *Deep peace, grey wind of the west to you;*
> *Deep peace, dark wind of the north from you;*
> *Deep peace, blue wind of the south to you!*
> *Deep peace, pure red of the flame to you;*
> *Deep peace, pure white of the moon to you;*
> *Deep peace, pure green of the grass to you;*
> *Deep peace, pure brown of the earth to you;*
> *Deep peace, pure grey of the dew to you,*
> *Deep peace, pure blue of the sky to you!*

---

43 The Haughty Father is one of the many names of the dark god Fiona created called Dalua.

Deep peace of the running wave to you,
Deep peace of the flowing air to you,
Deep peace of the quiet earth to you,
Deep peace of the sleeping stones to you!
Deep peace of the Yellow Shepherd to you,
Deep peace of the Wandering Shepherdess to you,
Deep peace of the Flock of Stars to you,
Deep peace from the Son of Peace to you,
Deep peace from the heart of Mary to you,
And from Bridget of the Mantle
Deep peace, deep peace!
And with the kindness too of the Haughty Father,
Peace!
In the name of the Three who are One,
Peace!
And by the will of the King of the Elements,
Peace! Peace!"[44]

Then, for a time he prayed: and, as he prayed, a white and beautiful Image stood beside him, and put soft moon-white hands upon the brow of the Amadan. In this wise the beauty of Alan Dall's spirit, that had become a prayer, was created by God into a new immortal spirit.

The Image was as a wavering reed of light, before it stooped and kissed the soul of Alasdair, and was at one with it.

Alasdair opened his eyes.

God had healed him.

---

44 See my book *The Chronicles of the Sidhe* for an in-depth discussion on this important rune.

Section Three

IONA & ST. COLUMBA

IONA & ST. COLUMBA

This selection of tales all concern Iona and the 6th century Irish Saint Columba. He arrived on the Isle of Iona, Scotland in 563 AD, started a monastic community and, from there, sent out missionaries all over Scotland, Ireland, England and even into Continental Europe. His hagiography was written within a hundred years of his death and since then more and more stories have been added to his already colourful and eventful life. He is one of the most popular saints in the Highlands and Islands and many oral stories still abound, usually having something to do with the area in which the story-teller lives. Fiona mentions St Columba frequently throughout her earlier stories but none of these authentic-sounding vignettes are to be found anywhere else. However they all ring true to the style and subject matter of the 'original' tales of the saint's doings and sayings.

The first piece is an abbreviated version of a long essay simply called *Iona* which appeared in the November and December 1899 issues of the *Fortnightly Review* magazine. This rather rambling piece covers the factual and spiritual history of the Scottish Isle of Iona but also diverges off into many other topics. I have cut out several sections that go into great details about the proper use of the Gaelic language plus several short sections that repeat material to be found elsewhere in her writings. It is clear from this essay just how important tiny Iona was to Fiona – Sharp at one time claimed that Fiona was born and raised there – and many people today would echo the same sentiments. It is indeed a very mystical and beautiful place.

The following three tales, *The Festival of the Birds*, *The Sabbath of the Fishes and the Flies* and *The Moon-Child*, were published together in the 1895 collection *The Sin-Eater* under the group heading of *The Three Marvels of Hy*. Hy is an old Celtic name usually given to the Otherworld but here refers to the sacred Isle of Iona. All three tales contain a clear, easy and comfortable mixing of the Christian and pre-Christian beliefs and practices and, indeed, the early biographies of Columba contain similar mixings of traditions that today we would consider hostile to each other.

Alexander Carmichael's great collection *Carmina Gadelica*, a mass of oral stories, runes, sayings and blessings collected in the mid-19th century from the Gaelic-speaking Highlanders and Islanders, likewise is a mish-mash of accepted Christian canon and early pre-Christian Celtic mythology and folklore all sitting quite easily and happily with each other. This was important to Fiona and is a common background theme in most of her writings. She also wrote several vignettes of the early life of Christ which again relate tales not to be found anywhere else, tales that are certainly not the normal stuff of Sunday School teaching, but which add a new and fulfilling dimension to his life and work on earth. I look at several of these beautiful tales in my book *The Chronicles of the Sidhe*.

Iona

A few places in the world are to be held holy, because of the love which consecrates them and the faith which enshrines them. Their names are themselves talismans of spiritual beauty. Of these is Iona.

The Arabs speak of Mecca as a holy place before the time of the prophet, saying that Adam himself lies buried here: and, before Adam, that the Sons of Allah, who are called Angels, worshipped; and that when Allah Himself stood upon perfected Earth it was on this spot. And here, they add, when there is no man left upon earth, an angel shall gather up the dust of this world, and say to Allah, "There is nothing left of the whole earth but Mecca: and now Mecca is but the few grains of sand that I hold in the hollow of my palm, O Allah."

In spiritual geography Iona is the Mecca of the Gael.

It is but a small isle, fashioned of a little sand, a few grasses salt with the spray of an ever-restless wave, a few rocks that wade in heather and upon whose brows the sea-wind weaves the yellow lichen. But since the remotest days sacrosanct men have bowed here in worship. In this little island a lamp was lit whose flame lighted pagan Europe, from the Saxon in his fens to the swarthy folk who came by Greek waters to trade the Orient. Here Learning and Faith had their tranquil home, when the shadow of the sword lay upon all lands, from Syracuse by the Tyrrhene Sea to the rainy isles of Orcc. From age to age, lowly hearts have never ceased to bring their burthen here. Iona herself has given us for remembrance a fount of youth more wonderful than that which lies under her own boulders of Dûn-I. And here Hope waits.

To tell the story of Iona is to go back to God, and to end in God.

But to write of Iona, there are many ways of approach. No place that has a spiritual history can be revealed to those who know nothing of it by facts and descriptions. The approach may be through the obscure glens of another's mind and so out by the moonlit way, as well as by the track that thousands travel. I have nothing to say of Iona's acreage, or fisheries, or pastures: nothing of how the islanders live. These things are the accidental. There is small difference in simple life anywhere. Moreover, there are many to tell all that need be known.

There is one Iona, a little island of the west. There is another Iona, of which I would speak. I do not say that it lies open to all. It is as we come that we find. If we come, bringing nothing with us, we go away ill-content, having seen and heard nothing of what we had vaguely expected to see or hear. It is another Iona than the Iona of sacred memories and prophecies: Iona the metropolis of dreams. None can understand it who does not see it through its pagan light, its Christian light, its singular blending of paganism and romance and spiritual beauty. There is, too, an Iona that is more than Gaelic, that is more than a place rainbow-lit with the seven desires of the world, the Iona that, if we will it so, is a mirror of your heart and of mine.

History may be written in many ways, but I think that in days to come the method of spiritual history will be found more suggestive than the method of statistical history. The one will, in its own way, reveal inward life, and hidden significance, and palpable destiny: as the other, in the good but narrow way of convention, does with exactitude delineate features, narrate facts, and relate events. The true interpreter will as little despise the one as he will claim all for the other.

And that is why I would speak here of Iona as befalls my pen, rather than as perhaps my pen should go: and choose legend and remembrance, and my own and other memories and associations, and knowledge of my own and others, and hidden meanings, and beauty and strangeness surviving in dreams and imaginations, rather than facts and figures, that others could adduce more deftly and with more will.

When I think of Iona I think often, too, of a prophecy once connected with Iona; though perhaps current no more in a day when prophetical hopes are fallen dumb and blind.

It is commonly said that, if he would be heard, none should write in advance of his times. That I do not believe. Only, it does not matter how few listen. I believe that we are close upon a great and deep spiritual change. I believe a new redemption is even now conceived of the Divine Spirit in the human heart, that is itself as a woman, broken in dreams, and yet sustained in faith, patient, long-suffering, looking towards home. I believe that though the Reign of Peace may be yet a long way off, it is drawing near: and that Who shall save us anew shall come divinely as a Woman, to save as Christ saved but not, as He did, to bring with Her a sword. But whether this Divine Woman, this Mary of so many passionate hopes and dreams, is to come through mortal birth, or as an immortal Breathing upon our souls, none can yet know.

Sometimes I dream of the old prophecy that Christ shall come again upon Iona, and of that later and obscure prophecy which foretells, now as the Bride of Christ, now as the Daughter of God, now as the Divine Spirit embodied through mortal birth in a Woman, as once through mortal birth in a Man, the coming of a new Presence and Power: and dream that this may be upon Iona, so that the little Gaelic island may become as the little Syrian Bethlehem. But more wise it is to dream, not of hallowed ground, but of the hallowed gardens of the soul wherein She shall appear white and radiant. Or, that upon the hills, where we are wandered, the Shepherdess shall call us home.

From one man only, on Iona itself, I have heard any allusion to the prophecy as to the Saviour who shall yet come: and he in part was obscure, and confused the advent of Mary into the spiritual world with the possible coming again to earth of Mary, as another Redeemer, or with a descending of the Divine Womanhood upon the human heart as a universal spirit descending upon awaiting souls. But in intimate remembrance I recall the words and faith of one or two whom I loved well. Nor must I forget that my old nurse, Barabal, used to sing a strange "oran," to the effect that when St. Bride came again to Iona it would be to bind the hair and wash the feet of the Bride of Christ.

One of those to whom I allude was a young Hebridean priest, who died in Venice, after troubled years, whose bitterest vicissitude was the clouding of his soul's hope by the wings of a strange multitude of dreams — one of whom and whose end I have elsewhere written: and he told me once how, "as our forefathers and elders believed and still believe, that Holy Spirit shall come again which once was mortally born among us as the Son of God, but, then, shall be the Daughter of God. The Divine Spirit shall come again as a Woman. Then for the first time the world will know peace." And when I asked him if it were not prophesied that the Woman is to be born in Iona, he said that if this prophecy had been made it was doubtless of an Iona that was symbolic, but that this was a matter of no moment, for She would rise suddenly in many hearts, and have her habitation among dreams and hopes. The other who spoke to me of this Woman who is to save was an old fisherman of a remote island of the Hebrides, and one to whom I owe more than to any other spiritual influence in my childhood, for it was he who opened to me the three gates of Beauty. Once this old man, Seumas Macleod, took me with him to a lonely haven in the rocks, and held me on his knee as we sat watching the sun sink and the moon climb out of the eastern wave.

I saw no one, but abruptly he rose and put me from him, and bowed his grey head as he knelt before one who suddenly was standing in that place. I asked eagerly who it was. He told me that it was an Angel. Later, I learned (I remember my disappointment that the beautiful vision was not winged with great white wings) that the Angel was one soft flame of pure white, and that below the soles of his feet were curling scarlet flames. He had come in answer to the old man's prayer. He had come to say that we could not see the Divine One whom we awaited. "But you will yet see that Holy Beauty," said the Angel, and Seumas believed, and I too believed, and believe. He took my hand, and I knelt beside him, and he bade me repeat the words he said. And that was how I first prayed to Her who shall yet be the Balm of the World.

And since then I have learned, and do see, that not only prophecies and hopes, and desires unclothed yet in word or thought, foretell her coming, but already a multitude of spirits are in the gardens of the soul, and are sowing seed and calling upon the wind of the south; and that everywhere are watching eyes and uplifted hands, and signs which cannot be mistaken, in many lands, in many peoples, in many minds; and, in the heaven itself that the soul sees, the surpassing signature.

I recall one whom I knew, a fisherman of the little green island: and I tell this story of Coll here, for it is to me more than the story of a dreaming islander. One night, lying upon the hillock that is called Cnoc-nan-Aingeal, because it is here that St. Colum was wont to hold converse with an angel out of heaven, he watched the moonlight move like a slow fin through the sea: and in his heart were desires as infinite as the waves of the sea, the moving homes of the dead.

And while he lay and dreamed, his thoughts idly adrift as a net in deep waters, he closed his eyes, muttering the Gaelic words of an old line,

"In the Isle of Dreams God shall yet fulfil Himself anew."

Hearing a footfall, he stirred. A man stood beside him. He did not know the man, who was young, and had eyes dark as hill-tarns, with hair light and soft as thistledown; and moved light as a shadow, delicately treading the grass as the wind treads it. In his hair he had twined the fantastic leaf of the horn-poppy.

The islander did not move or speak: it was as though a spell were upon him.

"God be with you," he said at last, uttering the common salutation.

"And with you, Coll mac Coll," answered the stranger. Coll looked at him. Who was this man, with the sea-poppy in his hair, who, unknown, knew him by name? He had heard of one whom he did not wish to meet, the Green Harper: also of a grey man of the sea whom islesmen seldom alluded to by name: again, there was the Amadan Dhu ... but at that name Coll made the sign of the cross, and remembering what Father Allan had told him in South Uist, muttered a holy exorcism of the Trinity.

The man smiled.

"You need have no fear, Coll mac Coll," he said quietly.

"You that know my name so well are welcome, but if you in turn would tell me your name I should be glad."

"I have no name that I can tell you," answered the stranger gravely; "but I am not of those who are unfriendly. And because you can see me and speak to me, I will help you to whatsoever you may wish."

Coll laughed.

"Neither you nor any man can do that. For now that I have neither father nor mother, nor brother nor sister, and my lass too is dead, I wish neither for sheep nor cattle, nor for new nets and a fine boat, nor a big house, nor as much money as MacCailein Mòr has in the bank at Inveraora."

"What then do you wish for, Coll mac Coll?"

"I do not wish for what cannot be, or I would wish to see again the dear face of Morag, my lass. But I wish for all the glory and wonder and power there is in the world, and to have it all at my feet, and to know everything that the Holy Father himself knows, and have kings coming to me as the crofters come to MacCailein Mòr's factor."

"You can have that, Coll mac Coll," said the Green Harper, and he waved a withe of hazel he had in his hand.

"What is that for?" said Coll.

"It is to open a door that is in the air. And now, Coll, if that is your wish of all wishes, and you will give up all other wishes for that wish, you can have the sovereignty of the world. Ay, and more than that: you shall have the sun like a golden jewel in the hollow of your right hand, and all the stars as pearls in your left, and have the moon as a white shining opal above your brows, with all knowledge behind the sun, within the moon, and beyond the stars."

Coll's face shone. He stood, waiting. Just then he heard a familiar sound in the dusk. The tears came into his eyes.

"Give me instead," he cried, "give me a warm breast-feather from that grey dove of the woods that is winging home to her young." He looked as one moon-dazed. None stood beside him. He was alone. Was it a dream, he wondered? But a weight was lifted from his heart. Peace fell upon him as dew upon grey pastures. Slowly he walked homeward. Once, glancing back, he saw a white figure upon the knoll, with a face noble and beautiful. Was it Colum himself come again? he mused: or that white angel with whom the Saint was wont to discourse, and who brought him intimacies of God? or was it but the wave-fire of his dreaming mind, as lonely and cold and unreal as that which the wind of the south makes upon the wandering hearths of the sea?

I tell this story of Coll here, for, as I have said, it is to me more than the story of a dreaming islander. He stands for the soul of a race. It is because, to me, he stands for the sorrowful genius of our race, that I have spoken of him here. Below all the strife of lesser desires, below all that he has in common with other men, he has the livelong unquenchable thirst for the things of the spirit. This is the thirst that makes him turn so often from the near securities and prosperities, and indeed all beside, setting his heart aflame with vain, because illimitable, desires. For him, the wisdom before which knowledge is a frosty breath: the beauty that is beyond what is beautiful. For, like Coll, the world itself has not enough to give him. And at the last, and above all, he is like Coll in this, that the sun and moon and stars themselves may become as trampled dust, for only a breast-feather of that Dove of the Eternal, which may have its birth in mortal love, but has its evening home where are the dews of immortality.

"The Dove of the Eternal." It was from the lips of an old priest of the Hebrides that I first heard these words. I was a child, and asked him if it was a white dove, such as I had seen fanning the sunglow in Icolmkill.

"Yes," he told me, "the Dove is white, and it was beloved of Colum, and is of you, little one, and of me."

"Then it is not dead?"

"It is not dead."

I was in a more wild and rocky isle than Iona then, and when I went into a solitary place close by my home it was to a stony wilderness so desolate that in many moods I could not bear it. But that day, though there were no sheep lying beside boulders as grey and still, nor whinnying goats (creatures that have always seemed to me strangely homeless, so that, as a child, it was often my noon-fancy on hot days to play to them on a little reed-flute I was skilled in making, thwarting the hill-wind at the small holes to the fashioning of a rude furtive music, which I believed comforted the goats, though why I did not know, and probably did not try to know): and though I could hear nothing but the soft, swift, slipping feet of the wind among the rocks and grass and a noise of the tide crawling up from a shore hidden behind crags (beloved of swallows for the small honey-flies which fed upon the thyme): still, on that day, I was not ill at ease, nor in any way disquieted. But before me I saw a white rock-dove, and followed it gladly. It flew it circling among the crags, and once I thought had passed seaward; but it came again, and alit on a boulder.

I went upon my knees, and prayed to it, and, as nearly as I can remember, in these words: —

"O Dove of the Eternal, I want to love you, and you to love me: and if you live on Iona, I want you to show me, when I go there again, the place where Colum the Holy talked with an angel. And I want to live as long as you, Dove" (I remember thinking this might seem disrespectful, and that I added hurriedly and apologetically), "Dove of the Eternal."

That evening I told Father Ivor what I had done. He did not laugh at me. He took me on his knee, and stroked my hair, and for a long time was so silent that I thought he was dreaming. He put me gently from him, and kneeled at the chair, and made this simple prayer which I have never forgotten: "O Dove of the Eternal, grant the little one's prayer."

That is a long while ago now, and I have sojourned since in Iona, and there and elsewhere known the wild doves of thought and dream. But I have not, though I have longed, seen again the White Dove that Colum so loved. For long I thought it must have left Iona and Barra too, when Father Ivor died.

Yet I have not forgotten that it is not dead.

"I want to live as long as you," was my child's plea: and the words of the old priest, knowing and believing were, "O Dove of the Eternal, grant the little one's prayer."

It was not in Barra, but in Iona, that, while yet a child, I set out one evening to find the Divine Forges. A Gaelic sermon, preached on the shoreside by an earnest man, who, going poor and homeless through the west, had tramped the long roads of Mull over against us, and there fed to flame a smouldering fire, had been my ministrant in these words. The "revivalist" had spoken of God as one who would hammer the evil out of the soul and weld it to good, as a blacksmith at his anvil: and suddenly, with a dramatic gesture, he cried: "This little island of Iona is this anvil;

God is your blacksmith: but oh, poor people, who among you knows the narrow way to the Divine Forges?"

There is a spot on Iona that has always had a strange enchantment for me. Behind the ruined walls of the Columban church, the slopes rise, and the one isolated hill of Iona is there, a steep and sudden wilderness. It is commonly called Dûn-I *(Doon-ee)*, for at the summit in old days was an island fortress; but the Gaelic name of the whole of this uplifted shoulder of the isle is Slibh Meanach. Hidden under a wave of heath and boulder, near the broken rocks, is a little pool. From generation to generation this has been known, and frequented, as the Fountain of Youth.

There, through boggy pastures, where the huge-horned shaggy cattle stared at me, and up through the ling and roitch, I climbed: for, if anywhere, I thought that from there I might see the Divine Forges, or at least might discover a hidden way, because of the power of that water, touched on the eyelids at sunlift, at sunset, or at the rising of the moon.

From where I stood I could see the people still gathered upon the dunes by the shore, and the tall, ungainly figure of the preacher. In the narrow strait were two boats, one being rowed across to Fionnphort, and the other, with a dun sail burning flame-brown, hanging like a bird's wing against Glas Eilean, on the tideway to the promontory of Earraid. Was the preacher still talking of the Divine Forges? I wondered; or were the men and women in the ferry hurrying across to the Ross of Mull to look for them among the inland hills? And the Earraid men in the fishing-smack: were they sailing to see if they lay hidden in the wilderness of rocks, where the muffled barking of the seals made the loneliness more wild and remote?

I wetted my eyelids, as I had so often done before (and not always vainly, though whether vision came from the water, or from a more quenchless spring within, I know not), and looked into the little pool. Alas! I could see nothing but the reflection of a star, too obscured by light as yet for me to see in the sky, and, for a moment, the shadow of a gull's wing as the bird flew by far overhead. I was too young then to be content with the symbols of coincidence, or I might have thought that the shadow of a wing from Heaven, and the light of a star out of the East, were enough indication. But, as it was, I turned, and walked idly northward, down the rough side of Dun Bhuirg (at Cul Bhuirg, a furlong westward, I had once seen a phantom, which I believed to be that of the Culdee, Oran, and so never went that way again after sundown) to a thyme-covered mound that had for me a most singular fascination.

It is a place to this day called Dûn Mananain. Here, a friend who told me many things, a Gaelic farmer named Macarthur, had related once a fantastic legend about a god of the sea. Manaun was his name, and he lived in the times when Iona was part of the kingdom of the Suderöer. Whenever he willed he was like the sea, and that is not wonderful, for he was born of the sea. Thus his body was made of a green wave. His hair was of wrack and tangle, glistening with spray; his robe was of windy foam; his feet, of white sand. That is, when he was with his own, or when he willed; otherwise, he was as men are. He loved a woman of the south so beautiful that she was named Dèarsadh-na-Ghréine (Sunshine). He captured her and brought her to Iona in September, when it is the month of peace. For one month she was happy: when the wet gales from the west set in, she pined for her own land: yet in the dream-days of November, she smiled so often that Manaun hoped; but when Winter was come, her lover saw that she could not live. So he changed her into a seal. "You shall be a sleeping woman by day," he said, "and sleep in my dûn here on Iona: and by night, when the dews fall, you shall be a seal, and hear me calling to you from a wave, and shall come out and meet me."

They have mortal offspring also, it is said.

Probably some thought was in my mind that there, by Dûn Mananain, I might find a hidden way. That summer I had been thrilled to the inmost life by coming suddenly, by moonlight, on a seal moving across the last sand-dune between this place and the bay called Port Ban. A strange voice, too, I heard upon the sea. True, I saw no white arms upthrown as the seal plunged into the long wave that swept the shore; and it was a grey skua that wailed above me, winging inland; yet had I not had a vision of the miracle?

But alas! that evening there was not even a barking seal. Some sheep fed upon the green slope of Manaun's mound.

So, still seeking a way to the Divine Forges, I skirted the shore and crossed the sandy plain of the Machar, and mounted the upland district known as Sliav Starr (the Hill of Noises), and walked to a place, to me sacred. This was a deserted green airidh between great rocks. From here I could look across the extreme western part of Iona, to where it shelved precipitously around the little Port-na-Churaich, the Haven of the Coracle, the spot where St. Columba landed when he came to the island.

I knew every foot of ground here, as every cave along the wave-worn shore. How often I had wandered in these solitudes, to see the great spout of water rise through the grass from the caverns beneath, forced upward when tide and wind harried the sea-flocks from the north; or to look across the ocean to the cliffs of Antrim, from the Carn cul Ri Eirinn, the Cairn of the Hermit King of Ireland, about whom I had woven many a romance.

I was tired, and fell asleep. Perhaps the Druid of a neighbouring mound, or the lonely Irish King, or Colum himself (whose own Mound of the Outlook was near), or one of his angels who ministered to him, watched, and shepherded my dreams to the desired fold. At least I dreamed, and thus: —

The skies to the west beyond the seas were not built of flushed clouds, but of transparent flame. These flames rose in solemn stillness above a vast forge, whose anvil was the shining breast of the sea. Three great Spirits stood by it, and one lifted a soul out of the deep shadow that was below; and one with his hands forged the soul of its dross and welded it anew; and the third breathed upon it, so that it was winged and beautiful. Suddenly the glory-cloud waned, and I saw the multitude of the stars. Each star was the gate of a long, shining road. Many — a countless number — travelled these roads. Far off I saw white walls, built of the pale gold and ivory of sunrise. There again I saw the three Spirits, standing and waiting. So these, I thought, were not the walls of Heaven, but the Divine Forges.

That was my dream. When I awaked, the curlews were crying under the stars.

When I reached the shadowy glebe, behind the manse by the sea, I saw the preacher walking there by himself, and doubtless praying. I told him I had seen the Divine Forges, and twice; and in crude, childish words told how I had seen them.

"It is not a dream," he said.

I know now what he meant.

Strange, that to this day none knows with surety the derivation or original significance of the name Iona. Many ingenious guesses have been made, but of these some are obviously far-fetched, others are impossible in Gaelic, and all but impossible to the mind of any Gael speaking his ancient tongue. Nearly all these guesses concern the Iona of Columba: few attempt the name of the sacred island of the Druids. Another people once lived here with a forgotten faith; possibly before the Picts there was yet another, who worshipped at strange altars and bowed down before Shadow and Fear, the earliest of the gods.

The most improbable derivation is one that finds much acceptance. When Columba and his few followers were sailing northward from the isle of Oronsay, in quest, it is said, of this sacred island of the Druids, suddenly one of the monks cried *sud i (? siod e !)* "yonder it!" With sudden exultation Columba exclaimed, *Mar sud bithe I, goir thear II*, "Be it so, and let it be called I" (I or EE). We are not the wiser for this obviously monkish invention. It accounts for a syllable only, and seems like an effort to explain the use of *I* (II, Y, Hy, Hee) for "island" in place of the vernacular Innis, Inch, Eilean, etc. Except in connection with Iona I doubt if *I* for island is ever now used in modern Gaelic. Icolmkill is familiar: the anglicised Gaelic of the Isle of Colum of the Church. But it is doubtful if any now living has ever heard a Gael speak of an island as *I*; I doubt if an instance could be adduced. On the other hand, *I* might well have been, and doubtless is, used in written speech as a sign for Innis, as *'s* is the common writing of *agus*, 'and'. As for the ancient word *Idh* or *Iy*, I do not know that its derivation has been ascertained, though certain Gaelic linguists claim that *Idh* and Innis are of the same root.

I do not know on what authority, but an anonymous Gaelic writer, in an account of Iona in 1771, alludes to the probability that Christianity was introduced there before St. Columba's advent, and that the island was already dedicated to the Apostle St. John, "for it was originally called *I'Eoin*, i.e. the Isle of John, whence Iona." *I'eoin* certainly is very close in sound, as a Gael would pronounce it, to Iona, and there can be little doubt that the island had druids (whether Christian monks also with or without) when Columba landed. Before Conall, King of Alba (as he was called, though only Dalriadic King of Argyll), invited Colum to Iona, to make that island his home and sanctuary, there were certainly Christian monks on the island. Among them was the half-mythical Odran or Oran, who is chronicled in the *Annals of the Four Masters* as having been a missionary priest, and as having died in Iona fifteen years before Colum landed. Equally certainly there were druids at this late date, though discredited of the Pictish king and his people, for a Cymric priest of the old faith was at that time Ard-Druid. This man Gwendollen, through his bard or second-druid Myrddin (Merlin), deplored the persecution to which he was subject, in that now he and his no longer dared to practise the sacred druidical rites "in raised circles" — adding bitterly, "the grey stones themselves, even, they have removed."

Again, Davies in his *Celtic Researches* speaks of Colum as having on his settlement in Iona burnt a heap of druidical books. It is at any rate certain that druidical believers (helots perhaps) remained to Colum's time, even if the last druidic priest had left. In the explicit accounts which survive there is no word of any dispossession of the druidic priests. It is more than likely that the Pictish king, who had been converted to Christianity, and gave the island to Columba by special grant, had either already seen Irish monks inhabit it, or at least had withdrawn the lingering priests of the ancient faith of his people. Neither Columba nor Adamnan nor any other early chronicler speaks of Iona as held by the Druids when the little coracle with the cross came into Port-na-Churaich.

Others have derived the name from *Aon*, an isthmus, but the objections to this are that it is not applicable to the island, and perhaps never was; and, again, the Gaelic pronunciation. Some have thought that the word, when given as *I-Eoin*, was intended, not for the Isle of John, but the Isle of Birds. Here, again, the objection is that there is no reason why Iona should be called by a designation equally applicable to every one of the numberless isles of the west. To the mountaineers of Mull, however, the little low-lying seaward isle must have appeared the haunt of the myriad sea-fowl of the Moyle; and if the name thus derives, doubtless a Mull man gave it.

Again, it is said that Iona is a miswriting of *Ioua*, "the avowed ancient name of the island." It is easy to see how the scribes who copied older manuscripts might have made the mistake; and easy to understand how, the mistake once become the habit, fanciful interpretations were adduced to explain "Iona."

There is little reasonable doubt that *Ioua* was the ancient Gaelic or Pictish name of the island. I have frequently seen allusions to its having been called Innis nan Dhruidnechean, or Dhruidhnean, the Isle of the Druids: but that is not ancient Gaelic, and I do not think there is any record of Iona being so called in any of the early manuscripts. Doubtless it was a name given by the Shenachies or bardic story-tellers of a later date, though of course it is quite possible that Iona was of old commonly called the Isle of the Druids. In this connection I may put on record that a few years ago I heard an old man of the western part of the Long Island (Lewis), speak of the priests and ministers of to-day as "druids"; and once, in either Coll or Tiree, I heard a man say, in English, alluding to the Established minister, "Yes, yes, that will be the way of it, for sure, for Mr. — is a wise druid." It might well be, therefore, that in modern use the Isle of Druids signified only the Isle of Priests. There is a little island of the Outer Hebrides called Innis Chailleachan Dhubh — the isle of the black old women; and a legend has grown up that witches once dwelt here and brewed storms and evil spells. But the name is not an ancient name, and was given not so long ago, because of a small sisterhood of black-cowled nuns who settled there.

St. Adamnan, ninth Abbot of Iona, writing at the end of the seventh century, invariably calls the island *Ioua* or the *Iouan Island*. Unless the hypothesis of the careless scribes be accepted, this should be conclusive.

On one other occasion I have heard the name *Ioua* used by a fisherman. I was at Strachur, on Loch Fyne, and was speaking to the skipper of a boat's crew of Macleods from the Lews, when I was attracted by an old man. He knew my Uist friend, then at Strachur, who told me more than one strange legend of the Sliochd-nan-Ron, the seal-men. I met the old man that night before the peat-glow, and while he was narrating a story of a Princess of Spain who married the King of Ireland's son, he spoke incidentally of their being wrecked on Iona, "that was then called Ioua, ay, an' that for one hundred and two hundred and three hundred years and thrice a hundred on the top o' that before it was Icolmkill."

I did not know him, but a friend told me that the late Mr. Cameron, the minister of Brodick, in Arran, had the MS. of an old Iona (or Hebridean) iorram, in the refrain of which *Ioua* was used throughout.

Neither do I think the name the island now bears has anything in common with *Ioua*. In a word, I am sure that the derivations of Iona are commonly fanciful, and that the word is simply Gaelic for the Isle of Saints, and was so given it because of Columba and the abbots and monks who succeeded him and his. In Gaelic, the letters *sh* at the beginning of a word are invariably mute; so that *I-shona*, the Isle of Saints, would be pronounced *Iona*. I think that any lingering doubt I had about the meaning of the name went when I got the old map of which I have spoken, and found that in the left corner was written in large rude letters *II-SHONA*.

How great a man was the Irish monk Crimthan, called Colum, the Dove: Columcille, the Dove of the Church. One may read all that has been written of him since the sixth century, and not reach the depths of his nature. I doubt if any other than a Gael can understand him aright. More than any Celt of whom history tells, he is the epitome of the Celt. In war, Cuchullin himself was not more brave and resourceful. Finn, calling his champions to the pursuit of Grania, or Oisín boasting of the Fianna before Patrick, was not more arrogant, yet his tenderness could be as his Master's was, and he could be as gentle as a young mother with her child, and had a child's simplicity. He knew the continual restlessness of his race. He was forty-two when he settled in Iona, and had led a life of frequent and severe vicissitude, often a wanderer, sometimes with blood against him and upon his head, once in extremity of danger, an outlaw, excommunicated. But even in his haven of Iona he was not content. He journeyed northward through the Pictish realms, a more dangerous and obscure adventure then than to cross Africa to-day. He sailed to "the Ethican island" as St. Adamnan calls Tiree, and made of it a sanctuary, where prayer might rise as a continual smoke from quiet homes. No fear of the savage clans of Skye — where a woman had once reigned with so great a fame in war that even the foremost champion of Ireland went to her in his youth to learn arms and battle-wisdom — restrained him from facing the island Picts. Long before Hakon the Dane fought the great sea fight off Largs on the mainland, Colum had built a church there. In the far Perthshire wilds, before Macbeth slew Duncan the king, the strong abbot of Iona had founded a monastery in that thanedom. At remote Inbhir Nis, the Inverness of to-day, he overcame the King of the Picts and his sullen Druids, by his daring, the fierce magnetism of his will, his dauntless resource. Once, in a savage region far north-eastward, towards the Scandinavian sea, he was told that there his Cross would not long protect either wattled church or monk's cell: on that spot he built the monastery of Deir, that stood for a thousand years, and whose priceless manuscript is now one of the treasures of Northumbria.

Columba was at once a saint, a warrior, a soldier of Christ, a great abbot, a dauntless explorer, and militant Prince of the Church; and a student, a man of great learning, a poet, an artist, a visionary, an architect, administrator, law-maker, judge, arbiter. As a youth this prince, for he was of royal blood, was so beautiful that he was likened to an angel. In mature manhood, there was none to equal him in stature, manly beauty, strength, and with a voice so deep and powerful that it was like a bell and could be heard on occasion a mile away, and once, indeed, at the court of King Bruidh, literally overbore and drowned a concerted chorus of sullen druids. These had tried to outvoice him and his monks, little knowing what a mighty force the sixty-fourth Psalm could be in the throat of this terrible Culdee, who to them must have seemed much more befitting his house-name, Crimthan (Wolf), than "the Dove"!

For one thing of great Gaelic import, Columba has been given a singular pre-eminence — not for his love of country, pride of race, passionate loyalty to his clan, to every blood-claim and foster-claim, and friendship claim, though in all this he was the very archetype of the clannish Gael — but because (so it is averred) he was the first of our race of whom is recorded the systematic use of the strange gift of spiritual foresight, "second-sight." It has been stated authoritatively that he is the first of whom there is record as having possessed this faculty; but that could only be averred by one ignorant of ancient Gaelic literature. Even in Adamnan's chronicle, within some seventy years after the death of Columba, there is record of others having this faculty.

There is something strangely beautiful in most of these "second-sight" stories of Columba. The faculty itself is so apt to the spiritual law that one wonders why it is so set apart in doubt. It would, I think, be far stranger if there were no such faculty.

That I believe, it were needless to say, were it not that these words may be read by many to whom this quickened inward vision is a superstition, or a fantastic glorification of insight. I believe; not only because there is nothing too strange for the soul, whose vision surely I will not deny, while I accept what is lesser, the mind's prescience, and, what is least, the testimony of the eyes. That I have cause to believe is perhaps too personal a statement, and is of little account; but in that interior wisdom, which is no longer the flicker of one little green leaf but the light and sound of a forest, of which the leaf is a part, I know that to be true, which I should as soon doubt as that the tide returns or that the sap rises or that dawn is a ceaseless flashing light beneath the circuit of the stars. Spiritual logic demands it.

It would ill become me to do otherwise. I would as little, however, deny that this inward vision is sometimes imperfect and untrustworthy, as I would assert that it is infallible. There is no common face of good or evil and in like fashion the aspect of this so-called mystery is variable as the lives of those in whom it dwells. With some it is a prescience, more akin to instinct than to reason, and obtains only among the lesser possibilities, as when one beholds another where in the body none is; or a scene not possible, there, in that place; or a face, a meeting of shadows, a disclosure of hazard or accident, a coming into view of happenings not yet fulfilled. With some it is simply a larger sight, more wide, more deep; not habitual, because there is none of us who is not subject to the law of the body; and sudden, because all tense vision is a passion of the moment. It is as the lightning, whose sustenance is sure for all that it has a second's life. With a few it is a more constant companion, a dweller by the morning thought, by the moon reverie, by the evening dream. It lies upon the pillow for some: to some it is as though the wind disclosed pathways of the air; a swaying branch, a dazzle on the wave, the quick recognition in unfamiliar eyes, is, for others, sufficient signal. Not that these accidents of the manner need concern us much. We have the faculty, or we do not have it. Nor must we forget that it can be the portion of the ignoble as well as of those whose souls are clear. When it is in truth a spiritual vision, then we are in company of what is the essential life, that which we call divine.

It was this that Columba had, this serene perspicuity. That it was a conscious possession we know from his own words, for he gave this answer to one who marvelled: "Heaven has granted to some to see on occasion in their mind, clearly and surely, the whole of earth and sea and sky."

It is not unlikely that in the seventy years which elapsed between Colum's death and the writing of that lovely classic of the Church, Adamnan's *Vita St. Columbæ*, some stories grew around the saint's memory which were rather the tribute of childlike reverence and love than the actual experiences of the holy man himself. What then? A field in May is not the less a daughter of Spring, because the cowslip-wreaths found there may have been brought from little wayward garths by children who wove them lovingly as they came.

Many of these strange records are mere coincidences; others reveal so happy a surety in the simple faith of the teller that we need only smile, and with no more resentment than at a child who runs to say he has found stars in a wayside pool. Others are rather the keen insight of a ceaseless observation than the seeing of an inward sense. But, and perhaps oftener, they are not inherently incredible. I do not think our forebears did ill to give haven to these little ones of faith, rather than to despise, or to drive them away.

I have already spoken of Columba as another St. Francis, because of his tenderness for creatures. I recall now the lovely legend (for I do not think Colum himself attributed "second-sight" to an animal) which tells how the old white pony which daily brought the milk from the cow-shed to the monastery came and put its head in the lap of the aged and feeble abbot, thus mutely to bid farewell. Let Adamnan tell it: "This creature then coming up to the saint, and knowing that his master would soon depart from him, and that he would see his face no more, began to utter plaintive moans, and, as if a man, to shed tears in abundance into the saint's lap, and so to weep, frothing greatly. Which when the attendant saw, he began to drive away that weeping mourner. But the saint forbade him, saying, 'Let him alone! As he loves me so, let him alone, that into this my bosom he may pour out the tears of his most bitter lamentation. Behold, thou, a man, that hast a soul, yet in no way hast knowledge of my end save what I have myself shown thee; but to this brute animal the Master Himself hath revealed that his master is about to go away from him.' And so saying, he blessed his sorrowing servant the horse."

If there be any to whom the aged Colum comforting the grief of his old white pony is a matter of disdain or derision, I would not have his soul in exchange for the dumb sorrow of that creature. One would fare further with that sorrow, though soulless, than with the soul that could not understand that sorrow.

If one were to quote from Adamnan's three Books of the Prophecies, Miracles, and Visions of Columba, there would be another book. Amid much that is childlike, and a little that is childish, what store of spiritual beauty and living symbol in these three books — the Book of Prophetic Revelations, the Book of Miracles of Power, the Book of Angelic Visitations.

It would take a book indeed to tell all the stories of Columba's visionary and prophetic powers. That I write at this length concerning him, indeed, is because he is himself Iona. Columba is Christian Iona, as much as Iona is Icolmkill. I have often wondered (because of a passage in Adamnan) if the island be not indeed named after him, the Dove: for as Adamnan says incidentally, the name Columba is identical with the Hebrew name Jonah, also signifying a Dove, and by the Hebrews pronounced Iona.

It is enough now to recall that this man, so often erring but so human always, in whose life we see the soul of Iona as in a glass, is become the archetype of his race, as Iona is the microcosm of the Gaelic world. That he came into this life heralded by dreams and visions, that from his youth onward to old age he knew every mystery of dream and vision, and that before and after his death his soul was revealed to others through dreams and visions, is but an added hieratic grace: yet we do well to recall often how these dreams before and these visions after were angelical, and nobly beautiful: how there was left of him, and to his little company, and to us for remembrance, that last signal vision of a blaze of angelic wings, more intolerable than the sun at noon, the tempestuous multitude trembling with the storm of song.

Columba and Oran ... these are the two great names in Iona. Love and Faith have made one immortal; the other lives also, clothed in legend. I am afraid there is not much definite basis for the popular Iona legend of Oran. It is now the wont of guides and others to speak of the Réilig Odhrain, Oran's burial-place, as that of Columba's friend (and victim), but it seems likelier that the Oran who lies there is he who is spoken of in the *Annals of the Four Masters* as having died in the year 548, that is fifteen years before Colum came to the island. This, however, might well be a mistake: what is more convincing is that Adamnan never mentions the episode, nor even the name of Oran, nor is there mention of him in that book of Colum's intimate friend and successor, Baithene, which Adamnan practically incorporated. On the other hand, the Oran legend is certainly very old. The best modern rendering we have of it is that of Mr. Whitley Stokes in his *Three Middle-Irish Homilies*, and readers of Dr. Skene's valuable *Celtic Scotland* recollect the translation there redacted. The episode occurs first in an ancient Irish life of St. Columba. The legend, which has crystallised into a popular saying, "Ùir, ùir, air sùil Odhrain! mu'n labhair e tuille comhraidh" — "Earth, earth, on Oran's eyes, lest he further blab" — avers that three days after the monk Oran or Odran was entombed alive (some say in the earth, some in a cavity), Colum opened the grave, to look once more on the face of the dead brother, when to the amazed fear of the monks and the bitter anger of the abbot himself, Oran opened his eyes and exclaimed, "There is no such great wonder in death, nor is Hell what it has been described." (Ifrinn, or Ifurin — the word used — is the Gaelic Hell, the Land of Eternal Cold.) At this, Colum straightway cried the now famous Gaelic words, and then covered up poor Oran again lest he should blab further of that uncertain world whither he was supposed to have gone. In the version given by Mr. Whitley Stokes there is no mention of Odran's grave having been uncovered after his entombment. But what is strangely suggestive is that both in the oral legend and in that early monkish chronicle alluded to, Columba is represented as either suggesting or accepting immolation of a living victim as a sacrifice to consecrate the church he intended to build.

One story is that he received a divine intimation to the effect that a monk of his company must be buried alive, and that Odran offered himself. In the earliest known rendering, "Colum Cille said to his people: 'It is well for us that our roots should go underground here'; and he said to them, 'It is permitted to you that some one of you go under the earth of this island to consecrate it. 'Odran rose up readily, and thus he said: 'If thou wouldst accept me,' he said, 'I am ready for that.' ... Odran then went to heaven. Colum Cille then founded the Church of Hii."

It would be a dark stain on Columba if this legend were true. But apart from the fact that Adamnan does not speak of it or of Oran, the probabilities are against its truth. On the other hand, it is, perhaps, quite as improbable that there was no basis for the legend. I imagine the likelier basis to be that a druid suffered death in this fashion under that earlier Odran of whom there is mention in the *Annals of the Four Masters*: possibly, that Odran himself was the martyr, and the Ard-Druid the person who had "the divine intimation." Again, before it be attributed to Columba, one would have to find if there is record of such an act having been performed among the Irish of that day. We have no record of it. It is not improbable that the whole legend is a symbolical survival, an ancient teaching of some elementary mystery through some real or apparent sacrificial rite.

Among the people of Iona to-day there is a very confused idea about St. Oran. To some he is a saint: to others an evil-doer: some think he was a martyr, some that he was punished for a lapse from virtue. Some swear by his grave, as though it were almost as sacred as the Black Stone of Iona: to others, perhaps most, his is now but an idle name.

By the Black Stone of Iona! One may hear that in Icolmkill or anywhere in the west. It used to be the most binding oath in the Highlands, and even now is held as an indisputable warrant of truth. In Iona itself, strangely enough, one would be much more likely to hear a statement affirmed "by St. Martin's Cross." On this stone — the old Druidic Stone of Destiny, sacred among the Gael before Christ was born — Columba crowned Aidan King of Argyll. Later, the stone was taken to Dunstaffnage, where the Lords of the Isles were made princes: thence to Scone, where the last of the Celtic Kings of Scotland was crowned on it. It now lies in Westminster Abbey,[45] a part of the Coronation Chair, and since Edward I every British monarch has been crowned upon it. If ever the Stone of Destiny be moved again, that writing on the wall will be the signature of a falling dynasty; but perhaps, like Iona in the island saying, this can be left to the Gaelic equivalent of Nevermas, "gus am bi MacCailein na' rìgh," "till Argyll be a king."

---

45 The Stone of Destiny was returned to Scotland and the Scottish people in 1997, exactly seven hundred years after it had been taken to England. It now lies in Edinburgh Castle where it is on public display along with the Scottish Crown jewels.

My earliest knowledge of the heroic cycle of Celtic mythology and history came to me, as a child, when I spent my first summer in Iona. How well I remember a fantastic legend I was told: how that the far blue mountains on Skye, the Coolins, so freaked into a savage beauty, were due to the sword-play of Cuchullin. And this happened because the Queen o' Skye had put a spear through the two breasts of his love, so that he went in among her warrior women and slew every one and severed the head of Sgàyah herself, and threw it into Coruisk, where to this day it floats as Eilean Dubh, the dark isle. Thereafter, Cuchullin hewed the mountain-tops into great clefts, and trampled the hills into a craggy wilderness, and then rushed into the waves and fought with the sea-hordes till far away the bewildered and terrified stallions of the ocean dashed upon the rocks of Man and uttermost shores of Erin.

This magnificent mountain range can be seen better still from Lunga near Iona, whence it is a short sail with a southerly wind. In Lunga there is a hill called Cnoc Cruit or Dun Cruit, and thence one may see, as in a vast illuminated missal whose pages are of deep blue with bindings of azure and pale gold, innumerable green isles and peaks and hills of the hue of the wild plum. When last I was there it was a day of cloudless June. There was not a sound but the hum of the wild bee foraging in the long garths of white clover, and the continual sighing of a wave. Listening, I thought I heard a harper playing in the hollow of the hill. It may have been the bees heavy with the wine of honey, but I was content with my fancy and fell asleep, and dreamed that a harper came out of the hill, at first so small that he seemed like the green stalk of a lily and had hands like daisies, and then so great that I saw his breath darkening the waves far out on the Hebrid sea. He played, till I saw the stars fall in a ceaseless, dazzling rain upon Iona. A wind blew that rain away, and out of the wave that had been Iona I saw thousands upon thousands of white doves rise from the foam and fly down the four great highways of the wind. When I woke, there was no one near. Iona lay like an emerald under the wild-plum bloom of the Mull mountains. The bees stumbled through the clover; a heron stood silver-grey upon the grey-blue stone; the continual wave was, as before, as one wave, and with the same hushed sighing.

Of all the saints of the west, from St. Molios or Molossius (Maol-Iosa? the servant by Jesus?) who has left his name in the chief township in Arran, to St. Barr, who has given his to the largest of the Bishop's

Isles, as the great Barra island-chain in the South Hebrides used to be called, there is none so commonly remembered and so frequently invoked as St. Micheil. There used to be no festival in the Western Isles so popular as that held on 29th September, "La' Fheill Mhicheil," the Day of the Festival of Michael; and the Eve of Michael's Day is still in a few places one of the gayest nights in the year, though no longer is every barn turned into a dancing place or a place of merrymaking or, at least, a place for lovers to meet and give betrothal gifts. The day itself, in the Catholic Isles, was begun with a special Mass, and from hour to hour was filled with traditional duties and pleasures.

The whole of the St. Micheil ceremonies were of a remote origin, and some, as the ancient and almost inexplicable dances, and their archaic accompaniment of word and gesture far older than the sacrificial slaying of the Michaelmas Lamb. It is, however, not improbable that this latter rite was a survival of a pagan custom long anterior to the substitution of the Christian for the Druidic faith.

The "Iollach Mhicheil" — the triumphal song of Michael — is quite as much pagan as Christian. We have here, indeed, one of the most interesting and convincing instances of the transmutation of a personal symbol. St. Michael is on the surface a saint of extraordinary powers and the patron of the shores and the shore-folk: deeper, he is an angel, who is upon the sea what the angelical saint, St. George, is upon the land: deeper, he is a blending of the Roman Neptune and the Greek Poseidon: deeper, he is himself an ancient Celtic god: deeper, he is no other than Manannan, the god of ocean and all waters, in the Gaelic Pantheon: as, once more, Manannan himself is dimly revealed to us as still more ancient, more primitive, and even as supreme in remote godhead, the Father of an immortal Clan.

To this day Micheil is sometimes alluded to as the god Micheil, and I have seen some very strange Gaelic lines which run in effect: —

"It was well thou hadst the horse of the god Micheil
Who goes without a bit in his mouth,
So that thou couldst ride him through the fields of the air,
And with him leap over the knowledge of Nature"—

presumably not very ancient as they stand, because of the use of *steud* for horse, and *naduir* for nature, obvious adaptations from English and Latin. Certainly St. Michael has left his name in many places, from the shores of the Hebrides to the famous Mont St. Michel of Brittany, and

I doubt not that everywhere an earlier folk, at the same places, called him Manannan. In a most unlikely place to find a record of old hymns and folk-songs, one of the volumes of Reports of the Highlands and Islands Commission, Mr. Carmichael many years ago contributed some of his unequalled store of Hebridean reminiscence and knowledge. Among these old things saved, there is none that is better worth saving than the beautiful Catholic hymn or invocation sung at the time of the midsummer migration to the hill-pastures. In this shealing-hymn the three powers who are invoked are St. Micheil (for he is a patron saint of horses and travel, as well as of the sea and seafarers), St. Columba, guardian of Cattle, and the Virgin Mary, "Mathair Uain ghil," "Mother of the White Lamb," as the tender Gaelic has it, who is so beautifully called the golden-haired Virgin Shepherdess.

It is pleasant to think of Columba, who loved animals, and whose care for his shepherd-people was always so great, as having become the patron saint of cattle. It is thus that the gods are shaped out of a little mortal clay, the great desire of the heart, and immortal dreams.

I may give the whole hymn in English, as rendered by Mr. Carmichael:

I

Thou gentle Michael of the white steed,
Who subdued the Dragon of blood,
For love of God and the Son of Mary,
Spread over us thy wing, shield us all!
Spread over us thy wing, shield us all!

II

Mary beloved! Mother of the White Lamb,
Protect us, thou Virgin of nobleness,
Queen of beauty! Shepherdess of the flocks!
Keep our cattle, surround us together,
Keep our cattle, surround us together.

III

Thou Columba, the friendly, the kind,
In name of the Father, the Son, and the Holy Spirit,
Through the Three-in-One, through the Three,
Encompass us, guard our procession,
Encompass us, guard our procession.

IV

Thou Father! Thou Son! Thou Holy Spirit!
Be the Three-One with us day and night,
On the machair plain, on the mountain ridge,
The Three-one is with us, with His arm around our head,
The Three-One is with us, with His arm around our head."

I have heard a paraphrase of this hymn, both in Gaelic and English, on Iona; and once, off Soa, a little island to the south of Icolmkill, took down a verse which I thought was local, but which I afterwards found (with very slight variance) in Mr. Carmichael's Governmental Uist-Record. It was sung by Barra fishermen, and ran in effect "O Father, Son, and Holy Ghost! O Holy Trinity, be with us day and night. On the crested wave as on the mountain-side! Our Mother, Holy Mary Mother, has her arm under our head; our pillow is the arm of Mary, Mary the Holy Mother."

It is perhaps the saddest commentary that could be made on what we have lost that the children of those who were wont to go to rest, or upon any adventure, or to stand in the shadow of death, with some such words as

"My soul is with the Light on the mountains,
Archangel Micheil shield my soul!"

now go or stand in a scornful or heedless silence, or without remembrance, as others did who forgot to trim their lamps.

Who now would go up to the hill-pastures singing the Beannachadh Buachailleag, the Herding Blessing? With the passing of the old language the old solemnity goes, and the old beauty, and the old patient, loving wonder. I do not like to think of what songs are likely to replace the Herding Blessing, whose first verse runs thus:

"I place this flock before me
As ordained by the King of the World,
Mary Virgin to keep them, to wait them, to watch them.
On hill and glen and plain,
On hill, in glen, on plain."

In the maelstrom of the cities the old race perishes, drowns. How common the foolish utterance of narrow lives, that all these old ways of thought are superstitious. To have a superstition is, for these, a worse ill than to have a shrunken soul. I do not believe in spells and charms and foolish incantations, but I think that ancient wisdom out of the simple and primitive heart of an older time is not an ill heritage: and if to believe in the power of the spirit is to be superstitious, I am well content to be of the company that is now forsaken.

But even in what may more fairly be called superstitious, have we surety that we have done well in our exchange?

A short while ago I was on the hillside above one of the much-frequented lochs in eastern Argyll. Something brought to my mind, as I went further up into the clean solitudes, one of the verses of the Herding Blessing:

"From rocks, from snow-wreaths, from streams,
From crooked ways, from destructive pits,
From the arrows of the slim fairy women,
From the heart of envy, the eye of evil,
Keep us, Holy St. Bride."

"From the arrows of the slim fairy women." And I — do I believe in that? At least it will be admitted that it is worth a belief; it is a pleasant dream; it is a gate into a lovely world; it is a secret garden, where are old sweet echoes; it has the rainbow-light of poetry. Is it not poetry? And I — oh yes, I believe it, that superstition: a thousand-fold more real is it, more believable, than that coarse-tongued, ill-mannered, boorish people, desperate in slovenly pleasure. For that will stay, and they will go. And if I am wrong, then I will rather go with it than stay with them. And yet — surely, surely the day will come when this sordidness of life as it is so often revealed to us will sink into deep waters, and the stream become purified, and again by its banks be seen the slim fairy women of health and beauty and all noble and dignified things.

This is a far cry from Iona! And I had meant to write only of how I heard so recently as three or four summers ago a verse of the Uist Herding Chant. It was recited to me, over against Dûn-I, by a friend who is a crofter in that part of Iona. It was not quite as Mr. Carmichael translates it, but near enough. The Rann Buachhailleag is, I should add, addressed to the cattle.

"The protection of God and Columba
Encompass your going and coming,
And about you be the milkmaid of the smooth white palms,
Bridget of the clustering hair, golden brown."

On Iona however, there is, so far as I remember, no special spot sacred to St. Micheil but there is a legend that on the night Columba died Micheil came over the waves on a rippling flood of light, which was a cloud of angelic wings, and that he sang a hymn to the soul of the saint before it took flight for its heavenly fatherland. No one heard that hymn save Colum, but I think that he who first spoke of it remembered a more ancient legend of how Manannan came to Cuchullin when he was in the country of the Shee, when Liban laughed.

I spoke of Port-na-Churaich, the Haven of the Coracle, a little ago. How strange a history is that of Iona since the coming of the Irish priest, Crimthan, or Crimmon as we call the name, surnamed Colum Cille, the Dove of the Church. Perhaps its unwritten history is not less strange. God was revered on Iona by priests of a forgotten faith before the Cross was raised. The sun-priest and the moon-worshipper had their revelation here. I do not think their offerings were despised. Colum, who loved the Trinity so well that on one occasion he subsisted for three days on the mystery of the mere word, did not forego the luxury of human sacrifice, though he abhorred the blood-stained altar. For, to him, an obstinate pagan slain was to the glory of God. The moon-worshipper did no worse when he led the chosen victim to the dolmen. But the moon-worshipper was a Pict without the marvel of the written word; so he remained a heathen, and the Christian named himself saint or martyr.

None knows with surety who dwelled on this mysterious island before the famous son of Feilim of Clan Domnhuil, great-grandson of Niall of the Nine Hostages, came with his fellow-monks and raised the Cross among the wondering Picts. But the furthest record tells of worship. Legend itself is more ancient here than elsewhere. Once a woman was worshipped. Some say she was the moon, but this was before the dim day of the moon-worshippers. (In Gaelic too, as with all the Celtic peoples, it is not the moon but the sun that is feminine.) She may have been an ancestral Brighde, or that mysterious Anait whose Scythian name survives elsewhere in the Gaelic west, and nothing else of all her ancient glory but that shadowy word. Perhaps, here, the Celts remembered one whom they had heard of in Asian valleys or by the waters of Nilus, and called upon Isis under a new name.

The Haven of the Coracle! It was not Colum and his white-robe company who first made the isle sacred. I have heard that when Mary Macleod (our best-loved Hebridean poet) was asked what she thought of Iona, she replied that she thought it was the one bit of Eden that had not been destroyed, and that it was none other than the central isle in the Garden untouched of Eve or Adam, where the angels waited.

Many others have dreamed by that lonely cairn of the Irish king, before Colum, and, doubtless, many since the child who sought the Divine Forges.

Years afterwards I wrote, in the same place, after an absence wherein Iona had become as a dream to me, the story of St. Bridget, in the Hebrides called Bride, under the love name commonly given her, Muime Chriosd — Christ's Foster-Mother.

(ed. I have removed the abbreviated version of this tale which now follows but give it in full in Section Four.)

Elsewhere I have told how a good man of Iona sailed along the coast one Sabbath afternoon with the Holy Book, and put the Word upon the seals of Soa: and, in another tale, how a lonely man fought with a sea-woman that was a seal: as, again, how two fishermen strove with the sea-witch of Earraid: and, in *The Dàn-nan-Ròn*, of a man who went mad with the sea-madness, because of the seal-blood that was in his veins, he being a MacOdrum of Uist, and one of the Sliochd nan Ron, the Tribe of the Seal. And those who have read the tale, twice printed, once as *The Annir Choille*, and again as *Cathal of the Woods*, will remember how, at the end, the good hermit Molios, when near death in his sea-cave of Arran, called the seals to come out of the wave and listen to him, so that he might tell them the white story of Christ; and how in the moonshine, with the flowing tide stealing from his feet to his knees, the old saint preached the gospel of love, while the seals crouched upon the rocks, with their brown eyes filled with glad tears: and how, before his death at dawn, he was comforted by hearing them splashing to and fro in the moon-dazzle, and calling one to the other, "We, too, are of the sons of God."

What has so often been written about is a reflection of what is in the mind: and though stories of the seals may be heard from the Rhinns of Islay to the Seven Hunters (and I first heard that of the MacOdrums, the seal-folk, from a Uist man), I think, that it was because of what I heard of the sea-people on Iona, when I was a child, that they have been so much with me in remembrance.

In the short tale of the Moon-child, I told how two seals that had been wronged by a curse which had been put upon them by Columba, forgave the saint, and gave him a sore-won peace. I recall another (unpublished) tale, where a seal called Domnhuil Dhu — a name of evil omen — was heard laughing one Hallowe'en on the rocks below the ruined abbey, and calling to the creatures of the sea that God was dead: and how the man who heard him laughed, and was therewith stricken with paralysis, and so fell sidelong from the rocks into the deep wave, and was afterwards found beaten as with hammers and shredded as with sharp fangs.

When I was a child I used to throw offerings — small coins, flowers, shells, even a newly caught trout, once a treasured flint arrow-head — into the sea-loch by which we lived. My Hebridean nurse had often told me of Shony, a mysterious sea-god, and I know I spent much time in wasted adoration: a fearful worship, not unmixed with disappointment and some anger. Not once did I see him. I was frighted time after time, but the sudden cry of a heron, or the snort of a pollack chasing the mackerel, or the abrupt uplifting of a seal's head, became over-familiar, and I desired terror, and could not find it by the shore. Inland, after dusk, there was always the mysterious multitude of shadow. There too, I could hear the wind leaping and growling. But by the shore I never knew any dread, even in the darkest night. The sound and company of the sea washed away all fears.

I was amused not long ago to hear a little girl singing, as she ran wading through the foam of a troubled sunlit sea, as it broke on those wonderful white sands of Iona—

"Shanny, Shanny, Shanny,
Catch my feet and tickle my toes!
And if you can, Shanny, Shanny, Shanny,
I'll go with you where no one knows!"

I have no doubt this daintier Shanny was my old friend Shony, whose more terrifying way was to clutch boats by the keel and drown the sailors, and make a death-necklace of their teeth. An evil Shony; for once he netted a young girl who was swimming in a loch, and when she would not give him her love he tied her to a rock, and to this day her long brown hair may be seen floating in the shallow green wave at the ebb of the tide. One need not name the place!

The Shanny song recalls to me an old Gaelic alphabet rhyme, wherein a *Maighdeann-Mhara*, or Mermaid, stood for M, and a *Suire* (also a mermaid) stood for S; and my long perplexities as to whether I would know a shuera from a midianmara when I saw either. It also recalls to me that it was from a young schoolmaster priest, who had come back from Ireland to die at home, that I first heard of the Beth-Luis-Nuin, the Gaelic equivalent of "the A B C." Every letter in the Gaelic alphabet is represented by a tree, and Beithe and Luis and Nuin are the Birch, the

Rowan, and the Ash. The reason why the alphabet is called the Beth-Luis-Nuin is that B, L, N, and not A, B, C, are its first three letters. It consists of eighteen letters and in ancient Gaelic seventeen, for H (the Uath, or Whitethorn) does not exist there, I believe: and these run, B, L, N, F, S (H), D, T, C, M, G, P, R, A, O, U, E, I — each letter represented by the name of a tree, Birch, Rowan, Ash, etc. Properly, there is no C in Gaelic, for though the letter C is common, it has always the sound of K.

Since this page first appeared I have had so many letters about the Gaelic alphabet of to-day that I take the opportunity to add a few lines. To-day as of old all the letters of the Gaelic alphabet are called after trees, from the oak to the shrub-like elder, with the exception of G, T, and U, which stand for Ivy, Furze and Heather. It no longer runs B, L, N, etc., but in sequence follows the familiar and among western peoples, universal A, B, C, etc. It is, however, short of our Roman alphabet by eight letters J, K, Q, V, W, X, Y and Z. On the other hand, each of these is represented, either by some other letter having a like value or by a combination: thus K is identical with C, which does not exist in Gaelic as a soft sound any more than it does in Greek, but only as the C in English words such as *cat* or *cart*, or in combination with h as a gutteral as in *loch* — while v, as common a sound in Gaelic as the hiss of s in English, exists in almost every second or third word, as *bh* or *mh*. The Gaelic A, B, C of to-day, then, runs as follows: Ailm, Beite, Coll, Durr, Eagh, Fearn, Gath, Huath, Togh, Luis, Muin, Nuin, Oir, Peith, Ruis, Suil, Teine, Ur — which again is equivalent to saying Elm, Birch, Hazel, Oak, Aspen, Alder, Ivy, Whitethorn, Yew, Rowan or Quicken, Vine, Ash, Spindle-tree, Pine, Elder, Willow, Furze, Heath.

The little girl who knew so much about Shanny knew nothing about her own A B C. But I owe her a debt, since through her I came upon my good friend "Gunainm."[46] From her I heard first, there on Iona, on a chance visit of a few summer days, of two of the most beautiful of the ancient Gaelic hymns, the Fiacc Hymn and the Hymn of Broccán. My friend had delineated them as missals, with a strangely beautiful design to each. How often I have thought of one, illustrative of a line in the Fiacc Hymn: "There was pagan darkness in Eiré in those days: the people adored Faerie." In the Broccán Hymn (composed by one Broccán in the time of Lugaid, son of Loegaire, A.D. 500) is one particularly lovely line: "Victorious Bride (Bridget) loved not this vain world: here, ever, she sat the seat of a bird on a cliff."

---

46 Properly spelt 'gun ainm' meaning 'without a name' - i.e. anonymous.

In a dream I dream frequently, that of being the wind, and drifting over fragrant hedgerows and pastures, I have often, through unconscious remembrance of that image of St. Bride sitting the seat of a bird on the edge of the cliff that is this world, felt myself, when not lifted on sudden warm fans of dusk, propelled as on a swift wing from the edge of a precipice.

I would that we had these winds of dream to command. I would, now that I am far from it, that this night at least I might pass over Iona, and hear the sea-doves by the ruins making their sweet mournful croon of peace, and lift, as a shadow gathering phantom flowers, the pale orchids by the lapwing's nest.

Nothing is more strange than the confused survival of legends and pagan faiths and early Christian beliefs, such as may be found still in some of the isles. A Tiree man, whom I met some time ago on the boat that was taking us both to the west, told me there's a story that Mary Magdalene lies in a cave in Iona. She roamed the world with a blind man who loved her, but they had no sin. One day they came to Knoidart in Argyll. Mary Magdalene's first husband had tracked her there, and she knew that he would kill the blind man. So she bade him lie down among some swine, and she herself herded them. But her husband came and laughed at her. "That is a fine boar you have there," he said. Then he put a spear through the blind man. "Now I will take your beautiful hair," he said. He did this and went away. She wept till she died. One of Colum's monks found her, and took her to Iona, and she was buried in a cave. No one but Colum knew who she was. Colum sent away the man, because he was always mooning and lamenting. She had a great wonderful beauty to her.

It is characteristic enough, even to the quaint confusion that could make Mary Magdalene and St. Columba contemporary. But as for the story, what is it but the universal Gaelic legend of Diarmid and Grania? They too wandered far to escape the avenger. It does not matter that their "beds" are shown in rock and moor, from Glenmoriston to Loch Awe, from Lora Water to West Loch Tarbert, with an authenticity as absolute as that which discovers them almost anywhere between Donegal and Clare; nor that the death-place has many sites betwixt Argyll and Connemara. In Gaelic Scotland everyone knows that Diarmid was wounded to the death on the rocky ground between Tarbert of Loch Fyne and the West Loch. Everyone knows the part the boar played, and the part Finn played.

Doubtless the story came by way of the Shannon to the Loch of Shadows, or from Cuchullin's land to Dûn Sobhairce on the Antrim coast, and thence to the Scottish mainland. In wandering to the isles, it lost something both of Eiré and Alba. The Campbells, too, claimed Diarmid; and so the Hebrideans would as soon forget him. So, there, by one byplay of the mind or another, it survived in changing raiment. Perhaps an islesman had heard a strange legend about Mary Magdalene, and so named Grania anew. Perhaps a storyteller consciously wove it the new way. Perhaps an Iona man, hearing the tale in distant Barra or Uist, in Coll or Tiree, "buried" Mary in a cave of Icolmkill.

The notable thing is, not that a primitive legend should love fantastic raiment, but that it should be so much alike, where the Syrian wanders from waste to waste, by the campfires of the Basque muleteers, and in the rainy lands of the Gael.

In Mingulay, one of the south isles of the Hebrides, in South Uist, and in Iona, I have heard a practically identical tale told with striking variations. It is a tale so widespread that it has given rise to a pathetic proverb, "Is mairg a loisgeadh a chlarsach dut," "Pity on him who would burn the harp for you."

In Mingulay, the "harper" who broke his harp "for a woman's love" was a young man, a fiddler. For three years he wandered out of the west into the east, and when he had made enough money to buy a good share in a fishing boat, or even a boat itself, he came back to Mingulay. When he reached his Mary's cottage, at dusk, he played her favourite air, an "oran leannanachd,"[47] but when she came out it was with a silver ring on her left hand and a baby in her arms. Thus poor Padruig Macneill knew Mary had broken her troth and married another man, and so he went down to the shore and played a "marbh-rann,"[48] and then broke his fiddle on the rocks; and when they came upon them in the morning he had the strings of it round his neck. In Uist, the instrument is more vaguely called a "tiompan," and here, on a bitter cold night in a famine time, the musician breaks it so as to feed the fire to warm his wife — a sacrifice ill repaid by the elopement of the hard woman that night. In Iona, the tale is of an Irish piper who came over to Icolmkill on a pilgrimage, and to lay his pipes on "the holy stones"; but, when there, he got word that his young wife was ill, so he "made a loan of his clar," and with the money returned to Derry, only to find that his dear had gone away with a soldier for the Americas.

47 'song for a sweetheart.'
48 'death poem.'

The legendary history of Iona would be as much Pagan as Christian. To-day, at many a ceilidh by the warm hearths in winter, one may hear allusions to the Scandinavian pirates, or to their more ancient and obscure kin, the Fomór. ... The Fomór or Fomórians were a people that lived before the Gael, and had their habitations on the isles: fierce prowlers of the sea, who loved darkness and cold and storm, and drove herds of wolves across the deeps. In other words, they were elemental forces. But the name is sometimes used for the Norse pirates who ravaged the west, from the Lews to the town of the Hurdle-ford.[49]

In poetic narration "the men of Lochlin" occurs oftener: sometimes the Summer-sailors, as the Vikings called themselves; sometimes, perhaps oftenest, the Danes. The Vikings have left numerous personal names among the islanders, notably the general term in "summer-sailors," *somerlédi*, which survives as Somerled. Many Macleods and Macdonalds are called Somerled, Torquil (also Torcall, Thorkill), and Mànus (Magnus), and in the Hebrides surnames such as Odrum betray a Norse origin. A glance at any good map will reveal how largely the capes and promontories and headlands, and small bays and havens of the west, remember the lords of the Suderöer.

The fascination of this legendary history is in its contrast of the barbaric and the spiritual. Since I was a child I have been held spellbound by this singular union. To see the Virgin-Mary in the sombre and terrible figure of the Washer of the Ford, or spiritual destiny in that of the Woman with the Net, was natural: as to believe that the same Columba could be as tender as St. Bride or gentle as St. Francis, and yet could thrust the living Oran back into his grave, or prophesy, as though himself a believer in the druidic wisdom, by the barking of a favourite hound that had a white spot on his forehead — *Donnalaich chon chinain*.

At times, I doubt not, there must have been weaker brethren among these simple and devoted Culdees of Iona, though in Colum's own day there was probably none (unless it were Oran) who was not the visible outward shrine of a pure flame.

Thinking of such an one, and not without furtive pagan sympathy, I wrote the other day these lines, which I may also add here as a further side-light upon that half-Pagan, half-Christian basis upon which the Columban Church of Iona stood.

---

49 Dublin in Ireland.

Balva the old monk I am called: when I was young, Balva Honeymouth.
That was before Colum the White came to Iona in the West.
She whom I loved was a woman whom I won out of the South.
And I had a good heaven with my lips on hers and with breast to breast.

Balva the old monk I am called: were it not for the fear
That the soul of Colum the White would meet my soul in the Narrows
That sever the living and dead, I would rise up from here,
And go back to where men pray with spears and arrows.

Balva the old monk I am called: ugh! ugh! the cold bell of the matins — 'tis dawn!
Sure it's a dream I have had that I was in a warm wood with the sun ashine,
And that against me in the pleasant greenness was a soft fawn,
And a voice that whispered "Balva Honeymouth, drink, I am thy wine!"

As I write, here on the hill-slope of Dûn-I, the sound of the furtive wave is as the sighing in a shell. I am alone between sea and sky, for there is no other on this bouldered height, nothing visible but a single blue shadow that slowly sails the hillside. The bleating of lambs and ewes, the lowing of kine, these come up from the Machar that lies between the West slopes and the shoreless sea to the west; these ascend as the very smoke of sound. All round the island there is a continuous breathing; deeper and more prolonged on the west, where the open sea is but audible everywhere. The seals on Soa are even now putting their breasts against the running tide; for I see a flashing of fins here and there in patches at the north end of the Sound, and already from the ruddy granite shores of the Ross there is a congregation of seafowl — gannets and guillemots, skuas and herring-gulls, the long-necked northern diver, the tern, the cormorant. In the sunblaze, the waters of the Sound dance their blue bodies and swirl their flashing white hair o' foam; and, as I look, they seem to me like children of the wind and the sunshine, leaping and running in these flowing pastures, with a laughter as sweet against the ears as the voices of children at play.

The joy of life vibrates everywhere. Yet the Weaver does not sleep, but only dreams. He loves the sun-drowned shadows. They are invisible thus, but they are there, in the sunlight itself. Sure, they may be heard: as, an hour ago, when on my way hither by the Stairway of the Kings — for so sometimes they call here the ancient stones of the mouldered princes of long ago — I heard a mother moaning because of the son that had had to go over sea and leave her in her old age; and heard also a child sobbing, because of the sorrow of childhood — that sorrow so unfathomable, so incommunicable. And yet not a stone's-throw from where I lie, half hidden beneath an overhanging rock, is the Pool of Healing. To this small, black-brown tarn, pilgrims of every generation, for hundreds of years, have come. Solitary, these; not only because the pilgrim to the Fount of Eternal Youth must fare hither alone, and at dawn, so as to touch the healing water the moment the first sunray quickens it — but solitary, also, because those who go in quest of this Fount of Youth are the dreamers and the Children of Dream, and these are not many, and few come now to this lonely place. Yet, an Isle of Dream Iona is, indeed. Here the last sun-worshippers bowed before the Rising of God; here Columba and his hymning priests laboured and brooded; and here Oran or his kin dreamed beneath the monkish cowl that pagan dream of his. Here, too, the eyes of Fionn and Oisìn, and of many another of the heroic men and women of the Fiànna, may have lingered; here the Pict and the Celt bowed beneath the yoke of the Norse pirate, who, too, left his dreams, or rather his strangely beautiful soul-rainbows, as a heritage to the stricken; here, for century after century, the Gael has lived, suffered, joyed, dreamed his impossible, beautiful dream; as here, now, he still lives, still suffers patiently, still dreams, and through all and over all, broods upon the incalculable mysteries. He is an elemental, among the elemental forces. He knows the voices of wind and sea: and it is because the Fount of Youth upon Dûn-I of Iona is not the only wellspring of peace, that the Gael can front destiny as he does, and can endure. Who knows where its tributaries are? They may be in your heart, or in mine, and in a myriad others.

I would that the birds of Angus Òg might, for once, be changed, not, as fabled, into the kisses of love, but into doves of peace, that they might fly into the green world, and nest there in many hearts, in many minds, crooning their incommunicable song of joy and hope.

A doomed and passing race. I have been taken to task for these words. But they are true, in the deep reality where they obtain. Yes, but true only in one sense, however vital that is. The Breton's eyes are slowly turning from the enchanted West, and slowly his ears are forgetting the whisper of the wind around menhir and dolmen. The Manxman has ever been the mere yeoman of the Celtic chivalry but even his rude dialect perishes year by year. In Wales, a great tradition survives; in Ireland, a supreme tradition fades through sunset-hued horizons; in Celtic Scotland, a passionate regret, a despairing love and longing, narrows yearly before a dull and incredibly selfish alienism. The Celt has at last reached his horizon. There is no shore beyond. He knows it. This has been the burden of his song since Malvina led the blind Oisìn to his grave by the sea. "Even the Children of Light must go down into darkness." But this apparition of a passing race is no more than the fulfilment of a glorious resurrection before our very eyes. For the genius of the Celtic race stands out now with averted torch, and the light of it is a glory before the eyes, and the flame of it is blown into the hearts of the stronger people. The Celt fades, but his spirit rises in the heart and the mind of the Anglo-Celtic peoples, with whom are the destinies of generations to come.

I stop, and look seaward from this hill slope of Dûn-I. Yes, even in this Isle of Joy, as it seems in this dazzle of golden light and splashing wave, there is the like mortal gloom and immortal mystery which moved the minds of the old seers and bards. Yonder, where that thin spray quivers against the thyme-set cliff, is the Spouting Cave, where to this day the Mar-Tarbh, dread creature of the sea, swims at the full of the tide. Beyond, out of sight behind these craggy steeps, is Port-na-Churaich, where, a thousand years ago, Columba landed in his coracle. Here, eastward, is the landing-place, for the dead of old, brought hence out of Christendom for sacred burial in the Isle of the Saints. All the story of the Gael is here. Iona is the microcosm of the Gaelic world.

Last night, about the hour of the sun's going, I lay upon the heights near the Cave, overlooking the Machar — the sandy, rock-frontiered plain of duneland on the west side of Iona, exposed to the Atlantic. There was neither bird nor beast, no living thing to see, save one solitary human creature. The man toiled at kelp-burning. I watched the smoke till it merged into the sea-mist that came creeping swiftly out of the north, and down from Dûn-I eastward. At last nothing was visible. The mist shrouded everything. I could hear the dull, rhythmic beat of the waves. That was all. No sound, nothing visible.

It was, or seemed, a long while before a rapid thud-thud trampled the heavy air.

Then I heard the rush, the stamping and neighing, of some young mares, pasturing there, as they raced to and fro, bewildered or perchance in play. A glimpse I caught of three, with flying manes and tails; the others were blurred shadows only. A swirl, and the mist disclosed them; a swirl, and the mist enfolded them again. Then, silence once more.

Abruptly, though not for a long time thereafter, the mist rose and drifted seaward.

All was as before. The kelp-burner still stood, straking the smouldering seaweed. Above him a column ascended, bluely spiral, dusked with shadow.

The kelp-burner: who was he but the Gael of the Isles? Who but the Gael in his old-world sorrow? The mist falls and the mist rises. He is there all the same, behind it, part of it; and the column of smoke is the incense out of his longing heart that desires Heaven and Earth, and is dowered only with poverty and pain, hunger and weariness, a little isle of the seas, a great hope, and the love of love.

But ... to the island-story once more!

Some day, surely, the historian of Iona will appear.

How many "history-books" there are like dead leaves. The simile is a travesty. There is no little russet leaf of the forest that could not carry more real, more intimate knowledge. There is no leaf that could not reveal mystery of form, mystery of colour, wonder of structure, secret of growth, the law of harmony; that could not testify to birth, and change, and decay, and death; and what history tells us more? — that could not, to the inward ear, bring the sound of the south wind making a greenness in the woods of Spring, the west wind calling his brown and red flocks to the fold.

What a book it will be! It will reveal to us the secret of what Oisìn sang, what Merlin knew, what Columba dreamed, what Adamnan hoped: what this little "lamp of Christ" was to pagan Europe; what incense of testimony it flung upon the winds; what saints and heroes went out of it; how the dust of kings and princes were brought there to mingle with its sands; how the noble and the ignoble came to it across long seas and perilous countries. It will tell, too, how the Danes ravaged the isles of the west, and left not only their seed for the strengthening of an older race, but imageries and words, words and imageries so alive to-day that the listener in the mind may hear the cries of the Viking above the voice of the Gael and the more ancient tongue of the Pict. It will tell, too, how the nettle came to shed her snow above kings' heads, and the thistle to wave where bishops' mitres stood; how a simple people out of the hills and moors, remembering ancient wisdom or blindly cherishing forgotten symbols, sought here the fount of youth; and how, slowly, a long sleep fell upon the island, and only the grasses shaken in the wind, and the wind itself, and the broken shadows of dreams in the minds of the old, held the secret of Iona. And, at the last — with what lift, with what joy — it will tell how once more the doves of hope and peace have passed over its white sands, this little holy land! This little holy land! Ah, white doves, come again! A thousand thousand wait.

The Three Marvels of Hy

I

THE FESTIVAL OF THE BIRDS

BEFORE dawn, on the morning of the hundredth Sabbath after Colum the White had made glory to God in Hy, that was theretofore called Ioua and thereafter I-shona and is now Iona, the Saint beheld his own Sleep in a vision.

Much fasting and long pondering over the missals, with their golden and azure and sea-green initials and earth-brown branching letters, had made Colum weary. He had brooded much of late upon the mystery of the living world that was not man's world.

On the eve of that hundredth Sabbath, which was to be a holy festival in Iona, he had talked long with an ancient greybeard out of a remote isle in the north, the wild Isle of the Mountains, where Scathach[50] the Queen hanged the men of Lochlin[51] by their yellow hair.

This man's name was Ardan, and he was of the ancient people. He had come to Hy because of two things. Maolmòr, the King of the northern Picts, had sent him to learn of Colum what was this god-teaching he had brought out of Eire: and for himself he had come, with his age upon him, to see what manner of man this Colum was, who had made Ioua, that was "Innis-nan-Dhruidhneach" — the Isle of the Druids — into a place of new worship.

For three hours Ardan and Colum had walked by the sea-shore. Each learned of the other. Ardan bowed his head before the wisdom. Colum knew in his heart that the Druid saw mysteries.

In the first hour they talked of God. Colum spake, and Ardan smiled in his shadowy eyes.

"It is for the knowing," he said, when Colum ceased.

"Ay, sure," said the Saint: "and now, O Ardan the wise, is my God thy God?"

But at that Ardan smiled not. He turned the grave, sad eyes of him to the west. With his right hand he pointed to the Sun that was like a great golden flower. "Truly, He is thy God and my God." Colum was silent.

---

50 Scathach was a warrior queen in Celtic legend. The name is pronounced "sky-ah" and the Scottish Isle of Skye (where she lived with her warrior women compatriots) still bears her name.

51 Lochlin, or Lochlann, is the Gaelic name for Norway. 'Men of Lochlin' are the Vikings.

Then he said: "Thee and thine, O Ardan, from Maolmòr the Pictish king to the least of thy slaves, shall have a long weariness in Hell. That fiery globe yonder is but the Lamp of the World: and sad is the case of the man who knows not the torch from the torch-bearer."

And in the second hour they talked of Man. Ardan spake, and Colum smiled in his deep, grey eyes.

"It is for laughter that," he said, when Ardan ceased.

"And why will that be, O Colum of Eiré?" said Ardan. Then the smile went out of Colum's grey eyes, and he turned and looked about him.

He beheld, near, a crow, a horse, and a hound.

"These are thy brethren," he said scornfully.

But Ardan answered quietly, "Even so."

The third hour they talked about the beasts of the earth and the fowls of the air.

At the last Ardan said : "The ancient wisdom hath it that these are the souls of men and women that have been, or are to be."

Whereat Colum answered: "The new wisdom, that is old as eternity, declareth that God created all things in love. Therefore are we at one, O Ardan, though we sail to the Isle of Truth from the West and the East. Let there be peace between us."

"Peace," said Ardan.

That eve, Ardan of the Picts sat with the monks of Iona. Colum blessed him and said a saying. Oran of the Songs sang a hymn of beauty. Ardan rose, and put the wine of guests to his lips, and chanted this rune:

O Colum and monks of Christ
It is peace we are having this night
Sure, peace is a good thing,
And I am glad with the gladness.

We worship one God,
Though ye call him *Dè* —
And I say not, *O Dia!*
But cry *Bea'uil!*

For it is one faith for man,
And one for the living world,
And no man is wiser than another —
And none knoweth much.

None knoweth a better thing than this:
The Sword, Love, Song, Honour, Sleep.
None knoweth a surer thing than this
Birth, Sorrow, Pain, Weariness, Death.

Sure, peace is a good thing
Let us be glad of Peace:
We are not men of the Sword,
But of the Rune and the Wisdom.

I have learned a truth of Colum,
He hath learned of me:
All ye on the morrow shall see
A wonder of the wonders.

The thought is on you, that the Cross
Is known only of you:
Lo, I tell you the birds know it
That are marked with the Sorrow.

Listen to the Birds of Sorrow,
They shall tell you a great joy[52]
It is Peace you will be having,
With the Birds.

No more would Ardan say after that, though all besought him.

Many pondered long that night. Oran made a song of mystery. Colum brooded through the dark; but before dawn he slept upon the fern that strewed his cell. At dawn, with waking eyes, and weary, he saw his Sleep in a vision. It stood grey and wan beside him.

"What art thou, O Spirit?" he said.

"I am thy Sleep, Colum."

"And is it peace?"

"It is peace."

"What wouldest thou?"

"I have wisdom. Thy heart and thy brain were closed. I could not give you what I brought. I brought wisdom."

"Give it."

"Behold!"

And Colum, sitting upon the strewed fern that was his bed, rubbed his eyes that were heavy with weariness and fasting and long prayer. He could not see his Sleep now. It was gone as smoke that is licked up by the wind.

But on the ledge of the hole that was in the eastern wall of his cell he saw a bird. He leaned his elbow upon the leabhar-aifrionn[53] that was by his side. Then he spoke.

---

52 See my book *The Chronicles of the Sidhe* for Fiona's frequent, and deliberate, use of the terms 'sorrow' and 'joy' in prose and poem.

53 Book of the Mass.

"Is there song upon thee, O Bru-dhearg?"[54]

Then the Red-breast sang, and the singing was so sweet that tears came into the eyes of Colum, and he thought the sunlight that was streaming from the east was melted into that lilting sweet song. It was a hymn that the Bru-dhearg sang, and it was this:

Holy, Holy, Holy,
Christ upon the Cross
My little nest was near,
Hidden in the moss.

Holy, Holy, Holy,
Christ was pale and wan
His eyes beheld me singing
Bron, Bron, mo Bron![55]

Holy, Holy, Holy,
"Come near, O wee brown bird!"
Christ spake: and lo, I lighted
Upon the Living Word.

Holy, Holy, Holy,
I heard the mocking scorn
But *Holy, Holy, Holy*
I sang against a thorn!

Holy, Holy, Holy,
Ah, his brow was bloody:
Holy, Holy, Holy,
All my breast was ruddy.

Holy, Holy, Holy,
Christ's-Bird shalt thou be:
Thus said Mary Virgin
There on Calvary.

Holy, Holy, Holy,
A wee brown bird am I:
But my breast is ruddy
For I saw Christ die.

Holy, Holy, Holy,
By this ruddy feather,
Colum, call thy monks, and
All the birds together.

---

54 'red breast' - the robin.
55 'Grief! Grief! My Grief!'

And at that Colum rose. Awe was upon him, and joy.

He went out and told all to the monks. Then he said Mass out on the green sward. The yellow sunshine was warm upon his grey hair. The love of God was warm in his heart.

"Come, all ye birds!" he cried.

And lo, all the birds of the air flew nigh. The golden eagle soared from the Cuchullins in far-off Skye, and the osprey from the wild lochs of Mull; the gannet from above the clouds, and the fulmar and petrel from the green wave: the cormorant and the skua from the weedy rock, and the plover and the kestrel from the machar: the corbie and the raven from the moor, and the snipe and the bittern and the heron: the cuckoo and cushat from the woodland : the crane from the swamp, the lark from the sky, and the mavis and the merle from the green bushes: the yellowyite, the shilfa, and the lintie, the falcon and the wren and the redbreast, one and all, every creature of the wings, they came at the bidding.

"Peace!" cried Colum.

"Peace!" cried all the Birds, and even the Eagle, the Kestrel, the Corbie, and the Raven cried *Peace, Peace!*

"I will say the Mass," said Colum the White.

And with that he said the Mass. And he blessed the birds.

When the last chant was sung, only the Bru-dhearg remained.

"Come, O Ruddy-Breast," said Colum, "and sing to us of the Christ."

Through a golden hour thereafter the Redbreast sang. Sweet was the joy of it.

At the end Colum said, "Peace! In the name of the Father, the Son, and the Holy Ghost."

Thereat Ardan the Pict bowed his head, and in a loud voice repeated —

"Sìth (shee)! An ainm an Athar, 's an mhic, 's an Spioraid Naoimh!"

And to this day the song of the Birds of Colum, as they are called in Hy, is Sìth — Sìth — Sìth — an — ainm — Chriosd —

"Peace-Peace-Peace-in the name of Christ!"[56]

II
THE SABBATH OF THE FISHES AND THE FLIES

For three days Colum had fasted, save for a mouthful of meal at dawn, a piece of ryebread at noon, and a mouthful of dulse and spring-water at sundown. On the night of the third day, Oran and Keir came to him

---

56 There is a pun in Gaelic here. The word 'sith' (also given as 'sidhe') means peace but also means Faery.

in his cell. Colum was on his knees, lost in prayer. There was no sound there, save the faint whispered muttering of his lips, and on the plastered wall the weary buzzing of a fly.

"Master!" said Oran in a low voice, soft with pity and awe, "Master!"

But Colum took no notice. His lips still moved, and the tangled hairs below his nether lip shivered with his failing breath.

"Father!" said Keir, tender as a woman, "Father!"

Colum did not turn his eyes from the wall. The fly droned his drowsy hum upon the rough plaster. It crawled wearily for a space, then stopped. The slow hot drone filled the cell.

"Master," said Oran, "it is the will of the brethren that you break your fast. You are old, and God has your glory. Give us peace."

"Father," urged Keir, seeing that Colum kneeled unnoticingly, his lips still moving above his black beard, with the white hair of him falling about his head like a snowdrift slipping from a boulder. "Father, be pitiful! We hunger and thirst for your presence. We can fast no longer, yet have we no heart to break our fast if you are not with us. Come, holy one, and be of our company, and eat of the good broiled fish that awaiteth us. We perish for the benediction of thine eyes."

Then it was that Colum rose, and walked slowly towards the wall.

"Little black beast," he said to the fly that droned its drowsy hum and moved not at all; "little black beast, sure it is well I am knowing what you are. You are thinking you are going to get my blessing, you that have come out of hell for the soul of me!"

At that the fly flew heavily from the wall, and slowly circled round and round the head of Colum the White.

"What think you of that, brother Oran, brother Keir?" he asked in a low voice, hoarse because of his long fast and the weariness that was upon him.

"It is a fiend," said Oran.

"It is an angel," said Keir.

Thereupon the fly settled upon the wall again, and again droned his drowsy hot hum.

"Little black beast," said Colum, with the frown coming down into his eyes, "is it for peace you are here, or for sin? Answer, I conjure you in the name of the Father, the Son, and the Holy Ghost!"

"An ainm an Athar, 's an mhic, 's an Spioraid Naoimh,"[57] repeated Oran below his breath.

---

57 'In the name of the Father, and of the Son, and of the Holy Spirit.'

"An ainm an Athar, 's an mhic, 's an Spioraid Naoimh," repeated Keir below his breath.

Then the fly that was upon the wall flew up to the roof and circled to and fro. And it sang a beautiful song, and its song was this:

I

Praise be to God, and a blessing too at that, and a blessing!
For Colum the White, Colum the Dove, hath worshipped;
Yea, he hath worshipped and made of a desert a garden,
And out of the dung of men's souls hath made a sweet savour of burning.

II

A savour of burning, most sweet, a fire for the altar,
This he hath made in the desert ; the hell-saved all gladden.
Sure he hath put his benison, too, on milch-cow and bullock,
On the fowls of the air, and the man-eyed seals, and the otter.

III

But where in his Dûn in the great blue mainland of Heaven
God the All-Father broodeth, where the harpers are harping his glory;
There where He sitteth, where a river of ale poureth ever,
His great sword broken, His spear in the dust, He broodeth.

IV

And this is the thought that moves in his brain, as a cloud filled with thunder
Moves through the vast hollow sky filled with the dust of the stars:
What boots it the glory of Colum, since he maketh a Sabbath to bless me,
And hath no thought of my sons in the deeps of the air and the sea?

And with that the fly passed from their vision. In the cell was a most wondrous sweet song, like the sound of far-off pipes over water.

Oran said in a low voice of awe, "O our God!"

Keir whispered, white with fear, "O God, my God!"

But Colum rose, and took a scourge from where it hung on the wall. "It shall be for peace, Oran," he said, with a grim smile flitting like a bird above the nest of his black beard; "it shall be for peace, Keir!"

And with that he laid the scourge heavily upon the bent backs of Keir and Oran, nor stayed his hand, nor let his three days' fast weaken the deep piety that was in the might of his arm, and because of the glory to God.

Then, when he was weary, peace came into his heart, and he sighed "Amen!"

"Amen!" said Oran the monk.

"Amen!" said Keir the monk.

"And this thing hath been done," said Colum, "because of the evil wish of you and the brethren, that I should break my fast, and eat of fish, till God willeth it. And lo, I have learned a mystery. Ye shall all witness to it on the morrow, which is the Sabbath."

That night the monks wondered much. Only Oran and Keir cursed the fishes in the deeps of the sea and the flies in the deeps of the air.

On the morrow, when the sun was yellow on the brown sea-weed, and there was peace on the isle and upon the waters, Colum and the brotherhood went slowly towards the sea.

At the meadows that are close to the sea, the Saint stood still. All bowed their heads.

"O winged things of the air," cried Colum, "draw near!"

With that the air was full of the hum of innumerous flies, midges, bees, wasps, moths, and all winged insects. These settled upon the monks, who moved not, but praised God in silence. "Glory and praise to God," cried Colum, "behold the Sabbath of the children of God that inhabit the deeps of the air! Blessing and peace be upon them."

"Peace! Peace!" cried the monks, with one voice.

"In the name of the Father, the Son, and the Holy Ghost!" cried Colum the White, glad because of the glory to God.

"An ainm an Athar, 's an mhic, 's an Spioraid Naoimh," cried the monks, bowing reverently, and Oran and Keir deepest of all, because they saw the fly that was of Colum's cell leading the whole host, as though it were their captain, and singing to them a marvellous sweet song.

Oran and Keir testified to this thing, and all were full of awe and wonder, and Colum praised God.

Then the Saints and the brotherhood moved onward and went upon the rocks. When all stood ankle-deep in the sea-weed that was swaying in the tide, Colum cried:

"O finny creatures of the deep, draw near!"

And with that the whole sea shimmered as with silver and gold.

All the fishes of the sea, and the great eels, and the lobsters and the crabs, came in a swift and terrible procession. Great was the glory.

Then Colum cried, "O fishes of the Deep, who is your king?"

Whereupon the herring, the mackerel, and the dog-fish swam forward, and each claimed to be king. But the echo that ran from wave to wave said, *The Herring is King.*

Then Colum said to the mackerel: "Sing the song that is upon you!"

And the mackerel sang the song of the wild rovers of the sea, and the lust of pleasure.

Then Colum said, "But for God's mercy, I would curse you, O false fish."

Then he spake likewise to the dog-fish: and the dog-fish sang of slaughter and the chase, and the joy of blood.

And Colum said: "Hell shall be your portion."

And there was peace. And the Herring said :

"In the name of the Father, the Son, and the Holy Ghost!"

Whereat all that mighty multitude, ere they sank into the deep, waved their fins and their claws, each after his kind, and repeated as with one voice:

"An ainm an Athar, 's an mhic, 's an Spioraid Naoimh!"

And the glory that was upon the Sound of Iona was as though God trailed a starry net upon the waters, with a shining star in every little hollow, and a flowing moon of gold on every wave.

Then Colum the White put out both his arms, and blessed the children of God that are in the deeps of the sea and that are in the deeps of the air.

That is how Sabbath came upon all living things upon Hy that is called Iona, and within the air above Hy, and within the sea that is around Hy.

And the glory is Colum's.

III
THE MOON-CHILD

A year and a day before God bade Colum arise to the Feast of Eternity, Pòl the Freckled, the youngest of the brethren, came to him, on a night of the nights.

"The moon is among the stars, O Colum. By his own will, and yours, old Murtagh that is this day with God, is to be laid in the deep dry sand at the east end of the isle."

So the holy Saint rose from his bed of weariness, and went and blessed the place that Murtagh lay in, and bade neither the creeping worm nor any other creature to touch the sacred dead. "Let God only," he said "let God alone strip that which he made to grow."

But on his way back sleep passed from him. The sweet salt smell of the sea was in his nostrils: he heard the running of a wave in all his blood.

At the cells he turned, and bade the brethren go in. "Peace be with you," he sighed wearily.

Then he moved downwards towards the sea.

A great tenderness of late was upon Colum the Bishop. Ever since he had blessed the fishes and the flies, the least of the children of God, his soul had glowed in a whiter flame. There were deep seas of compassion in his grey-blue eyes. One night he had waked, because God was there.

"O Christ," he cried, bowing low his old grey head. "Sure, ah sure, the gladness and the joy, because of the hour of the hours."

But God said: "Not so, Colum, who keepest me upon the Cross. It is Murtagh, Murtagh the Druid that was, whose soul I am taking to the glory."

With that Colum rose in awe and great grief. There was no light in his cell. In the deep darkness, his spirit quailed. But lo, the beauty of his heart wrought a soft gleam about him, and in that moonshine of good deeds he rose and made his way to where Murtagh slept.

The old monk slept indeed. It was a sweet breath he drew — he, young and fair now, and laughing with peace under the apples in Paradise.

"O Murtagh," Colum cried, "and thee I thought the least of the brethren, because that thou wast a Druid, and loved not to see thy pagan kindred put to the sword if they would not repent. But, true, in my years I am becoming as a boy who learns, knowing nothing. God wash the sin of pride out of my life!"

At that a soft white shining, as of one winged and beautiful, stood beside the dead.

"Art thou Murtagh?" whispered Colum, in deep awe.

"No, I am not Murtagh," came as the breath of vanishing song.

"What art thou?"

"I am Peace," said the glory.

Thereupon Colum sank to his knees, sobbing with joy, for the sorrow that had been and was no more.

"Tell me, O White Peace," he murmured, "can Murtagh hearken, there under the apples where God is?"

"God's love is a wind that blows hitherward and hence. Speak, and thou shalt hear."

Colum spake. "O Murtagh my brother, tell me in what way it is that I still keep God crucified upon the Cross."

There was a sound in the cell as of the morning-laughter of children, of the singing of birds, of the sunlight streaming through the blue fields of Heaven.

Then Murtagh's voice came out of Paradise, sweet with the sweetness: honey-sweet it was, and clothed with deep awe because of the glory.

"Colum, servant of Christ, arise!"

Colum rose, and was as a leaf there, a leaf that is in the wind.

"Colum, thine hour is not yet come. I see it, bathing in the white light which is the Pool of Eternal Life, that is in the abyss where deep-rooted are the Gates of Heaven."

"And my sin, O Murtagh, my sin?"

"God is weary because thou hast not repented."

"O my God and my God! Sure, Murtagh, if that is so, it is so, but it is not for knowledge to me. Sure, O God, it is a blessing I have put on man and woman, on beast and bird and fish, on creeping things and flying things, on the green grass and the brown earth and the flowing wave, on the wind that cometh and goeth, and on the mystery of the flame! Sure, O God, I have sorrowed for all my sins: there is not one I have not fasted and prayed for. Sorrow upon me! — Is it accursed I am, or what is the evil that holdeth me by the hand?"

Then Murtagh, calling through sweet dreams and the rainbow-rain of happy tears that make that place so wondrous and so fair, spake once more:

"O Colum, blind art thou. Hast thou yet repented because after that thou didst capture the great black seal, that is a man under spells, thou, with thy monks, didst crucify him upon the great rock at the place where, long ago, thy coracle came ashore?"

"O Murtagh, favoured of God, will you not be explaining to Him that is King of the Elements, that this was because the seal who was called Black Angus wrought evil upon a mortal woman, and that of the sea-seed was sprung one who had no soul?"

But no answer came to that, and when Colum looked about him, behold there was no soft shining, but only the body of Murtagh the old monk. With a heavy heart, and his soul like a sinking boat in a sea of pain, he turned and went out into the night.

A fine, wonderful night it was. The moon lay low above the sea, and all the flowing gold and flashing silver of the rippling running water seemed to be a flood going that way and falling into the shining hollow splendour.

Through the sea-weed the old Saint moved, weary and sad. When he came to a sandy place he stopped. There, on a rock, he saw a little child. Naked she was, though clad with soft white moonlight. In her hair were brown weeds of the sea, gleaming golden because of the glow. In her hands was a great shell, and at that shell was her mouth. And she was singing this song; passing sweet to hear it was, with the sea-music that was in it:

A little lonely child am I
That have not any soul:
God made me but a homeless wave,
Without a goal.

A seal my father was, a seal
That once was man:
My mother loved him tho' he was
'Neath mortal ban.

He took a wave and drownèd her,
She took a wave and lifted him
And I was born where shadows are
I' the sea-depths dim.

All through the sunny blue-sweet hours
I swim and glide in waters green;
Never by day the mournful shores
By me are seen.

But when the gloom is on the wave
A shell unto the shore I bring:
And then upon the rocks I sit
And plaintive sing.

O what is this wild song I sing,
With meanings strange and dim?
No soul am I, a wave am I,
And sing the Moon-Child's hymn.

Softly Colum drew nigh.

"Peace," he said. "Peace, little one. Ah tender little heart, peace!"

The child looked at him with wide sea-dusky eyes.

"Is it Colum the Holy you will be?"

"No, my fawn, my white dear babe: it is not Colum the Holy I am, but Colum the poor fool that knew not God!"

"Is it you, O Colum, that put the sorrow on my mother, who is the Sea-woman that lives in the whirlpool over there?"

"Ay, God forgive me!"

"Is it you, O Colum, that crucified the seal that was my father: him that was a man once, and that was called Black Angus?"

"Ay, God forgive me!"

"Is it you, O Colum, that bade the children of Hy run away from me, because I was a moon-child, and might win them by the sea-spell into the green wave?"

"Ay, God forgive me!"

"Sure, dear Colum, it was to the glory of God, it was?"

"Ay, He knoweth it, and can hear it, too, from Murtagh, who died this night."

"Look!"

And at that Colum looked, and in a moongold wave he saw Black Angus, the seal-man, drifting dark, and the eyes in his round head were the eyes of love. And beside the man-seal swam a woman fair to see, and she looked at him with joy, and with joy at the Moon-Child that was her own, and at Colum with joy.

Thereupon Colum fell upon his knees and cried —

"Give me thy sorrow, wild woman of the sea!"

"Peace to you, Colum," she answered, and sank into the shadow-thridden wave.

"Give me thy death and crucifixion, O Angus-dhu!" cried the Saint, shaking with the sorrow.

"Peace to you, Colum," answered the man-seal, and sank into the dusky quietudes of the deep.

"Ah, bitter heart o' me! Teach me the way to God, O little child," cried Colum the old, turning to where the Moon-Child was!

But lo, the glory and the wonder!

It was a little naked child that looked at him with healing eyes, but there were no seaweeds in her hair, and no shell in the little wee hands of her. For now, it was a male Child that was there, shining with a light from within: and in his fair sunny hair was a shadowy crown of thorns, and in his hand was a pearl of great price.

"O Christ, my God," said Colum, with failing voice.

"It is thine now, O Colum," said the Moon-Child, holding out to him the shining pearl of great price.

"What is it, O Lord my God?" whispered the old servant of God that was now glad with the gladness: "what is this, thy boon?"

"Perfect Peace."

And that is all.
(To God be the Glory. Amen.)

Section Four

MYSTICAL AND AUTOBIOGRAPHICAL TALES

MYSTICAL AND AUToBI?GRAPHICAL TALES

Many of Fiona Macleod's short stories and essays deal with mystical themes and introduce episodes from the life of St. Columba and the early life of Christ that are her own creations but which nonetheless ring true from a deeper mystical point of view. Woven into many of these narratives are detailed episodes from her own life, which is no mean feat considering that she never existed. However these incidents and episodes are taken directly from the factual life of William Sharp who inserted them to further the illusion of Fiona being a real person with a history, preferences, friendships etc that one would expect from such a seasoned traveller and commentator on life in the remote Highlands and Islands. Having said that, I should point out that there are occasional biographical details that are not from William Sharp's life but which nonetheless have an air of validity in their own right. In the following selection of writings I have added footnotes as appropriate to fill out more detail on exactly whose biography we are really dealing with.

William Sharp was very interested in all things spiritual, mystical and magical and it is only natural that this interest should spill over into Fiona Macleod's output. He was friends with several other authors, mystics and magicians who were involved with the Victorian magical group called The Golden Dawn and many of these were also involved in the political struggle of the day for Irish independence. Whereas Sharp was committed to being active in both of these circles, Fiona was clearly not. Interesting.

The tale *Muime Chriosd* is given in abbreviated form in the Iona essay (see Section Three) but I have given it in full below as it is an important tale. There are many stories of St Brigid current in the Gaelic speaking areas of both Scotland and Ireland and she has been called the "Mary of the Gael" as in many ways she surpasses even the Virgin Mary in importance. Fiona's version of her life is clearly anachronistic and mingles Gaelic speaking Highlanders, complete with bagpipes, into the arid deserts of the Holy Land as if this was completely normal. To her it probably was. Despite this, the tale flows easily and lays out in a clear and concise manner many of the fragmentary beliefs concerning Brigid to be found in *Carmina Gadelica* and even amongst the prayers intoned by modern Gaels. She also manages to weave in some interesting pieces of folklore explaining how the Gaelic names for the dandelion and the oyster-catcher came to be.

The tales *The Fisher of Men* and *The Last Supper* both appear in the collection *The Sin-Eater* and are two Christ-stories that are not taken from the Gaelic folklore and are definitely not part of the accepted canon regarding the Christ. The first emphasizes the loneliness and quiet of life in one of the thousands of small crofts that are scattered throughout the brooding glens of the Highlands and Islands. It also shows beautifully the crofters' deep and profound belief in the life of Christ as being as lonely and without joy as their own. The old woman of the story knows that even though the Son of the Carpenter is the Son of God he nevertheless has no home on this earth and wanders the hillsides like the lost sheep and the frightened little birds. It is a touching little vignette of the last days of an old mother and the aging son now left alone in the empty croft.

The Last Supper is not directly connected to *The Fisher of Men* but is a good example of how Fiona took the Gaelic belief in the poor, wandering Christ and added to the corpus a story which is new and her own but which manages to slip seamlessly into the Gaelic story-tellers' repertoire. The young child is shown great wonders by Christ and given an insight into his mission and his followers that is not given out by the institutionalized church. A tale we shall encounter later, *The Wayfarer*, shows in an uncharacteristically vitriolic way how much William Sharp and Fiona Macleod disliked the Church of Rome and the Church of Scotland and the way that both institutions deliberately crushed any inclination that their members might have in developing a very deep, and very personal, relationship with Christ - without the need for priest or minister.

The short tale *The Man on the Moor* first appeared in the 1905 collection *The Sunset of Old Tales* and is in keeping with the other previously unknown tales of Jesus and his followers given here. The first part, which has nothing to do with the main story, is at first familiar to us in that Fiona spends some time describing the hillside over which she has travelled. But it is different from her many earlier descriptions which focused on emptiness, bleakness, loneliness etc. Now she describes a much softer and more appealing place, one with beauty that must be looked for but which is definitely there. Her later work moved away from the darkness, loneliness and horror of her earlier material and started to soften considerably. This is a good example of such a change. It also includes a small autobiographical reference in that William Sharp had been to Italy several times throughout his life and this is brought up in the conversation Fiona has with the gentleman she had gone to visit.

The next tale, *The Archer*, is important for several rather complicated reasons which I deal with in detail in *The Little Book of the Great Enchantment*. It was written before Fiona's first book *Pharais* was published in 1894 and originally bore the title *The Last Phantasy of James Achanna*. She offered it to the *Scots Observer* magazine, that did not publish it but did have kind words to say of it. This early version ends with the death of one of the male characters but has no mention of stars or a woman archer as is found in the later version. In August 1896 Sharp's Irish literary acquaintances William Butler Yeats and Edward Martyn (who did not know Fiona's true identity) both had a dream of a woman archer firing arrows at the stars. Later, Fiona revealed that she too had had the same dream at the same time although she was in Scotland and had no knowledge of Yeats' and Martyn's joint experience. It was then that she added the ending given in the version below, at least two full years after penning the first version. Patrick Geddes published the longer version in his collection *Re-issue of the Shorter Tales of Fiona Macleod, Rearranged with Additional Tales* in 1897 and it appeared again in 1899 in the collection called *The Dominion of Dreams*.

The tale is an autobiographical piece based on events that were happening in the life of William Sharp, which had nothing to do with stars and archers but had everything to do with illicit love affairs. The struggle of the two male characters, Ian and Seumas, over the woman Silis reflected the struggle Sharp was going through with his own wife Elizabeth and his lover Edith Rinder, while at the same time Yeats was struggling to be accepted as lover by Maud Gonne. Fiona added the ending involving the woman archer for no other reason than to convince Yeats that she was on the same psychic wavelength as he was; this was important to her. However it is highly unlikely that she ever had the archer dream as she later claimed. She saw an opportunity to use this story with the new ending to make Yeats believe they were psychically linked and the ruse worked.

The Book of the Opal was published in the 1899 volume *The Dominion of Dreams* and contains much that is autobiographical and relevant to the time at which Fiona wrote this piece. In 1899 William Sharp was experimenting a great deal with magic and psychic phenomena in an effort to understand what was happening to him regarding the Fiona

Macleod personality that he was aware of yet knew not what she was going to say, do or write. There is a telling sentence near the beginning of this tale that reveals much, "I believe more readily now that a man or woman may be possessed: or, that two spirits may inhabit the same body, as fire and air together inhabit a jet of flame." He continued to struggle with the sheer effort of thinking and writing as two people yet all the time desperately hiding the secret of who Fiona Macleod really was. The latter part of the tale also introduces the four magical elements and weapons that he would have been so familiar with thanks to his Golden Dawn connections. The book of the title, The Book of the Opal, never existed and it can be put together with two other books Fiona drew upon frequently that likewise never existed (at least not in this world) namely *The Little Book of the Great Enchantment* and *The Chronicles of the Sidhe*.

The next tale *The Wells of Peace* is also from *The Dominion of Dreams* and is a typical example of a little vignette from a lonely Gael's life, a subject dear to Fiona's heart. As in many of these tales, she lists several conditions for the achieving of peace or whatever the particular desire of the subject of the tale may be. Often these lists are enumerated by a person we have encountered elsewhere in Fiona's writings. In this case it is Art, the little child from the mystical tale *The Last Supper*, who is grown up now but wise beyond his years with Inner Wisdom. What happens to Ian Mòr after he and Art go their own ways? We do not know. It does not matter.

The Dominion of Dreams is also the source for *The Wind, the Shadow, and the Soul*, an intense mystical piece mingling evocative descriptions of a simple seaside cove with the deep broodings of the narrator's thoughts and soul. Who is the narrator and who is the lost loved? They are all lovers, they are all mystics, they are everyone who can see the detailed beauty of a simple seashore and grassy path.

From the 1900 collection *The Divine Adventure* comes an autobiographical piece, being a short description of William Sharp's childhood nurse, Barbara Macleod, here called "Barabal." Also mentioned briefly in the tale is another Macleod, Seumas Macleod, who was an old fisherman living on one of the Inner Hebridean islands, probably the Isle of Eigg. He and Barbara were responsible for teaching the young William Sharp the Gaelic language (he was born and raised in an area of Scotland where the Gaelic is not spoken) and all the many proverbs, runes and sayings that Fiona Macleod would use so prolifically later in his life. It is also from them that he took the surname Macleod, to be added to the personal name Fiona, his own invention, and they could rightly be described as Fiona Macleod's parents. However, the tale tells us almost nothing of the subject, Barbara, but instead gives us a linguistic discussion on some of the popular proverbs the old nurse is alleged to have passed on to young William. In reality nearly all of these 'ancient Gaelic proverbs' are the creation of Fiona Macleod. The subject of the Four Winds and the Four Stars were clearly of great importance to Fiona as she used them in several of her writings across her entire career. They are also to be found many times in William Sharp's personal notebooks and diaries but, as far as I have been able to ascertain, are not to be found in the writings or oral recordings of any other Gaelic-speaking writer, poet or croft-dwelling story teller.

The essay *Mäya* was published in Volume 5 of *The Collected Works of Fiona Macleod* in 1911. It is a deep, questioning piece that provides no answers. Perhaps there are no answers to such inadequate questioning but the final paragraphs, dealing with the Celtic god of the sea Mânan, give us a glimpse as to why the sea and all waters appear so often in the writings of Fiona Macleod.

The final piece *The Distant Country* is from *The Dominion of Dreams* and was clearly very important to Fiona. See the final entry in Section Seven for a comment on this intense and deep essay.

Note to Muime Chriosd

This legendary romance is based upon the ancient and still current (though often hopelessly contradictory) legends concerning Brighid, or Bride, commonly known as "Muime Chriosd," — i.e. the Foster-Mother of Christ. From the universal honour and reverence in which she was and is held — second only in this respect to the Virgin herself — she is also called "Mary of the Gael." Another name, frequent in the West, is "Brighde-nam-Brat" — i.e. St Bride of the Mantle, a name explained in the course of my legendary story. Brighid, the Christian saint should not, however, be confused with a much earlier and remoter Brighid, the ancient Celtic Muse of Song.

ST BRIDE OF THE ISLES
SLOINNEADH BRIGHDE, MUIME CHRIOSD

Brighde nighean Dughaill Duinn,
'Ic Aoidth, 'ic Arta, 'ic Cuinn.
Gach la is gach oidhche
Ni mi cuimhneachadh air sloinneadh Brighde.
Cha mharbhar mi,
Cha ghuinear mi,
Cha ghonar mi,
Cha mho dh' fhagas Criosd an dearmad mi;
Cha loisg teine gniomh Shatain mi;
'S cha bhath uisge no saile mi;
'S mi fo chomraig Naoimh Moire
'S me chaomh mhuime, Brighde.

The Genealogy of St Bridget or St Bride, Foster-Mother of Christ.

St Bridget, the daughter of Dùghall Donn,
Son of Hugh, son of Art, son of Conn.
Each day and each night
I will meditate on the genealogy of St Bridget.
[Whereby] I will not be killed,
I will not be wounded,
I will not be bewitched
Neither will Christ forsake me;
Satan's fire will not burn me;
Neither water nor sea shall drown me;
For I am under the protection of the Virgin Mary,
And my gentle foster-mother, St Bridget.

Muime Chriosd

To the beautiful memory of
S. F. Alden.

I

BEFORE ever St. Colum came across the Moyle to the island of Iona, that was then by strangers called Innis-nan-Dhruidhneach, the Isle of the Druids, and by the natives Ioua, there lived upon the south-east slope of Dun-I a poor herdsman named Dùvach.[58] Poor he was, for sure, though it was not for this reason that he could not win back to Ireland, green Banba, as he called it: but because he was an exile thence, and might never again smell the heather blowing over Sliabh-Gorm in what of old was the realm of Aoimag.

He was a prince in his own land, though none on Iona save the Arch-Druid knew what his name was. The high priest, however, knew that Dùvach was the royal Dùghall, called Dùghall Donn, the son of Hugh the King, the son of Art, the son of Conn. In his youth he had been accused of having done a wrong against a noble maiden of the blood. When her child was born he was made to swear across her dead body that he would be true to the daughter for whom she had given up her life, that he would rear her in a holy place, but away from Eiré, and that he would never set foot within that land again. This was a bitter thing for Dùghall Donn to do: the more so as, before the King, and the priests, and the people, he swore by the Wind, and by the Moon, and by the Sun, that he was guiltless of the thing of which he was accused. There were many there who believed him because of that sacred oath: others, too, forasmuch as that Morna the Princess had herself sworn to the same effect. Moreover, there was Aodh of the Golden Hair, a poet and seer, who avowed that Morna had given birth to an immortal, whose name would one day be as a moon among the stars for glory. But the King would not be appeased, though he spared the life of his youngest son. So it was that, by the advice of Aodh of the Druids, Dùghall Donn went northwards through the realm of Clanadon and so to the sea-loch that was then called Loch Feobal. There he took boat with some wayfarers bound for Alba. But in the Moyle a tempest arose, and the frail galley

---

58 This name means gloom or despair.

was driven northward, and at sunrise was cast like a fish, spent and dead, upon the south end of Ioua, that is now Iona. Only two of the mariners survived: Dùghall Donn and the little child. This was at the place where, on a day of the days in a year that was not yet come, St. Colum landed in his coracle, and gave thanks on his bended knees.

When, warmed by the sun, they rose, they found themselves in a waste place. Ill was Dùghall in his mind because of the portents, and now to his fear and amaze the child Bridget knelt on the stones, and, with claspt hands, small and pink as the sea-shells round about her, sang a song of words which were unknown to him. This was the more marvellous, as she was yet but an infant, and could say no word even of Erse, the only tongue she had heard.

At this portent, he knew that Aodh had spoken seeingly. Truly this child was not of human parentage. So he, too, kneeled, and, bowing before her, asked if she were of the race of the Tuatha de Danann, or of the older gods, and what her will was, that he might be her servant. Then it was that the kneeling babe looked at him, and sang in a low sweet voice in Erse:

> I am but a little child,
> Dùghall, son of Hugh, son of Art,
> But my garment shall be laid
> On the lord of the world,
> Yea, surely it shall be that He
> The King of the Elements Himself
> Shall lean against my bosom,
> And I will give him peace,
> And peace will I give to all who ask
> Because of this mighty Prince,
> And because of his Mother that is the Daughter of Peace.

And while Dùghall Donn was still marvelling at this thing, the Arch-Druid of Iona approached, with his white-robed priests. A grave welcome was given to the stranger. While the youngest of the servants of God was entrusted with the child, the Arch-Druid took Dùghall aside and questioned him. It was not till the third day that the old man gave his decision. Dùghall Donn was to abide on Iona if he so willed: but the child was to stay. His life would be spared, nor would he be a bondager of any kind, and a little land to till would be given him, and all that he might need. But of his past he was to say no word. His name was to become as nought, and he was to be known simply as Dùvach. The child, too, was to be named Bride, for that was the way the name Bridget was called in the Erse of the Isles.

To the question of Dùghall, that was thenceforth Dùvach, as to why he laid so great stress on the child, that was a girl, and the reputed offspring of shame at that, Cathal the Arch-Druid replied thus: "My kinsman Aodh of the Golden Hair who sent you here, was wiser than Hugh the King and all the Druids of Aoimag. Truly, this child is an Immortal. There is an ancient prophecy concerning her: surely of her who is now here, and no other. There shall be, it says, a spotless maid born of a virgin of the ancient immemorial race in Innisfail. And when for the seventh time the sacred year has come, she will hold Eternity in her lap as a white flower. Her maiden breasts shall swell with milk for the Prince of the World. She shall give suck to the King of the Elements. So I say unto you, Dùvach, go in peace. Take unto thyself a wife, and live upon the place I will give thee on the east side of Ioua. Treat Bride as though she were thy spirit, but leave her much alone, and let her learn of the sun and the wind. In the fulness of time the prophecy shall be fulfilled."

So was it, from that day of the days. Dùvach took a wife unto himself, who weaned the little Bride, who grew in beauty and grace, so that all men marvelled. Year by year for seven years the wife of Dùvach bore him a son, and these grew apace in strength, so that by the beginning of the third year of the seventh cycle of Bride's life there were three stalwart youths to brother her, and three comely and strong lads, and one young boy fair to see. Nor did anyone, not even Bride herself, saving Cathal the Arch-Druid, know that Dùvach the herdsman was Dùghall Donn, of a princely race in Innisfail.

In the end, too, Dùvach came to think that he had dreamed, or at the least that Cathal had not interpreted the prophecy aright. For though Bride was of exceeding beauty, and of a strange piety that made the young Druids bow before her as though she were a bàndia, yet the world went on as before, and the days brought no change. Often, while she was still a child, he had questioned her about the words she had said as a babe, but she had no memory of them. Once, in her ninth year, he came upon her on the hillside of Dun-I singing these self-same words. Her eyes dreamed far away. He bowed his head, and, praying to the Giver of Light, hurried to Cathal. The old man bade him speak no more to the child concerning the mysteries.

Bride lived the hours of her days upon the slopes of Dun-I, herding the sheep, or in following the kye upon the green hillocks and grassy dunes of what then as now was called the Machar. The beauty of the world was her daily food. The spirit within her was like sunlight behind a white flower. The birdeens in the green bushes sang for joy when they saw her blue eyes. The tender prayers that were in her heart for all the beasts and birds, for helpless children, and tired women, and for all who were old, were often seen flying above her head in the form of white doves of sunshine.

But when the middle of the year came that was, though Dùvach had forgotten it, the year of the prophecy, his eldest son, Conn, who was now a man, murmured against the virginity of Bride, because of her beauty and because a chieftain of the mainland was eager to wed her. "I shall wed Bride or raid Ioua," was the message he had sent. So one day, before the great fire of the summer-festival, Conn and his brothers reproached Bride.

"Idle are these pure eyes, O Bride, not to be as lamps at thy marriage-bed."

"Truly, it is not by the eyes that we live," replied the maiden gently, while to their fear and amazement she passed her hand before her face and let them see that the sockets were empty.

Trembling with awe at this portent, Dùvach intervened.

"By the Sun I swear it, O Bride, that thou shalt marry whomsoever thou wilt and none other, and when thou willest, or not at all if such be thy will."

And when he had spoken, Bride smiled, and passed her hand before her face again, and all there were abashed because of the blue light as of morning that was in her shining eyes.

II

The still weather had come, and all the isles lay in beauty. Far south, beyond vision, ranged the coasts of Eiré: westward, leagues of quiet ocean dreamed into unsailed wastes whose waves at last laved the shores of Tir-ná'n-Òg, the Land of Eternal Youth: northward, the spell-bound waters sparkled in the sunlight, broken here and there by purple shadows, that were the isles of Staffa and Ulva, Lunga and the isles of the columns, misty Coll, and Tiree that is the land beneath the wave; with, pale blue in the heat-haze, the mountains of Rûm called Haleval, Haskeval, and Oreval, and the sheer Scuir-na-Gillian and the peaks of the Cuchullins in remote Skye.

All the sweet loveliness of a late spring remained, to give a freshness to the glory of summer. The birds had song to them still.

It was while the dew was yet wet on the grass that Bride came out of her father's house, and went up the steep slope of Dun-I. The crying of the ewes and lambs at the pastures came plaintively against the dawn. The lowing of the kye arose from the sandy hollows by the shore, or from the meadows on the lower slopes. Through the whole island went a rapid trickling sound, most sweet to hear: the myriad voices of twittering birds, from the dotterel in the seaweed to the larks climbing the blue spirals of heaven.

This was the morning of her birth, and she was clad in white. About her waist was a girdle of the sacred rowan, the feathery green leaves of it flickering dusky shadows upon her robe as she moved. The light upon her yellow hair was as when morning wakes, laughing low with joy amid the tall corn. As she went she sang, soft as the crooning of a dove. If any had been there to hear he would have been abashed, for the words were not in Erse, and the eyes of the beautiful girl were as those of one in a vision.

When, at last, a brief while before sunrise, she reached the summit of the Scuir, that is so small a hill and yet seems so big in Iona where it is the sole peak, she found three young Druids there, ready to tend the sacred fire the moment the sun-rays should kindle it. Each was clad in a white robe, with fillets of oak leaves; and each had a golden armlet. They made a quiet obeisance as she approached. One stepped forward, with a flush in his face because of her beauty, that was as a sea-wave for grace, and a flower for purity, and sunlight for joy, and moonlight for peace, and the wind for fragrance.

"Thou mayst draw near if thou wilt, Bride, daughter of Dùvach," he said, with something of reverence as well as of grave courtesy in his voice: "for the holy Cathal hath said that the Breath of the Source of All is upon thee. It is not lawful for women to be here at this moment, but thou hast the law shining upon thy face and in thine eyes. Hast thou come to pray?"

But at that moment a low cry came from one of his companions. He turned, and rejoined his fellows. Then all three sank upon their knees, and with outstretched arms hailed the rising of God.

As the sun rose, a solemn chant swelled from their lips, ascending as incense through the silent air. The glory of the new day came soundlessly. Peace was in the blue heaven, on the blue-green sea, on the green land. There was no wind, even where the currents of the deep moved in shadowy purple. The sea itself was silent, making no more than a sighing slumber-breath round the white sands of the isle, or a hushed whisper where the tide lifted the long weed that clung to the rocks.

In what strange, mysterious way, Bride did not see; but as the three Druids held their hands before the sacred fire there was a faint crackling, then three thin spirals of blue smoke rose, and soon dusky red and wan yellow tongues of flame moved to and fro. The sacrifice of God was made. Out of the immeasurable heaven He had come, in His golden chariot. Now, in the wonder and mystery of His love, He was re-born upon the world, re-born a little fugitive flame upon a low hill in a remote isle. Great must be His love that He could die thus daily in a thousand places: so great His love that He could give up His own body to daily death, and suffer the holy flame that was in the embers He illumined to be lighted and revered and then scattered to the four quarters of the world.

Bride could bear no longer the mystery of this great love. It moved her to an ecstasy. What tenderness of divine love that could thus redeem the world daily: what long-suffering for all the evil and cruelty done hourly upon the weeping earth: what patience with the bitterness of the blind fates! The beauty of the worship of Be'al was upon her as a golden glory. Her heart leaped to a song that could not be sung. The inexhaustible love and pity in her soul chanted a hymn that was heard of no Druid or mortal anywhere, but was known of the white spirits of Life.

Bowing her head, so that the glad tears fell warm as thunder-rain upon her hands, she rose and moved away.

Not far from the summit of Dun-I is a hidden pool, to this day called the Fountain of Youth. Hitherward she went, as was her wont when upon the hill at the break of day, at noon, or at sundown. Close by the huge boulder, which hides it from above, she heard a pitiful bleating, and soon the healing of her eyes was upon a lamb which had become fixed in a crevice in the rock. On a crag above it stood a falcon, with savage cries, lusting for warm blood. With swift step Bride drew near. There was no hurt to the lambkin as she lifted it in her arms. Soft and warm was it there, as a young babe against the bosom that mothers it. Then with quiet eyes she looked at the falcon, who hooded his cruel gaze.

"There is no wrong in thee, Seobhag,"[59] she said gently; "but the law of blood shall not prevail for ever. Let there be peace this morn."

And when she had spoken this word, the wild hawk of the hills flew down upon her shoulder, nor did the heart of the lambkin beat the quicker, while with drowsy eyes nestled as against its dam. When she stood by the pool she laid the little woolly creature among the fern. Already the

---

59 The Gaelic word for hawk.

bleating of it was sweet against the forlorn heart of a ewe. The falcon rose, circled above her head, and with swift flight sped through the blue air. For a time Bride watched its travelling shadow: when it was itself no more than a speck in the golden haze, she turned, and stooped above the Fountain of Youth.

Beyond it stood then, though for ages past there has been no sign of either, two quicken-trees. Now they were gold-green in the morning light, and the brown-green berries that had not yet reddened were still small. Fair to see was the flickering of the long finger-shadows upon the granite rocks and boulders.

Often had Bride dreamed through their foliage; but now she stared in amaze. She had put her lips to the water, and had started back because she had seen, beyond her own image, that of a woman so beautiful that her soul was troubled within her, and had cried its inaudible cry, worshipping. When, trembling, she had glanced again, there was none beside herself. Yet what had happened? For, as she stared at the quicken-trees, she saw that their boughs had interlaced, and that they now became a green arch. What was stranger still was that the rowan-clusters hung in blood-red masses, although the late heats were yet a long way off.

Bride rose, her body quivering because of the cool sweet draught of the Fountain of Youth, so that almost she imagined the water was for her that day what it could be once in each year to every person who came to it, a breath of new life and the strength and joy of youth. With slow steps she advanced towards the arch of the quickens. Her heart beat as she saw that the branches at the summit had formed themselves into the shape of a wreath or crown, and that the scarlet berries dropped therefrom a steady rain of red drops as of blood. A sigh of joy breathed from her lips when, deep among the red and green, she saw the white merle of which the ancient poets sang, and heard the exceeding wonder of its rapture, which was now the pain of joy and now the joy of pain.

The song of the mystic bird grew wilder and more sweet as she drew near. For a brief while she hesitated. Then as a white dove drifted slow before her under and through the quicken-boughs, a dove white as snow but radiant with sunfire, she moved forward to follow, with a dream-smile upon her face and her eyes full of the sheen of wonder and mystery, as shadowy waters flooded with moonshine.

And this was the passing of Bride, who was not seen again of Dùvach or her foster brothers for the space of a year and a day. Only Cathal, the aged Arch-Druid, who died seven days thence, had a vision of her, and wept for joy.

III

When the strain of the white merle ceased, though it had seemed to her scarce longer than the vanishing song of the swallow on the wing, Bride saw that the evening was come. Through the violet glooms of dusk she moved soundlessly, save for the crispling of her feet among the hot sands. Far as she could see to right or left there were hollows and ridges of sand; where, here and there, trees or shrubs grew out of the parched soil, they were strange to her. She had heard the Druids speak of the sunlands in a remote, nigh unreachable East, where there were trees called palms, trees in a perpetual sunflood yet that perished not, also tall dark cypresses, black-green as the holy yew. These were the trees she now saw. Did she dream, she wondered? Far down in her mind was some memory, some floating vision only, mayhap, of a small green isle far among the northern seas. Voices, words, faces, familiar yet unfamiliar when she strove to bring them near, haunted her.

The heat brooded upon the land. The sigh of the parched earth was "Water, water."

As she moved onward through the gloaming she descried white walls beyond her: white walls and square white buildings, looming ghostly through the dark, yet home-sweet as the bells of the cows on the sea-pastures, because of the yellow lights every here and there agleam.

A tall figure moved towards her, clad in white, even as those figures which haunted her unremembering memory. When he drew near she gave a low cry of joy. The face of her father was sweet to her.

"Where will be the pitcher, Brighid?" he said, though the words were not the words that were near her when she was alone. Nevertheless she knew them, and the same manner of words was upon her lips.

"My pitcher, father?"

"Ah, dreamer, when will you be taking heed! It is leaving your pitcher you will be, and by the Well of the Camels, no doubt: though little matter will that be, since there is now no water, and the drought is heavy upon the land. But ... Brighid ..."

"Yes, my father?"

"Sure now, it is not safe for you to be on the desert at night. Wild beasts come out of the darkness, and there are robbers and wild men who lurk in the shadow. Brighid ... Brighid ... is it dreaming you are still?"

"I was dreaming of a cool green isle in northern seas, where ..."

"Where you have never been, foolish lass, and are never like to be. Sure, if any wayfarer were to come upon us you would scarce be able to tell him that yonder village is Bethlehem, and that I am Dùghall Donn the innkeeper, Dùghall, the son of Hugh, son of Art, son of Conn. Well, well, I am growing old, and they say that the old see wonders. But I do not wish to see this wonder, that my daughter Brighid forgets her own town, and the good inn that is there, and the strong sweet ale that is cool against the thirst of the weary. Sure, if the day of my days is near it is near. 'Green be the place of my rest,' I cry, even as Oisìn the son of Fionn of the hero-line of Trenmor cried in his old age; though if Oisìn and the Fionn were here not a green place would they find now, for the land is burned dry as the heather after a hill-fire. But now, Brighid, let us go back into Bethlehem, for I have that for the saying which must be said at once."

In silence the twain walked through the gloaming that was already the mirk, till they came to the white gate, where the asses and camels breathed wearily in the sultry darkness, with dry tongues moving round parched mouths. Thence they fared through narrow streets, where a few white-robed Hebrews and sons of the desert moved silently, or sat in niches. Finally, they came to a great yard where more than a score of camels lay huddled and growling in their sleep. Beyond this was the inn, which was known to all the patrons and friends of Dùghall Donn as the "Rest and Be Thankful," though formerly as the Rest of Clan-Ailpean, for was he not himself through his mother MacAlpine of the Isles, as well as blood-kin to the great Cormac the Ard-Rìgh, to whom his father, Hugh, was feudatory prince?

As Dùghall and Bride walked along the stone flags of a passage leading to the inner rooms, he stopped and drew her attention to the water-tanks.

"Look you, my lass," he said sorrowfully, "of these tanks and barrels nearly all are empty. Soon there will be no water whatever, which is an evil thing though I whisper it in peace, to the Stones be it said. Now, already the folk who come here murmur. No man can drink ale all day long, and those wayfarers who want to wash the dust of their journey from their feet and hands complain bitterly. And ... what is that you will be saying? The kye? Ay, sure, there is the kye; but the poor beasts are o'ercome with the heat, and there's not a Cailliach[60] on the hills who could win a drop more of milk from them than we squeeze out of their udders now, and that only with rune after rune till all the throats of the milking lassies are as dry as the salt grass by the sea.

---

60 Cailliach has three (related) meanings -an old woman, a witch and a nun.

"Well, what I am saying is this: 'tis months now since any rain will be falling, and every crock of water has been for the treasuring as though it had been the honey of Moy-Mell itself. The moon has been full twice since we had the good water brought from the mountain-springs; and now they are for drying up too. The seers say that the drought will last. If that is a true word, and there be no rain till the winter comes, there will be no inn in Bethlehem called 'The Rest and Be Thankful'; for already there is not enough good water to give peace even to your little thirst, my birdeen. As for the ale, it is poor drink now for man or maid, and as for the camels and asses, poor beasts, they don't understand the drinking of it."

"That is true, father; but what is to be done?"

"That's what I will be telling you, my lintie. Now, I have been told by an oganach[61] out of Jerusalem, that lives in another place close by the great town, that there is a quenchless well of pure water, cold as the sea with a north wind in it, on a hill there called the Mount of Olives. Now, it is to that hill I will be going. I am for taking all the camels and all the horses and all the asses, and will lade each with a burthen of water-skins and come back home again with water enough to last us till the drought breaks."

That was all that was said that night. But at the dawn the inn was busy, and all the folk in Bethlehem were up to see the going abroad of Dùghall Donn and Ronald McIan, his shepherd, and some Macleans and Maccallums that were then in that place. It was a fair sight to see as they went forth through the white gate that is called the Gate of Nazareth. A piper walked first, playing the Gathering of the Swords: then came Dùghall Donn on a camel, and McIan on a horse, and the herdsmen on asses, and then there were the collies barking for joy.

Before he had gone, Dùghall took Bride out of the hearing of the others. There was only a little stagnant water, he said; and as for the ale, there was no more than a flagon left of what was good. This flagon and the one jar of pure water he left with her. On no account was she to give a drop to any wayfarer, no matter how urgent he might be; for he, Dùghall, could not say when he would get back, and he did not want to find a dead daughter to greet him on his return, let alone there being no maid of the inn to attend to customers. Over and above that, he made her take an oath that she would give no one, no, not even a stranger, accommodation at the inn, during his absence.

---

61 A young man.

Afternoon and night came, and dawn and night again, and yet again. It was on the afternoon of the third day, when even the crickets were dying of thirst, that Bride heard a clanging at the door of the inn.

When she went to the door she saw a weary grey-haired man, dusty and tired. By his side was an ass with drooping head, and on the ass was a woman, young, and of a beauty that was as the cool shadow of green leaves and the cold ripple of running waters. But beautiful as she was it was not this that made Bride start: no, nor the heavy womb that showed the woman was with child. For she remembered her of a dream — it was a dream, sure — when she had looked into a pool on a mountain-side, and seen, beyond her own image, just this fair and beautiful face, the most beautiful that ever man saw since Nais, of the Sons of Usna, beheld Deirdré in the forest — ay, and lovelier far even than she, the peerless among women.

"Gu'm beannaicheadh Dia an tigh," said the grey-haired man in a weary voice, "the blessing of God on this house."

'Soraidh leat," replied Bride gently, "and upon you likewise."

"Can you give us food and drink, and, after that, good rest at this inn? Sure it is grateful we will be. This is my wife Mary, upon whom is a mystery: and I am Joseph, a carpenter in Arimathea."

"Welcome, and to you, too, Mary: and peace. But there is neither food nor drink here, and my father has bidden me give shelter to none who comes here against his return."

The carpenter sighed, but the fair woman on the ass turned her shadowy eyes upon Bride, so that the maiden trembled with joy and fear.

"And is it forgetting me you will be, Brighid-Alona," she murmured, in the good sweet Gaelic of the Isles; and the voice of her was like the rustle of leaves when a soft rain is falling in a wood.

"Sure, I remember," Bride whispered, filled with deep awe. Then without a word she turned, and beckoned them to follow: which, having left the ass by the doorway, they did.

"Here is all the ale that I have," she said, as she gave the flagon to Joseph: "and here, Mary, is all the water that there is. Little there is, but it is you that are welcome to it."

Then, when they had quenched their thirst she brought out oatcakes and scones and brown bread, and would fain have added milk, but there was none.

"Go to the byre, Brighid," said Mary, "and the first of the kye shall give milk."

So Bride went, but returned saying that the creature would not give milk without a sian or song, and that her throat was too dry to sing.

"Say this sian," said Mary:

Give up thy milk to her who calls
Across the low green hills of Heaven
And stream-cool meads of Paradise!

And sure enough, when Bride did this, the milk came: and she soothed her thirst, and went back to her guests rejoicing. It was sorrow to her not to let them stay where they were, but she could not, because of her oath.

The man Joseph was weary, and said he was too tired to seek far that night, and asked if there was no empty byre or stable where he and Mary could sleep till morning. At that, Bride was glad: for she knew there was a clean cool stable close to the byre where her kye were: and thereto she led them, and returned with peace at her heart.

When she was in the inn again, she was afraid once more: for lo, though Mary and Joseph had drunken deep of the jar and the flagon, each was now full as it had been. Of the food, too, none seemed to have been taken, though she had herself seen them break the scones and the oatcakes.

It was dusk when her reverie was broken by the sound of the pipes. Soon thereafter Dùghall Donn and his following rode up to the inn, and all were glad because of the cool water, and the grapes, and the green fruits of the earth, that they brought with them.

While her father was eating and drinking, merry because of the ale that was still in the flagon, Bride told him of the wayfarers. Even as she spoke, he made a sign of silence, because of a strange, unwonted sound that he heard.

"What will that be meaning?" he asked, in a low, hushed voice.

"Sure it is the rain at last, father. That is a glad thing. The earth will be green again. The beasts will not perish. Hark, I hear the noise of it coming down from the hills as well." But Dùghall sat brooding.

"Ay," he said at last, "is it not foretold that the Prince of the World is to be born in this land, during a heavy falling of rain, after a long drought? And who is for knowing that Bethlehem is not the place, and that this is not the night of the day of the days? Brighid, Brighid, the woman Mary must be the mother of the Prince, who is to save all mankind out of evil and pain and death!" And with that he rose and beckoned to her to follow. They took a lantern, and made their way through the drowsing camels and and horses, and past the byres where the kye lowed gently, and so to the stable.

"Sure that is a bright light they are having," Dùghall muttered uneasily; for, truly, it was as though the shed were a shell filled with the fires of sunrise.

Lightly they pushed back the door. When they saw what they saw they fell upon their knees. Mary sat with her heavenly beauty upon her like sunshine on a dusk land: in her lap, a Babe, laughing sweet and low.

Never had they seen a Child so fair. He was as though wrought of light. "Who is it?" murmured Dùghall Donn, of Joseph, who stood near, with rapt eyes.

"It is the Prince of Peace."

And with that Mary smiled, and the Child slept.

"Brighid, my sister dear" — and, as she whispered this, Mary held the little one to Bride. The fair girl took the Babe in her arms, and covered it with her mantle. Therefore it is that she is known to this day as Brighde-nam-Brat, St Bride of the Mantle.

And all through that night, while the mother slept, Bride nursed the Child with tender hands and croodling crooning songs. And this was one of the songs that she sang:

Ah, Baby Christ, so dear to me,
    Sang Bridget Bride:
How sweet thou art,
My baby dear,

Heart of my heart!
Heavy her body was with thee,
Mary, beloved of One in Three,
    Sang Bridget Bride —
Mary, who bore thee, little lad
But light her heart was, light and glad
With God's love clad.

Sit on my knee,
    Sang Bridget Bride:
Sit here
O Baby dear,
Close to my heart, my heart
For I thy foster-mother am,
My helpless lamb!
O have no fear,
    Sang good St Bride.

None, none,
No fear have I
So let me cling
Close to thy side,
Whilst thou dost sing,
O Bridget Bride!

My Lord, my Prince I sing:
My baby dear, my King!
    Sang Bridget Bride.

It was on this night that, far away in Iona, the Arch-Druid Cathal died. But before the breath went from him he had his vision of joy, and his last words were:

Brighde 'dol air a glùn,
Righ nan dùl a shuidh 'na h-uchd!
(Bridget Bride upon her knee,
The King of the Elements asleep on her breast!)

At the coming of dawn Mary awoke, and took the Child. She kissed Bride upon the brows, and said this thing to her: "Brighid, my sister dear, thou shalt be known unto all time as Muime Chriosd."

IV

No sooner had Mary spoken than Bride fell into a deep sleep. So profound was this slumber that when Dùghall Donn came to see to the wayfarers, and to tell them that the milk and the porridge were ready for the breaking of their fast, he could get no word of her at all. She lay in the clean, yellow straw beneath the manger, where Mary had laid the Child. Dùghall stared in amaze. There was no sign of the mother, nor of the Babe that was the Prince of Peace, nor of the douce, quiet man that was Joseph the carpenter. As for Bride, she not only slept so sound that no word of his fell against her ears, but she gave him awe. For as he looked at her he saw that she was surrounded by a glowing light. Something in his heart shaped itself into a prayer, and he knelt beside her, sobbing low. When he rose, it was in peace. Mayhap an angel had comforted his soul in its dark shadowy haunt of his body.

It was late when Bride awoke, though she did not open her eyes, but lay dreaming. For long she thought she was in Tir-Tairngire,[62] the Land

---

62 One of the many names for the World of Faery.

of Promise, or wandering on the honey-sweet plain of Magh-Mell; for the wind of dreamland brought exquisite odours to her, and in her ears was a most marvellous sweet swinging.

All round her there was a music of rejoicing. Voices, lovelier than any she had ever heard, resounded; glad voices full of praise and joy. There was a pleasant tumult of harps and trumpets, and as from across blue hills and over calm water came the sound of the bagpipes. She listened with tears. Loud and glad were the pipes at times, full of triumph, as when the heroes of old marched with Cuchulain or went down to battle with Fionn: again, they were low and sweet, like humming of bees when the heather is heavy with the honey-ooze. The songs and wild music of the angels lulled her into peace: for a time no thought of the woman Mary came to her, nor of the Child that was her foster-child.

Suddenly it was in her mind as though the pipes played the chant that is called the "Aoibhneas a Shlighe," "the joy of his way," a march played before a bridegroom going to his bride.

Out of this glad music came a solitary voice, like a child singing on the hillside. "The way of wonder shall be thine, O Brighid Naomha!"

This was what the child-voice sang. Then it was as though all the harpers of the west were playing "air clàrsach": and the song of a multitude of voices was this:

"Blessed art thou, O Brighid, who nursed the King of the Elements in thy bosom: blessed thou, the Virgin Sister of the Virgin Mother, for unto all time thou shalt be called Muime Chriosd, the Foster-Mother of Jesus that is the Christ."

With that, Bride remembered all, and opened her eyes. Nought strange was there to see, save that she lay in the stable. Then as she noted that the gloaming had come, she wondered at the soft light that prevailed in the shed, though no lamp or candle burned there. In her ears, too, still lingered a wild and beautiful music.

It was strange. Was it all a dream, she pondered. But even as she thought thus, she saw half of her mantle lying upon the straw in the manger. Much she marvelled at this, but when she took the garment in her hand she wondered more. For though it was no more than a half of the poor mantle wherewith she had wrapped the Babe, it was all wrought with mystic gold lines and with precious stones more glorious than ever Arch Druid or Island Prince had seen. The marvel gave her awe at last, when, as she placed the garment upon her shoulder, it covered her completely.

She knew now that she had not dreamed, and that a miracle was done. So with gladness she went out of the stable, and into the inn. Dùghall

Donn was amazed when he saw her, and then rejoiced exceedingly.

"Why are you so merry, my father," she asked.

"Sure it is glad that I am. For now the folk will be laughing the wrong way. This very morning I was so pleased with the pleasure, that while the pot was boiling on the peats I went out and told every one I met that the Prince of Peace was come, and had just been born in the stable behind the 'Rest and Be Thankful.' Well, that saying was just like a weasel among the rabbits, only it was an old toothless weasel: for all Bethlehem mocked me, some with jeers, some with hard words, and some with threats. Sure, I cursed them right and left. No, not for all my cursing — and by the blood of my fathers, I spared no man among them, wishing them sword and fire, the black plague and the grey death — would they believe. So back it was that I came, and going through the inn I am come to the stable. 'Sorrow is on me like a grey mist,' said Oisìn, mourning for Oscur, and sure it was a grey mist that was on me when not a sign of man, woman, or child was to be seen, and you so sound asleep that a March gale in the Moyle wouldn't have roused you. Well, I went back, and told this thing, and all the people in Bethlehem mocked at me. And the Elders of the People came at last, and put a fine upon me: and condemned me to pay three barrels of good ale, and a sack of meal, and three thin chains of gold, each three yards long: and this for causing a false rumour, and still more for making a laughing-stock of the good folk of Bethlehem. There was a man called Murdoch-Dhu, who is the chief smith in Nazareth, and it's him I'm thinking will have laughed the Elders into doing this hard thing."

It was then that Bride was aware of a marvel upon her, for she blew an incantation off the palm of her hand, and by that frith she knew where the dues were to be found.

"By what I see in the air that is blown off the palm of my hand, father, I bid you go into the cellar of the inn. There you will find three barrels full of good ale, and beside them a sack of meal, and the sack is tied with three chains of gold, each three yards long."

But while Dùhall Donn went away rejoicing, and found that which Bride had foretold, she passed out into the street. None saw her in the gloaming, or as she went towards the Gate of the East. When she passed by the Lazar-house she took her mantle off her back and laid it in the place of offerings. All the jewels and fine gold passed into invisible birds with healing wings: and these birds flew about the heads of the sick all night, so that at dawn every one arose, with no ill upon him, and went on his way rejoicing. As each went out of Bethlehem that morning of the mornings he found a clean white robe and new sandals at the first mile; and, at the second, food and cool water; and, at the third, a gold piece and a staff.

The guard that was at the Eastern Gate did not hail Bride. All the gaze of him was upon a company of strange men, shepherd-kings, who said they had come out of the East led by a star. They carried rare gifts with them when they first came to Bethlehem: but no man knew whence they came, what they wanted, or whither they went.

For a time Bride walked along the road that leads to Nazareth. There was fear in her gentle heart when she heard the howling of hyenas down in the dark hollows, and she was glad when the moon came out and shone quietly upon her.

In the moonlight she saw that there were steps in the dew before her. She could see the black print of feet in the silver sheen on the wet grass, for it was on a grassy hill that she now walked, though a day ago every leaf and sheath there had lain brown and withered, The footprints she followed were those of a woman and of a child.

All night through she tracked those wandering feet in the dew. They were always fresh before her, and led her away from the villages, and also where no wild beasts prowled through the gloom. There was no weariness upon her, though often she wondered when she should see the fair wondrous face she sought. Behind her also were footsteps in the dew, though she knew nothing of them. They were those of the Following Love. And this was the Lorgadh-Brighde of which men speak to this day: the Quest of the holy St. Bride.

All night she walked; now upon the high slopes of a hill. Never once did she have a glimpse of any figure in the moonlight, though the steps in the dew before her were newly made, and none lay in the glisten a short way ahead.

Suddenly she stopped. There were no more footprints. Eagerly she looked before her. On a hill beyond the valley beneath her she saw the gleaming of yellow stars. These were the lights of a city. "Behold, it is Jerusalem," she murmured, awe-struck, for she had never seen the great town.

Sweet was the breath of the wind that stirred among the olives on the mount where she stood. It had the smell of heather, and she could hear the rustle of it among the bracken on a hill close by.

"Truly, this must be the Mount of Olives," she whispered, "The Mount of which I have heard my father speak, and that must be the hill called Calvary."

But even as she gazed marvelling, she sighed with new wonder; for now she saw that the yellow stars were as the twinkling of the fires of the sun along the crest of a hill that is set in the east. There was a living joy in the dawntide. In her ears was a sweet sound of the bleating of ewes and lambs. From the hollows in the shadows came the swift singing rush of the flowing tide. Faint cries of the herring gulls filled the air; from the weedy boulders by the sea the skuas called wailingly.

Bewildered, she stood intent. If only she could see the footprints again, she thought. Whither should she turn, whither go? At her feet was a yellow flower. She stooped and plucked it.

"Tell me, O little sun-flower, which way shall I be going?" and as she spoke a small golden bee flew up from the heart of it, and up the hill to the left of her. So it is that from that day the dandelion is called am-Bèarnàn-Bhrighde.

Still she hesitated. Then a sea-bird flew by her with a loud whistling cry.

"Tell me, O eisireùn," she called, "which way shall I be going?"

And at this the eisireùn[63] swerved in its flight, and followed the golden bee, crying, "This way, O Bride, Bride, Bride, Bride, Bri-i-i-ide!" So it is that from that day the oyster catcher has been called the Gille-Bhrighde, the Servant of St. Bridget.

Then it was that Bride said this sian:

Dia romham;
Moire am dheaghuidh;
'S am Mac a thug Righ nan Dul!
Mis' air do shlios, a Dhia,
Is Dia ma'm luirg.
Mac' 'oire, a's Righ nan Dul,
A shoillseachadh gach ni dheth so,
Le a ghras, mu'm choinneamh.

God before me
The Virgin Mary after me;
And the Son sent by the King of the Elements.
I am to windward of thee, O God!
And God on my footsteps.
May the Son of Mary, King of the Elements,
Reveal the meaning of each of these things
Before me, through His grace.

---

63 The oyster-catcher.

And as she ended she saw before her two quicken-trees, of which the boughs were inter-wrought so that they made an arch. Deep in the green foliage was a white merle that sang a wondrous sweet song. Above it the small branches were twisted into the shape of a wreath or crown, lovely with the sunlit rowan-clusters, from whose scarlet berries red drops as of blood fell.

Before her flew a white dove, all aglow as with golden light. She followed, and passed beneath the quicken arch.

Sweet was the song of the merle, that was then no more; sweet the green shadow of the rowans, that now grew straight as young pines. Sweet the far song in the sky, where the white dove flew against the sun.

Bride looked, and her eyes were glad. Bonnie the blooming of the heather on the slopes of Dun-I. Iona lay green and gold, isled in her blue waters. From the sheiling of Dùvach, her father, rose a thin column of pale blue smoke. The collies, seeing her, barked loudly with welcoming joy.

The bleating of the sheep, the lowing of the kye, the breath of the salt wind from the open sea beyond, the song of the flowing tide in the Sound beneath: dear the homing.

With a strange light in her eyes she moved down through the heather and among the green bracken : white, wonderful, fair to see.

The Fisher of Men

HEN old Sheen nic Lèoid came back to the croft, after she had been to the burn at the edge of the green airidh, where she had washed the *claar* that was for the potatoes at the peeling, she sat down before the peats.

She was white with years. The mountain wind was chill, too, for all that the sun had shone throughout the midsummer day. It was well to sit before the peat-fire.

The croft was on the slope of a mountain, and had the south upon it. North, south, east, and west, other great slopes reached upward like hollow green waves frozen into silence by the very wind that curved them so, and freaked their crests into peaks and jagged pinnacles. Stillness was in that place for ever and ever. What though the Gorromalt Water foamed down Ben Nair, where the croft was, and made a hoarse voice for aye surrendering sound to silence? What though at times the stones fell from the ridges of Ben Chaisteal and Maolmòr, and clattered down the barren declivities till they were slung in the tangled meshes of whin and juniper? What though on stormy dawns the eagle screamed as he fought against the wind that graved a thin line upon the aged front of Ben Mulad, where his eyrie was: or that the kestrel cried above the rabbit-burrows in the strath: or that the hill-fox barked, or that the curlew wailed, or that the scattered sheep made an endless mournful crying? What were these but the ministers of silence?

There was no blue smoke in the strath except from the one turf cot. In the hidden valley beyond Ben Nair there was a hamlet, and nigh upon three-score folk lived there; but that was over three miles away. Sheen Macleod was alone in that solitary place, save for her son Alasdair Mòr Òg. "Young Alasdair" he was still, though the grey feet of fifty years had marked his hair. Alasdair Òg he was while Alasdair Ruadh mac Chalum mhic Lèoid, that was his father, lived. But when Alasdair Ruadh changed, and Sheen was left a mourning woman, he that was their son was Alasdair Òg still.

She had sore weariness that day. For all that, it was not the weight of the burden that made her go in and out of the afternoon sun and sit by the red glow of the peats, brooding deep.

When, nigh upon an hour later, Alasdair came up the slope, and led the kye to the byre, she did not hear him: nor had she sight of him, when his shadow flickered in before him and lay along the floor.

"Poor old woman," he said to himself, bending his head because of the big height that was his, and he there so heavy and strong, and tender, too, for all the tangled black beard and the wild hill-eyes that looked out under bristling grey-black eyebrows.

"Poor old woman, and she with the tired heart that she has. Ay, ay, for sure the weeks lap up her shadow, as the sayin' is. She will be thinking of him that is gone. Ay, or maybe the old thoughts of her are goin' back on their own steps, down this glen an' over that hill an' away beyont that strath, an' this corrie an' that moor. Well, well, it is a good love, that of the mother. Sure a bitter pain it will be to me when there's no old grey hair there to stroke. It's quiet here, terrible quiet, God knows, to Himself be the blessin' for this an' for that; but when she has the white sleep at last, then it'll be a sore day for me, an' one that I will not be able to bear to hear the sheep callin', callin', callin' through the rain on the hills here, and Gorromalt Water an' no other voice to be with me on that day of the days.

She heard a faint sigh, and stirred a moment, but did not look round.

"Muim'-à-ghraidh,[64] is it tired you are, and this so fine a time, too?"

With a quick gesture, the old woman glanced at him.

"Ah, child, is that you indeed? Well, I am glad of that, for I have the trouble again."

"What trouble, Muim' ghaolaiche?"[65]

But the old woman did not answer. Wearily she turned her face to the peat-glow again.

Alasdair seated himself on the big wooden chair to her right. For a time he stayed silent thus, staring into the red heart of the peats. What was the gloom upon the old heart that he loved? What trouble was it?

At last he rose and put meal and water into the iron pot, and stirred the porridge while it seethed and sputtered. Then he poured boiling water upon the tea in the brown jenny, and put the new bread and the sweet-milk scones on the rude deal board that was the table.

"Come, dear tired old heart," he said, "and let us give thanks to the Being."

"Blessings and thanks," she said, and turned round.

---

64 Muim'-à-ghraidh - a term of endearment, literally "foster mother of love." The fostering of children with other clans and families was a common practice in the Highlands and Islands. The bond a child had with its foster parents was considered stronger than that with its biological parents.
65 Muim' ghaolaiche - term of endearment, literally 'darling mother.'

Alasdair poured out the porridge, and watched the steam rise. Then he sat down, with a knife in one hand and the brown-white loaf in the other.

"O God," he said, in the low voice he had in the kirk when the Bread and Wine were given — "O God, be giving us now thy blessing, and have the thanks. And give us peace."

Peace there was in the sorrowful old eyes of the mother. The two ate in silence. The big clock that was by the bed tick-tacked, tick-tacked. A faint sputtering came out of a peat that had bog-gas in it. Shadows moved in the silence, and met and whispered and moved into deep, warm darkness. There was peace.

There was still a red flush above the hills in the west when the mother and son sat in the ingle again.

"What is it, mother-my-heart?" Alasdair asked at last, putting his great red hand upon the woman's knee.

She looked at him for a moment. When she spoke she turned away her gaze again, "Foxes have holes, and the fowls of the air have their places of rest, but the Son of Man hath not where to lay his head."

"And what then, dear? Sure, it is the deep meaning you have in that grey old head that I'm loving so."

"Ay, lennav-aghray, there is meaning to my words. It is old I am, and the hour of my hours is near. I heard a voice outside the window last night. It is a voice I will not be hearing, no, not for seventy years. It was cradle-sweet, it was."

She paused, and there was silence for a time.

"Well, dear," she began again, wearily, and in a low, weak voice, "it is more tired and more tired I am every day now this last month. Two Sabbaths ago I woke, and there were bells in the air: and you are for knowing well, Alasdair, that no kirk-bells ever rang in Strath-Nair. At edge o' dark on Friday, and by the same token the thirteenth day it was, I fell asleep, and dreamed the moles were on my breast, and that the roots of the white daisies were in the hollows where the eyes were that loved you, Alasdair, my son."

The man looked at her with troubled gaze. No words would come. Of what avail to speak when there is nothing to be said? God sends the gloom upon the cloud, and there is rain: God sends the gloom upon the hill, and there is mist: God sends the gloom upon the sun, and there is winter. It is God, too, sends the gloom upon the soul, and there is change. The swallow knows when to lift up her wing overagainst the shadow that creeps out of the north: the wild swan knows when the smell of snow is behind the sun: the salmon, lone in the brown pool among the hills, hears the deep sea, and his tongue pants for salt, and his fins quiver, and he knows that his time is come, and that the sea calls. The doe knows when the fawn hath not yet quaked in her belly: is not the violet more deep in the shadowy dewy eyes? The woman knows when the babe hath not yet stirred a little hand: is not the wild-rose on her cheek more often seen, and are not the shy tears moist on quiet hands in the dusk? How, then, shall the soul not know when the change is nigh at last? Is it a less thing than a reed, which sees the yellow birch-gold adrift on the lake, and the gown of the heather grow russet when the purple has passed into the sky, and the white bog-down wave grey and tattered where the loneroid grows dark and pungent — which sees, and knows that the breath of the Death-Weaver at the Pole is fast faring along the frozen norland peaks. It is more than a reed, it is more than a wild doe on the hills, it is more than a swallow lifting her wing against the coming of the shadow, it is more than a swan drunken with the savour of the blue wine of the waves when the green Arctic lawns are white and still. It is more than these, which has the Son of God for brother, and is clothed with light. God doth not extinguish at the dark tomb what he hath litten in the dark womb.

Who shall say that the soul knows not when the bird is aweary of the nest, and the nest is aweary of the wind? Who shall say that all portents are vain imaginings? A whirling straw upon the road is but a whirling straw: Yet the wind is upon the cheek almost ere it is gone.

It was not for Alasdair Òg, then, to put a word upon the saying of the woman that was his mother, and was age-white, and could see with the seeing of old wise eyes.

So all that was upon his lips was a sigh, and the poor prayer that is only a breath out of the heart.

"You will be telling me, grey sweetheart," he said lovingly, at last — "You will be telling me what was behind the word that you said: that about the foxes that have holes for the hiding, poor beasts, and the birdeens wi' their nests, though the Son o' Man hath not where to lay his head?"

"Ay, Alasdair, my son that I bore long syne an' that I'm leaving soon, I will be for telling you that thing, an' now too, for I am knowing what is in the dark this night of the nights."

Old Sheen put her head back wearily on the chair, and let her hands lie, long and white, palm-downward upon her knees. The peat-glow warmed the dull grey that lurked under her closed eyes and about her mouth, and in the furrowed cheeks. Alasdair moved nearer and took her right hand in his, where it lay like a tired sheep between two scarped rocks. Gently he smoothed her hand, and wondered why so frail and slight a creature as this small old wizened woman could have mothered a great swarthy man like himself — he a man now, with his two score and ten years, and yet but a boy there at the dear side of her.

"It was this way, Alasdair-mochree," she went on in her low thin voice — like a wind-worn leaf, the man that was her son thought. "It was this way. I went down to the burn to wash the *claar*, and when I was there I saw a wounded fawn in the bracken. The big sad eyes of it were like those of Maisie, poor lass, when she had the birthing that was her going-call. I went through the bracken, and down by the Gorromalt, and into the Shadowy Glen.

"And when I was there, and standing by the running water, I saw a man by the stream-side. He was tall, but spare and weary: and the clothes upon him were poor and worn. He had sorrow. When he lifted his head at me, I saw the tears. Dark, wonderful, sweet eyes they were. His face was pale. It was not the face of a man of the hills. There was no red in it, and the eyes looked in upon themselves. He was a fair man, with the white hands that a woman has, a woman like the Bantighearna of Glenchaisteal over yonder. His voice, too, was a voice like that: in the softness, and the sweet, quiet sorrow, I am meaning.

"The word that I gave him was in the English: for I thought he was like a man out of Sasunn, or of the southlands somewhere. But he answered me in the Gaelic: sweet, good Gaelic like that of the Bioball[66] over there, to Himself be the praise.

"'And is it the way down the Strath you are seeking,' I asked: 'and will you not be coming up to the house yonder, poor cot though it is, and have a sup of milk, and a rest if it's weary you are?'

"'You are having my thanks for that,' he said, 'and it is as though I had both the good rest and the cool sweet drink. But I am following the flowing water here.'

"'Is it for the fishing?' I asked.

"'I am a Fisher,' he said, and the voice of him was low and sad.

"He had no hat on his head, and the light that streamed through a rowan-tree was in his long hair. He had the pity of the poor in his sorrowful grey eyes.

"'And will you not sleep with us?' I asked again: 'that is, if you have

66 The Bible.

no place to go to, and are a stranger in this country, as I am thinking you are; for I have never had sight of you in the home-straths before.'

"'I am a stranger,' he said, 'and I have no home, and my father's house is a great way off.'

"'Do not tell me, poor man,' I said gently, for fear of the pain, 'do not tell me if you would fain not; but it is glad I will be if you will give me the name you have.'

"'My name is Mac-an-t'-Saoir,'[67] he answered with the quiet deep gaze that was his. And with that he bowed his head, and went on his way, brooding deep.

"Well, it was with a heavy heart I turned, and went back through the bracken. A heavy heart, for sure, and yet, oh peace too, cool dews of peace. And the fawn was there: healed, Alasdair, healed, and whinny-bleating for its doe, that stood on a rock wi' lifted hoof an' stared down the glen to where the Fisher was.

"When I was at the burnside, a woman came down the brae. She was fair to see, but the tears were upon her.

"'Oh,' she cried, 'have you seen a man going this way?'

"'Ay, for sure,' I answered, 'but what man would he be?'

"'He is called Mac-an-t'-Saoir.'

"'Well, there are many men that are called Son of the Carpenter. What will his own name be?'

"'Iosa,'[68] she said.

"And when I looked at her, she was weaving the wavy branches of a thorn near by, and sobbing low and it was like a wreath or crown that she made.

"'And who will you be, poor woman?' I asked.

"'O my Son, my Son,' she said, and put her apron over her head and went down into the Shadowy Glen, she weeping sore, too, at that, poor woman.

"So now, Alasdair, my son, tell me what thought you have about this thing that I have told you. For I know well whom I met on the brae there, and who the Fisher was. And when I was at the peats here once more I sat down, and my mind sank into myself. And it is knowing the knowledge I am."

"Well, well, dear, it is sore tired you are. Have rest now. But sure there are many men called Macintyre."

---

67 Mac-an-t'-Saoir - Gaelic = 'Son of the Carpenter' but can also be translated as 'Son of peace.' In English this name is given as MacIntyre.
68 Iosa is Gaelic for Jesus.

"Ay, an' what Gael that you know will be for giving you his surname like that."

Alasdair had no word for that. He rose to put some more peats on the fire. When he had done this, he gave a cry.

The whiteness that was on the mother's hair was now in the face. There was no blood there, or in the drawn lips. The light in the old, dim eyes was like water after frost.

He took her hand in his. Clay-cold it was. He let it go, and it fell straight by the chair, stiff as the cromak he carried when he was with the sheep.

"Oh my God and my God," he whispered white with the awe, and the bitter cruel pain.

Then it was that he heard a knocking at the door.

"Who is there?" he cried hoarsely.

"Open, and let me in." It was a low, sweet voice, but was that grey hour the time for a welcome?

"Go, but go in peace, whoever you are. There is death here."

"Open, and let me in."

At that, Alasdair, shaking like a reed in the wind, unclasped the latch. A tall fair man, ill-clad and weary, pale, too, and with dreaming eyes, came in.

"Beannachd Dhe an Tigh," he said, "God's blessing on this house, and on all here."

"The same upon yourself," Alasdair said, with the weary pain in his voice. "And who will you be? and forgive the asking."

"I am called Mac-an-t'-Saoir, and Iosa is the name I bear — Jesus, the Son of the Carpenter."

"It is a good name. And is it good you are seeking this night?"

"I am a Fisher."

"Well, that's here an' that's there. But will you go to the Strath over the hill, and tell the good man that is there, the minister, Lachlan MacLachlan, that old Sheen nic Lèoid, wife of Alasdair Ruadh, is dead."

"I know that, Alasdair Òg."

"And how will you be knowing that, and my name too, you that are called Macintyre?"

"I met the white soul of Sheen as it went down by the Shadowy Glen a brief while ago. She was singing a glad song, she was. She had green youth in her eyes. And a man was holding her by the hand. It was Alasdair Ruadh."

At that Alasdair fell on his knees. When he looked up there was no one there. Through the darkness outside the door, he saw a star shining white, and leaping like a pulse.

It was three days after that day of shadow that Sheen Macleod was put under the green turf.

On each night, Alasdair Òg walked in the Shadowy Glen, and there he saw a man fishing, though ever afar off. Stooping he was, always, and like a shadow at times. But he was the man that was called Iosa Mac-an-t'-Saoir — Jesus, the Son of the Carpenter.

And on the night of the earthing he saw the Fisher close by.

"Lord God," he said, with the hush on his voice, and deep awe in his wondering eyes: "Lord God!"

And the Man looked at him.

"Night and day, Alasdair MacAlasdair," he said, "night and day I fish in the waters of the world. And these waters are the waters of grief, and the waters of sorrow, and the waters of despair. And it is the souls of the living I fish for. And lo, I say this thing unto you, for you shall not see me again: *Go in peace.* Go in peace, good soul of a poor man, for thou hast seen the Fisher of Men."

The Last Supper

THE last time that the Fisher of Men was seen in Strath-Nair was not of Alasdair Macleod but of the little child, Art Macarthur, him that was born of the woman Mary Gilchrist, that had known the sorrow of women. He was a little child, indeed, when, because of his loneliness and having lost his way, he lay sobbing among the bracken by the streamside in the Shadowy Glen.

When he was a man, and had reached the gloaming of his years, he was loved of men and women, for his songs are many and sweet, and his heart was true, and he was a good man and had no evil against any one.

It is he who saw the Fisher of Men when he was but a little lad: and some say that it was on the eve of the day that Alasdair Òg died, though of this I know nothing. And what he saw, and what he heard, was a moon-beam that fell into the dark sea of his mind, and sank therein, and filled it with light for all the days of his life. A moonlit mind was that of Art Macarthur: him that is known best as Ian Mòr, Ian Mòr of the Hills, though why he took the name of Ian Cameron is known to none now but one person, and that need not be for the telling here. He had music always in his mind. I asked him once why he heard what so few heard, but he smiled and said only: "When the heart is full of love, cool dews of peace rise from it and fall upon the mind: and that is when the song of joy is heard."

It must have been because of this shining of his soul that some who loved him thought of him as one illumined. His mind was a shell that held the haunting echo of the deep seas: and to know him was to catch a breath of the infinite ocean of wonder and mystery and beauty of which he was the quiet oracle. He has peace now, where he lies under the heather upon a hillside far away: but the Fisher of Men will send him hitherward again, to put a light upon the wave and a gleam upon the brown earth.

I will tell this sgeul[69] as Ian Mòr that was the little child Art Macarthur, told it to me.

Often and often it is to me all as a dream that comes unawares. Often and often have I striven to see into the green glens of the mind whence it comes, and whither, in a flash, in a rainbow gleam, it vanishes. When I seek to draw close to it, to know whether it is a winged glory out of the

---

69 A narrated story.

soul, or was indeed a thing that happened to me in my tender years, lo —
it is a dawn drowned in day, a star lost in the sun, the falling of dew.

But I will not be forgetting: no, never: no, not till the silence of the
grass is over my eyes: I will not be forgetting that gloaming.

Bitter tears are those that children have. All that we say with vain
words is said by them in this welling spray of pain. I had the sorrow that
day. Strange hostilities lurked in the familiar bracken. The soughing of
the wind among the trees, the wash of the brown water by my side, that
had been companionable, were voices of awe. The quiet light upon the
grass flamed.

The fierce people that lurked in shadow had eyes for my helplessness.
When the dark came I thought I should be dead, devoured of I knew not
what wild creature. Would mother never come, never come with saving
arms, with eyes like soft candles of home?

Then my sobs grew still, for I heard a step. With dread upon me, poor
wee lad that I was, I looked to see who came out of the wilderness. It
was a man, tall and thin and worn, with long hair hanging adown his
face. Pale he was as a moonlit cot on the dark moor, and his voice was
low and sweet. When I saw his eyes I had no fear upon me at all. I saw
the mother-look in the grey shadow of them.

"And is that you, Art lennavan-mo?"[70] he said, as he stooped and
lifted me. I had no fear. The wet was out of my eyes.

"What is it you will be listening to now, my little lad?" he whispered,
as he saw me lean, intent, to catch I know not what.

"Sure," I said, "I am not for knowing: but I thought I heard a music
away down there in the wood." I heard it, for sure. It was a wondrous
sweet air, as of one playing the *feadan* in a dream. Callum Dall,[71] the
piper, could give no rarer music than that was; and Callum was a seventh
son, and was born in the moonshine.

"Will you come with me this night of the nights, little Art?" the man
asked me, with his lips touching my brow and giving me rest.

"That I will indeed and indeed," I said.

And then I fell asleep.

When I awoke we were in the huntsman's booth, that is at the far end
of the Shadowy Glen.

There was a long rough-hewn table in it, and I stared when I saw
bowls and a great jug of milk and a plate heaped with oat-cakes, and
beside it a brown loaf of rye-bread.

---

70 A term of endearment.
71 Blind Malcolm.

"Little Art," said he who carried me, "are you for knowing now who I am?"

"You are a prince, I'm thinking," was the shy word that came to my mouth.

"Sure, lennav-aghrày, that is so. It is called the Prince of Peace I am."

"And who is to be eating all this?" I asked.

"This is the last supper," the prince said, so low that I could scarce hear; and it seemed to me that he whispered, "For I die daily, and ever ere I die the Twelve break bread with me." It was then I saw that there were six bowls of porridge on the one side and six on the other.

"What is your name, O prince?"

"Iosa."

"And will you have no other name than that?"

"I am called Iosa mac Dhe."[72]

"And is it living in this house you are?"

"Ay. But Art, my little lad, I will kiss your eyes, and you shall see who sup with me."

And with that the prince that was called Iosa kissed me on the eyes, and I saw.

"You will never be quite blind again," he whispered, and that is why all the long years of my years I have been glad in my soul.

What I saw was a thing strange and wonderful. Twelve men sat at that table, and all had eyes of love upon Iosa. But they were not like any men I had ever seen. Tall and fair and terrible they were, like morning in a desert place; all save one, who was dark, and had a shadow upon him and in his wild eyes. It seemed to me that each was clad in radiant mist. The eyes of them were as stars through that mist. And each, before he broke bread, or put spoon to the porridge that was in the bowl before him, laid down upon the table three shuttles. Long I looked upon that company, but Iosa held me in his arms, and I had no fear.

"Who are these men?" he asked me.

"The Sons of God," I said, I not knowing what I said, for it was but a child I was.

He smiled at that. "Behold," he spoke to the twelve men who sat at the table, "behold the little one is wiser than the wisest of ye." At that all smiled with the gladness and the joy, save one; him that was in the shadow. He looked at me, and I remembered two black lonely tarns upon the hillside, black with the terror because of the kelpie and the drowner.

"Who are these men?" I whispered, with the tremor on me that was

---

72 Jesus Son of God.

come of the awe I had.

"They are the Twelve Weavers, Art, my little child."

"And what is their weaving?"

"They weave for my Father, whose web I am."

At that I looked upon the prince, but I could see no web. "Are you not Iosa the Prince?"

"I am the Web of Life, Art lennavan-mo."

"And what are the three shuttles that are beside each Weaver?"

I know now that when I turned my child's eyes upon these shuttles I saw that they were alive and wonderful, and never the same to the seeing.

"They are called *Beauty* and *Wonder* and *Mystery*."

And with that Iosa mac Dhe sat down and talked with the Twelve. All were passing fair, save him who looked sidelong out of dark eyes. I thought each, as I looked at him, more beautiful than any of his fellows but most I loved to look at the twain who sat on either side of Iosa.

"He will be a Dreamer among men," said the prince; "so tell him who ye are."

Then he who was on the right turned his eyes upon me. I leaned to him, laughing low with the glad pleasure I had because of his eyes and shining hair, and the flame as of the blue sky that was his robe. "I am the Weaver of Joy," he said. And with that he took his three shuttles that were called Beauty and Wonder and Mystery, and he wove an immortal shape, and it went forth of the room and out into the green world, singing a rapturous sweet song.

Then he that was upon the left of Iosa the Life looked at me, and my heart leaped. He, too, had shining hair, but I could not tell the colour of his eyes for the glory that was in them. "I am the Weaver of Love," he said, "and I sit next the heart of Iosa." And with that he took his three shuttles that were called Beauty and Wonder and Mystery and he wove an immortal shape, and it went forth of the room and into the green world singing a rapturous sweet song.

Even then, child as I was, I wished to look on no other. None could be so passing fair, I thought, as the Weaver of Joy and the Weaver of Love.

But a wondrous sweet voice sang in my ears, and a cool, soft hand laid itself upon my head, and the beautiful lordly one who had spoken said, "I am the Weaver of Death," and the lovely whispering one who had lulled me with rest said, "I am the Weaver of Sleep." And each wove with the shuttles of Beauty and Wonder and Mystery, and I knew not which was the more fair, and Death seemed to me as Love, and in the eyes of Dream I saw Joy.

My gaze was still upon the fair wonderful shapes that went forth from these twain — from the Weaver of Sleep, an immortal shape of star-eyed Silence, and from the Weaver of Death a lovely Dusk with a heart of hidden flame — when I heard the voice of two others of the Twelve. They were like the laughter of the wind in the corn, and like the golden fire upon that corn. And the one said, "I am the Weaver of Passion," and when he spoke I thought that he was both Love and Joy, and Death and Life, and I put out my hands. "It is Strength I give," he said, and he took and kissed me. Then, while Iosa took me again upon his knee, I saw the Weaver of Passion turn to the white glory beside him, him that Iosa whispered to me was the secret of the world, and that was called "The Weaver of Youth." I know not whence nor how it came, but there was a singing of skiey bird, when these twain took the shuttles of Beauty and Wonder and Mystery, and wove each an immortal shape, and bade it go forth out of the room into the green world, to sing there for ever and ever in the ears of man a rapturous sweet song.

"O Iosa," I cried, "are these all thy brethren? for each is fair as thee, and all have lit their eyes at the white fire I see now in thy heart."

But, before he spake, the room was filled with music. I trembled with the joy, and in my ears it has lingered ever, nor shall ever go. Then I saw that it was the breathing of the seventh and eighth, of the ninth and the tenth of those star-eyed ministers of Iosa whom he called the Twelve: and the names of them were the Weaver of Laughter, the Weaver of Tears, the Weaver of Prayer, and the Weaver of Peace. Each rose and kissed me there.

"We shall be with you to the end, little Art," they said: and I took hold of the hand of one, and cried, "O beautiful one, be likewise with the woman my mother," and there came back to me the whisper of the Weaver of Tears: "I will, unto the end."

Then, wonderingly, I watched him likewise take the shuttles that were ever the same and yet never the same, and weave an immortal shape. And when this Soul of Tears went forth of the room, I thought it was my mother's voice singing that rapturous sweet song, and I cried out to it. The fair immortal turned and waved to me. "I shall never be far from thee, little Art," it sighed, like summer rain falling on leaves: "but I go now to my home in the heart of women."

There were now but two out of the Twelve. Oh the gladness and the joy when I looked at him who had his eyes fixed on the face of Iosa that was the Life! He lifted the three shuttles of Beauty and Wonder and Mystery, and he wove a Mist of Rainbows in that room; and in the glory I saw that even the dark twelfth one lifted up his eyes and smiled.

"O what will the name of you be?" I cried, straining my arms to the beautiful lordly one.

But he did not hear, for he wrought Rainbow after Rainbow out of the mist of glory that he made, and sent each out into the green world, to be for ever before the eyes of men.

"He is the Weaver of Hope," whispered Iosa mac Dhe; "and he is the soul of each that is here."

Then I turned to the twelfth, and said "Who art thou, O lordly one with the shadow in the eyes?"

But he answered not, and there was silence in the room. And all there, from the Weaver of Joy to the Weaver of Peace, looked down, and said nought. Only the Weaver of Hope wrought a rainbow, and it drifted into the heart of the lonely Weaver that was twelfth.

"And who will this man be, O Iosa mac Dhe?" I whispered.

"Answer the little child," said Iosa, and his voice was sad.

Then the Weaver answered: "I am the Weaver of Glory — ," he began, but Iosa looked at him, and he said no more.

"Art, little lad," said the Prince of Peace, "he is the one who betrayeth me for ever. He is Judas, the Weaver of Fear."

And at that the sorrowful shadow-eyed man that was the twelfth took up the three shuttles that were before him.

"And what are these, O Judas?" I cried eagerly, for I saw that they were black.

When he answered not, one of the Twelve leaned forward and looked at him. It was the Weaver of Death who did this thing.

"The three shuttles of Judas the Fear-Weaver, O little Art," said the Weaver of Death, "are called Mystery, and Despair, and the Grave."

And with that Judas rose and left the room. But the shape that he had woven went forth with him as his shadow: and each fared out into the dim world, and the Shadow entered into the minds and into the hearts of men, and betrayed Iosa that was the Prince of Peace.

Thereupon, Iosa rose and took me by the hand, and led me out of that room. When, once, I looked back I saw none of the Twelve save only the Weaver of Hope, and he sat singing a wild sweet song that he had learned of the Weaver of Joy, sat singing amid a mist of rainbows and weaving a radiant glory that was dazzling as the sun.

And at that I woke, and was against my mother's heart, and she with the tears upon me, and her lips moving in a prayer.

The Man on the Moor

ON the mainland of Ardnamurchan there is a house by the shore, built of grey stones, against which the yellow flags and gallingale run up like surf, and behind which a long slope of bracken looks like the green sea beyond rocks when the wind is heavy on it, though with no more to see than a myriad wrinkling. There is no other house near, nor boat on the shore; and I saw or heard never a sheep, but the few thin beasts of Anndra MacCaskill browsing the salt grass by the long, broken, wandering dune where the rocks lie in a heavy jumble. It is a desolate place. I saw no birds in all the bramble, never a finch in the undershaws, nor shilfa in the tansy-wastes. Even on the shore the white wings of the gulls and terns were not catching the light: I saw nothing but three birds, a dotterel flying and wailing, a scart black-green on a weedy rock, and a grey skua hawking the sighing suck of the ebb. The light was that of storm, though the twilight was already gathering in every corrie and hollow: and in October the day falls soon.

The sea south was a dark, tossing waste, with long, irregular dykes of foam that ran and merged when you looked at them, but were like broken walls on fields of black rye when you saw them only through the side of the eyes. South-west and west, long splashes of red flame ruddied the wild sea and brought the black to blue. It was not this year, nor last, nor the year before, that I heard that of which I now write: but I remember it all as though it were of yesterday. A bit of loneroid, gale or bog-myrtle as it is called in the south, wet, with the light green and the dark green on the same stem, will often, in a moment, bring Tighnaclachan[73] before me, so that I see just that desolate shore and no other shore, and hear the scattered lamenting of the few sheep yonder, and see that scart on the weedy rock plucking at its black-green feathers, or that grey skua with its melancholy cry hawking the sighing shallows of the ebb beyond the ledges, to this side of the house itself, half windowless yet it may be, and with the byre-doors open and falling back and rotting.

It was a matter of no moment that took me there: partly to meet one coming another way, partly to see Dionaid Maclure, a frail old woman who kept the place for Neil McNeil, her brother. I had walked some three miles, and was tired; not with the distance, but with a something

---

73 House of the Stones.

in the wind, and perhaps from the singular gloom of the place at that hour in that grey loneliness, caught between deserted lands and a sea never quiet, an angry troubled waste, perpetually lamenting, continually shaken with fierce wraths.

As I came close to Tighnaclachan, I saw no smoke above the boulder-held thatch. The ragged pony I had seen there before was not in the airidh beyond. It was with relief I heard the clucking of a hen somewhere. The only other living thing I saw was a magpie by a pool of rain-water, stalking with sharp cries of anger its own restless image.

Yet it was here that, before I heard the tale Neil McNeil told me, I heard words from old Janet which put a beauty into that lonely unhomely place on me, then and for always. I forget what led to the beauty in the old heart, and stirred it: but I remember the shape it took on the old lips.

She had given me tea, and we had sat awhile in the brown dusk by the comforting red glow of the peats, and then I told her something, I forget what — perhaps of someone we knew, perhaps a bit of a tale, or a song maybe, likely the sigh of a ballad or song — when she leaned to me and said, "It's a blessing they are, a healing and a blessing: ay, so they are, the moonlight and the dew. When we're young, summer's sweet wi' them: when we're old, they're in the heart still. It's the song left, the memory o' the song, a sweet air, when the bird's flown for aye. Ay, my dear, an' there's more than that to be said. God made the sun an' the day: the Holy Spirit, the night an' the stars; but Christ made the moonlight an' the dew."

She was tender and sweet, old Dionaid: fair in life and fair in death. Strange that the beauty of a single thought can thenceforth clothe the desolation in loveliness, and change the grey air and the grey sea and the grey face of a seared land into a sanctuary of peace, as though unknown birds builded there, doves of the spirit. I remember, once, on the waste of Subasio behind Assisi, that someone near me said the barrenness was terrible, more lifeless and sad than any other solitude. To me, at that moment, as it happened, this was not so: the hill glowed with the divine light, that came, not from the east welling it or the west gathering it, but from the immortal life of the heart of St. Francis — and a storm of white doves rose with flashing wings, so that I was dazzled: and only when I saw that they were not there did I know I had seen the prayers and joys of a multitude of hearts, children of him to whom the wind was "brother" and the grass "sister."

But now I must go back to that of which I meant to write. I have given the lonely setting of the place where, when we came in at day fall for the porridge, Neil McNeil — a tired man, tall, gaunt, grey-black, with cold blue eyes like the solander's — told me of the man MacRoban, or MacRobany.

There is no need to tell of what kept me there till long after dark was come, with the flowing tide making so heavy a noise among the loose rock that at times our words sounded hollow and far away: nor of all that we three, waiting there, talked nor what dreams and thoughts came into that flame-lit dark room in the desolate house by the sea. When Neil spoke once, unquestioned, it was after a long silence, when we were unconsciously listening to the loud *tick-tack, tick-tack* of the great wall clock as though we were eager almost to a strained anxiety to hear urgent tidings, some news expected or feared, or half-guessed, coming mysteriously, on quivering lips: with a foreign sound, broken, meshed in obscurity — hearing at the same time the gathering clamour in the sea's voice, the hoarse scroach-an-scroach of the flung surge on the dragged reluctant beach, and the loud demanding cry of the wind behind the confused and trampling noise of the tide, that by the sound was in the house itself and away inland.

"I can't tell you much about what you asked," he began slowly. "There isn't much to tell. You've been in or near that place away in the Italian country, and may know more than I know. It was this way, then, since I must tell you the little I know. You thought, that day we talked about it, the name was MacCroban. But I'm not knowing if there's any such name: any way it is not the man's name, the man I'm thinking of, the man I have in my mind. His name was MacRóban, or MacRóbany."

"Was ?"

"Ay."

Tick-tack ... tick-tack ... and the loud anger of the sea at the door. I was glad when Neil went on.

"He had no home. I met him a long way inland — on the Moss of Achnacree, beyond Morven, across the Sound of Lorne. It was at the edge o' dark, and he was lying with his head on a stone. I stooped and spoke to him. 'Poor man, have you the heavy sickness on you?' I asked, and again in the English, when he did not answer.

"'It is dying you are,' I said. 'I fear, poor man, it is near death you will be if you lie there.'

"'I will give you all things,' he said in a thin voice, weary as a three-day wind in the east: 'Ay, I will give you secrets and all things, if you will give me death.'

"'And for why that?' I asked.

"'I die like this every night,' he said, 'and there are three of us. I am not knowing where my two brothers will be, in what land, west or east: my brother John, and my brother Raphael. But they, too, are like this, like what I am, like what you see me here. They have their heads on stones, in a waste place. They call upon death if a man stoops as you do, over John, my brother, he will say what I say — "I will give you all, I will give you all secrets, I will give you knowledge and power, if you will give me one thing, if you will give me death." And if any man stoops over Raphael, my brother, he will say that also — that John our brother would say, and that I say.'

"At that I thought the poor man had the black trouble."

"'No,' he said, as though he knew my thought. 'It is not madness I have, but old, old weariness.'

"'And what will your name be? I asked."

"'Here I have been, in this country, for seven years, wandering. And hear my name, by some chance of change, is MacRóban, or MacRóbany. And that is no ill change, for it means son of Robani or Robany, and that is what I am. But no,' he added, 'it is not the name you have now in your mind. It is an older name than that. It is a name that has the sand of the desert on its feet. It is a name written on the weeping wall in the Holy City of Zion.'

"I looked at the man, though the darkness was fast falling through the greyness. I remember a crying of many curlews in that waste place, and the suddenness of snipe drumming in a wet hollow a stone's-throw beyond where two lapwings never stopped wheeling and wailing."

"'And who will you be?' I said. My voice was hard, for the cold of a fear was in my bones."

"'My name is Robani,' he said, 'Daniel Robani. I am Daniel Robani, and my brother John is Johannes Robani, and my brother Raphael is Raphael Robani. And there's no weariness like our weariness. And every night we lie down to die, but we never die.'

"Then I knew the poor man was mad, and seeing I could not lift him, I gave him my cloak and hurried on to the clachan of Ledaig beyond the Moss to get help. I saw the minister, a stranger come for a month, but a good man and kind. He came with me. We saw no man. We found my cloak, but no man."

"Next day the minister had me into his room. 'Tell me again what words he spoke,' he said to me. I told him. Then he leaned from his chair, and said to me 'Neil McNeil, you have dreamed a dream or seen a mystery. Best go to your home now, and in silence: ay, go away without a word of this. For I do not know what is dream and what is vision, and what is truth and what is madness. But hear this: In the tenth year of this century we live in, a great vase or jar of marble was found in the excavated ruin of an ancient city in the southlands of Italy, called Aquila — which is to say, Iolair, Eagle — and in that jar was a copper plate. On the one side was engraved in the Hebrew, "A plate like this has gone unto every tribe." On the other side, and also in the Hebrew, was engraved the Death Warrant of Jesus of Nazareth, called Jesus the Christ. And of the four witnesses who signed the condemnation of the Christ the names of three were the names of three brothers, Daniel Robani, and Johannes Robani, and Raphael Robani."'

Neil ceased abruptly. The noise of the waves was as a multitude of hands batting the walls of the house: the wail and cry of the wind was like a dreadful Spirit. Before the red glow of the peat-fire we sat silent. *Tick-tack, tick-tack:* and the calling of the sea, the calling of the sea.

The Archer

HE man who told me this thing was Coll McColl,[74] an islander of Barra, in the Southern Hebrides. He spoke in the Gaelic, and it was while he was mending his net; and by the same token I thought at the time that his words were like herring-fry in that net, some going clean through, and others sticking fast by the gills. So I do not give it exactly as I heard it, but in substance as Coll gave it.

He is dead now, and has perhaps seen the Archer. Coll was a poet, and the island-folk said he was mad: but this was only because he loved beyond the reach of his fate.

There were two men who loved one woman. It is of no mere girl with the fair looks upon her I am speaking, but of a woman, that can put the spell over two men. The name of the woman was Silis:[75] the names of the men were Seumas[76] and Ian.[77]

Both men were young; both were of the strong, silent, island-race, but Ian Macleod was the taller. He had, too, the kiss of Dermid[78] on his brow, the fire of Angus[79] in his heart, and was a poet.

Silis was the wife of Seumas. So Seumas had his home, for her breast was his pillow when he willed it: and he had her voice for daily music: and his eyes had never any thirst, for they could drink of her beauty by day and by night. But Ian had no home. He saw his home afar off, and his joy and his strength failed, because the shining lights of it were not for him.

One night the two men were upon the water. It was a dead calm, and the nets had been laid. There was no moon at all, and only a star or two up in the black corner of the sky. The sea had wandering flames in it: and

---

74 Coll in the Gaelic language is the name for the hazel tree. In Gaelic mythology hazel nuts are believed to hold all wisdom. Hence, Coll McColl implies a very wise person indeed and, therefore, what he says must be true.

75 Silis is a woman's name, not very common nowadays, but it also means tear drops. An indication of the weeping and tragedy she is unwittingly about to release.

76 James.

77 John.

78 Dermid/Diarmed is a tragic figure from early Gaelic literature. He elopes with Grainne and unwittingly brings death and ruin. Another indication which way this tale is about to go.

79 Angus, or Aonghus, is the Celtic god of love.

when the big jellyfish floated by, they were like the tidelamps that some say the dead bear on their drowned faces.

"Some day I may be telling you a strange thing, Seumas," said Ian, after the long silence there had been since the last net had sent a little cloud of sparkles up from the gulfs.

"Ay?" said Seumas, taking his pipe from his mouth, and looking at the spire of smoke rising just forward o' the mast. The water slipped by, soft and slow. It was only the tide feeling its way up the sea-loch, for there was not a breath of wind. Here and there were dusky shadows: the boats of the fishermen of Inchghunnais.[80] Each carried a red light, and in some were green lanterns slung midway up the mast.

No other word was said for a long time.

"And I'm wondering," said Ian at last: "I'm wondering what you'll think of that story."

Seumas made no answer to that. He smoked, and stared down into the dark water. After a time he rose, and leaned against the mast. Though there was no light of either moon or lamp, he put his hand above his eyes, as his wont was.

"I'm thinking the mackerel will be coming this way to-night. This is the third time I've heard the snoring of the pollack ... away yonder, beyond Peter Macallum's boat."

"Well, Seumas, I'll sleep a bit. I had only the outside of a sleep last night."

With that Ian knocked the ash out of his pipe, and lay over against a pile of rope, and shut his eyes, and did not sleep at all because of the sick dull pain of the homeless man he was — home, home, home, and Silis the name of it.

When, an hour or more later, he grew stiff he moved, and opened his eyes. His mate was sitting at the helm, but the light in his pipe was out, though he held the pipe in his mouth, and his eyes were wide staring open.

"I would not be telling me that story, Ian," he said.

Ian answered nothing, but shifted back to where he was before, for all his cramped leg. He closed his eyes again.

At the full of the tide, in the deep dark hour before the false dawn, as the first glimmer is called, the glimmer that comes and goes, both men got up, and moved about, stamping their feet. Each lit his pipe, and the smoke hung long in little greyish puffs, so dead-still was it.

---

80 This name in Gaelic means 'The Island of No Going Back.' There is no such place in this world.

On the *Brudhearg*, John Macalpine's boat, young Neil Macalpine sang. The two men on the *Eala* could hear his singing. It was one of the strange songs of Ian Mòr.

O, she will have the deep dark heart, for all her face is fair,
As deep and dark as though beneath the shadow of her hair:
For in her hair a spirit dwells that no white spirit is,
And hell is in the hopeless heaven of that lost spirit's kiss.

She has two men within the palm, the hollow of her hand:
She takes their souls and blows them forth as idle drifted sand:
And one falls back upon her breast that is his quiet home,
And one goes out into the night and is as wind-blown foam.

Seumas leaned against the tiller of the *Eala*, and looked at Ian. He saw a shadow on his face. With his right foot the man tapped against a loose spar that was on the starboard deck.

When the singer ceased, Ian raised his arm and shook menacingly his clenched fist, over across the water to where the *Brudhearg* lay.

There were words on his lips, but they died away when Neil Macalpine broke into a love song, *Mo nighean donn*.[81]

"Can you be telling me, Ian," said Seumas, who was the man that made that song about the homeless man?"

"Ian Mòr."

"Ian Mòr of the Hills?"

"Ay."

"They say he had the shadow upon him?"

"Well, what then?"

"Was it because of love?"

"It was because of love."

"Did the woman love him?"

"Ay."

"Did she go to him?"

"No."

"Was that why he had the mind-dark?"

"Ay."

"But he loved her, and she loved him?"

"He loved her, and she loved him."

For a time Seumas kept silence. Then he spoke again.

---

81 'My Brown-Haired Girl,' a well-known Gaelic love song.

"She was the wife of another man?"

"Ay; she was the wife of another man."

"Did *he* love her?

"Yes, for sure."

"Did she love him?"

"Yes ... yes."

"Whom, then, did she love? For a woman can love one man only."

"She loved both."

"That is not a possible thing: not the one deep love. It is a lie, Ian Macleod."

"Yes, it is a lie, Seumas Maclean."

"Which man did she love?"

Ian slowly shook the ash from his pipe, and looked for a second or two at a momentary quiver in the sky in the northeast.

"The dawn will be here soon now, Seumas."

"Ay. I was asking you, Ian, which man did she love?"

"Sure she loved the man who gave her the ring."

"Which man did she love?

"O for sure, man, you're asking me just like the lawyer who has the trials away at Balliemore on the mainland yonder."

"Well, I'll tell you that thing myself, Ian Macleod, if you'll tell me the name of the woman."

"I am not knowing the name."

"Was it Mary ... or Jessie ... or mayhap was it Silis, now?"

"I am not knowing the name."

"Well, well, it might be Silis, then?"

"Ay, for sure it might be Silis. As well Silis as any other."

"And what would the name of the other man be?"

"What man?"

"The man whose ring she wore?"

"I am not remembering that name."

"Well, now, would it be Padruig, or mayhap Ivor, or or ... perhaps, now, Seumas?"

"Ay, it might be that."

"Seumas?"

"Ay, as well that as any other."

"And what was the end?"

"The end o' what?"

"The end of that loving?"

Ian Macleod gave a low laugh. Then he stooped to pick up the pipe he had dropped. Suddenly he rose without touching it. He put his heel on the warm clay, and crushed it.

"That is the end of that kind of loving," he said. He laughed low again as he said that.

Seumas leaned and picked up the trodden fragments. "They're warm still, Macleod."

"Are they?" Ian cried at that, his eyes with a red light coming into the blue: "Then they will go where the man in the song went, the man who sought his home for ever and ever and never came any nearer than into the shine of the window-lamps."

With that he threw the pieces into the dark water that was already growing ashy-grey.

"'Tis a sure cure, that, Seumas Maclean."

"Ay, so they say ... and so, so: ay, as you were saying, Ian Mòr went into the shadow because of that home he could not win?"

"So they say. And now we'll take the nets. 'Tis a heavy net that comes out black, as the sayin' is. They're heavy for sure, after this still night, an' the wind southerly, an' the pollack this way an' that."

"Well, now, that's strange."

"What is strange, Seumas Maclean?"

"That you should say that thing."

"And for why that?"

"Oh, just this. Silis had a dream the other night, she had. She dreamed she saw you standing alone on the *Eala*: and you were hauling hard a heavy net, so that the sweat ran down your face. Your face was dead-white pale, she said. An' you hauled an' you hauled. An' someone beside you that she couldn't see laughed an' laughed: an' ..."

With a stifled oath, Ian broke in upon the speaker's words: "Why, man alive, you said he, the man, myself it is, was alone on the *Eala*."

"Well, Silis saw no one but yourself, Ian Macleod."

"But she heard some one beside me laughing an' laughing."

"So she said. And you were dead-white, she said: with the sweat pouring down you. An' you pulled an' you pulled. Then you looked up at her and said: '*It's a heavy net that comes up black, as the sayin' is.*'"

Ian Macleod made no answer to that, but slowly began to haul at the nets. A swift moving light slid hither and thither well away to the north-east. The sea greyed. A new, poignant, salt smell came up from the waves. Sail after sail of the smacks ceased to be a blur in the dark: each lifted a brown shadowy wing against a dusk through which a flood of myriad drops of light steadily oozed.

Now from this boat, now from that, hoarse cries resounded.

The *Mairi Ban* swung slowly round before the faint dawn-wind, and lifted her bow homeward with a little slapping splash. The *Maggie*, the *Trilleachan*, the *Eilid*, the *Jessie*, and the *Mairi Donn* followed one by one.

In silence the two men on the *Eala* hauled in their nets. The herring made a sheet of shifting silver as they lay in the hold. As the dawn lightened, the quivering silver mass sparkled. The decks were mailed with glittering scales: these, too, gleamed upon the legs, arms, and hands of the two fishermen.

"Well, that's done!" exclaimed Seumas at last. "Up with the helm, Ian, and let us make for home."

The *Eala* forged ahead rapidly when once the sail had its bellyful of wind. She passed the *Tern*, then the *Jessie Macalpine,* caught up the big, lumbering *Maggie*, and went rippling and rushing along the wake of the *Eilid*, the lightest of the Inchghunnais boats.

Off shore, the steamer *Osprey* met the smacks, and took the herring away, cran by cran. Long before her screw made a yeast of foam athwart the black-green inshore water, the *Eala* was in the little haven and had her nose in the shingle at Craigard point.

In silence Seumas and Ian walked by the rock-path to the isolated cottage where the Macleans lived. The swallows were flitting hither and thither in front of its low, whitewashed wall, like flying shuttles against a silent loom. The luminous, pale gold of a rainy dawn lit the whiteness with a vivid gleam. Suddenly Ian stopped.

"Will you be telling me now, Seumas, which man it was that she loved?"

Maclean did not look at the speaker, though he stopped too. He stared at the white cottage, and at the little square window with the geranium-pot on the lintel.

But while he hesitated, Ian Macleod turned away, and walked swiftly across the wet bracken and bog-myrtle till he disappeared over Cnoc-na-Hurich, on the hidden slope of which his own cottage stood amid a wilderness of whins.

Seumas watched him till he was out of sight. It was then only that he answered the question.

"I'm thinking," he muttered slowly, "I'm thinking she loved Ian Mòr."

"Yes," he muttered again later, as he took off his sea-soaked clothes, and lay down on the bed in the kitchen, whence he could see into the little room where Silis was in a profound sleep: "Yes, I'm thinking she loved Ian Mòr."

He did not sleep at all, for all his weariness.

When the sunlight streamed in across the red sandstone floor, and crept toward his wife's bed, he rose softly and looked at her. He did not need to stoop when he entered the room, as Ian Macleod would have had to do.

He looked at Silis a long time. Her shadowy hair was all about her face. She had never seemed to him more beautiful. Well was she called "Silis the Fawn" in the poem that some one had made about her.

The poem that some one had made about her? ... yes, for sure, how could he be forgetting who it was. Was it not Ian, and he a poet, too, another Ian Mòr they said.

"Another Ian Mòr." As he repeated the words below his breath, he bent over his wife. Her white breast rose and fell, the way a moonbeam does in moving water.

Then he knelt. When he took the slim white hand in his she did not wake. It closed lovingly upon his own.

A smile slowly came and went upon the dreaming face — ah, lovely, white, dreaming face, with the hidden starry eyes. There was a soft flush, and a parting of the lips. The half-covered bosom rose and fell as with some groundswell from the beating heart.

"Silis," he whispered. "Silis ... Silis ..."

She smiled. He leaned close above her lips.

"Ah, heart o' me," she whispered, "O Ian, Ian, mo rùn, mo ghray,[82] Ian, Ian, Ian!"

Seumas drew back. He too was like the man in her dream, for it was dead-white he was, with the sweat in great beads upon his face. He made no noise as he went back to the hearthside, and took his wet clothes from where he had hung them before the smoored peats, and put them on again. Then he went out.

It was a long walk to Ian Macleod's cottage that few-score yards: a long, long walk.

When Seumas stood on the wet grass round the flagstones he saw that the door was ajar. Ian had not lain down. He had taken his ash-lute, and was alternately playing and singing low to himself.

Maclean went close up to the wall, and listened. At first he could hear no more than snatches of songs. Then suddenly the man within put down his ash-lute, and stirred. In a loud vibrant voice he sang:

---

82 Terms of endearment equivalent to 'my heart, my love.'

O far away upon the hills at the lighting of the dawn
I saw a stirring in the fern and out there leapt a fawn:
And O my heart was up at that and like a wind it blew
Till its shadow hovered o'er the fawn as 'mid the fern it flew.

And *Silis! Silis! Silis!* was the wind-song on the hill,
And *Silis! Silis! Silis!* did the echoing corries fill:
My hunting heart was glad indeed, at the lighting of the dawn,
For O it was the hunting then of my bonnie, bonnie Fawn!

For some moments there was dead silence. Then a heavy sigh came from within the cottage. Seumas Maclean at last made a step forward, and before his shadow fell across the doorway Ian breathed a few melancholy notes and began a slow, wailing song:

O heart that is breaking,
    Breaking, breaking,
O for the home that I canna, canna win:
O the weary aching,
    The weary, weary aching
To be in the home that I canna, canna win!

Seumas' face was white and tired. It is weary work with the herring, no doubt.

He lifted a white stone and rapped loudly on the door. Ian came out, and looked at him. The singer smiled, though that smiling had no light in it. It was dark as a dark wave it was.

"Well?" he said.

"May I come in?"

"Come in, and welcome. And what will you be wanting, Seumas Maclean?"

"Sure, it's too late to sleep, an' I'm thinking I would like to hear now that story you were to tell me."

The man gave no answer to that. Each looked at the other with luminous, unwinking eyes.

"It will not be a fair thing," said Ian slowly, at last. "It will not be a fair thing: for I am bigger and stronger."

"There is another way, Ian Macleod."

"Ay?"

"That you or I go to her, and tell her all, and then at the last say: 'Come with me, or stay with him.'"

"So be it."

So there and then they drew for chance. The gaining of that hazard was with Seumas Maclean. Without a word Ian turned and went into the house. There he took his *feadan*, and played low to himself, staring into the red heart of the smouldering peats. He neither smiled nor frowned; once only he smiled, and that was when Seumas came back, and said, "Come."

So the two walked in silence across the dewy grass. There was a loud calling of skuas and terns, and the raucous laughing cry of the great herring-gull, upon the weedy shore of Craigard. The tide bubbled and oozed through the wilderness of wrack. Farther off there were the cackling of hens, the lowing of restless kye, and the bleating of the sheep on the slopes of Melmonach. A shrewd salt air tingled in the nostrils of the two men. At the closed door Seumas made a sign of silence. Then he unfastened the latch, and entered.

"Silis," he said in a low voice, but clear. "Silis, I've come back again. Dry your tears, my lass, and tell me once again for I'm dying to hear the blessed truth once again — tell me once again if it's me you love best, or Ian Macleod."

"I have told you, Seumas."

Without, Ian heard her words and drew closer.

"And it is a true thing that you love me best, and that since the choice between him and me has come, you choose me?"

"It is a true thing."

A shadow fell across the room. Ian Macleod stood in the doorway. Silis turned the white, beautiful face of her, and looked at the man. He smiled. She was no coward, his Silis: that was the thought which sang in his mind.

"Is — it — a — true — thing, Silis?" he asked slowly.

She looked at Seumas, then at Ian, then back at her husband.

"It might kill Seumas," she muttered below her breath, so that neither heard her: "it might kill him," she repeated. Then, with a swift turn of her eyes, she spoke.

"Yes, it is a true thing, Ian. I abide by Seumas."

That was all.

She was conscious of the wave of relief that went into Seumas' face. She saw the rising of a dark, strange tide in the eyes of Ian. He stared at her. Perhaps he did not hear? Perhaps he was dreaming still? He was a dreamer, a poet: perhaps he could not understand.

"A ghraidh mo chridhe — dear love of my heart," he whispered hoarsely. But Silis was frozen.

Ian stood awhile, strangely tremulous. She could see his nerves quivering below his clothes. He was a big, strong giant of a lover: but he trembled now like a fawn himself, she thought. His blue eyes were suddenly grown cloudy and dim. Then the deadly frost of her lie slew that in him without which life is nothing.

Ian turned. He stumbled through the blinding white light beyond the door. In his ears the faint lapsing noise of the tide stormed in the doorway. Seumas did not look at Silis. They listened, till they no more heard the sound of Ian's feet across the shingle that led to the haven.

He was quite white and still when they found him three days later. He seemed a giant of a man as he lay, face upward, among the green flags by the water-edge. The chill starlight of three nights had got into the quiet of his face.

That night, resumed Coll McColl, after a long pause — that night he, Coll, was walking in the moonlight across the hither slope of Melmonach.

He stood under a rowan-tree, and watched a fawn leaping wildly through the fern. While he watched, amazed, he saw a tall, shadowy woman pass by. She stopped, and drew a great bow she carried, and shot an arrow. It went through the air with a sharp whistling sound — just like Silis-Silis-Silis, Coll said, to give me an idea of it.

The arrow went right through the fawn.

But here was a strange thing. The fawn leapt away sobbing into the night: while its heart suspended, arrow-pierced, from the white stem of a silver birch.

"And to this day," said Coll at the last, "I am not for knowing who that archer was, or who that fawn. You think it was these two who loved? Well, 'tis Himself knows. But I have this thought of my thinking: that it was only a vision I saw, and that the fawn was the poor suffering heart of Love, and that the Archer was the great Shadowy Archer that hunts among the stars, For in the dark of the morrow after that night I was on Cnoc-na-Hurich, and I saw a woman there shooting arrow after arrow against the stars. At dawn she rose and passed away, like smoke, beyond those pale wandering fires."

The Book of the Opal

WHEN my kinsman Ambrose Stuart died last year, he left me many papers, family documents, and the MS. of a book, the third and final part of it unfinished. He died, where for some years he had lived, in Venice. I remember when he went: it was to join his intimate friend and foster-brother, Carolan Stuart, spiritual head of a House of Rest there: and he left his birth-isle in the Hebrides because he could no longer be a priest, having found a wisdom older than that he professed, and gods more ancient than his own, and a vision of beauty, that was not greater than that which dreaming souls see through the incense of the Church — because there is no greater or lesser beauty in the domain of the spirit, but only Beauty — that was to him higher in its heights and deeper in its depths.

The first part of this book is his own story, from childhood to manhood: a story of a remote life, remotely lived; of a singular and pathetic loneliness. The second deals with his thoughts and dreams in Rome during his novitiate, his life in Paris, his priesthood in the Southern Hebrides. The third, and much the longest, though unfinished, is less a narrative than a journal, and begins from the day when he first knew that the prayers in his mind shaped themselves otherwise than as they came to his lips; and that old forgotten wisdom of his people came nearer to his spirit than many sacred words, which, to him, were not the wind, but the infinite circling maze of leaves blown before the wind.

The papers were, for the most part, pages written during those dull days of idle or perplexed thought which came between this change and his abrupt relinquishing of the priesthood. A bitter spirit inhabits them: a spirit of the flesh, and the things of the flesh, and of the dust. Among the latest are one or two of which I am glad, for they show that he sought evil, or if not evil, the common ways of evil, as a man will take a poison to avert death.

The third part of the book comes to within a few days of his death. It deals with his life in Venice: with his inner life, for he lived solitary, and went little among his fellows, and for the most part dwelled with Father Carolan at the Casa San Spirito in the Rio del Occidente. It was there I saw him a week before his death. I was in Italy, where I had gone for a light and warm air, after a northern winter damp and bleak beyond any I have known: and when I had a letter from him, begging me leave my

227

friends and to come to Venice to see him before death put him beyond these too many dreams, I went.

From these papers, from that unfinished book, I learned much of a singular and perplexing nature. I believe more readily now that a man or woman may be possessed: or, that two spirits may inhabit the same body, as fire and air together inhabit a jet of flame.

"I am shaken with desire," he writes in one place, "and not any wind can blow that fire out of my heart. There is no room for even one little flaming word of God in my heart. When I am not shaken with desires, it is only because I am become Desire. And my desire is all evil. It is not of the mind or of the body only, but is of the mind and the body and the spirit. It is my pleasure to deny God. I have no fear."

And yet, within a page or two of where these words are, and written later on the same day, I find: "There is a star within me which guides me through all darkness. Pride is evil, but there is a pride which great angels know, they who do not stoop, who hear but do not listen. What are all desires but dust to the feet? I fear above all things the unforgiving love of Him who has dominion. But great love, great hope, these touch with immortal lips my phantom frailties. What day can be vain when I know within myself that I am kin to spirits who do not pass as smoke and flame?"

But because one can understand a man better from what height he may have reached, than from any or all of his poor fallings away, I learned more from a vellum-bound MS. book, written also on vellum, as though he held it as his particular and most intimate utterance, which he gave me the day before he died. For there are many among us who become transparent through the light of their imaginations: who, when they mould images of thought and dream, reveal their true selves with an insight that is at once beautiful and terrible. My friend was of these: and I recall seldom, and with ever less heed, the morbid agonies and elations, the bitter perversities, the idle veering of shaken thought, but remember what he wrote, not openly of himself or his apparent life and yet poignantly and convincingly of himself, and of one whom he loved, in *The Book of the Opal.*

He gave me also the rare and beautiful stone after which he had named his book. He told me that it possessed occult powers, but whether of itself, or in the making of its perfect beauty, he could not say; or simply because of its beauty, and because perfect beauty has an infinite radiation and can attract not only influences, but powers. It may well be so.

I read often in this *Book of the Opal*. It is, to me, as the sea is, or the wind: for, like the unseen and homeless creature which in the beginning God breathed between the lips of Heat and Cold, it is full of unbidden meanings and has sighs and laughters: and, like the sea, it has limits and shallows, but holds the stars, and has depths where light is dim and only the still, breathless soul listens; and has a sudden voice that is old as day and night, and is fed with dews and rains, and is salt and bitter.

It was not his will that it should be given to others. "I would like three to read it," he said: "then, in time, it will be moonlight in many minds, and, through the few, thousands will know all in it that has deep meaning for any but myself. For now I am a husbandman who knows he shall not reap what he has sown, but is content if even one seed only sink and rise. I see a forest of souls staring at the stars which are the fruit of the tree that shall grow from that single seed."

This that he desired may or not be: for there is another Husbandman who garners in His own way and at His own time.

When I reached him I saw in his face the shadow of that ill which none may gainsay. He was on a sofa which had been drawn close to the window. The house was in a poor and unfrequented part, but the windows looked across the Laguna Morte, and from the roof garden one might see at sundown the spires of Padua, like white gossamer caught in that vast thicket of flame and delicate rose which was the West. It was at this hour, at a sundown such as this, that I saw him. Already the sweat of death was on his brow, though he lived, as in a tremulous, uncertain balance of light and shadow, for seven days.

His mind dwelled almost wholly upon secret things: ancient mysteries, old myths, the forgotten gods and the power and influences starry and demoniacal, dreams, and the august revelation of eternal beauty. One afternoon he gave me four small objects, of which three were made of ivory and gold, and the fourth was a rounded stone of basalt double-sphered with gold. I asked him what meaning they had, for I knew he gave them with meaning.

"Do you not know?" he said. One was the small image of a sword, the other of a spear, the third of a cup. Then I knew that he had given me the symbols of the four quarters of the earth, and of all the worlds of the universe: the stone for the North, the sword for the East, the spear for the South, and the cup for the West.

"Hold the sword against the light that I may see it," he whispered; adding, after a while: "I am tired of all thoughts of glory and wonder, of power, and of love that divides."

The next day, at sundown, he asked me to hold the little gold and ivory spear against the light. "I am tired," he said, "of all thoughts of dominion, of great kingdoms and empires that come and pass, of insatiable desires, and all that goes forth to smite and to conquer."

On the day that followed I held before his dimmed eyes the little gold and ivory cup, white as milk in the pale gold of a rain-cleat, windy set. "I am tired," he said, "of all thoughts of dreams that outlive the grave, and of fearless eyes looking at the stars, and of old heroisms, and mystery, and the beauty of all beauty."

It was on the next day he died. At noon his faint breath bade me lift the stone of basalt, though he could not see that which I held before his eyes. I saw the shadow in his closed eyelids become tremulous and pale blue, like faint, wind-shaken smoke. When I put the stone on the marble by his side, not more still or white than that other silent thing which lay beside it, I knew that of the eternal symbols of which he has so often written in *The Book of the Opal*, one he had forever relinquished. With him in that new passage, he had the spear, and the sword, and the little infinite cup that the tears of one heart might fill and yet not all the dews of the incalculable stars cause to overflow.

Among the impersonal episodic parts of *The Book of the Opal* I found much diffuse and crude material, often luminous with living thought — the swimming thought of timeless imagination out of which an old-time romance of two worlds has been woven: two worlds, the one as the other remote from us now, though each in degree to be recovered, if neither till after a deeper "sea-change" than any modern world has yet known.

Though the soul is the still-water in which each of us may dimly discern this "sea-change"; Art, which is the symbolic language of the soul, is alone, now, the common mirror with which all may look. And Art, we must remember, is the continual recovery of a bewildered tradition, the tradition of Beauty and of joy and of Youth, that like the Aztec word Ahecatl — which signifies the Wind, and the Breath, and the Soul — are but the three mortal names for one immortal Word.

The Wells of Peace

WHEN Ian Mòr, of whom elsewhere I have spoken so often, was a man in the midway of life, he sought the Wells of Peace.

All his life long he had desired other things. But when a man has lived deeply he comes at last to long for rest. Beauty, joy, life, these may be his desire: but soon or late he will seek the Wells of Peace.

I speak of a man such as Ian Mòr was. There is too vast a concourse of those who herd ignobly among the low levels of desire: of these I do not speak, knowing little of them, for there are stars in my inner life that guide my stumbling feet elsewhere and otherwise. He has quiet now. There is sleep upon his brain that was so tired. There is balm upon his spirit. He has peace, there, where he lies in deep, unheeding rest, under a rowan on a green hillside.

When he was ill with the death-weariness, though none saw signs of that, for it was from within, I asked him once what was the thing he remembered best out of life — who had lived so deeply, and was a poet and dreamer, and had loved with the great love. He answered me in the Gaelic he loved. It is a saying of the people; but to me never common now, who see in the words the colour of his deep enduring loneliness.

"Deireadh gach comuinn, sgaoileadh; deireadh gach cogaidh, sìth" — the end of all meetings, parting: the end of all striving, peace. "Deireadh gach cogaidh, sìth": I have slept often to the quiet music of that.

When he was in the midway of life, Ian Mòr went deep and far into the dark valley of weariness. The beauty of the world, the mystery of the human soul, the flame-like ecstasy of his dream: these sustained him. And when, at last, the radiance was without mystery, and the mystery without vista; when the loveliness of light and shadow over all the green earth and ancient hills and ever-changeful, unchanging sea, was a mere idle pageant for tired eyes — then was he sustained only by the star of his love. Far away she was. God knows in what unplumbed, fathomless depths of loneliness the following love pursues its quest. Afar off, he loved. Fair star of his redemption: he could always discern that light through the darkness of his homeless heart.

She was of the old heroic mould. "Joy and deep love," he said to her once, "these will be our stars." She smiled gravely in whispering back, "And strength and endurance."

Through how many strange gulfs he had sailed, through what hazardous straits, against what adverse winds and tides, before he set his course for the one haven he had never found; that port which each mariner on the sea of life has heard of, which many have descried across the running wave, which ever and again a few have found and entered: the blue quietudes of the haven of Peace.

I do not remember when it was that Ian Mòr went forth upon his quest. He was in the midway of life, that I know; and he arose one day from where he lay upon the hillside, dreaming an old, sweet, impossible dream. It is enough.

He went down the hillside of Ben Maiseach, through the still purpled heather and the goldening bracken. Behind him the slopes rose pale blue, with isles of deeper azure where a few drifting clouds trailed their shadows across the upland moors. Beneath him, and just beyond the Glen of the Willows, the Gorromalt Water made a few shimmering curves of light among the green of hazel-thickets and fern; farther, the low hills broke into a serrated crest, as of a spent and broken billow. Beyond, lay a single, long, suspensive wave, immutable, pale as turquoise, ethereal as blue smoke. It was the sea.

A quiet region. Few crofts lightened the hillsides. Scanty pastures twisted this way and that among the granite boulders and endless green surf of fern. On that solitary way, from the end of Monanair to where the path of the Glen of the Willows diverges, Ian Mòr met no one. In the glen itself he passed a woman, a tinker's wife, dishevelled, with sullen eyes and ignoble mien, carrying wearily a sleeping child. He spoke, but she gave no other answer than a dull stare. He passed her, dreaming his dream. A redbreast, who had found his fall-o'-the-leaf song, flew before him a while, fluting brief cries.

"Ah, birdeen, birdeen," he cried, "be the bird of the rainbow and lead me to my love."

But the redbreast fluttered idly into a thicket of red-brown bramble, and Ian walked slowly on. Something lay upon his heart.

"Lead me to my love," he muttered over and over.

Suddenly he turned and moved swiftly back. When he came upon the woman he smiled, and said again in the sweet, homely Gaelic, "God be with you, and a quiet night." The sullen eyes wandered idly over him.

"Let me help you," he asked.

She held out her hand, the hollow palm upward. But when he said simply that he had no money, she cursed him.

"You are weary, poor woman," he added, taking no notice of her bitter words. "Let me carry the child for you a bit. Sure, 'tis a heavy weight at the end o' the day, but not so heavy as the burden o' want and the hand o' sorrow."

The woman looked at Ian suspiciously, but at last she gave him the child. For a time they walked in silence, side by side.

"Is the child a lass or a boy?" Ian asked after a while.

"A lassie, worse luck."

His heart yearned. He looked into the little one's eyes, for she had wakened, and the last light of day was in those deep-blue pools, so fathomless and quiet. Ian remembered a song he had made, years and years before, when his life was green as June, and his heart glad as May, and his thought light as April. The memory came running like a freshet over a barren course. Tears welled from his heart into his eyes. And so, remembering, he sang in a low, murmuring voice:

"Ah, Eilidh, Eilidh, Eilidh,[83] dear to me, dear and sweet,
In dreams I am hearing the sound of your little running feet;
The sound of your running feet that like the sea-hoofs beat
A music by day and night, Eilidh, on the sands of my heart, my sweet.

Eilidh, Eilidh, Eilidh, put off your wee hands from the heart o' me;
It is pain they are making there, where no more pain should be:
For little running feet, an' wee white hands, an' croodlin' as of the sea,
Bring tears to my eyes ... tears, tears, out o' the heart o' me,
        Mo lennav-a-chree,
        Mo lennav-a-chree!"

While he sang, low as it was, the woman trudged on seemingly unhearing. When he ceased she spoke, with choking words and a gasp in her throat.

"Sing those last lines over again."

Ian glanced at her. Putting the child over into the hollow of his right arm, he slipped his hand into that of the tattered, dishevelled woman, as she tramped wearily on, her sullen eyes now red. He sang low:

"For little running feet, an' wee white hands, an' croodlin' as of the sea,
Bring tears to my eyes ... tears, tears, out o' the heart o' me,
        Mo lennav-a-chree,
        Mo lennav-a-chree!"

---

83 Eilidh is Gaelic for Helen.

"Why is there weeping upon you, poor woman?" he asked of her, in the kindly idiom of those who have the Gaelic.

Suddenly she stopped, and leaned against a birch; her breast shook with sobs. For long she sobbed with bitter tears.

Gently Ian soothed her out of the deep, warm pity that was ever in his heart for poor, sorrowful women. Soon she told him. The child he carried was not hers, but that of the woman her tinker-husband had taken to himself when, she, his wife, proved barren.

"An' I've only one hope," she cried, "an' only one dream, an' that's to feel the wee white hands, an' to hear the running feet, and to hear the croodlin' as of the sea, of my own, own bairn."

Looking upon the poor vagrant, Ian's heart melted in pity. Deep, wonderful love of the mother, that could court hunger and privation and misery and all else as dross only for the kiss of little lips, the light in little eyes, the mothering touch. The poor, uncomely wench he thought: for sure, for sure, Mary, the Mother of All, called to her from afar off, with sister-sweet whispering and deep compassionate love. They talked no more till they came to the little inn at the far end of the Glen of the Willows. The man there knew Ian Mòr, and so promised readily to give the woman shelter and food for that day, and the morrow, which was the Sabbath.

At the rising of the moon Ian left her. She had no speech, but she stammered piteous, ungracious words. Peradventure he understood right well. When he kissed the child, she put her little arms round his neck, and clung to him like a white butterfly against a bole of pine.

As he left the last birches of the Glen of the Willows, and heard the vague, inland rumour of the sea echoing through a gully in the shoreward hills, another wayfarer joined him. It was Art, the son of Mary Gilchrist, he who as a little lad had been found, weary, in that very place, by a stranger who had taken him to a forest booth and shown him the mystery of the Twelve Weavers, who every day of the days meet at the Last Supper — for with them who are immortal there is no last or first.

For a brief while they spoke of one another. Then Ian told Art his friend that his weariness had become a burden too great to be borne; and that, tired even of hope — he had come forth to seek the Wells of Peace.

"And Art," he added, "if you will tell me where I may find these, you will have all the healing love that is in my heart."

"There are seven Wells of Peace, Ian Mòr. Four you found long since, blind dreamer; and of one you had the sweet, cool water a brief while ago; and the other is where your hour waits; and the seventh is under the rainbow."

Ian Mòr turned his eager, weary eyes upon the speaker.

"The Wells of Peace," he muttered, "which I have dreamed or — which I have dreamed of through tears and longing, and old, familiar pain, and sorrow too deep for words."

"Even so, Ian. Poet and dreamer, you too have been blind, for all your seeing eyes and wonder-woven brain and passionate dream."

"Tell me! What are the four Wells of Peace I have already passed and drunken of and not known?"

"They are called 'Love,' 'Beauty,' 'Dream,' and 'Endurance.'"

Ian bowed his head. Tears dimmed his eyes.

"Art," he whispered. "Art, bitter, bitter waters were those that I drank in that fourth Well of Peace. For I knew not the waters were sweet, then. And even now, even now, my heart faints at that shadowy well."

"It is the Well of Strength, Ian, and its waters rise out of that of Love, which you found so passing sweet."

"And what is that of which I drank a brief while ago?"

"It was in the Glen of the Willows. Your felt its cool breath when you turned and went back to that poor, outcast woman, and saw her sorrow, and looked into the eyes of the little one. And you drank of it when you gave the woman peace. It is the well where the Son of God sits forever, dreaming His dream. It is called 'Compassion.'"

And so, Ian thought, he had been at the Well of Peace that is called Compassion, and not known it.

"Tell me, Art, what are the sixth and seventh?"

"The sixth is where your hour waits. It is the Well of Rest; deep, deep sleep; deep, deep rest; balm for the weary brain, the weary heart, the spirit that hath had weariness for comrade and loneliness as a bride. It is a small well that, and shunned of men, for its portals are those of the grave, and the soft breath of it steals up through brown earth and the ancient, dreadful quiet of the underworld."

"And the seventh? That which is under the rainbow in the West?"

"Ian, you know the old, ancient tales. Once, years ago, I heard you tell that of Ulad the Lonely. Do you remember what was the word on the lips of his dream when, after long years, he saw her again when both met at last under the rainbow?"

"Ay, for sure. It was the word of triumph, of joy, the whisper of peace: *There is but one love.*"

235

"When you hear that, Ian, and from the lips of her whom you have loved and love, then you shall be standing by the Seventh Well."

They spoke no more, but moved slowly onward through the dusk. The sound of the sea deepened. The inland breath rose, as on a vast wing, but waned, and passed like perishing smoke against the starry regions in the gulfs above.

When the moon sank behind the ridge-set pines of Benallan, and darkness oozed out of every thicket and shadowy place, and drowned the black-green boughs and branches in a massed obscurity, Ian turned.

His quest was over. Not beyond those crested hills, nor by the running wave on the shore, whose voice filled the night as though it were the dark whorl of a mighty shell: not there, nor in this nor that far place, were the Wells of Peace.

Love, Beauty, Dream, Endurance, Compassion, Rest, Love-Fulfilled; for sure the Wells of Peace were not far from home.

So Ian Mòr went back to his loneliness and his pain and his longing.

The Wind, the Shadow, and the Soul

THERE are dreams beyond the thrust of the spear, and there are dreams and dreams; of what has been or what is to be, as well as the more idle fantasies of sleep. And this, perhaps, is of those dreams whose gossamer is spun out of the invisible threads of sorrow; or it may be, is woven out of the tragic shadows of unfulfilled vicissitude. It is of little moment.

One who was, now is not. That "is the sting, the wonder."

One who was, now is not. The soul and the shadow have both gone away upon the wind.

I write this in a quiet sea-haven. Tall cliffs half enclose it, in two white curves, like the wings of the solander when she hollows them as she breasts the north wind.

These sun-bathed cliffs, with soft hair of green grass, against whose white walls last year the swallows, dusky arrowy shuttles, slid incessantly, and where tufts of sea-lavender hung like breaths of stilled smoke, now seem to me merely tall cliffs. Then, when we were together, they were precipices which fell into seas of dream, and at their bases was for ever the rumour of a most ancient, strange, and penetrating music. It is I only, now, who do not hear: doubtless, in those ears, it fashions new meanings, mysteries, and beauty: there, where the music deepens beyond the chime of the hours, and Time itself is less than the whisper of the running wave. White walls, which could open, and where the sea-song became a spirit, still with the foam-bells on her hair, but with a robe green as grass, and in her band a white flower.

Symbols: yes. To some, foolish; to others clear as the noon, the clearness that is absolute in light, that is so obvious, and is unfathomable.

Last night the wind suddenly smote the sea. There had been no warning. The sun had set beneath narrow peninsulas of lemon and pale mauve; overagainst the upper roseate glow, the east was a shadowy opal wilderness, with one broad strait of luminous green wherein a star trembled. At the furtive suffusion of the twilight from behind the leaves, a bat, heedless of the season, flittered through the silent reaches; and when it too was lost in the obscurity, and darkness was silence and silence darkness, the continuous wave upon the shore was but the murmurous voice of that monotony. Three hours later a strange confused sound was audible. At midnight there was a sudden congregation of voices; a myriad scream tore the silence; the whole sea was uplifted, and it was as though the whirling body of the tide was rent therefrom and flung upon the land.

I did not sleep, but listened to the wind and sea. My dreams and thoughts, children of the wind, were but ministers of a mind wrought in shadow. They did "the will of beauty and regret."

At dawn the tempest was over. But for an hour thereafter the sea was in a shroud of scud and spray: I could see nothing but this shimmering, dreadful whiteness.

Why do I write this? It is because in this past night of tempest, in this day of calm, I have come close to one of whom I speak, and would image in this after-breath, as a sudden fragrance of violets in an unexpected place, a last fragrance of memory. Yet, I would not have written these last words to this book if it were not for the keen resurrection of my sorrow in the very haven of today's noontide.

I was in a hollow in the eastern cliff, a hollow filled with pale blue shadow, and with a faint sea-rumour clinging invisibly to the flint bosses and facets of sun-warmed chalk. Before me rose gradually a grass-green path, the aslant upon the upward slope. There was absolute stillness in the air. The trouble of the waters made this landward silence as peace within peace.

Out of the blue serenities, where nothing, not even the moving whiteness of a vanishing wing, was visible; out of the heat and glory of the day; out of that which is beyond — an eddy of wind swiftly descended. I saw the grasses shiver along the green path. A few broken sprays and twigs whirled this way and that. In my own land this has one open meaning. Those invisible ones whom we call the hidden people — whom so many, instinctively ever reducing what is great to what is small, what is of mystery and tragic wonder to what is fantastic and unthinkable, call "the fairies" — have passed by.

There are too many who inhabit the world that from our eyes is hidden, for us to know who pass, in times, on occasions like this. The children of light and darkness tread the same way. But to-day it was not one of those unseen and therefore unfamiliar kindred.

For when I looked again, I saw that the one whom I had lost moved slowly up the path; but not alone. Behind, or close by, moved another.

It was this other who turned to me. The image stooped, and lifted a palmful of dust in the hollow of its hand. This it blew away with a little sudden breath; and I saw that it was not the shadow, nor the phantom, but the soul of that which I had loved. Yet my grief was for that sweet perished mortality when I saw the eddy-spiralled greying dust was all that remained.

But for a second I had seen them together, so much one, so incommunicably alien. In that moment of farewell, all that was of mortal beauty passed into the starry eyes of the comrade who had forgotten the little infinite change. It was then, it was thus, I saw Eternity. That is why I write.

Then, as a film of blue smoke fades into the sky, what I had seen was not; and the old bewilderment was mine again, and I knew not which was the shadow or which the soul, or whether it was but the wind which had thus ceased to be.

Barabal: A Memory

I have spoken in 'Iona' and elsewhere of the old highland woman who was my nurse. She was not really old, but to me seemed so, and I have always so thought of her. She was one of the most beautiful and benignant natures I have known.

I owe her a great debt. In a moment, now, I can see her again, with her pale face and great dark eyes, stooping over my bed, singing 'Woe's me for Prince Charlie,' or an old Gaelic Lament, or that sad, forgotten, beautiful and mournful air that was played at Fotheringay when the Queen of Scots was done to death, 'lest her cries should be heard.' Or, later, I can hear her telling me old tales before the fire; or, later still, before the glowing peats in her little island-cottage, speaking of men and women, and strange legends, and stranger dreams and visions. To her, and to an old islander, Seumas Macleod, of whom I have elsewhere spoken in this volume, I owe much more than to any other influences in my childhood.

Perhaps it is from her that in part I have my great dislike of towns. There is no smoke in the lark's house, to use one of her frequent sayings — one common throughout the west.

I never knew any one whose speech, whose thought, was so coloured with the old wisdom and old sayings and old poetry of her race. To me she stands for the Gaelic woman, strong, steadfast, true to 'her own,' her people, her clan, her love, herself. 'When you come to love,' she said to me once, 'keep always to the one you love a mouth of silk and a heart of hemp.'

Her mind was a storehouse of proverbial lore. Had I been older and wiser, I might have learned less fugitively. I cannot attempt to recall adequately even the most characteristic of these proverbial sayings; it would take overlong.

Most of them, of course, would be familiar to our proverb-loving people. But, among others of which I have kept note, I have not anywhere seen the following in print. 'You could always tell where his thoughts would be ... pointing one way like the hounds of Finn' (*i.e.* the two stars of the north, the pointers): 'It's a comfort to know there's nothing missing, as the wren said as she counted the stars': 'The dog's howl is the stag's laugh'; and again, 'I would rather cry with the plover than laugh with the dog' (both meaning that the imprisoned comfort of towns is not to be compared with the life of the hills, for all its wildness). 'True love is like a mountain-tarn; it may not be deep, but that's deep enough that can hold the sun, moon, and stars': 'It isn't silence where the lark's song ceases': 'St. Bride's Flower, St. Bride's Bird, and St. Bride's Gift make a fine spring and a good year.' (*Am Beàrnan Bhrìgde 'us Gille-Bhrìgde 'us Lunn-Bata Bhrìgde*, etc. — the dandelion, the oyster-catcher, and the cradle* — because the dandelion comes with the first south winds and in a sunny spring is seen everywhere, and because in a fine season the oyster-catcher's early breeding-note foretells prosperity with the nets, and because a birth in spring is good luck for child and mother.') 'It seems easier for most folk to say *Lus Bealtainn* than *La' Bealtainn*': i.e. people can see the small things that concern themselves better than the great things that concern the world; literally, "It's easier to say marigold than may-day' — in Gaelic, a close play upon words: '*Cuir do lamh leinn*,' 'Lend us a hand,' as the fox in the ditch said to the duckling on the roadside: '*Gu'm a slàn gu'n till thu*,' 'May you return in health,' as the young man said when his conscience left him: 'It's only a hand's-turn from *eunadair* to *eunadan*' (from the bird-snarer to the cage): 'Saying *eud* is next door to saying *eudail*,' as the girl laughed back to her sweetheart (*eud* is jealousy, and *eudail* is my Treasure): 'The lark doesn't need *broggan* (shoes) to climb the stairs of the sky.'

Among those which will not be new to some readers, I have note of a rhyme about the stars of the four seasons, and a saying about the three kinds of love, and the four stars of destiny.

Wind comes from the spring star, runs the first; heat from the summer star, water from the autumn star, and frost from the winter star. Barabal's variant was 'wind (air) from the spring star in the east; fire (heat) from the summer star in the south; water from the autumn star in the west; wisdom, silence, and death from the star in the north.' Both the season-rhyme and that of the three kinds of love are well known. The latter runs:

Gaol nam fear-dìolain, mar shruth-lionaidh na mara;
Gaol nam fear-fuadain, mar ghaoith tuath 'thig o'n charraig;
Gaol nam fear-posda, mar luing a' seòladh gu cala.

---

* It is probably in the isles only that the pretty word *Lunn-Bata* is used for *cra-all* (*creathall*), a cradle. It might be best rendered as boat-on-a-billow, *lunn* being a heaving billow.

Lawless love is as the wild tides of the sea;
And the roamer's love cruel as the north wind blowing from barren rocks;
But wedded love is like the ship coming safe home to haven.

I have found these two and many others of Barabal's sayings and rhymes, except those I have first given, in collections of proverbs and folklore, but do not remember having noted another, though doubtless 'The Four Stars of Destiny (or Fate)' will be recalled by some. It ran somewhat as follows:

Reul Near (Star of the East), Give us kindly birth;
Reul Deas (Star of the South), Give us great love;
Reul Siar (Star of the West), Give us quiet age;
Reul Tuath (Star of the North), Give us Death.

It was from her I first heard of the familiar legend of the waiting of Fionn and the Fèinn (popularly now Fingal and the Fingalians), 'fo-gheasaibh,' spellbound, till the day of their return to the living world. In effect the several legends are the same. That which Barabal told was as an isleswoman would more naturally tell it. A man so pure that he could give a woman love and yet let angels fan the flame in his heart, and so innocent that his thoughts were white as a child's thoughts, and so brave that none could withstand him, climbed once to the highest mountain in the Isles, where there is a great cave that no one has ever entered. A huge white hound slept at the entrance to the cave. He stepped over it, and it did not wake. He entered, and passed four tall demons, with bowed heads and folded arms, one with great wings of red, another with wings of white, another with wings of green, and another with wings of black. They did not uplift their dreadful eyes. Then he saw Finn and the Fèinn sitting in a circle.

Their long hair trailed on the ground; their eyebrows fell to their beards; their beards lay upon their feet, so that nothing of their bodies was seen but hands like scarped rocks that clasped gigantic swords. Behind them hung an elk-horn with a mouth of gold. He blew this horn, but nothing happened, except that the huge white hound came in, and went to the hollow place round which the Fèinn sat, and in silence ate greedily of treasures of precious stones. He blew the horn again, and Fionn and all the Fèinn opened their great, cold, grey, lifeless eyes, and stared upon him; and for him it was as though he stood at a grave and the dead man in the grave put up strong hands and held his feet, and as though his soul saw Fear.

But with a mighty effort he blew the horn a third time. The Fèinn leaned on their elbows, and Fionn said, 'Is the end come?' But the man could wait no more and turned and fled, leaving that ancient mighty company leaning upon its elbows, spellbound thus, waiting for the end. So they shall be found. The four demons fled into the air, and tumultuous winds swung him from that place. He was found lying dead in a pasture in the little island that was his home. I recall this here because the legend was plainly in Barabal's mind when her last ill came upon her. In her delirium she cried suddenly, "The Fèinn! The Fèinn! they are coming down the hill!'

'I hear the bells of the ewes,' she said abruptly, just before the end: so by that we knew she was already upon far pastures, and heard the Shepherd calling upon the sheep to come into the fold.

Mäya

LESS has been written of the psychology of waking dreams than of the psychology of the dreams of sleep. Surely they are more wonderful, and less lawless, if that can be without law which is invariable in disorder. I do not mean the dreams which one controls, as the wind herds the clouds which rise from the sea-horizons: but the dreams which come unawares, as, when one is lying on the grass and idly thinking, there may appear in the passing of a moment the shadow of a hawk hovering unseen. They are not less irresponsible and unaccountable — they come, reinless and wild, across unknown plains, and one hardly hears the trampling of their feet or sees the flashing of tameless eyes before the imagination is carried away by them. In a twinkling, the world that was is no more, and the world that now is has neither frontiers nor height nor depth, and the dancing stars may be underfoot, and from the zenith to the horizons may lean the greenness of the domed sea, and clouds be steadfast as the ancient hills, and dreams and passion and emotions be the winged creatures who move through gulfs of light and shadow.

Sometimes it happens that, in sleep, dreams have a rhythmical order, a beauty as of sculpture. It is rare: for when the phantoms of the silent house are not wild or fantastic or futile, they move commonly as to a music, unheard of us, and are radiant or sombre as though an unseen painter touched them with miraculous dyes. But, once perhaps, the dreamer may rejoice in a subtle and beautiful spiritual architecture: and look upon some completed vision of whose advent he has had no premonition, of whose mysterious processes he has no gleam, and whose going will be as lordly as its coming, without touch of ruin or of faded beauty.

Who builds these perfected dreams? What wings, in the impenetrable shadow wherein one has sunk, have lifted them to the verge where the unsleeping soul can perceive, and, perceiving, perhaps understand?

These are not the distempered images of broken remembrance: they are not the foam idly fretting the profound suspense of the deep. Nor is the mind consciously at work, building, or shaping, or controlling. As the shadow comes, they come: but as the shadow of some shape or beauty thrown in moonlight in some enchanted garden, a garden wherein one has never been, a shape upon which none has ever looked, a thing of life, complete and wonderful. Strange imaginations arise, as birds winged with flame and with heads like flowers: the unknown is become familiar. When not an image is made by that subtle artificer within; when not a thought steals out to whisper or to shape; when the mind is as a hushed child in the cradle, hearing a new and deep music and unknowing the sea, listening to a lullaby beyond the mother-song and unknowing the wind ... who, then, fashions those palaces upon the sea, those walls of green ice among the rose-garths of June, those phantoms of bright flame sleeping in peace among dry grass or moving under ancient trees of the unfailing branch and the unfading leaf?

Surely in these is a mystery beyond that of the unquiet brain in a body ill at ease, or beyond that of the mind when like a sleuthhound it slips out on the trail of old dreams and fleeing imaginations?

When first I began to notice these lamps of beauty hung in unexpected paths, whether in the twilights of bodily sleep or when the mind was in that trance of the spirit akin to the slumber of the body, I strove to understand, to trace, to go up to the hidden altars and look on the forbidden ecstasy. But, soon, an inward wisdom withheld me. And so for years I have known what has been my whim to call by a name: *The Secret Garden, the White Company*, and *Music*.

Of what I have seen there, and what music heard, and by whom I have been met and with whom gone, it is not my purpose to speak. Dreamland is the last fantasy of the unloosened imagination, or its valley of Avalon, or the *via sacra* for the spirit, accordingly as one finds it, or with what dower one goes to it. The ways are hidden to all save to those who themselves find. "*Thou canst not travel on the Path till thou hast become the Path itself.*"

If these unaccountable waking and unsought dreams bore any immediate or later relation to the things held by the mind, or recently held, or foreseen, one would the more readily believe that the inner mind was working slowly and in its own way at what the outer intelligence had not reached or had ignored. But sometimes they have no recognisable bearing. Sometimes, indeed, they are as fragmentary as the phantasmagoria of sleep. A friend told me this: — "Speaking to a friend on ordinary matters, suddenly I saw him quite clearly walking swiftly along a shore-road unknown to me, a road northern in feature and yet in detail as unfamiliar to me as though set in an unvisited land. He was wild and unkempt, but walked with uplifted head and swiftly. His head and right shoulder were meshed in a net, which trailed behind him. His left arm gleamed as though it were of silver, or mailed like a salmon. His left hand was a flame of fire that was as though entranced, for it neither hurt the unconscious walker nor burned anything with which it came in contact. The vision came and went more swiftly than I have taken time to tell of it, and had no bearing, so far as I know, then or later, on anything concerning either him or myself. A few days later, certainly, he told me that he had been thinking some time before of the symbolism of Nuada of the Dedannan, Nuada of the Silver Hand, a Gaelic divinity of uncertain attributes, but whom some take to be a Celtic Hephaistos. Whether this is any clue I cannot say: or why, since it came, it could not come with more obvious bearing, in a less obscure symbolism. And why, too, should the large round stones on the shore, the peculiar wind-waved line of old yews, the stranded fishing-coble, and other details be so extraordinarily vivid — so vivid that though I know I have never seen this headland I could not possibly mistake it were I some day to come upon its like."

Dreams or visions such as this, are, I fancy, of a kind that have not necessarily any significance. There are curlews of the imagination that suddenly go crying through waste places in the mind.

Of another, I think differently. "In the middle of a commonplace action of daily life suddenly I saw a woodland glade in twilight. A man lay before a fire, but when I looked closer I saw that what I thought was a fire was a mass of continually revolving leaves, though no leaf was blown from the maze, which was like an ever whirling yet never advancing wheel in that forest silence. He took up a reed-pipe or something of the kind. He played, and I saw the stars hang on the branches of the trees. He played, and I saw the great boles of the oaks become like amber filled with moonlight. He played, and then suddenly I realised that it was a still music, and had its life for me only in the symbol of colour. Flowers and plants and tree-growths of shape and hue such as I had never seen, and have never imagined, arose in the glade, which was now luminous as a vast shell behind which burned torches of honey-coloured flame.

"These changed continually, as the red foliage of fire continually renews itself. Then the player rose, and was a changing flame, and was gone. Another player was in the glade, where all was moveless shadow and old darkness. 'It is I, now, who am God,' he said. Then he in turn was like a shadow of a reed in the wind, that a moment is, and is not. And I looked, and in the heart of the darkness saw a white light continually revolving: and in the silence was a voice ... 'And I — I am Life.'"

Here, obviously, clear or not, there is the symbolic imagination at work. I do not think an interpreter of dreams need seek here for other than spiritual significance. It is, surely, an effort of the soul to create in symbolic vision a concept of spiritual insight such as the mind cannot adequately realise within its restricted terms, or what is beyond the reach of words. For these, though children of air and fire, have mortal evasive wings, and bands of impalpable dew, and feet wandering and uncertain as the eddying leaf.

It is less easy to interpret or accept either the rounded and complete dream of sleep — that all too rare visitor in the night of the body — or the waking dream that comes not less mysteriously, unsought, clanless among the tribes of the day's thoughts, an exile from a forbidden land, a prince who will not be commanded in his going or coming, who knows not any law of ours but only his own law.

It is to write of one such vision that I took up my pen and have written these things. It was a dream in sleep, but so potent an image, that, with both body and mind alert in startled wakefulness, I saw it not less clearly, not less vividly, not less overwhelmingly near and present. Its strangeness was in its living nearness in vision, and perhaps neither in aspect nor relation may appeal to others. Perhaps, even, it will seem no more than a luminous phantasy, void of significance. But, to me, it appeared, later, as an effort on the part of the spirit to complete in symbol what I had failed to do in words, while I have been writing these foregoing pages on the children of water of those in whose hearts is the unresting wave, and whom the tides of happy life lift and leave, and whose longing is idle as foam, and whose dreams are as measureless as all the waters of the world.

I saw, suddenly, greenness come out of the sea, and then the sea pass like a dewdrop in the heat of the sun. A vast figure stood on the bare under-strand of ocean, and leaned on his right arm along a mountain-brow so high that it seemed to me Himalaya or the extreme Cordillera. As he leaned, I could not see the face, for the Titan stared beyond the rim of the world. But he leaned negligently, as though idly watching, idly waiting. There was nothing of him but was green water, fluent as the homeless wave yet held in unwavering columnar suspense. Not a limb but was moulded in strength and beauty, not a muscle of man's mortal body but was there: yet the white coral of the depths gleamed through the titanic feet sculptured as in green jade, and the floating brown weed of the perpetual tide cast a wavering shadow among the sculptured green ridges and valleys of that titanic head. But it was not an image I saw: it was not an image of life, but life. There was not an ocean withheld in that bended arm, in that lifted shoulder, which could not have yielded in flying wave and soaring billow, or heaved with a slow mighty breath sustaining navies and argosies as drifting shells. When thought stirred behind the unseen brows, tides moved within these columnar deeps: and I do not doubt that the vast heart was a maelstrom where the inrush and outrush of tempestuous surges made a throb that shook the coasts of worlds beyond our own.

Looking on the greatness of this upbuilded sea, this titanic statue of silence and water, I thought I beheld the most ancient of the gods: the most ancient of the gods, the greatest of the gods.

Suddenly I heard breaths of music, and a sound as of a multitude of swift feet around me and beyond. I turned. There was no one. But a low voice, that ran through me like fire, spoke.

"Look, child of water, at your god."

Again I heard breaths of music rise, like thin spirals of smoke, but I did not see whence they came.

While the music breathed, I saw the Titan stand back from the rim of the world. His face slowly turned. But a whiteness as of foam was against my eyes, and a sudden intolerable fear bowed my head. When I looked again I saw only an illimitable sea that reached from my feet, green as grass: and on the west of the world the unloosened rains and dews hung like a veil.

The unseen one beside me stooped, and lifted a wave, and threw it into my heart.

Then I knew that I was made of the kinship of Mânan, and should never know peace, but should have the homeless wave for my heart's brother, and the salt sea as my cup to drink, and the wilderness of waters as the symbol of all vain ungovernable longings and desires.

And I woke, still looking out of time into eternity, and saw a Titan figure of living green water sculptured like jade, with feet set in the bed of ancient oceans; leaning, with averted face, on a mountain-brow, vast as Andes, vast as Himalaya.

The Distant Country

*"He has loved, perhaps; of a surety he has suffered.
Inevitably must he too have heard the 'sounds that
come from the distant country of Splendour and Terror;
and many an evening has he bowed down in silence
before laws that are deeper than the sea."*

THERE is a poet's tale that I love well, and have often recalled; and of how in the hour of death love may be so great that it transcends the height of hills and the waste of deserts and the salt reaches of the sea.

Last night I dreamed of Ithel and Bronwen: confusedly, for a noise of waves and the crying of an inland bird were continuously wrought into the colours and fragrances of places remote from moor and sea, with the colours and fragrances of a land of orchards and pastures and quiet meres, and with the thin, poignant fragrances and acute breadths of colour of the sun-wrought East.

And when I woke, I knew it was not really Ithel and Bronwen, Red Ithel and Pale-Bronwen, of whom I had been dreaming. Nor yet of an old grey day, nor of the remote East, but of two whom I knew well, and of this West of rains and rainbows, of tears and hopes, which I love as a child loves a widowed mother.

Then I slept again, and before dawn dreamed, and again awoke. But it was not of Bronwen and Ithel now that I dreamed, but of Aillinn and Bailê the Sweet-Spoken.

Among the stories of the Gael there is one that women love most. It is that of Bailê the Sweet-Spoken. When Bailê, who lived in one part of the country of the Gaels, suffered in any wise, Aillinn, who lived in another part, suffered also and with the same suffering. So great was their love that distance between them was no more than a flow of water between two other flows in a narrow stream. That is love, that cannot live apart. But in an evil hour the hate of a base nature caused a death-image to appear to Aillinn and to Bailê Honeymouth. And when Bailê the Sweet-Spoken saw his dead love, his heart broke, and the grass was less cold than was that which lay upon it. And when Aillinn saw her dead love, her life went away in a breath, and she was more white than were the white daisies in the grass where her great beauty lay like a stilled flame. Each was buried where each fell. Then this wonder was known throughout the lands of the Gaels, that an apple-tree straightway grew out of the grave of Aillinn, which the wind and the sun and moon and unseen powers moulded at the top into the form and head of Bailê; and that out of the grave of Bailê grew a yew-tree, of the upper leaves and branches of which the unseen powers and the moon and the sun and the wind wrought the fair, beautiful head of Aillinn. That is love, that cannot dream apart. That is love, that forever remoulds love nearer and nearer to the desire of the heart.

And when seven years had passed, the yew-tree and the apple-tree were laid low. It may be that one who loved not with the great love bade this to be done: for it is only the few who love as Aillinn and Bailê loved, and the smaller or weaker the soul is, the more does it abhor or be troubled by the white flame. But the poets and seers made tablets of the apple-wood and the yew-wood, and wrote thereon amorous and beautiful words. Later, it happened that the Ardrigh summoned the poets to bring these tablets before him at the House of the Kings. But hardly had he touched them when the yew-wood and the apple-wood were suddenly one wood, swift in their coming together as when two waves meet at sea and are one wave. And the king and those about him could see the pale apple-wood inwoven with the dark yew-wood, nor could any magic or incantation undo that miracle. So the Ardrigh bade the wood of the love of Aillinn and Bailê be taken to the treasury, and be kept there with the sacred emblems of great powers and demons and gods and the trophies of the heroes. And that is love, that heeds neither the word of man, nor the bitterness of death, nor the open law, nor the law that is secret and inscrutable.

But when I heard a mavis singing above the dew on the white wild-roses, and saw the blue light like a moving blue flame underslidden with running gold, and knew that it was day, I thought no more of Aillinn and of Bailê the Sweet-Spoken, nor of Red Ithel and Pale Bronwen, nor of the far, dim East where Ithel lay among the sands and Bronwen's love flickered like a shadow; nor of the dim day of those four lovers of dream; but of two whom I loved well and who had their day in this West of rains and rainbows, of tears and hopes.

Love is at once so great and so frail that there is perhaps no thought which can at the same time so appal and uplift us. And there is in love, at times, for some an unfathomed mystery. That which can lead to the stars can lead to the abyss. There is a limit set to mortal joy as well as to mortal suffering, and the flame may overleap itself in one as in the other. The most dread mystery of a love that is overwhelming is its death through its own flame.

This is an "untold story" that I write. None could write it. A few will understand: to most it will be at once as real and as unreal as foam, as no more than the phosphorescence of emotion. One may see, and yet deny: as one may see in the nocturnal wave a flame that is not there, or a star caught momentarily in the travelling hollow, and know that there is no flame but only a sudden gleam of infinitesimal, congregated life; no star, but only a wandering image. But, also, one may deny that which is not phantasmal. He who is colour-blind cannot see colour: he who is blind to that infinite flame of life which creates the blue mist of youth and love and romance cannot discern in youth or love or romance the names of those primitive ecstasies that in themselves are immortal things, though we see only their fruitions and decays: and he whose soul is obscure, or whose spirit is blind, cannot see those things which pertain to the spirit, or understand those things wherein the spirit expresses itself.

But for the some who care, I write these few words: not because I know a mystery, and would reveal it, but because I have known a mystery, and am to-day as a child before it, and can neither reveal nor interpret it.

They loved each other well, the two of whom I speak. It was no lesser love, though upheld by desires and fed with flame; but knew these, and recognised in them the bodily images of a flame that was not mortal and of desires that were not finite. They knew all of joy and sorrow that can come to man and woman through the mysterious gates of Love, which to some seem of dusk and to some seem of morning or the radiances of noon.

Year by year their love deepened. I know of no love like theirs. It was, in truth, a flame.

One hears everywhere that passion is but unsatisfied desire, that love is but a fever. So, too, as I have heard, the moles, which can see in twilight and amid the earthy glooms they inhabit, cannot see the stars even as shining points upon the branches of trees, nor these moving branches even, nor their wind-lifted shadows.

Their love did not diminish, but grew, through tragic circumstances. As endurance became harder — for love deepened and passion became as the bird of prey that God sets famished in the wilderness, while the little and great things of common life came in upon this love like a tide — it seemed to each that they only withdrew the more into that which was for them not the most great thing in life, but life.

To her, he was not only the man she loved: to whom she had given the inward, unnameable life as well as that which dwelled in the heart and in the mind, in the pulse and the blood and the nerves. He was Love itself; and when sometimes he whispered in her hair, she heard other words, and knew that a greater than he whom she loved spoke with hidden meanings.

How could she tell what she was to him? She was a flame to his mind as well as to his life: that she knew. But he could not tell her what words fail to tell. She could feel his heart beat: his pulse rose to her eyes as a wave to the moon: in those eyes of his she could see that which was in her own heart, but which she had to blind and lead blindfold, because a woman cannot look upon that which is intolerable. Doubtless it was not so with him. This she could not know. But she knew her own heart. The untranslatable call was there. She heard it in those silences where women listen.

Sometimes she looked at him, wondering: at times, even with a sudden fear. She did not fear him whom she loved, but unknown forces behind him. He spoke to her sometimes of that which cannot pass: of love more enduring than the hills, of passion, of the spirit, of deathless things. She feared them. She did not fear with the mind: that leaped, as a doe to the water-springs. She did not fear with the body, for that abhorred death and the ending of dreams. But something within her feared. These things he spoke of were too great and terrible a wind for a little, wandering flame.

Did he not think thus himself? she wondered. Was it because he was a man that he spoke, blithely of these far-off, beautiful and terrible things?

Once they were lying on a grassy slope, on a promontory, on a warm, moonlit night. A single pine-tree grew on the little, rocky buttress: and against this they leaned, and looked through the branches at the pale, uncertain stars, or into the moving, dark, mysterious water.

"It is our love," he whispered to her: "we are on the granite rock: and through the tree of our little world we look at the unchanging stars: and this moving tide is the mystery that is forever about us, and whispers so much, and tells so little."

It was sweet to hear: and she loved him who whispered: and the thought was her own. But that night she lay thinking for hour upon hour, or, rather, her mind was but a swimming thought; a thought that swam idly on still seas in deep darkness. How wonderful were these dreams that love whispered: how ...

But when at sunrise she woke, it was with a sense that the horizons of life crept closer and closer. She smiled sadly as she thought of how measurable are the mortalities we flatter with infinitude: the sands of the desert, the green hair of the grass, the waves of the sea.

Often, of late, she knew that he who loved her was strangely disquieted. "Too many dreams," he said once, with double meaning, smiling as he looked at her, but with an unexpressed trouble in his eyes.

More and more, because of the great, enduring, pitiless flame of love, she turned to the little things of the hour and the moment. It is the woman's way, and is a law. And more and more, wrought by longings and desires, he whom she loved turned to the inward contemplation of the things that are immortal, to the longings and desires that have their roots in the soul, but whose tendrils reach beyond the stars, and whose flowers grow by the waters of life in Edens beyond dream. It may not be men's way; and he had the fatal gift of the imagination, which is to men what great beauty is to women — a crown of stars and a slaying sword.

They turned the same way, not knowing it. How could they know, being blind? Blind children they were.

He feared the flame would consume them. She feared it would consume itself.

Therein lay the bitterness. But for her, being a woman, the depths were deeper. He had his dreams.

When, at last, the end came — a tragic, an almost incredible end, perhaps, for love did not change, passion was not slain, but translated to a starry dream, and every sweet and lovely intercourse was theirs still — the suffering was too great to be borne. Yet neither death nor tragic mischance came with veiled healing.

Love, won at a supreme hazard (and again, I do not tell the story of these two, who had, and now in the further silences have, their own secret, forever sacred), proved a stronger force than life. Life that can be measured, that is so measurable, is as a child before the other unknown power, that is without measure. The man did not understand. He fed the flame with dreams upon dreams, with hopes upon hopes; with more dreams and more hopes.

Once, dimly foreseeing the end, she said, "Love can be slain. It is mortal." He answered, almost with anger, that sooner could the soul die. She looked at him, wondering that he, whose imagination was so much greater than hers, could not understand.

She loved to the edge of death by will. Will can control the mortal things of love. Instinct wore her heart by day and by night. She put her frail strength into the balance, then her dreams, then her memories. Before the end, hesitating, but not for herself, she put her whole mind there. Still, life weighed lower and lower the scale.

One day they talked of immaterial things. Suddenly he asked her a question.

She was silent. The room was in darkness, for the fire had burned low. He could see only the ruddy gleam on the white skirt; the two white hands; the little restless flame in an opal.

Then, quietly, she told him. She had not ceased to love: it was not that.

Simply, love had been too great a flame. At the last, at that moment, she had striven to save all: she had already put all in the balance, all but her soul. That, too, she had now put there with swift and terrible suddenness.

The balance trembled, then Life weighed the scale lower, and lower.

It was gone. That had gone away upon the wind, which was light as it, homeless as it, as mysterious. Out of the balance she took back what else she had put there: her mind, quiet, sane, serene now, if that can be serene that neither fears nor cares because it does not feel: and the dreams and desires, that had turned to loosened fragrances and shadows: and hopes, grey as the ashes of wood, that fell away and were no more.

She was the same and yet not the same. He trembled, but dare not understand. In his mind were falling stars.

"I will give you all I have to give," she said; "to you, who have had all I had to give, I give that which is left. It is an image that has no life."

When he walked that night alone under the stars he understood. Love can come, not in his mortal but in his immortal guise: as a spirit of flame. There is no alchemy of life which can change that tameless and fierce thing, that power more intense than fire, that creature whose breath consumes what death only silences.

It had come close and looked at them. Long ago he had prayed that it might be so. In answer, the immortal had come to the mortal. How little of all that was to be he had foreseen when, by a spiritual force, he accomplished that too intimate, that too close union, in which none may endure! I speak of a mystery. That it may be, that to many, if not all, this thing that I say will be meaningless, I know. But I do not try to explain what is not a matter of words: nay, I could not, for though I believe, I know of this mystery only through those two who broke (or of whom one broke) some occult but imperious spiritual law.

They lived long after this great change. Their love never faltered. Each, as before, came close to the other, as day and night ceaselessly meet in dawns and twilights.

But that came to her no more which had gone. For him, he grew slowly to understand a love more great than his. His had not known the innermost flame, that is pure fire.

Strange and terrible thoughts came to him at times. The waste places of the imagination were peopled.

Often, as he has told me, through sleepless nights a solemn marching as of a vast throng rose and fell, a dreadful pulse. But, for him, life was fulfilled. I know that he had always one changeless hope. I do not know what, in the end clouded or unclouded that faithful spirit. But I, too, who knew them, who loved them, have my assured faith: the more, not the less, now that they are gone to that "distant country of Splendour and Terror." Love is more great than we conceive, and Death is the keeper of unknown redemptions. Of her, I have had often, I have ever, in my mind the words wherewith I begin one of the tales in this book: "It is God that builds the nest of the blind bird."

Section Five

DESCRIPTIONS OF THE NATURAL WORLD

DESCRIPTIONS OF THE NATURAL WORLD

All of the short essays in this section were originally published in the magazine *Country Life* during the years 1903-05 and were first published as a collection in 1906 shortly after the death of William Sharp. I include here her dedication to Mr. P. Anderson Graham who was a frequent correspondent with Fiona Macleod and who encouraged her to submit her natural and mystical essays to *Country Life*. This dedication spells out that the true source of her writings was, as far as she was concerned, the Realm of Faery. Many of her books contain such dedications and they are often more revealing of her inner nature than her other published works.

Several of these pieces were published in other magazines and journals across Europe in English, French, German, Swedish and Italian.

Not many writers could write over 2,200 words in explaining the wonderful nature and fascination of common, everyday grass but Fiona achieves this magnificently in *The Clans of the Grass*. This is another of those tales that has woven into it stories of Christ that are not to be found in the Bible, and Gaelic proverbs and sayings that are Fiona's own creations.

The Sea Spell deals with the fascination Fiona had for the oceans and seas in the same manner the previous essay dealt with her musings on common grass. Woven into this essay is a section dealing with four cities - not to be found in this world - which are an integral and basic part of the mythology of the Faeries. I deal with these four cities in depth in my book *The Chronicles of the Sidhe*. Note how seamlessly and comfortably these ancient Faery myths blend with the other poetic descriptions of the sea scattered across the essay.

The theme of the sea crops up in the next piece, *The Gardens of the Sea*, but here Fiona concentrates on the flora of the oceans, the seaweed. As we have seen, the sea and lochs appear frequently throughout Fiona's writings but often in a threatening and dangerous manner. Here the tone is much softer as she muses on how seaweed came into being and that despite its proclivity we know so little about it. Fiona's apparent negative attitude towards the sea may have been influenced somewhat by an incident in the life of William Sharp where he came across the corpse of a drowned sailor entangled in seaweed in the little fishing village of Crail in Scotland.

The Children of Wind and The Clan of Peace is another example of old Gaelic sayings that are not truly old, and events from the life of Jesus that are not to be found anywhere else. The story is different from her other stories and essays however, in that her companion at the beginning of the story, John Logan, is clearly a Lowlander who speaks English with a smattering of the Scottish Lowland dialect known as Lallans. Normally Fiona's sources are Gaelic-speaking Highlanders and Islanders. However she soon switches to a Gaelic source when she introduces John's Gaelic speaking mother. Her tale is yet another explanation of how things came to be as they are in the "Green World," the world of nature, a topic dear to Fiona's heart.

The final short piece in this section is a fragment called simply *The Star of Rest*. It is presumably the last thing Fiona was working on before the death of William Sharp as it was found lying on his desk in Castello di Maniace where he died on December 12th 1905.

DEDICATION
to
MR. P. ANDERSON GRAHAM

Dear Mr. Graham — To whom so fittingly as to you could I inscribe this book? It was you who suggested it; you who in *Country Life* published at intervals, no longer or shorter as the errant spirit of composition moved me, the several papers which make it one book; you without whose encouragement and good counsel this volume would probably not have been written. Then, perchance, it might have gone to that Y-Brasil[84] Press in the Country of the Young wherefrom are issued all the delightful books which, though possible and welcome in Tir-na-n'Òg,[85] are unachieved in this more difficult world, except in dreams and hopes. It would be good to have readers among the kindly Shee[86] ... do not the poets there know an easy time, having only to breathe their thought on to a leaf and to whisper their music to a reed, and lo the poem is public from the caverns of Tir-fo-Tuin[87] to the hills of Flatheanas![88] ... but, till one gets behind the foam yonder, the desire for the heart is for comrades here. These hours of beauty have meant so much to me, somewhat in the writing, but much more in the long, incalculable hours and days out of which the writing has risen like the blue smoke out of woods, that I want to share them with others, who may care for the things written of as you and I care for them, and among whom may be a few who, likewise, will be moved to garner from each day of the eternal pageant one hour of unforgettable beauty.

FIONA MACLEOD

---

84 Y-Brasil is one of the many names for the Realm of Faery.
85 Another name for the Realm of Faery, literally the Land of Youth.
86 Anglicized version of the Gaelic word *Sidhe* which means Faeries.
87 Another name for the Realm of Faery, literally Land under Waves.
88 An old Gaelic name for Heaven.

The Clans of the Grass

O F all the miracles of the green world none surpasses that of the grass. It has many names, many raiments even, but it is always that wonderful thing which the poets of all time have delighted in calling the green hair of earth. "Soft green hair of the rocks," says a Breton poet. Another Celtic poet has used the word alike for the mosses which clothe the talons of old trees and for the forests themselves. No fantastic hyperbole this: from a great height forests of pine and oak seem like reaches of sombre grass. To the shrewmouse the tall grasses of June are green woods, and the slim stems of the reddening sorrels are groves of pine-trees. I remember having read somewhere of a lovely name given to the grass by the Arabs of the desert ... "the Bride of Mahomet." What lovelier and more gracious thing in the world, in their eyes, than this soft cool greenness of the oasis, this emerald carpet below the green shadowy roof of waving palms; and as of all women in the world there could be but one, according to the old legend, worthy to be the supreme bride of the Prophet, what poetic name for her so fitting as this exquisite apparition of the desert, so beautiful, so evernew in itself, so welcome for its association with sweet waters and shade and coolness. A Gaelic poet calls the grass the Gift of Christ, literally slender-greenness of Christ (uain-eachd-caol Chriosde), and another has written of how it came to be called Green-Peace — both from an old tale (one of the many ebbed, forgotten tales of the isles) that, when God had created the world, Christ said: "Surely one thing yet lacks, my Father: soft greenness for the barren mountain, soft greenness for rocks and cliffs, soft greenness for stony places and the wilderness, soft greenness for the airidhs of the poor." Whereupon God said, "Let thy tenderness be upon these things, O my Son, and thy peace be upon them, and let the green grass be the colour of peace and of home" — and thereafter, says the taleteller, the Eternal Father turned to the Holy Spirit and said of the Son that from that hour He should be named the Prince of Peace, Prionnsa na Sioth-cainnt canar ris.

Grass is as universal as dew, as commonplace as light. That which feels the sea wind in the loneliest Hebrides is brother to that which lies on Himalaya or is fanned by the hot airs of Asian valleys. That which covers a grey scarp in Iceland is the same as that on Adam's Peak in Ceylon, and that which in myriad is the prairie of the north is in myriad the pampas of the south; that whose multitude covers the Gaelic hills is that whose multitude covers the Russian steppes. It is of all the signature of Nature that which to us is nearest and homeliest. The green grass after long voyaging, the grass of home-valley or hillside after long wayfaring, the green grass of the Psalmist to souls athirst and weary, the grass of El Dorado to the visionary seeking the gold of the spirit, the grass of the Fortunate Isles, of the Hills of Youth, to the poets and dreamers of all lands and times ... everywhere and ever has this omnipresent herb that withereth and yet is continually reborn, been the eternal symbol of that which passes like a dream, the symbol of everlasting illusion, and yet, too, is the symbol of resurrection, of all the old divine illusion essayed anew, of the inexplicable mystery of life recovered and everlastingly perpetrated.

When we speak of grass we generally mean one thing, the small slim green herb which carpets the familiar earth. But there are many grasses, from the smooth close-set herb of our lawns or the sheep-nibbled downy greenness of mountain-pastures, to the forest-like groves which sway in the torrid winds of the south. Of these alone much might be written. I prefer, however, that name I have placed at the head of this article — taken, if I remember rightly, from a poem by the Gaelic mountain-poet, Duncan Ban Macintyre — and used in the sense of the original. In this sense, the Clans of the Grass are not only the grasses of the pasture, the sand-dune, the windy down, not only the sorrel-red meadow grass or the delicate quaking-grass, but all the humbler green growth which covers the face of the earth. In this company are the bee-loved clover, the trailing vetch, the yellow-sea clover and the sea-pink; the vast tribe of the charlock or wild mustard which on showery days sometimes lights up field or hill-meadow with yellow flame so translucent that one thinks a sudden radiant sunflood burns and abides there. In it too are all the slim peoples of the reed and rush, by streams and pools and lochans: of the yellow iris by the sea-loch and the tall flag by the mountain-tarn: the grey thistle, the sweet-gate, and all the tribe of the bog-cotton or canna (ceann-bàn-a-mhonaidh, the white head of the hillside, as we call it in Gaelic), those lovers of the wilderness and boggy places. With these is the bind weed that with the salt bent holds the loose shores. With these are all the shadow-loving clans of the fern, from the bracken, whose April-glow lightens the glens and whose autumnal brown and dull gold make the hillsides so resplendent, to the stonewort on the dykes, the lady-fern in the birch-woods, the maidenhair by springs and falls, the hart's-tongue in caverns, the Royal fern whose broad fronds are the pride of heather-waste and morass. The mosses, too, are from this vast clan of the earth-set, from the velvet-soft edging of the oak-roots or the wandering greenness of the swamp to the ashy tresses which hang on spruce or hemlock or the grey fringes of the rocks by northern seas. And with them are the lichens, that beautiful secret company who love the shadow-side of trees, and make stones like flowers, and transmute the barrenness of rock and boulder with dyes of pale gold and blazing orange and timber, rich as the brown hearts of tarns, and pearl-grey delicate as a cushat's breast, and saffron as yellow-green as the sunset-light after the clearing of rains. To all these, indeed, should be added the greater grasses which we know as wheat and oats, as rye and maize. Thus do we come to "the waving hair of the ever-wheeling earth," and behold the unresting mother as in a vision, but with the winds of space for ever blowing her waving tresses in a green gladness, or in a shimmer of summer-gold, or in the bronze splendour of the columnal passage.

But the grasses proper, alone: the green grass itself — what a delight to think of these, even if the meaning of the title of this paper be inclusive of them and them only. What variety, here, moreover. The first spring-grass, how welcome it is. What lovely delicacy of green. It is difficult anywhere to match it. Perhaps the first greening of the sallow, that lovely hair hung over ponds and streams or where sloping lawns catch the wandering airs of the south: or the pale green-flame of the awakening larch: or the tips of bursting hawthorn in the hedgerows — perhaps, these are nearest to it in hue. But with moonlight it may become almost the pale-yellow of sheltered primroses, or yellow-green as the cowslip before its faint gold is minted, and in the mellowing afternoon it may often be seen as illuminated (as with hidden delicate flame) as the pale-emerald candelabra of the hellebore. How different is the luxuriant grass in hollows and combs and along watered meadows in June, often dark as pine-greens or as sunlit jade, and in shadowy places or a twilight sometimes as lustrously sombre-grey as the obsidian, that precious stone of the Caucasus now no longer a rarity among us. How swiftly, too, that changes after the heats of midsummer, often being threaded with grey light before the dog-days are spent. Moreover, at any season there is a difference between down-grass and mountain-grass, between sea-grass and valley-grass, between moor-grass and wood-grass. It may be slight, and not in kind but only in shadowy dissemblances of texture and hue; still one may note the difference. More obvious, of course, is the difference between, say, April-grass and the same grass when May or June suffuses it with the red glow of the seeding sorrel, or between the sea-grass that has had the salt wind upon it since its birth, the bent as it is commonly called, and its brother among the scarps and cliff-edges of the hills, so marvellously soft and hairlike for all that it is not long since the snows have lifted or since sleet and hail have harried the worn faces of boulder and crag. Or, again, between even the most delicate wantonness of the seeding hay, fragrant with white clover and purple vetch, and the light aerial breathfulness, frail as thistledown, of the quaking-grass. How it loves the wood's-edge, this last, or sheltered places by the hedgerows, the dream-hollows of sloping pastures, meadow-edges where the cow-parsley whitens like foam and the meadow-sweet floats cream-white and the white campions hang in clotted froth over the long surge of daisies: or, where, like sloops of the nautilus on tropic seas, curved blossoms of the white wild-rose motionlessly suspend or idly drift, hardly less frail, less wantonly errant than the white bloomy dust of the dandelion.

Caran-cheann-air-chrith, "little friend of the quaking-grass," is one of the Gaelic names of the wagtail, perhaps given to it because of a like tremulous movement, as though invisible wings of gossamer shook ever in a secret wind. Or given to it, perhaps, because of a legend which puts the common grass, the quaking-grass, the wagtail, the cuckoo, the aspen, and the lichen in one traditional company. In the Garden of Gethsemane, so runs the Gaelic folk-tale as I heard it as a child, all Nature suddenly knew the Sorrow of Christ. The dew whispered it: it was communicated in the dusk: in pale gold and shaken silver it stole from moon and star into the green darkness of cypress and cedar. The grass-blades put all their green lips into one breath, and sighed, "Peace, Brother!" Christ smiled in His sorrow, and said, "Peace to you for ever."

But here and there among the grasses, as here and there among the trees, and as here and there among the husht birds, were those who doubted, saying, "It is but a man who lies here. His sorrow is not our sorrow." Christ looked at them, and they were shaken with the grief of all grief and the sorrow of all sorrow. And that is why to this day the quaking-grass and the aspen are for ever a-tremble, and why the wagtail has no rest but quivers along the earth like a dancing shadow. But to those mosses of Gethsemane which did not give out the sympathy of their kin among the roots of cedar and oak, and to the cuckoo who rang from her nest a low chime of "All's well! All's well!" Christ's sorrowful eyes when He rose at dawn could not be endured. So the cuckoo rose and flew away across the Hill of Calvary, ringing through the morning twilight the bells of sorrow, and from that day was homeless and without power anywhere to make a home of her own. As for the mosses that had refused love, they wandered away to desolate places and hung out forlorn flags of orange-red and pale-yellow and faded-silver along the grey encampments of the rocks.

Often I have thought of this when lying in the mountain-grass beside one of those ancient lichened boulders which strew our hillsides. The lichen is the least of the grasses — and let us use the term in its poetic sense — but how lovely a thing it is; almost as lovely in endless variety of form as the frost-flower. In a sense they are strangely akin, these two; the frost-flower, which is the breath of Beauty itself, lasting a briefer hour than the noontide dew, and the moss-flower which the barren rock sustains through all the changing seasons.

Who is that Artificer who has subtly and diversely hidden the secret of rhythm in the lichen of the rock and in the rock's heart itself; in the frost-flower, so perfect in beauty that a sunbeam breathes it away; in the falling star, a snowflake in the abyss, yet with the miraculous curve in flight which the wave has had, which the bent poplar has had, which the rainbow has had, since the world began? The grey immemorial stone and the vanishing meteor are one. Both are the offspring of the Eternal Passion, and it may be that between the aeon of the one and the less than a minute of the other there shall not, in the divine reckoning, be more than the throb of a pulse. For who of us can measure even Time, that the gnat measures as well as we, or the eagle, or the ancient yew, or the mountain whose granite brows are white with ages — much less Eternity, wherein Time is but a vanishing pulse?

The Sea-Spell

OLD magical writers speak of the elemental affinity which is the veiled door in each of us. Find that door, and you will be on the secret road to the soul, they say in effect. Some are children of fire, and some of air, some are of earth, and some of water. They even resolve mortal strength and weakness, our virtue and our evil, into the movement of these elements. This virtue, it is of fire: this quality, it is of air: this frailty, it is of water.

Howsoever this may be, some of us are assuredly of that ancient clan in whose blood, as an old legend has it, is the water of the sea. Many legends, many poems, many sayings tell of the Chloinn-na-Mhara, the children of the sea. I have heard them from fishermen, from inland-shepherds, from moorlanders in inland solitudes where the only visitors from the mysterious far-off deep are the wandering sea-mews or the cloud that has climbed out of the south. Some tell of the terror of the sea, some of its mysteriousness, some of the evil and of the evil things that belong to it and are in it, some of its beauty, some of its fascination (as the Greeks of old time told of the sirens, who were the voices and fatal music and the strange and perilous loveliness of alien waters), some of the subtle and secret spell deep-buried in the hearts of certain men and women, the Chloinn-na-Mhara, a spell that will brood there, and give no peace, but will compel the spirit to the loneliness of the wind, and the outward life to the wayward turbulence of the wave. More than two thousand years ago the great Pindar had these in mind when he wrote of that strange tribe among men "who scorn the things of home, and gaze on things that are afar off, and chase a cheating prey with hopes that shall never be fulfilled."

Elsewhere I have written much of this sea-spell, of the Brònavara (to Anglicise an island word), or Sorrow of the Sea, and do not wish to write here of that strange passion or sinister affinity: but of that other and happier Spell of the Sea which so many of us feel, with pleasure always, with delight often, at times with exultation, as though in our very heart were the sharp briny splash of the blue wave tossing its white crest, or of the green billow falling like a tower of jade in a seething flood. But, first, I recall that old legend to which I have alluded. Perhaps some folklorist may recognise it as gathered out of the drift common to many shores, may trace it even to those Asian inlands where so many of our most ancient tales mysteriously arose; but I have nowhere met with it in print, nor seen nor heard allusion to it, other than in a crude fashioning on the lips of simple Gaelic folk, nor even there for years upon years.

There were once four cities (the Western Gael will generally call them Gorias and Falias, Finias and Murias), the greatest and most beautiful of the cities of those ancient tribes of beauty, the offspring of angels and the daughters of earth. The fair women were beautiful, but lived like flowers, and like flowers faded and were no more, for they were filled with happiness, as cups of ivory filled with sunlit dancing wine, but were soulless. Eve, that sorrowful loveliness, was not yet born. Adam was not yet lifted out of the dust of Eden. Finias was the gate of Eden to the South, Murias to the West: in the North, Falias was crowned by a great star: in the East, Gorias, the city of gems, flashed like sunrise. There the deathless clan of the sky loved the children of Lilith. On the day when Adam uttered the sacred name and became king of the world, a great sighing was heard in Gorias in the East and in Finias in the South, in Murias in the West and in Falias in the North: and when morn was come the women were no more awakened by the stirring of wings and the sunrise-flight of their angelic lovers. They came no more. And when Eve awoke, by the side of Adam, and he looked on her, and saw the immortal mystery in the eyes of this mortal loveliness, lamentations and farewells and voices of twilight were heard in Murias by the margin of the sea, and in Gorias high-set among her peaks; in the secret gardens of Falias, and where the moonlight hung like a spear above the towers of Finias upon the great plain. The Children of Lilith were gone away upon the wind, as lifted dust, as dew, as shadow, as the unreturning leaf. Adam rose, and bade Eve go to the four solitudes, and bring back the four ancient secrets of the world. So Eve went to Gorias and found nothing there but a flame of fire. She lifted it and hid it in her heart. At noon she came to Finias and found nothing there but a spear of white light. She took it and bid it in her mind. At dusk she came to Falias and found nothing there but a star in the darkness. She hid the darkness, and the star within the darkness, in her womb. At moonrise she came to Murias, by the shores of the ocean. There she saw nothing but a wandering light. So she stooped and lifted a wave of the sea and hid it in her blood. And when Eve was come again to Adam, she gave him the flame she had found in Gorias and the spear of light she had found in Finias.

"In Falias," she said, "I found that which I cannot give, but the darkness I have hidden shall be your darkness, and the star shall be your star."

"Tell me what you found in Murias by the sea?" asked Adam.

"Nothing," answered Eve. But Adam knew that she lied.

"I saw a wandering light," she said.

He sighed, and believed. But Eve kept the wave of the sea hidden in her blood. So has it been that a multitude of women have been homeless as the wave, and their heritage salt as the sea: and that some among their sons and daughters have been possessed by that vain cold fire, and that inappeasable trouble, and the restlessness of water. So it is that to the end of time some shall have the salt sea in the blood, and the troubled wave in the heart, and be homeless.

But thoughts like these, legends like these, are for the twilight hour, or for the silent people who live in isles and remote places. For most of us, for those of us who do not dwell by lonely shores and seldom behold the sea but in the quiet seasons, it is either a delight or an oppression. Some can no more love it, or can have any well-being or composure near it, than others can be well or content where vast moors reach from skyline to skyline, or amid the green solemnities of forests, or where stillness inhabits the hollows of hills. But for those who do love it, what a joy it is! *The Sea* ... the very words have magic. It is like the sound of a horn in woods, like the sound of a bugle in the dusk, like the cry of wind leaping the long bastions of silence. To many of us there is no call like it, no other such clarion of gladness.

But when one speaks of the sea it is as though one should speak of summer or winter, of spring or autumn. It has many aspects. It is not here what it is yonder, yonder it is not what it is afar off: here, even, it is not in August what it is when the March winds, those steel-blue courses, are unleashed; the grey-green calms of January differ from the purple-grey calms of September, and November leaning in mist across the dusk of wavering horizons is other than azure-robed and cirrus-crowned May moving joyously across a glorious tossing wilderness of blue and white. The blue sea frothed with wind has ever been a salutation of joy. Æschylos sounded the note of rapture which has since echoed through poetry and romance: that "multitudinous laughter" struck a vibration which time has never dulled nor lessened. It has been an exultation above all in the literatures of the north. Scandinavian poetry is full of the salt brine; there is not a Viking-saga that is not wet with the spray of surging seas. Through all the primitive tales and songs of the Gael one feels the intoxication of the blue wine of the running wave. In the Icelandic sagas it is like a clashing of shields. It calls through the Ossianic chants like a tide. Every Gaelic song of exile has the sound of it, as in the convolutions of a shell. The first Gaelic poet rejoiced at the call of the sea, and bowed before the chanting of a divine voice. In his madness, Cuchulain fought with the racing billows on the Irish Coast, striving with them as joy-intoxicated foes, laughing against their laughter; to the dark waves of Coruisk, in the Isle of Skye, he rushed with a drawn sword, calling to these wise warriors of the sea to advance in their proud hosts that he might slay them. Sigurd and Brynhild, Gunhild and Olaf, Torquil and Swaran and Haco, do they not sound like the names of waves? How good that old-world rejoicing in the great green wilderness of waters, in the foam-swept blue meads, in the cry of the wind and the chant of the billows and the sharp sting of flying scud?

It is of to-day also. A multitude of us rejoice as those of old rejoiced, though we have changed in so much with all the incalculable change of the years. To-day as then the poets of the isles ... the poet in the heart of each of us who loves the glory and beauty and in any degree feels the strong spell of the sea ... answer to that clarion-music: as in this *Evoë!* by one of the latest among them:

"*Oceanward, the sea-horses sweep magnificently, champing and whirling white foam about their green flanks, and tossing on high their manes of sunlit rainbow-gold, dazzling white and multitudinous, far as sight can reach.*

"*O champing horses of my soul, toss, toss on high your sunlit manes, your manes of rainbow-gold, dazzling white and multitudinous, for I too rejoice, rejoice!*"

And who of us will forget that great English poet of to-day, that supreme singer of —

"*Sky, and shore, and cloud, and waste, and sea,*"

who has written so often and so magically of the spell of the sea and of the elation of those who commit themselves to the sway and rhythm of its moving waters:

"The grey sky gleams and the grey seas glimmer,
Pale and sweet as a dream's delight,
As a dream's where darkness and light seem dimmer,
Touched by dawn or subdued by night.
The dark wind, stern and sublime and sad,
Swings the rollers to westward, clad

With lustrous shadow that lures the swimmer,
Lures and lulls him with dreams of light.

"Light, and sleep, and delight, and wonder,
Change, and rest, and a charm of cloud,
Fill the world of the skies whereunder
Heaves and quivers and pants aloud
All the world of the waters, hoary
Now, but clothed with its own live glory,
That mates the lightning and mocks the thunder
With light more living and word more proud.

"A dream, and more than a dream, and dimmer
At once and brighter than dreams that flee,
The moment's joy of the seaward swimmer
Abides, remembered as truth may be.
Not all the joy and not all the glory
Must fade as leaves when the woods wax hoary;
For there the downs and the sea-banks glimmer,
And here to south of them swells the sea."

What swimmer too, who loves this poet, but will recall the marvellous sea-shine line in "Thalassius":

"Dense water-walls and clear dusk waterways …
The deep divine dark dayshine of the sea — "

It is this exquisite miracle of transparency which gives the last secret of beauty to water. All else that we look upon is opaque: the mountain in its sundown purple or noon-azure, the meadows and fields, the gathered greenness of woods, the loveliness of massed flowers, the myriad wonder of the universal grass, even the clouds that trail their shadows upon the hills, or soar so high into frozen deeps of azure that they pass shadowless like phantoms or the creatures of dreams — the beauty of all these is opaque. But the beauty of water is that it is transparent. Think if the grass, if the leaves of the tree, if the rose and the iris and the pale horns of the honeysuckle, if the great mountains built of grey steeps of granite and massed purple of shadow were thus luminous, thus transparent! Think if they, too, as the sea, could reflect the passage of saffron-sailed and rose-flusht argosies of cloud, or mirror as in the calms of ocean the multitudinous undulation of the blue sky! This divine translucency is but a part of the Sea-Spell, which holds us from childhood to old age in wonder and delight, but that part is its secret joy, its incommunicable charm.

The Gardens of the Sea

(A MIDSUMMER NOON'S DREAM)

I recall a singular legend, where heard, where read, I do not remember, nor even am I sure of what race the offspring, of what land the denizen. It was to the effect that, in the ancient days of the world, flowers had voices, had song to them as the saying is: and that there were kingdoms among these populations of beauty, that in the course of ages (would they be flower-æons, and so of a measure in time different from our longer or shorter periods?) satraps revolted against the dominion of the Rose, and tropical princes led new hosts, and scarlet forest-queens filled the jungle and the savannah with their chants of victory. And the end was a conflict so great that even the isles of the sea were shaken by it, and the pale green moss of polar rocks whispered of the great world-war of the peoples of Flowry. At last, after the shadow-flitting passage of an æon, the gods were roused from their calm, and, looking down into the shaken mirror of the world, beheld all their dreams and visions and desires no longer children of loveliness and breaths of song. In these æons while they had slept in peace the Empire of Flowry had come to a dissolution: race fought with race, tribe with tribe, clan with clan. Among all the nations there was a madness for supremacy, so that the weed in the grass and the flame-crowned spire of the aloe were at one in a fierce discontent and a blind lust of dominion.

Thereupon the gods pondered among themselves. Kronos, who had been the last to wake and was already drowsy with old immemorial returning slumber, murmured: "A divine moment, O ye Brotherhood of Eternity, is a long time wherein to be disturbed by the mortal reflection of our dreams and the passions, and emotions of our enchanted hearts."

And as all the calm-eyed Immortals agreed, Kronos sighed out the mandate of silence, and turning his face to Eternity was again among the august dreams of the Everlasting Ones.

In that long moment — for, there in the other world, it was but a brief leaning on their elbows of the drowsy gods while the fans of Immortal Sleep for a second stayed the vast waves of Peace — the divine messengers, or were they the listening powers and dominions of the earth, fulfilled destiny? From every flower-nation, from every people by far waters, from every tribe in dim woods and the wilderness, from every clan habiting the most far hills beyond the ever-receding pale blue horizons, song was taken as stars are pluckt away from the Night by the grey fingers of the Dawn. The Rose breathed no more a flusht magic of sound; the Lily no more exhaled a foam-white cadence. Silence was come upon the wild chant of orchids in old, forgotten woods; stillness upon the tinkling cymbals of the little hands of the dim, myriad, incalculable host of blossom; a hush upon the songs of, meadow-flowers; a spell upon the singing of honeysuckles in the white dews at the rising of the moon. Everywhere, from all the green tribes, from all the glowing nations of Flowry, from each and every of the wandering folk of the Reed, the Moss, and the Lichen, from all the Clans of the Grass, the added loveliness of song was taken. Silence fell upon one and all: a strange and awful stillness came upon the woods and valleys. It was then that the God of Youth, wandering through the husht world, took the last song of a single rose that in a secret place had not yet heard the common doom, and with his breath gave it a body, and a pulse to its heart, and fashioned for it a feather covering made of down of the bog-cotton and the soft undersides of alder leaf and olive. Then, from a single blade of grass that still whispered in a twilight hollow, he made a like marvel, to be a mate to the first, and sent out both into the green world, to carry song to the woods and the valleys, the hills and the wildernesses, the furthest shores, the furthest isles. Thus was the nightingale created, the first bird, the herald of all the small clans of the bushes that have kept wild-song in the world, and are our delight.

But in the hearts of certain of the green tribes a sullen anger endured. So the mysterious Hand which had taken song and cadence away punished these sullen ones. From some, fragrance also was taken. There were orchid-queens of forest-loveliness from whom all fragrance suddenly passed like smoke: there were white delicate phantoms among the grasses, from whom sweet odour was lifted as summer dew: there were nomads of the hillways and gypsies of the plain to whom were given the rankness of the waste, the, smell of things evil, of corruption, of the grave. But to some, beautiful rebels of the peoples of the Reed, the Grass, and the Fern, the doom went out that henceforth their place should be in the waters ... the running waters of streams and rivers, the quiet waters of pools and lakes, the troubled waters of the seas along the coasts of the world, the ocean depths.

And that is how amid the salt bite of the homeless wave there grew the Gardens of the Sea. That is how it came about that the weed trailed in running waters, and the sea-moss swayed in brackish estuaries, and the wrack clung or swam in tangles of olive-brown and green and soft and dusky reds.

What a long preamble to the story of how the Seaweeds were once sweet-smelling blooms of the shores and valleys! Of how the flowers of meadow and woodland, of the sun-swept plain and the shadowy hill, had once song as well as sweet odours: how, of these, many lost not only fragrance but innocent beauty: and how out of a rose and a blade of grass and a breath of the wind the first birds were made, the souls of the green earth, winged, and voiced.

To-day I sit among deep, shelving rocks by the shore, in a desolate place where basaltic cliffs shut away the familiar world, and where, in front, the otherworld of the sea reaches beyond sight to follow the lifted wave against the grey skyline, or is it the grey lip of the fallen horizon? Looking down I can perceive the olive-brown and green seaweed swaying in the slow movement of the tide. Like drifted hair, the long thin filaments of the Mermaid's Locks (*Chorda Filum*) sinuously twist, intertwine, involve, and unfold. It is as though a seawoman rose and fell, idly swam or idly swung this way and that, asleep on the tide, nothing visible of her wave-grey body but only her long fatal hair, that so many a swimmer has had to cause dread, from whose embrace so many a swimmer has never risen. In the rock-set pools the flesh-hued fans of the dulse indolently stir. Wave-undulated over them are fronds of a lovely green weed, delicate, transparent: above these, two phantom fish, rock-cod or saithe, float motionless.

Idly watching, idly dreaming thus, I recall part of a forgotten poem about the woods of the sea, and the finned silent creatures that are its birds: and how there are stags and wolves in these depths, long hounds of the sea, mermen and merwomen and seal-folk. Others, too, for whom we have no name, we being wave-blind and so unable to discern these comers and goers of the shadow. Also, how old sea-divinities lie there asleep, and perilous phantoms come out of sunken ships and ancient weed-grown towns; and how there roams abroad, alike in the flowing wave and along the sheer green-darkening bodiless walls, an incalculable Terror that may be manifold, the cold implacable demons of the deep, or may be One, that grey timeworn Death whom men have called Poseidon and Mananan and by many names.

What a mysterious world this Tir-fo-Tuinn, this Land-Under-Wave. How little we know of it, for all that wise men have told us concerning the travelling tides, of currents as mysteriously steadfast in the comings and goings as the comets that from age to age loom briefly upon the stellar roads: how little, though they have put learned designations to a thousand weeds, and given names to ten thousand creatures to whom the whole world of man and all his hopes and dreams are less than a phantom, less than foam. The Gaelic poet who said that the man who goes to Tir-fo-Tuinn goes into another world, where the human soul is sand, and God is but the unloosened salt, tells us as much as the scientist who probes the ocean-mud and reveals dim crustacean life where one had believed to be only a lifeless dark. Above the weed-held palaces of Atlantis, over the soundless bells of Ys, above where Lyonesse is gathered in a foamless oblivion, the plummet may sink and lift a few broken shells, the drag-net may bring to the surface an unknown sea-snail or such a microscopic green Alga as that *Halosphoera viridis* which science has discovered in the great depths beyond the reach of sunlight: but who can tell, perchance how few who care to know, what Love was, long ago, when there were poets in Lyonesse: what worship was served by white-robed priests among the sunken fanes of Ys: what dreams withstayed and what passions beset the noble and the ignoble in drowned Atlantis, what empires rose and fell there, what gods were lauded and dethroned, and for how long Destiny was patient.

Even in the little pools that lie shoreward of the Gardens of the Sea what beauty there is, what obscure life, what fascinating "otherworld" association. This piece of kelp is at once *Fucus vesiculosus* and the long fingers of the Cailliach-Mhara, the Sea-Witch. This great smooth frond is ... I do not know, or forget: but it is the kale of Manan, in sea-groves of which that Shepherd pastures his roves of uncouth sea-swine. This green tracery has a Greek or Latin name, but in legend it is called the Mermaid's Lace. This little flame-like crest of undulating wrack has a designation longer than itself, but in tales of faerie we know it to be that of which the caps of the pool-elves are fashioned.

In the Isles seaweed has many local names, but is always mainly divided into Yellow Tails, Dark Tails, and Red Tails (*Feamainin bhuidhe*, *feamainn dubh*, and *feamainn dearg*). The first comprise all the yellowish, light-brown, and olive-brown seaware; the second all the dark-green, and also all green wrack; the third, the red. The common seaware or kelp or tang (*Fucus vesiculosus*) is generally called *propach*, or other variant signifying tangled: and the bladder-wrack, *feamainn bholgainn* or *builgeach*, "baggy-tails," have at times collected many local names of these weeds, and not a few superstitions and legends. Naturally the most poetic of these are connected with the *Chorda filum* or Dead Man's Hair, which has a score of popular names, from "corpsy-ropes" to the occasional Gaelic *gillemu lunn*, which may be rendered "the wave's gillie" or "servant of the wave": with the drifted gulf-weed, whose sea-grapes are called *uibhean sìthein*, fairy eggs, and are eagerly sought for: and with the *duileasg*, or dulse. Even to this day, in remote parts, an ancient seaweed-rite survives in the propitiatory offerings (now but a pastime of island children) to the Hebridean sea-god Shony at Samhain (Hallowmass). This Shony, whose favours were won by a cup of ale thrown into the sea in the dark of the night, is none other than Poseidon, Neptune, Manan; for he is the Scandinavian sea-god *Sjoni*, Viking-brought from Lochlin in the far-off days when the Summer-sailors raided and laid waste the Gaelic Isles.

It is singular how rarely seaweed has entered into the nomenclature and symbology of peoples, how seldom it is mentioned in ancient literature. Among our Gaelic clans there is only one (the M'Neil) which has seaware as a badge. Greek art has left us a few seaweed-filleted heads of Gorgons, and to sea-wrack the Latin poets have once or twice made but passing and contemptuous allusion. In the Bible ("whaur ye'll find everything frae a bat to a unicorn," as an old man said to me once) there is one mention of it only, in Jonah's words: "The depths closed me round about, the weeds were wrapped about my head."

The Children of Wind and the Clan of Peace

I was abroad on the moors one day in the company of a shepherd, and we were talking of the lapwing that were plentiful there, and were that day wailing continuously in an uneasy wavering flight. I had seen them act thus, in this excess of alarm, in this prolonged restless excitement, when the hill-falcons were hovering overhead in the nesting season: and, again, just before the unloosening of wind and rain and the sudden fires of the thundercloud. But John Logan the shepherd told me that now it was neither coming lightning nor drifting hawk nor eagle that made all this trouble among the "peewits."

"The wind's goin' to mak' a sudden veer," he said — adding abruptly a little later, "an' by the same token we'll have rain upon us soon."

I looked at the cold blue of the sky, and at the drift of the few clouds trailing out of the east or south-east, and could see no sign of any change of wind or likelihood of rain.

"What makes you think that?" I asked.

"Weel," he answered literally, "I don't think it, it's the peewits an' the craws that ken swifter than oursel; it's they that tell, an' I think they're better at the business than thae folk wha haver awa' in the papers, an' are sometimes richt because they canna help it an' oftener wrang because it's maistly guesswork."

"Well, what do the peewits and the crows say? — though I haven't seen crow or rook or corbie for the last hour."

"Thae peewits an' a' the plovers are a' the same. If the win's gaun to leap out of the east intae the sooth-wast, or slide quickly from the north intae the wast, they'll gang on wheelin' an' wailin' like you for an hour or mair, an' that afore there's the least sign o' a change. An' as for the craws ... weel, if ye had been lookin' up a wee whilie ago ye'd 'a seen a baker's dozen go by, slantin' on the edge o' the win', like boats before a stiff breeze. Aye, an' see there! ... there's a wheen mair comin' up overhead."

I glanced skyward, and saw some eight or ten rooks flying high and evidently making for the mountain-range about two miles away to our left.

"D'ye see that ... thae falling birds?"

"Yes," I answered, noticing a singular occasional fall in the general steady flight, as though the suddenly wheeling bird had been shot: "and what o' that, John?"

"It's just this. When ye see craws flyin' steady like that an' then yince in a while drapping oot like yon, ye may tak' it as meanin' there's heavy rain no that great way aff: onyways, when ye see the like when thae black deils are fleein' straight for the hills, ye maun feel sure frae the double sign that ye'll bae a good chance o' being drookit afore twa-three hours."

One question led to another, and I heard much crow and corbie lore from John Logan, some of it already familiar to me and some new to me or vaguely half-known — as the legend that the corbies or ravens, and with them all the crow-kind, were originally white, but at the time of the Deluge were turned sooty-black — because the head of the clan, when sent out by Noah from the Ark, did not return, but stayed to feed on the bodies of the drowned. "So the blackness of death was put on them, as my old mother has it in her own Gaelic."

"Your old mother, John?" I queried surprisedly: "I did not know you had any one at your croft."

"Aye, but I have that, though she's a poor frail auld body an' never gangs further frae the hoose than the byre an' the hen-yaird. If ye want to hear more aboot thae birds an' the auld stories forenenst them, she'd mak' you welcome, an' we'd be glad an' prood to offer ye tea: an' I'll just tell ye this, that ye'll gie her muckle pleasure if ye'll hae a crack wi' her in the Gaelic, an' let her tell her auld tales in't. She's Hielan', ye ken: tho' my faither was oot o' Forfar, Glen Isla way. She's never got hold o' the English yet varra weel, an' to my sorrow I've never learnt the auld tongue, takin' after my faither in that, dour Lowland body as he was. I ken enough to follow her sangs, an' a few words forbye, just enough to gie us a change as ye micht say."

I gladly accepted the shepherd's courteous offer; and so it was that an hour later we found ourselves at Scaur-vàn, as his croft was called, from its nearness to a great bleached crag that rose out of the heather like a light-ship in a lonely sea. By this time, his prognostications — or those rather of the wheeling and wailing lapwings, and the mountain-flying rooks — had come true. Across the wide desolate moors a grey wind soughed mournfully from the south-west, driving before it long slanting rains and sheets of drifting mist. I was glad to be out of the cold wet, and in the warm comfort of a room lit with a glowing peat-fire on which lay one or two spurtling logs of pine.

A dear old woman rose at my entrance. I could see she was of great age, because her face was like a white parchment seamed with myriad wrinkles, and her hands were so sere and thin that they were like wan leaves of October. But she was fairly active, and her eyes were clear — and even, if the expression may be used, with a certain quiet fire in their core — and her features were comely, with a light on them as of serene peace. The old-fashioned white mutch she wore enhanced this general impression, and I remember smiling to myself at the quaint conceit that old Mrs. Logan was like a bed-spirit of ancient slumber looking out from an opening of frilled white curtains.

It was pleasant to sit and watch her, as with deft hands she prepared the tea and laid on the table scones and butter and grey farrels of oatcake, while, outside, the wet wind moaned and every now and then a swirl of rain splashed against the narrow panes of the window, in whose inset stood three pots of geranium with scarlet flowers that caught the red flicker of the fire-flaucht and warmed the grey dusk gathering without.

Later, we began to speak of the things of which her son John and I had talked on the moor: and then of much else in connection with the legendary lore of the birds and beasts of the hills and high moorlands.

As it was so much easier for her (and so far more vivid and idiomatic) she spoke in Gaelic, delighted to find one who could understand the ancient speech: for in that part of the country, though in the Highlands, no Gaelic is spoken, or only a few words or phrases connected with sport, sheep-driving, and the like. I had won her heart by saying to her soon after the tea — up to which time she had spoken in the slow and calculated but refined Highland-English of the north-west — *Tha mi cinnteach gu bheil sibh aois mhòr* ... "I am sure that you have the great age on you." She had feared that because I had "the English way" I would not know, or remember, or care to remember, the old tongue: and she took my hand and stroked it while she said with a quiet dignity of pleasure, *Is taitneach leam nach 'eil 'ur Gàidhlig air meirgeadh* ... (in effect) "It is well pleased I am that your Gaelic has not become rusty."

It was after the tea-things had been set aside, and old Mrs. Logan had said reverently, *Iarramaid beannachadh* ("Let us ask a blessing"), that she told me, among other legendary things and fragments of old natural-history folklore, the following legend (or holy Christmas tale, as she called it) as to how the first crows were black and the first doves white.

I will tell it as simply but also with what beauty I can, because her own words, which I recall only as the fluctuating remembrance from a dream and so must translate from the terms of dream into the terms of prose, though simple, were beautiful with ancient idiom.

Thus she began: — *Feumaidh sinn dol air ar n'-ais dlùth fichead ceud bliadhna*, which is to say, "We must go back near two thousand (lit: twenty hundred) years.

Yes, it is nigh upon twenty hundred years that we must go back. It was in the last month of the last year of the seven years' silence and peace. When would that be, you ask? Surely what other would it be than the seven holy years when Jesus the Christ was a little lad. Do you not remember the lore of the elders? ... that in the first seven years of the life of the young Christ there was peace in the world, and that the souls of men were like souls in a dream, and that the hearts of women were at rest. In the second seven years it is said that the world was like an adder that sloughs its skin: for there was everywhere a troubled sense of new things to come. So wide and far and deep was this, that men in remote lands began moving across swamps and hills and deserts; that the wild beasts shifted their lairs and moaned and cried in new forests and upon untrodden plains; that the storks and swallows in their migration wearied their wings in high, cold, untravelled ways; that the narwhals and great creatures of the deep foamed through unknown seas; that the grasses of the world wandered and inhabited hills; that many waters murmured in the wilderness and that many waters mysteriously sank from pools and wellsprings. In the third seven years, men even on the last ocean-girdled shores were filled with further longing, and it is said that new stars were flung into the skies and ancient stars were whirled away, like dust and small stones beneath the wheels of a chariot. It was at the end of the third seven years that a Face looked out of Heaven, and that from the edges of the world men heard a confused and dreadful sound rising from the Abyss. Though the great and the small are the same, it is the great that withdraws from remembrance and the small that remains, and that may be why men have grown old with time, and have forgotten, and remember only the little things of the common life: as that in these years the Herring became the king of all fishes, because his swift gleaming clan carried the rumour of great tidings to the uttermost places of ocean; as that in these years the little fly became king over lions and panthers and eagles and over all birds and beasts, because it alone of all created things had remained tameless and fearless; as that in these years the wild-bees were called the Clan of Wisdom, because they carried the Word to every flower that grows and spread the rumour on all the winds of the world; as that in these years the Cuckoo was called the Herald of God, because in his voice are heard the bells of Resurrection.

But, as I was saying, it was in the last month of the last year of the seven years' silence and peace: the seventh year in the mortal life of Jesus the Christ. It was on the twenty-fifth day of that month, the day of His holy birth.

It was a still day. The little white flowers that were called Breaths of Hope and that we now call Stars of Bethlehem were so husht in quiet that the shadows of moths lay on them like the dark motionless violet in the hearts of pansies. In the long swards of tender grass the multitude of the daisies were white as milk faintly stained with flusht dews fallen from roses. On the meadows of white poppies were long shadows blue as the blue lagoons of the sky among drifting snow-white moors of cloud. Three white aspens on the pastures were in a still sleep: their tremulous leaves made no rustle, though there was a soundless wavering fall of little dusky shadows, as in the dark water of a pool where birches lean in the yellow hour of the frostfire. Upon the pastures were ewes and lambs sleeping, and yearling kids opened and closed their onyx eyes among the garths of white clover.

It was the Sabbath, and Jesus walked alone. When He came to a little rise in the grass He turned and looked back at the house where His parents dwelled. Joseph sat on a bench, with bent shoulders, and was dreaming with fixt gaze into the west, as seamen stare across the interminable wave at the pale green horizons that are like the grassy shores of home. Mary was standing, dressed in long white raiment, white as a lily, with her right hand shading her eyes as she looked to the east, dreaming her dream.

The young Christ sighed, but with the love of all love in His heart. "So shall it be till the day of days," He said aloud; "even so shall the hearts of men dwell among shadows and glories, in the West of passing things: even so shall that which is immortal turn to the East and watch for the coming of joy through the Gates of Life."

At the sound of His voice He heard a sudden noise as of many birds, and turned and looked beyond the low upland where He stood. A pool of pure water lay in the hollow, fed by a ceaseless wellspring, and round it and over it circled birds whose breasts were grey as pearl and whose necks shone purple and grass-green and rose. The noise was of their wings, for though the birds were beautiful they were voiceless and dumb as flowers.

At that edge of the pool stood two figures, whom He knew to be of the angelic world because of their beauty, but who had on them the illusion of mortality so that the child did not know them. But He saw that one was beautiful as Night, and one beautiful as Morning.

He drew near.

"I have lived seven years," He said, "and I wish to send peace to the far ends of the world."

"Tell your secret to the birds," said one.

"Tell your secret to the birds," said the other.

So Jesus called to the birds.

"Come," He cried; and they came.

Seven came flying from the left, from the side of the angel beautiful as Night. Seven came flying from the right, from the side of the angel beautiful as Morning.

To the first He said: "Look into my heart."

But they wheeled about him, and with newfound voices mocked, crying, "How could we see into your heart that is hidden" and mocked and derided, crying, "What is Peace? Leave us alone! Leave us alone!"

So Christ said to them: "I know you for the birds of Ahriman, who is not beautiful but is Evil. Henceforth ye shall be black, as night, and be children of the winds."

To the seven other birds which circled about Him, voiceless, and brushing their wings against His arms, He cried, "Look into my heart."

And they swerved and hung before Him in a maze of wings, and looked into His pure heart: and, as they looked, a soft murmurous sound came from them, drowsy-sweet, full of peace: and as they hung there like a breath in frost they became white as snow.

"Ye are the doves of the Spirit," said Christ, "and to you I will commit that which ye have seen. Henceforth shall your plumage be white and your voices be the voices of peace."

The young Christ turned, for He heard Mary calling to the sheep and goats, and knew that dayset was come and that in the valleys the gloaming was already rising like smoke from the urns of the twilight. When He looked back he saw by the pool neither the Son of Joy nor the Son of Sorrow, but seven white doves were in the cedar beyond the pool, cooing in low ecstasy of peace and awaiting through sleep and dreams the rose-red pathways of the dawn. Down the long grey reaches of the ebbing day He saw seven birds rising and falling on the wind, black as black water in caves, black as the darkness of night in the old pathless woods.

And that is how the first doves became white, and how the first crows became black and were called by a name that means the clan of darkness, the children of the wind.

The Star of Rest

REST — what an OCEANIC word! I have been thinking of the unfathomable, unpenetrable word with mingled longing, and wonder, and even awe.

What depths are in it, what infinite spaces, what vast compassionate sky, what tenderness of oblivions, what husht awakenings, what quiet sinkings and fadings into peace.

Waking early, I took the word as one might take a carrier-dove and loosed it into the cloudy suspense of the stilled mind — and it rose again and again in symbolic cloud-thought, now as an infinite green forest murmurous with a hidden wind, now in some other guise and once as Ecstasy herself, listening.

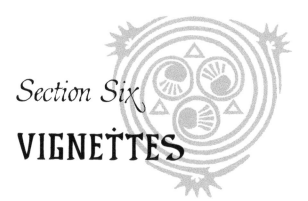

Section Six

VIGNETTES

VIGNETTES

Much of what Fiona Macleod wrote was no more than little snippets from the daily life of the Highlanders and Islanders she loved so much. Often the characters are not even named but some little insight into their world is revealed, and this was the purpose for the short tale or commentary. This section contains a small sampling of this style of her writing.

The first piece, *A Memory of Beauty* as it now stands, is all that William Sharp wished retained of the story entitled *The Daughter of the Sun* that originally formed a part of *The Sin-Eater*. The name of the child, Eilidh, is the Gaelic form of Helen. Was Fiona inspired to write this vignette by a real Helen or was she another creation of her fertile imagination? It does not matter. It stands up in its own right.

Lost is from *The Dominion of Dreams* and is a tragic tale concerning someone we today would call dysfunctional. The life-choices of the main character seem careless and downright stupid but they come across as believable and we can feel some sorrow and empathy for him. The way the narrative is laid out subtly keeps alive the belief that Fiona Macleod was a real person who allowed her readers to glimpse people and places they would probably otherwise never encounter.

The Sin-Eater is the source for *The Birdeen*, another snippet from the lives of several people we know nothing about other than the great inner beauty that seems to shine from many of Fiona's characters as if being born in the Scottish Highlands and Islands automatically gave you the beauty of a Helen and the inner tranquillity and wisdom of one of the old Celtic Saints.

The final piece in the section, *The Wayfarer* from *Cosmopolis Magazine*, uses several names with double-meanings in the Gaelic (explained in footnotes) and is one of Fiona's few commentaries on an identifiable event in time. In 1842 there was a schism within the members of the Church of Scotland and from this split came The Free Church of Scotland. The ministers of this breakaway movement adopted a harsh Calvinist approach to life and expected the same, if not more, from their congregation. William Sharp did not like the detrimental effect this was having on life and culture in the Highlands and Islands and makes his views clear in this short story.

A Memory of Beauty

MANY years ago a beautiful[89] dark woman came to Ardnathonn,[90] and lived there a while, and died, as she had lived, in silence.

None in that remote place knew who she was; nor of any there was ever known the name of the man who loved her, and died, or the name of another man who loved her, and died.

They called her "the foreign woman"; and where the nettle sheds her snow above the lichened stones in the little seaweed-sloping graveyard, there appear on one stone these words only: The Stranger.

In the ruined garden of Tighnardnathonn[91] stands a broken sundial. Here may still be deciphered the legend: Time Past: Time to Come.

Time past, time to come. It is the refrain of our mortality.

And Aileen? ... That great beauty of hers is no more. It is unthinkable. If loveliness can pass away as a breath ... nay, did not one in Asia of old, one of the seers of the world, interpret thus: "I am Beauty itself among beautiful things." The dream that is the body eternally perishes; only the dream that is the soul endures.

It is a commonplace that death is held most mournful when it is the seal of silence upon youth, upon what is beautiful. Peradventure, life incomplete may some day be revealed to us as the sole life that is complete. Howbeit we need not lament when love has been gloriously present. I think often of that old sundial inscription:

"Light and Shade by turns,
But Love always."

To have loved supremely! After all, the green, sweet world had been good to her, its daughter. She had loved and been loved, with the passion of passion. Nothing in the world could take away that joy; not any loss or sorrow, nor that last grief, the death of him whom she so loved; not the mysterious powers themselves that men call God, and that move and

---

89 'Beauty' is a synonym for the World of Faery. Still today we tell fairy tales about 'Sleeping Beauty' and 'Beauty and the Beast' and the tales of King Arthur are full of beautiful women and beautiful knights in shining armour.

90 'the headland of the waves,' another name for the World of Faery. A common variation on this is 'Tir fo Thonn' or 'Land under the Waves.'

91 'the house at the headland of the waves.'

live and have their blind will behind the blowing wind and the rising sap, behind the drifting leaf and the granite hills, behind the womb of woman and the mind of man, behind the miracle of day and night, behind life, behind death. This was hers. She had this supreme heritage. In truth she was crowned. And he ... from the first he wore the glory of her love, as morning wears the sunrise. It is enough.

Can love itself be as an idle bow upon our poor perishing heavens? Is love a dream, a dream within a dream? If so, the soul herself were a vain image, as fleeting as the travelling shadow of a wave.

Alas, how brief that lovely hour which was her life! It is only in what is loveliest, most fugitive, that eternity reveals, as in a sudden flame, as in the vanishing facet of a second, the beauty of all beauty; that it whispers, in the purple hollow of the dancing flame, the incommunicable word.

Strange mystery, that so many ages had to come and go, so many lives to be lived, so many ecstasies and raptures and sorrows and vicissitudes to flame and be and pass, just to produce one frail flower of perfection. I sometimes think of this unknown loveliness, this woman whose sole pulse now is in the sap of the grass over her head, not as a mortal joy, but as the breath or symbol of a most ancient and ever new mystery, the mystery of eternal beauty:

"...For I have seen
In lonely places, and in lonelier hours,
My vision of the rainbow-aureoled face
Of her whom men name Beauty: proud, austere:
Dim vision of the flawless, perfect face
Divinely fugitive, that haunts the world,
And lifts man's spiral thought to lovelier dreams."

She is gone now who was so fair. Can great beauty perish? The unlovely is as the weed that is everywhere under the sun. But that wind which blows the seed, alike of the unlovely and of the children of beauty — can it have failed to wed that exhaled essence to the glory of light, so that somewhere, somehow, that which was so beautiful is?

Lost

I had heard of Mànus Macleod before I met him, a year or more ago, in the South Isles. He had a tragic history. The younger fiùran[92] of the younger branch of a noble family, he was born and bred in poverty. At twenty he was studying for the priesthood; nearly two years later he met Margred Colquhoun; when he was twenty-two he was ordained; in his twenty-third year love carried him away on a strong and bitter tide; the next, he was unfrocked; the next again, Margred was dead, and her child too, and Mànus was a wandering broken man.

After some years, wherein he made a living none knows how, he joined a band of gypsies. They were not tinkers, but of the Romany clan, the Treubh-Siubhail or Wandering Race. He married a girl of that people, who was drowned while crossing the great ford of Uist; for she fell in the dusk, and was not seen, and the incoming tide took her while a swoon held her life below the heart. It was about this time that he became known as Mànus-am-Bard, Manus the poet, because of his songs, and his Cruit-Spànteach or guitar, which had belonged to the girl, and upon which she had taught him to play fantastic savage airs out of the East.

He must have been about forty when he became an outcast from the Romanies. I do not know the reason, but one account seems not improbable: that, in a drunken fit, he had tried to kill and had blinded Gillanders Caird, the brother of the girl whom he had lost.

Thereafter he became an idle and homeless tramp, a suspect even, but sometimes welcome because of his songs and music. A few years later he was known as Father Mànus, head of a dirty, wandering tribe of tinkers. He lived in the open, slept in a smoky, ill-smelling tent, had a handsome, evil, dishevelled woman as his mate, and three brown, otter-eyed offspring of his casual love.

It was at this period that a lawyer from Inveraray sought him out, and told him that because of several deaths he had become heir to the earldom of Hydallan: and asked if he would give up his vagrant life and make ready for the great change of estate which was now before him.

Mànus Macleod took the short, black cutty out of his mouth. "Come here, Dougal," he cried to one of his staring boys. The boy had a dead

---

92 A stripling or handsome young man.

cockerel in his hands, and was plucking it. "Tell the gentleman, Dougal, where you got that."

The boy answered sullenly that it was one o' dad's fowls.

"You lie," said his father; "speak out, or I'll slit your tongue for you."

"Well, then, for sure, I lifted it from Farmer Jamieson's henyard; an' by the same token you ca'ed me to do it."

Mànus looked at the lawyer.

"Now, you've seen me, an' you've seen my eldest brat. Go back an' tell my Lord Hydallan what you've seen. If he dies, I'll be Earl of Hydallan, an' that evil-eyed thief there would be master of Carndhu, an' my heir, if only he wasn't the bastard he is. An' neither now nor then will I change my way of life. Hydallan Chase will make fine camping-ground, an' with its fishings and shootings will give me an' my folk all we need, till I'm tired o' them, when others can have them; I mean others of *our* kind. As for the money ... well, I will be seeing to that in my own way, Mr. What's-your-name ... Finlay, are you for saying? ... Well, then, good-day to you, Mr. Finlay, an' you can let me know when my uncle's dead."

I suppose it was about a year after this that I found one day at a friend's house a little book of poems bearing my own surname, with Mànus before it as that of the author. The imprint showed that the book had been issued by a publisher in Edinburgh some twenty years back. It was the one achievement of Mànus, for whom all his kin had once so high hopes, and much of it seems to have been written when he was at the Scots College in Rome. I copied two of the poems. One was called "Cantilena Mundi," the other "The Star of Beauty." I quote the one I can remember:

> It dwells not in the skies,
>   My Star of Beauty!
> 'Twas made of her sighs,
> Her tears and agonies,
> The fire in her eyes,
>   My Star of Beauty!
>
> Lovely and delicate,
>   My Star of Beauty!
> How could she master Fate,
> Although she gave back hate
> Great as my love was great,
>   My Star of Beauty!

I loved, she hated, well,
 My Star of Beauty!
Soon, soon the passing bell:
She rose, and I fell:
Soft shines in deeps of hell
 My Star of Beauty!

I recalled this poem when, in Colonsay, I met Mànus Macleod, and remembered his story.

He was old and ragged. He had deserted, or been deserted by, his tinker herd; and wandered now, grey and dishevelled, from hamlet to hamlet, from parish to parish, from isle to isle. It was late October, and a premature cold had set in. The wind had shifted some of the snow on the mountains of Skye and Mull, and some had fallen among the old black ruins on Oronsay and along the Colonsay dunes of sand and salt bent. Mànus was in the inn kitchen, staring into the fire, and singing an old Gaelic song below his breath.

When my name was spoken, he looked up quickly.

An instinct made me say this:

"I can give you song for song, Mànus mac Tormod."

"How do you know that my father's name was Norman?" he asked in English.

"How do I know that as Tormod mhic Leoid's son, son of Tormod of Arrasay, you are heir to his brother Hydallan?"

Mànus frowned. Then he leaned over the fire, warming his thin, gaunt hands. I could see the flame-flush in them.

"What song can you give me for my song — which, for sure, is not mine at all, at all, but the old sorrowful song by Donull mac Donull of Uist, 'The Broken Heart'?"

"It is called 'The Star of Beauty'," I said, and quoted the first verse.

He rose and stooped over the fire. Abruptly he turned, and in swift silence walked from the room. His face was clay-white, and glistened with the streaming wet of tears.

The innkeeper's wife looked after him. "A bad evil wastrel that," she said; "these tinkers are ill folk at the best and Mànus Macleod is one o' the worst o' them. For sure, now, why should you be speaking to the man at all, at all? A dirty, ignorant man he is, with never a thought to him but his pipe an' drink an' other people's goods."

The following afternoon I heard that Mànus was still in the loft, where he had been allowed to rest. He was on death's lips, I was told.

I went to him. He smiled when he saw me. He seemed years and years younger, and not ill at all but for the leaf of flame on his white face and the wild shine in his great black eyes.

"Give me a wish," he whispered.

"Peace," I said.

He looked long at me.

"I have seen The Red Shepherd," he said.

I knew what he meant, and did not answer.

"And the dark flock of birds," he added. "And last night, as I came here out of Oronsay, I saw a white hound running before me till I came here."

There was silence for a time.

"And I have written this," he muttered hoarsely. "It is all I have written in all these years since she died whom I loved. You can put in the little book you know of if you have it." He gave me an old leathern case. In it was a dirty, folded sheet. He died that night. By the dancing yellow flame of the peats, while the wind screamed among the rocks, and the sea's gathering voices were more and more lamentable and dreadful, I read what he had given me. But in paraphrasing his simpler and finer Gaelic, I may also alter his title of "Whisperings (or secret Whisperings) in the Darkness" to "The Secrets of the Night" because the old Gaelic saying, "The Red Shepherd, the White Hound and the Dark Flock of Birds; the Three Secrets (or secret terrors) of the Night:"

In the great darkness where the shimmering stars
Are as the dazzle of the luminous wave
Moveth the shadow of the end of wars:
But mightly arises, as out of a bloody grave,
The Red Swineherd, he who has no name,
But who is gaunt, terrible, an awful flame
Fed upon blood and perishing lives and tears;
His feet are heavy with the bewildering years
Trodden dim bygone ages, and his eyes
Are black and vast and void as midnight skies.

Beware of the White Hound whose baying no man hears,
Though it is the wind that shakes the unsteady stars:
It is the Hound seen of men in old forlorn wars:
It is the Hound that hunts the stricken years.

Lost

Pale souls in the ultimate shadows see it gleam
Like a long lance o' the moon, and as a moon-white beam
It comes, and the soul is as blown dust within the wood
Wherein the White Hound moves where timeless shadows brood.

Have heed, too, of the flock of birds from twilight places,
The desolate haunted ways of ancient wars
Bewildered, terrible, winged, and shadowy faces
Of homeless souls adrift 'neath drifting stars.
But this thing surely I know, that he, the Red Flame,
And the White Hound, and the Dark Flock of Birds,
Appal me no more, who never, never again
Through all the rise and set and set and rise of pain
Shall hear the lips of her whom I loved uttering words,
Or hear my own lips in her shadowy hair naming her name.

The Birdeen

SOME other time I will tell the story of Isla and Morag McIan: Isla that was the foster brother and chief friend of Ian McIan the mountain-poet, known as Ian of the Hills, or simply as Ian Mòr, because of his great height and the tireless strength that was his. Of Morag, too, there is a story of the Straths, sweet as honey of the heather, and glad as the breeze that, blowing across it in summer, waves the purple into white-o'-the-wind and sea-change amethyst.

Isla was seven years older than Ian Mòr, and had been seven years married to Morag, when the sorrow of their friend's life came upon him. Of that matter I speak elsewhere.

They were happy, Isla and Morag. Though both were of Strachurmore of Loch Fyne, they lived at a small hill-farm on the west side of the upper fjord of Loch Long, and within sight of Arrochar, where it sits among its mountains. They could not see the fantastic outline of "The Cobbler," because of a near hill that shut them off, though from the loch it was visible and almost upon them. But they could watch the mists on Ben Arthur and Ben Maiseach, and when a flying drift of mackerel-sky spread upward from Ben Lomond, that was but a few miles eastward as the crow flies, they could tell of the good weather that was sure.

Before the end of the first year of their marriage, deep happiness came to them. "The Birdeen" was their noon of joy. When the child came, Morag had one regret only, that a boy was not hers, for she longed to see Isla in the child that was his. But Isla was glad, for now he had two dreams in his life: Morag whom he loved more and more, and the little one whom she had borne to him, and was for him a mystery and joy against the dark hours of the dark days that must be.

They named her Eilidh. One night, in front of the peats, and before her time was come, Morag, sitting with Isla and Ian Mòr, dreamed of the birthing. It was dark, save for the warm redness of the peat-glow. There was no other light, and in the dusky corners obscure velvety things that we call shadows moved and had their own life and were glad. Outside, the hill-wind was still at last, after a long wandering moaning that had not ceased since its westering, for, like a wailing hound, it had followed the sun all day. A soft rain fell. The sound of it was for peace.

Isla sat forward, his chin in his hands and his elbows on his knees. He was dreaming, too. 'Morag', 'Isla', deep love, deep mystery, the child that was already here, and would soon be against the breast; these were the circuit of his thoughts. Sure, Morag, sweet and dear as she was, was now more dear, more sweet. "Green life to her," he murmured below his breath, "and in her heart, joy by day and peace by night."

Ian sat in the shadow of the ingle, and looked now at one and now at the other, and then mayhap into the peat-flame or among the shadows. He saw what he saw. Who knows what is in a poet's mind? The echo of the wind that was gone was there, and the sound of the rain and the movement and colour of the fire, and something out of the earth and sea and sky, and great pitifulness and tenderness for women and children, and love of men and of birds and beasts, and of the green lives that were to him not less wonderful and intimate. And Ian, thinking, knew that the thoughts of Isla and Morag were drifting through his mind too; so that he smiled with his eyes because of the longing and joy in the life of the man, his friend; and looked through a mist of unshed tears at Morag, because of the other longing that shone in her eyes, and of the thinness of the hands now, and of the coming and going of the breath like a bird tired after a long flight. He was troubled, too, with the fear and the wonder that came to him out of the hidden glooms of her soul.

It was Ian who broke the stillness, though for sure his low words were parts of the peat-rustle and the dripping rain and the wash of the sea-loch, where it twisted like a black adder among the hills, and was now quick with the tide.

"But if the birdeen be after you, Morag, and not after Isla, what will you be for calling it?"

Morag started, glanced at him with her flame-lit eyes, and flushed. Then, with a low laugh, her whispered answer came.

"Now it is a true thing, Ian, that you are a wizard. Isla has often said that you can hear the wooing of the trees and the flowers, but sure I'm thinking you could hear the very stones speak, or at least know what is in their hearts. How did you guess that was the thought I was having?"

"It was for the knowing, lassikin."

"Ian, it is a wife you should have, and a child upon your knee to put its lips against yours, and to make your heart melt because of its little wandering hands," said Isla.

Ian made no sign, though his pulse leaped, for this was ever the longing that lay waiting behind heart and brain, and thrilled each along the wise, knowing nerves — our wise nerves that were attuned long, long ago, and play to us a march against the light, or down into the dark, and we unwitting, and not knowing the ancient rune of the heritage that the blood sings, an ancient, ancient song. Who plays the tune to which our dancing feet are led? It is behind the mist, that antique strain to which the hills rose in flame and marl, and froze slowly into granite silence, and to which the soul of man crept from the things of the slime to the palaces of the brain. It is for the hearing, that; in the shells of the human. Who knows the undersong of the tides in the obscure avenues of the sea? Who knows the immemorial tidal-murmur along the nerves — along the nerves even of a new-born child?

Seeing that he was silent, Morag added: "Ay, Ian dear, it is a wife and a child you must have. Sure no man that has all the loving little names you give to us can do without us!"

"Well, well, Morag-aghray, the hour waits, as they say out in the isles. But you have not given me the answer to what I asked?"

"And it is no answer that I have. Isla! — Isla, if a girl it is to be, you would be for liking the little one to be called Morag, because of me; but that I would not like; no, no, I would not. Is it forgetting, you are, what old Muim' Mary said, that a third Morag in line, like a third Seumas, would be born in the shadow, would have the gloom?"

"For sure, *muirnean*; it is not you or I that would forget that thing. Well, since there's Morag that was your mother, and Morag, that is you, there can be no third. But it is the same with Muireall that was the name of my mother and of the mother before her. See here now, dear, let Ian have the naming, if a girl it be — for all three of us know that, if a boy it is, his name will be Ian. So now, *mo-charaid*, what is the name that will be upon the wean?"

"*Wean*," repeated Ian, puzzled for a moment because of the unfamiliar word in the Gaelic, "ah, sure, yes: well, but it is Morag who knows best."

"No, no, Ian. The naming is to be with you. What names of women do you love best?"

"Morag."

"Ah, you know well that is not a true thing, but only a saying for the saying. Tell me true; what name do you love best?"

"Mona I like, and Lora, and Silis too; and of the old, old names, it's Brigid I am loving, and, too, Dearduil (*Darthula*) and Malmhin (*Malveen*); but of all names dear to me, and sweet in my ears, it is Eilidh (*Ei-lee*)."

And so it was. When, in the third week after that night, the child was born, and a woman-child at that, it was called Eilidh. But the first thing that Ian said when he entered the house after the birthing was: "How is the birdeen?"

And from that day Eilidh was "the birdeen," oftenest — even with
Isla and Morag.

Of the many songs that Ian made to Eilidh here is one:

Eilidh, Eilidh, Eilidh, dear to me, dear and sweet,
In dreams I am hearing the noise of your little running feet —
The noise of your running feet that like the sea-hoofs beat
A music by day and night, Eilidh, on the sands of my heart, my Sweet!

Eilidh, blue i' the eyes, as all babe-children are,
And white as the canna that blows with the hill-breast wind afar,
Whose is the light in thine eyes, the light of a star, a star
That sitteth supreme where the starry lights of heaven a glory are!

Eilidh, Eilidh, Eilidh, put off your wee hands from the heart o' me
It is pain they are making there, where no more pain should be;
For little running feet, an' wee white hands, an croodlin, as of the sea,
Bring tears to my eyes, Eilidh, tears, tears, out of the heart o' me —
                              Mo lennav-a-chree,
                              Mo lennav-a-chree!

This was for himself, and because of what was in his heart. But he
made songs to the Birdeen herself. Some were as simple-mysterious as
a wayside flower; others were strange, and with a note in them that all
who know the Songs of Ian will recognise. Here is one:

Lennavan-mo,
Lennavan-mo,
Who is it swinging you to and fro,
With a long low swing and a sweet low croon,
And the loving words of the mother's rune?

Lennavan-mo,
Lennavan-mo,
Who is it swinging you to and fro?
I'm thinking it is an angel fair,
The Angel that looks on the gulf from the lowest stair
And swings the green world upward by its leagues of sunshine-hair.

Lennavan-mo,
Lennavan-mo,

Who is it swings you and the Angel to and fro?
It is He whose faintest thought is a world afar,
It is He whose wish is a leaping seven-moon'd star,
It is He, Lennavan-mo,
To whom you and I and all things flow.

Lennavan-mo,
Lennavan-mo,
It is only a little wee lass you are, Eilidh-mo-chree
But as this wee blossom has roots in the depths of the sky,
So you are at one with the Lord of Eternity —
Bonnie wee lass that you are,
My Morning-star,
Eilidh-mo-chree, Lennavan-mo,
Lennavan-mo!

Once more let me give a song of his, this time also, like "Leanabhan-Mo," of those written while Eilidh was still a breast-babe.

Eilidh, Eilidh,
My bonnie wee lass;
The winds blow
And the hours pass.

But never a wind
Can do thee wrong,
Brown Birdeen, singing
Thy bird-heart song.

And never an hour
But has for thee
Blue of the heaven
And green of the sea —

Blue for the hope of thee,
Eilidh, Eilidh;
Green for the joy of thee,
Eilidh, Eilidh.

Swing in thy nest, then,
Here on my heart,
Birdeen, Birdeen,
Here on my heart,
Here on my heart!

But Eilidh was "the Birdeen" not only when she could be tossed high in the air in Ian's strong arms, or could toddle to him from *claar* to stool and from stool to chair; not only when she could go long walks with him upon the hills above Loch Long; but when, as a grown lass of twenty, she was so fair to see that the countryside smiled when it saw her, as at the first sunflood swallow, or as at the first calling across dewy meadows of the cuckoo after long days of gloom.

She was tall and slim, with a flower-like way with her: the way of the flower in the sunlight, of the wave on the sea, of the treetop in the wind. Her changing hazel eyes, now grey-green, now dusked with sea-gloom or a violet shadowiness; her wonderful arched eyebrows, dark so that they seemed black; the beautiful bonnie face of her, with her mobile mouth and white flawless teeth; the ears that lay against the tangle of her sun-brown shadowy hair, like pink shells on a drift of seaweed; the exquisite poise of head and neck and body: are not all these things to be read of her in the poems of Ian Mòr? Her voice, too, was sweet against the ears as the singing of hillside burns. But most she was loved for this: that she was ever fresh as the dawn, young as the morning, and alive in every fibre with the joy of life. The old dreamed they were young again, when she was with them; the weary opened their hearts, because she was sunshine; the young were glad and believed that all things might be. Who can tell the many names of the Birdeen? She was called Sunshine, Sunbeam, Way o' the Wind, and a score more of lovely and endearing names. But to every one there was one name that was common, the Birdeen.

"What has she done to, be so famous, both through Ian Mòr and others," was often said of her when, in later years, the first few threads of grey streaked the bonnie hair that was her pride. What has she done, this Eilidh, save what other women do? Ah, well, it is not Eilidh's story I am telling; and she living yet, and like to live till the young heart of her is still at last. It will be the going of a sunbeam, that.

But this is for the knowing, and, sure, can be said. She loved the green world with a deep enduring love. Earth, sea, and sky were comradely with her, as with few men and fewer women. And she loved men and women and children just as Ian Mòr loved them, and that was a way not far from the loving way that the Son of Man had, for it was tender and true and heeding little the evil, but rejoicing with laughter and tears over the good. Then, too, there is this: she loved the man to whom she gave herself, with deep passion, that was warm against all chill of change and time and death itself. How few of whom even this much can be said? For deep passion is rare, so rare that men have debased the flawless image to the service of a base coinage. She gave him love, and passion, and the longing of her woman's heart; and she was the flame that was in his brain, for he, too, like Ian Mòr, was a poet and dreamer. Then, after having given joy and strength and the flower of her life, so that he had the brain and the heart of two lives, she gave him the supreme gift she had for the giving, and that was their child, that is called Aluinn[93] because of his beauty, and is now the poet of a new day.

When she was married to the man whose love for her was almost worship, Ian Mòr said this to him: "Be proud, for she who has filled you with deep meanings and new powers, is herself a proud Queen in whose service you must either live or die with joy."

And to Eilidh herself he said, in a written word he gave her to take away with her: "Rhythms of the music of love for your brain, white-wing'd thoughts for the avenues of your heart, and the song of the White Merle be there!" And the Birdeen was glad at that, for she knew Ian, and all that he meant, and she would rather have had that word than any treasure of men.

To me, long years afterward, he said this: "I have known two women that were of the old race of the Tuatha De-Danann. They were as one, though she with whom my life rose and my life went was Ethlenn, and the other was Eilidh, the Birdeen at whose birthing I was, and who is comrade and friend to me, more than any man has been or any woman. Of each, this is my word: 'A woman beautiful, to be loved, honoured, revered, ay, scarce this side idolatry; but no weakling; made of heroic stuff, of elemental passions; strong to endure, but strong also to conquer and maintain.'"

Of what one who must be nameless wrote to her I have no right to speak, but here is one verse from his "Song of my Heart," ill-clad by me in this cold English out of the tender Gaelic that has won him the name "Mouth o' Honey." It is in prose I must give it, for I can find or make no rhythm to catch that strange sea-cadence of his:

"Come to my life that is already yours, and at one with you:
Come to my blood that leaps because of you,
Come to my heart that holds you, Eilidh,
Come to my heart that holds you as the green earth clasps and holds the
    sunlight,
Come to me! Come to me, Eilidh!"

---

93 Aluinn is an adjective meaning beautiful or very handsome. It is not normally given as a personal name.

But still — but still — "What has she done, this Eilidh, save what other women do?"

Sure, you must ask this elsewhere than of me. I know no reason for it other than what I have said. She was, and is, "the Birdeen." "Green life to her, green song to her, green joy to her," the old wish of Ian at her naming, has been fulfilled indeed. Why, for that matter, should she be called "the Birdeen"? There are other women as fair to see, as sweet and true, as dear to men and women. Why? Sure, for that, why was Helen, Helen; or Cleopatra, Cleopatra; or Deirdrê, Dierdrê?

And, too, why does the common familiar bow that is set in the heavens thrill us in each new apparition as though it were a sudden stairway to all lost or dreamed-of Edens? As I write I look seaward, and over Innisdûn, the dark precipitous isle that lies in these wide waters even as Leviathan itself, a rainbow rises with vast, unbroken sweep, a skyey flower fed from the innumerous hues of sunset woven this way and that on the looms of the sea. And I know that I have never seen a rainbow before, and of all that I may see I may never see another again as I have seen this. Yet it is a rainbow as others are, and have been and will be for all time past and to come.

Eilidh, that was "the Birdeen" when she laughed at the breast, and was "the Birdeen" when her own Aluinn first turned his father's eyes upon her, and is "the Birdeen" now when the white flower of age is belied by the young eyes and the young, young heart, Eilidh that I love, Eilidh that has the lilt of life in her brain as no woman I have known or heard of has ever had in like measure, Eilidh is my Rainbow.

The Wayfarer

I

AMONG those in the home-straths of Argyll who are now grey, and in the quiet places of whose hearts old memories live green and sweet, there must be some who recall that day when a stranger came into Strath Nair, and spoke of the life eternal.

This man, who was a minister of God, was called James Campbell.[94] He was what is called a good man, by those who measure the soul by inches and extol its vision by the tests of the purblind. He had rectitude of a kind, the cold and bitter thing that is not the sunlit integrity of the spirit. And he had the sternness that is the winter of a frozen life. In his heart, God was made in the image of John Calvin.

With this man the love of love was not even a dream. A poor strong man he was, this granite-clasped soul; and the sunlight faded out of many hearts, and hopes fell away to dust before the blight of the east wind of his spirit.

On the day after his coming to Strath Nair, the new minister went from cottage to cottage. He went to all, even to the hill-bothy of Peter Macnamara the shepherd; to all save one. He did not go to the cottage of Mary Gilchrist,[95] for the woman lived there alone, with the child that had been born to her. In the eyes of James Campbell she was evil. His ears heard, but not his heart, that no man or woman spoke harshly of her, for she had been betrayed.

On the morning of the Bell, as some of the old folk still call the morrow of the Sabbath, the glory of sunlight came down the Strath. For many days rain had fallen, hours upon hours at a time; or heavy, dropping masses of vapour had hung low upon the mountains, making the peaty uplands sodden, and turning the grey rocks into a wet blackness. By day and by night the wind had moaned among the corries along the high moors. There was one sound, more lamentable still: the incessant *mêhing* of the desolate, soaked sheep. The wind in the corries, on the moors, among the pines and larches; the plaintive cruel sorrow of the wandering

---

94 There is a play on words here. Campbell in Gaelic means 'crooked mouth' i.e. someone whose word cannot be trusted. As the tale unfolds this becomes clear.

95 Another double meaning. Gilchrist in Gaelic means 'Servant of Christ.' This coupled with the name Mary implies she is symbolic of the Virgin Mary with her own Son out of wedlock.

ewes; never was any other sound to be heard, save the distant wailing of curlews. Only, below all, as inland near the coast one hears continuously the murmur of the sea, so by night and day the Gorromalt Water made throughout the whole reach of Strath Nair an undertone as of a weary sighing.

But before nightfall on Saturday the rain ceased, and the wet wind of the south suddenly revolved upon itself beyond the spurs of Ben Maiseach. Long before the gloaming had oozed an earth-darkness to meet the falling dark, the mists had lifted. One by one, moist stars revealed hollows of violet, which, when the moon yellowed the fir-tops, disclosed a vast untravelled waste of blue, wherein slow silent waves of darkness continuously lapsed. The air grew full of loosened fragrances; most poignantly, of the bog-myrtle, the bracken, and the resinous sprays of pine and larch.

Where the road turns at the Linn o' Gorromalt there is an ancient disarray of granite boulders above the brown rushing water. Masses of wild rose grow in that place. On this June gloaming the multitudinous blooms were like pale wings, as though the fabled birds that live in rainbows, or the frail creatures of the falling dew, had alit there, tremulous, uncertain.

There that evening, the woman, Mary Gilchrist, sat, happy in the silences of the dusk. While she inhaled the fragrance of the wild roses, as it floated above the persistent green odour of the bent and the wet fern, and listened to the noise of Gorromalt Water foaming and surging out of the linn, she heard steps close by her. Glancing sidelong, she saw "the new minister," a tall, gaunt man, with lank, iron-grey hair above his white, stern, angular face.

He looked at her, not knowing who she was.

Mary Gilchrist did not speak. Her face, comely before, had become beautiful of late. "It's the sorrow," said the Strath folk simply, believing what they said.

Perhaps the dark eyes under the shadowy hair deepened. The minister, of course, could not see this, could not have noted so small a thing.

"God be with you, he said at last in Gaelic, and speaking slow and searchingly; "God be with you. This is a fine evening, at last."

"God be with you, too, Mr. Campbell."

"So; you know who I am?"

"For sure, sir, one cannot live alone here among the hills and not know who comes and who goes. What word is there, sir, of the old minister? Is he better?"

"No. He will never be better. He is old."

When he spoke these words, James Campbell uttered them as one drover answers another when asked about a steer or a horse. Mary Gilchrist noticed this, and with a barely audible sigh shrank a little among the granite boulders and wild roses.

The minister hesitated; then spoke again.

"You will be at the hill-preaching to-morrow? If fine, the Word will be preached on the slope of Monanair.[96] You will be there?"

"Perhaps."

He looked at her, leaning forward a little. Her answer perturbed him. The Rev. James Campbell thought no one should hesitate before the free offering of the bitter tribulation of his religion. Possibly she was one of that outcast race who held by Popish abominations. He frowned darkly.

"Are you of the true faith!"

"God alone knows that."

"Why do you answer me like that, woman? There is but one true faith."

"Mr. Campbell, will you be for telling me this? Do you preach the love of God?"

"I preach the love and hate of God, woman! His great love to the elect, his burning wrath against the children of Belial."

For a minute or more there was silence between them. The noise of the torrent filled the night. Beyond, all was stillness. The stars, innumerous now, flickered in pale uncertain fires. At last Mary Gilchrist spoke, whispered rather:

"Mr. Campbell, I am only a poor woman. It is not for me to be telling you this or that. But for myself, I know, ay, for sure, I know well, that everything God has to say to man is to be said in three words — and these were said long, long ago, an' before ever the Word came to this land at all. And these three words are, 'God is love.'"

The speech angered the minister. It was for him to say what was and what was not God's message to man, for him to say what was or was not the true faith. He frowned blackly awhile. Then, muttering that he would talk publicly of this on the morrow, was about to pass on his way. Suddenly he turned.

96　This story is set after the schism in 1843 when members of the Church of Scotland broke away to form The Free Church of Scotland. For a long time they had no formal church buildings and were forced to gather in the open air as is the case in the current tale. Despite the name 'Free' they were, and are, unrelentingly and strictly Calvinist in view and habit and repressive of anything joyful or happy.

"What will your name be? If you will tell me your name and where you live, my good woman, I will come to you and show you what fearful sinfulness you invite by speaking of God's providence as you do."

"I am Mary Gilchrist. I live up at the small croft called Annet-bhan."[97]

Without a word, Mr. Campbell turned on his heel, and moved whither away he was bound. He was glad when he was round the bend of the road, and going up the glen. God's curse was heavy on those who had made iniquity their portion. So this was the woman Gilchrist, whom already that day he had publicly avoided. A snare of the Evil One, for sure, that wayside meeting had been.

It had angered the new minister to find that neither man nor woman in Strath Nair looked upon Mary Gilchrist as accursed. A few blamed; all were sorrowful; none held her an outcast. To one woman, who replied that Mary was the sinned against, not the sinner, that black misfortune had been hers, Mr. Campbell answered harshly that the All Wise God took no store by misfortune — that at the last day no shivering human soul could trust to that plea. Even when John MacCallum, the hill-grieve, urged that, whether Mr. Campbell were right or wrong, it was clear nothing could be done, and would it not be wisest for one and all to let bygones be bygones, each man and woman remembering that in his or her heart evil dwelled somewhere — even then the minister was wrought to resentment, and declared that the woman, because of her sin, ought to be driven out of the Strath.

In the less than two days he had been in Strath Nair this man had brought upon that remote place a gloom worse than any that came out of the dark congregation of the clouds. In many a little croft the bright leaping flame of the pine-log or the comfortable glow of the peats had become lurid. For the eye sees what the heart fears.

Thus it was that when the Sabbath came in a glory of light, and the Strath, and the shadowy mountains and the vast sun-swept gulfs of blue overhead took on a loveliness as though on that very morrow God had recreated the earth and the universe itself, thus it was the people of the Strath were downcast. Poor folk, poor folk, that suffer so because of the blind shepherds.

But before that glory of a new day was come, and while he was still striding with bitter thoughts from the place where he had left the woman Gilchrist, Mr. Campbell had again cause for thought, for perplexed anger.

---

97 Another double meaning. 'Annet' has no meaning in written Gaelic but when spoken is identical in sound to the word 'Annaid' which means church. 'Ban' or 'Bhan' means fair or beautiful.

As he walked, he brooded sullenly. That this woman, this lost one, had ventured to bandy words with him! What was she, a fallen woman, she with an unhallowed child up there at her croft of Annetbhan, that she should speak to him, James Campbell, of what God's message was!

It was then that he descried a man sitting on a fallen tree by the side of the burn which runs out of the Glen of the Willows. He could not discern him clearly, but saw that he was not one of the Strath-folk with whom he had talked as yet. The man seemed young, but weary; yes, for sure, weary, and poor too. When he rose to his feet in courteous greeting, Mr. Campbell could see that he was tall. His long fair hair, and a mien and dress foreign to the straths, made him appear in the minister's eyes as a Wayfarer from the Lowlands.

"God be with you. Good evening," Mr. Campbell exclaimed abruptly, in the English tongue.

The man answered gravely, and in a low, sweet voice: "God be with you."

"Will you be for going my way?" the minister asked again, but now in the Gaelic, for he knew this would be a test as to whether the man was or was not of the Strath.

"No. I do not go your way. Peradventure you will yet come my way, James Campbell."

With a start of anger the minister took a step closer. What could the man mean, he wondered.

Still, the words were so gently said that hardly could he put offence into them.

"I do not understand you, my good man," he answered after a little; "but I see you know who I am. Will you be at the preaching of the Word at Monanair to-morrow; or, if wet, at the house of God close by the Mill o' Gorromalt?"

"What Word will you preach, James Campbell?"

"Look you, my man, you are no kinsman of mine to be naming me in that way. I am Mr. Campbell, the minister from Strathdree."

"What word will you preach, then, Mr. Campbell?"

"What word? There is but one Word. I will say unto you, as unto all men who hearken unto me on the morrow, that the Lord God is a terrible God against all who transgress His holy law, and that the day of repentance is well nigh gone. Even now it may be too late. Our God is a jealous God, who doth not brook delay. Woe unto those who in their hearts cry out, 'To-morrow! To-morrow!'"

For a brief while the man by the wayside was still. When he spoke, his voice was gentle and low.

"Rather do I believe the Word to be that which the woman Mary Gilchrist said to you yonder by the linn: that God is love."

And having said this, he moved quietly into the dusk of the gloaming, and was lost to sight.

James Campbell walked slowly on his way, pondering perplexedly. Twice that evening he had been told what the whole message of God was — an evil, blasphemous, fair-seeming doctrine, he muttered, more fit for the accursed courts of her who sitteth upon seven hills than for those who are within the sound of the Truth. And how had the false wisdom come? He smiled grimly at the thought of the wanton and the vagrant.

Before he slept that night he looked out upon the vast and solemn congregation of the stars. Star beyond star, planet beyond planet, strange worlds all, immutably controlled, unrelinquished day or night, age or æon, shepherded among the infinite deeps, moving orderly from a dawn a million years far off to a quiet fold a million years away, sheep shepherded beyond all change or chance, or no more than the dust of a great wind blowing behind the travelling feet of Eternity — what did it all mean? Shepherded starry worlds, or but the dust of Time? A Shepherd, or Silence? But he who had the wisdom of God, and was bearer of His message, turned to his bed and slept, muttering only that man in his wretchedness and sin was unworthy of those lamps suspended there to fill his darkness for sure, for God is merciful, but also to strike terror and awe and deep despair into the hearts of that innumerable multitude who go down daily into a starless night.

And when he had thought thus, he slept: till the fading bitterness of his thought was lost too in the noise of Gorromalt Water.

II

A great stillness of blue prevailed on the morrow. When sunrise poured over the shoulder of Ben Maiseach, and swept in golden foam among the pines of Strath Nair, it was as though a sweet, unknown, yet anciently familiar pastoral voice was uplifted — a voice full of solemn music, austerely glad, rejoicing with the deep rejoicing of peace.

The Strath was as one of the valleys of Eden. The rain-washed oaks and birches wore again their virginal green; the mountain ash had her June apparel; the larches were like the delicate green showers that fall out of the rainbow upon opal-hued clouds at sun setting; even the dusky umbrage of the pines filled slowly with light, as tidal sands at the flow.

The Gorromalt Water swept a blue arm round the western bend of the Strath; brown, foam-flecked, it emerged from the linn, tumultuous, whirling this way and that, leaping, surging.

In the wet loneroid, in the bracken, in the thyme-set grass, the yellow-hammers and stonechats remembered, perhaps for the last time in this summer-end, their nesting songs, their nestling notes.

From every green patch upon the hills the loud, confused, incessant bleating of the ewes and four-month lambs made a myriad single crying — a hill-music sweet to hear.

From the Mill o' Gorromalt, too, where little Sine Macrae danced in the sunlight, to the turfed cottage of Mary Gilchrist high on the furthest spur of Maiseach, where her child stretched out his hands to catch the sun-rays, resounded the laughter of children. The blue smoke from the crofts rose like the breath of stones.

A spirit of joy moved down the Strath. Even thus of old, men knew the wayfaring Breath of God.

It was then the new minister, the Interpreter, brought to the remembrance of every man and woman in the Strath that the Lord God moveth in shadow, and is a jealous God.

The water-bell of the Mill, that did duty on the preaching Sabbaths, began its monotonous call. Of yore, most who heard it had gone gladly to its summons. When John Campbell had preached the Word, all who heard him returned with something of peace, with something of hope. But now none went save unwillingly; some even with new suspicions the one against the other, some with bitter searchings, some with latent dark vanities that could not bloom in the light.

And so the man delivered the Gospel. He preached the Word, there, on the glowing hillside, where the sun shone with imperious beauty. Was it that while he preached, the sky darkened, that the hillside darkened, the sunglow darkened, the sun itself darkened? That the heart of each man and woman darkened, that the mind of each darkened, that every soul there darkened, yea, that even the white innocence of the little children grew dusked with shadow? And yet the sun shone as it had shone before the tolling of the bell. No cloud was in the sky. Beauty lay upon the hillside; the Gorromalt Water leaped and danced in the sunlight. Nothing darkened from without. The darkening was from within.

The Rev. James Campbell spoke for an hour with sombre eloquence. Out of the deep darkness of his heart he spoke. In that hour he slew many hopes, chilled many aspirations, dulled many lives. The old, hearing him, grew weary of the burden of years, and yet feared release as a more dreadful evil still. The young lost heart, relinquished hope.

There was one interruption. An old man, Macnamara by name, a shepherd, rose and walked slowly away from where the congregation sat in groups on the hillside. He was followed by his two collie dogs, who had sat patiently on their haunches while the minister preached his word of doom.

"Where will you be going, Peter Macnamara?" called Mr. Campbell, his voice dark with the same shadow that was in the affront on his face.

"I am going up into the hills," the old man answered quietly, "for I am too old to lose sight of God." Then, amid the breathless pause around him, he added: "And here, James Campbell, I have heard no word of Him."

"Go," thundered the minister, with outstretched arm and pointed finger. "Go, and when thine hour cometh thou shalt lament in vain that thou didst affront the most High God!"

The people sat awed. A spell was upon them. None moved. The eyes of all were upon the minister.

And, he, now, knew his power, and that he had triumphed. He spoke to or of now one, now another poor sinner, whose evildoing was but a weakness, a waywardness to guide, not a cancer inassuageable. Suddenly he remembered the woman, Mary Gilchrist.

Of her he spoke, till all there shuddered at her sin, and shuddered more at the chastisement of that sin. She was impure; she dwelt in the iniquity of that sin; she sought neither to repent nor to hide her shame. In that great flame of hell, which she would surely know, years hence — a hundred years hence — a thousand, ten thousand, immeasurably remote in eternity — she would know then, when too late, that God was, indeed, a jealous God — in unending torture, in ceaseless —

But at that moment a low hush grew into a rising crest of warning. The wave of sound spilled at the minister's feet. He stared, frowning.

"What is it?" he asked.

"Hush!" someone answered. "There's the poor woman herself coming this way."

And so it was. Over the slope beyond Monanair Mary Gilchrist appeared. She was walking slowly, and as though intent upon the words of her companion, who was the wayfarer with whom Mr. Campbell had spoken at the Glen of the Willows.

"Let her come," said the minister sullenly. Then, suddenly, being strangely uplifted by the cold night-wind in his heart, he resumed his bitter sayings, and spoke of the woman and her sin, and of all akin to her, from Mary Magdalene down to this Mary Gilchrist.

"Ay!" he cried, as the newcomers approached to within a few yards of where he stood, "and it was only by the exceeding overwhelming grace of God that the woman, Mary Magdalene, was saved at all. And often, ay, again and again, has the thought come to me that the mercy was hers only in this life."

A shudder went through the Strath-folk, but none stirred. A sudden weariness had come upon the minister, who had, indeed, spoken for a long hour and more. With a hurried blessing that sounded like a knell, for the last words were, "Beware the wrath of God," Mr. Campbell sat back in the chair which had been carried there for him.

Then, before any moved away, the stranger who was with Mary Gilchrist arose. None knew him. His worn face, with its large sorrowful eyes, his long, fair hair, his white hands, were all unlike those of a man of the hills; but when he spoke it was in the sweet homely Gaelic that only those spoke who had it from the mother's lips.

"Will you listen to me, men and women of Strath Nair?" he asked. He was obviously a poor man, and a wanderer; yet none there who did not realise he was one to whom all would eagerly listen. And so the man preached the Word. He, too, spoke of God and man, of the two worlds, of life and death, of time and eternity. As he spoke, it was as though he used, not the symbols of august and immortal things, but, in a still whiteness of simplicity, revealed these eternal truths themselves.

Was it that as he preached, the sky, the hillside, the sunglow, the sun itself lightened; that the heart of each man and woman lightened, that the mind of each lightened, that even the white innocence of the little children grew more fair to see?

The stranger, with the eyes of deep love and tenderness — so deep and tender that tears were in women's eyes, and the hearts of men were strained — spoke for long. Simple words he spoke, but none had ever been so moved. Out of the white beauty of his soul he spoke. In that hour he brought near to them many fair immortal things, clothed in mortal beauty; stilled shaken hearts; uplifted hopes grown dim or listless. The old, hearing him, smiled to think that age was but the lamp-lit haven, reached at last, with, beyond the dim strait, the shining windows of home. The young grew brave and strong; in the obscure trouble of each heart, new stars had arisen.

There was but one interruption. When the wayfarer said that they who could not read need not feel outcast from the Word of God, for all the Scriptures could be interpreted in one phrase — simply, "God is love" — the minister, James Campbell, rose and passed slowly through the groups upon the hillside.

"Listen," said the wayfarer, "while I tell you the story of Mary Magdalene."

Then he told the story again as any may read it in the Book, but with so loving words, and with so deep a knowledge of the pitifulness of life, that it was a revelation to all there. Tears were in the heart as well as in the eyes of each man and woman.

Then slowly he made out of the beauty of all their listening souls a wonderful thing.

Mary Gilchrist had kneeled by his side, and held his left hand in hers, weeping gently the while. A light was about her as of one glorified. It was, mayhap, the light from Him whose living words wrought a miracle there that day.

For as he spoke, all there came to know and to understand and to love. Each other they understood and loved, with a new love, a new understanding. And not one there but felt how sacred and beautiful in their eyes was the redemption of the woman Mary Gilchrist, who was now to them as Mary Magdalene herself.

The wayfarer spoke to one and all by name, or so to each it seemed; and to each he spoke of the sobbing woman by his side, and of the greatness and beauty of love and of the pitifulness of the sorrow of love, and of the two flames in the shame of love, the white flame and the red. The little green world, he said, this little whirling star, is held to all the stars that be, and these are held to every universe, and all universes surmised and yet undreamed of are held to God Himself, simply by a little beam of light — a little beam of Love. It is Love that is the following Thought of God. And it is love that is of sole worth in human life. This he said again and again, in familiar words become new and wonderful. Thus it was that out of the pain and sorrow, out of the passion and grief and despair of the heart of the woman Mary, and out of the heart of every man, woman, and child in that place, he wrought a vision of the Woman Mary, of Mary the Mother, of Mary whose name is Love, whose soul is Love, whose Breath is Love, who is wherever Love is, sees all and knows all and understands all; who has no weariness, and who solves all impurities and evils, and turns them into pure gold of love; who is the Pulse of Life, the Breath of Eternity, the Soul of God.

And when he had ceased speaking there was not one there — no, not one — who could see the glory of the beauty of his face because of the mist of tears that were in all eyes.

None saw him go. Quietly he moved down the path leading to the green birches at the hither end of the Glen of the Willows.

There he turned, and for a brief while gazed silent, with longing blue eyes full of dream, and pale face stilled by the ecstasy of prayer.

All stood beholding him. Slowly he raised his arms. Doves of peace flew out of his heart. In every heart there a white dove of peace nested. Mayhap he who stood under the green birches heard what none whom he had left on the hill-slope could hear — the whispering, the welling, the uplifted voice of spirits redeemed from their mortal to their immortal part.

For suddenly he smiled. Then he bowed his head, and was lost in the green gloom, and was seen no more.

But in the gloaming, in the dewy gloaming of that day, Mary Gilchrist walked alone, with her child in her arms, in the Glen of the Willows. And once she heard a step behind her, and a hand touched her shoulder.

"Mary!" said the low, sweet voice she knew so well, "Mary! Mary!"

Whereupon she sank upon her knees.

"Jesus of Nazareth, Son of God!" broke from her lips in faint, stammering speech.

For long she kneeled trembling. When she rose, none was there. White stars hung among the branches of the dusky green pyramids of the Glen of the Willows. On the hillside beyond, where her home was, the moonlight lay, quiet waters of peace. She bowed her head, and moved out of the shadow into the light.

Section Seven

POLITICAL COMMENTS & SOME FRAGMENTS

POLITICAL COMMENTS AND SOME FRAGMENTS

Towards the end of her 'life' Fiona wrote some comments on the political events of the day, particularly in reference to the struggle for Home Rule in Ireland, as well as the blossoming Celtic Twilight movement which was so popular amongst nationalists from not only Ireland but Scotland, Wales, Cornwall and Brittany as well. Up until then she had kept away from such subjects even after being personally invited to become actively involved by other great Celtic writers and activists of the day including William Butler Yeats.

However when she did capitulate and put pen to paper it caused much confusion and even anger amongst her new political readers. This was mainly because she was seen to be too 'airy-fairy,' too romantic and unworldly to be of much use to the hard and sometimes violent Celts she was trying to address. She did write apologies in which she tried to explain her comments in more detail but the damage had been done and she wisely decided to quietly drop from political circles and commentaries and return to her signature descriptions of nature, joy, sorrow and life in the Scottish Highlands and Islands.

The first essay in this section, *Celtic*, appeared in the *Contemporary Review Magazine* and caused a great amount of consternation. It seems to imply that all the die-hard Celtic writers are actually English writers and even if they should in fact be Celtic she personally does not want to be given that appellation. The second piece in this section, *For the Beauty of an Idea*, is an apology and rather unsuccessful attempt to explain what she really meant in the *Celtic* essay. It is clear from both of these why she wisely withdrew from the political debates of the day.

When William Sharp died he left behind dozens of notebooks, diaries and scraps of paper with all manner of ideas, sayings, outlines, magical bits and pieces that never made it into any of his or Fiona Macleod's published material but it is always clear whether they were intended for his own work or for Fiona's as the two styles are so distinctive. I give here a few random jottings from the notebooks of William Sharp but all in the style of his alter-ego Fiona Macleod.

Celtic

A writer might well be proud to be identified with a movement that is primarily spiritual and eager, a movement of quickened artistic life. I, for one, care less to be identified with any literary movement avowedly partisan. That is not the deliberate view of literature, which carries with it the heat and confused passions of the many. It is not the deliberate view, which confers passions that are fugitive upon that troubled Beauty which knows only a continual excellence. It is not the deliberate view, which would impose the penury of distracted dreams and desires upon those who go up to the treasure house and to white palaces.

But I am somewhat tired of an epithet that, in a certain association, is become jejune, through use and misuse. It has grown familiar wrongly; is often a term of praise or disdain, in each inept; is applied without moderation; and so now is sometimes unwelcome — even when there is none other so apt and right.

The 'Celtic Movement,' in the first place, is not, as so often confusedly stated, an arbitrary effort to reconstruct the past; though it is, in part, an effort to discover the past. For myself (as one imputed to this "movement") I would say that I do not seek merely to reproduce ancient Celtic presentments of tragic beauty and tragic fate, but do seek in nature and in life, and in the swimming thought of timeless imagination, for the kind of beauty that the old Celtic poets discovered and uttered. There were poets and mythmakers in those days; and to-day we may be sure that a new Mythus is being woven, though we may no longer regard with the old wonder, or in the old wonder imaginatively shape and colour the forces of Nature and her silent and secret processes; for the mythopoetic faculty is not only a primitive instinct but a spiritual need.

I do not suppose our Celtic ancestors — for all their high civilisation and development, so much beyond what obtained among the Anglo Saxon or Teutonic peoples at the same date — theorised about their narrative art; but from what we know of their literature, from the most ancient bardic chants to the *sgeul* of today, we cannot fail to see that the instinctive ideal was to represent beautiful life. It is an ideal that has lain below the spiritual passion of all great art in every period. Phidias knew it when he culled a white beauty from the many Athenian youth, and Leonardo when he discerned the inexplicable in woman's beauty and painted Mona Lisa, and Palestrina when from the sound of the pines and the voice of the wind in solitudes and the songs of labourers at sundown he wove a solemn music for cathedral aisles. With instinct the old Celtic poets and romanticists knew it: there are no Breton ballads nor Cymric Mabinogion nor Gaelic sgeulan which deal ignobly with pretty life. All the evil passions may obtain there, but they move against a spiritual background of pathetic wonder, of tragic beauty and tragic fate.

The ideal of art should be to represent beautiful life. If we want a vision of life that is not beautiful, we can have it otherwise: a multitude can depict the ignoble; the lens can replicate the usual.

It should be needless to add that our vision of the beautiful must be deep and wide and virile, as well as high and ideal. When we say that art should represent beautiful life, we do not say that it should represent only the beautiful in life, which would be to ignore the roots and the soil and the vivid sap, and account the blossom only. The vision of beautiful life is the vision of life seen not in impossible but in possible relief: of harmonious unity in design as well as in colour. To say that art should represent beautiful life is merely to give formal expression to the one passionate instinct in every poet and painter and musician, in every artist. There is no "art" saved by a moral purpose, though all true art is subtly informed of the spirit; but I know none, with pen or brush, with chisel or score, which, ignobly depicting the ignoble, survives in excellence.

In this, one cannot well go astray. Nor do I seek an unreal Ideal. In the kingdom of the imagination, says Calvert, one of our forgotten mystics, the ideal must ever be faithful to the general laws of nature — elsewhere adding a truth as immanent: "Man is not alone: the Angel of the Presence of the Infinite is with him." I do not, with Blake, look upon our world as though it were at best a basis for transcendental vision, while in itself "a hindrance and a mistake," but rather, as a wiser has said, to an Earth spiritualised, not a Heaven naturalised. With Calvert, too, I would say: "I have a fondness for the earth, and rather a Phrygian way of regarding it, despite a deeper yearning to see its glades receding into the Gardens of Heaven."

There is cause for deep regret when any word, that has peculiar associations of beauty or interest, or in which some distinction obtains, is lightly bandied. Its merit is then in convenience of signal rather than in its own significance. It is easy to recall some of these unfortunates; as our Scottish word "gloaming," that is so beautiful, and is now, alas, to be used rarely and with heed; as "haunting," with its implicit kinship with all mysteries of shadow, and its present low estate; as "melody," that has an outworn air, though it has three secrets of beauty; as others, that one or two use with inevitableness, and a small number deftly, till the journal has it, and it is come into desuetude.

We have of late heard so much of Celtic beauty and Celtic emotion that we would do well to stand in more surety as to what we mean and what we do not mean.

I do not myself know any beauty that is of art to excel than bequeathed to us by Greece. The marble has outlasted broken dynasties and lost empires; the word is to-day fresh as with dews of dawn. But through the heart I travel into another land. Through the heart I go to lost gardens, to mossed fountains, to groves where is no white beauty of still statue, but only the beauty of an old forgotten day remembered with quickened pulse and desired with I know not what of longing and weariness.

Is it remembrance, I wonder often, that makes many of us of the Celtic peoples turn to our own past with a longing so great, a love perfected through forgotten tribulations and familiar desires of the things we know to be impossible but so fair? Or do we but desire in memory what all primitive races had, and confuse our dreams with those which have no peace because they are immortal?

If one can think with surety but a little way back into the past, one can divine through both the heart and the mind. I do not think that our broken people had no other memories and traditions than other peoples had. I believe they stood more near to ancient forgotten founts of wisdom than others stood: I believe that they are the offspring of a race who were in a more fraternal communion with the secret powers of the world. I think their ancient writings show it, their ancient legends, their subtle and spiritual mythology. I believe that, in the East, they lit the primitive genius of their race at unknown and mysterious fires; that, in the ages, they have not wholly forgotten the ancestral secret; that, in the West, they may yet turn from the grey wave that they see, and the grey wave of time that they do not see, and again, upon new altars, commit that primeval fire.

But to believe is one thing, to convince is another. Those of us who believe thus have no warrant to show. It may well be that we do but create an image made after the desire and faith of the heart.

It is not the occasion to speak of what I do believe the peculiar and excelling beauty of the Celtic genius and Celtic literature to be; how deep its wellsprings, how full of strange new beauty to us who come upon it that is so old and remote. What I have just written will disclose that wherever else I may desire to worship, there is one beauty that has to me the light of home upon it; that there is one beauty from which, above all others now, I hope for a new revelation; that there is a love, there is a passion, there is a romance, which to me calls more suddenly and searchingly than any other ancient love or ancient passion or ancient romance.

But having said this, I am the more free to speak what I have in view. Let me say at once, then, that I am not a great believer in "movements," and still less in "renascences"; to be more exact, I hold myself in a suspicion towards these terms; for often, in the one, what we look for is riot implicit, and in the other, we are apt rather to find the excrescent and the deciduous.

So far as I understand the 'Celtic Movement,' it is a natural outcome, the natural expression of a freshly inspired spiritual and artistic energy. That this expression is coloured by racial temperament is its distinction; that it is controlled to novel usage is its opportunity. When we look for its source we find it in the usufruct of an ancient and beautiful treasure of national tradition. One may the more aptly speak thus collectively of a mythology and a literature, and a vast and wonderful legendary folklore, since to us now, it is in great part hidden behind veils of an all but forgotten tongue, and of a system of life and customs, ideals and thought, that no longer obtains.

I am unable, however, to see that it has sustenance in continuity of revolt. A new movement need not be a revolt, but rather a sortie to carry a fresh position. If a movement has any inherent force, it will not destroy itself in forlorn hopes, but, where the need is vital, will fall into line, and so achieve where alone the desired success can be achieved.

There is no racial road to beauty, nor to any excellence. Genius, which leads thither, beckons neither to tribe nor clan, neither to school nor movement, but only to one soul here and to another there; so that the Icelander hears and speaks in Saga, and the brown Malay hears and carves delicately in ivory; and the men in Europe, from the Serb and the Finn to the Basque and the Breton, hear, and each in his kind answers; and what the Englishman says in song and romance and the deep utterance of his complex life, his mountain-kindred say in Mabinogi or sgeul.

Even in those characteristics which distinguish Celtic literature — intimate natural vision; a swift emotion that is sometimes a spiritual ecstasy, but sometimes is also a mere intoxication of the senses; a peculiar sensitiveness to the beauty of what is remote and solitary; a rapt pleasure in what is ancient and in the contemplation of what holds an indwelling melancholy; a visionary passion for beauty, which is of the immortal things, beyond the temporal beauty of what is mutable and mortal — even in these characteristics it does not stand alone, and perhaps not preeminent. There is a beauty in the Homeric hymns that I do not find in the most beautiful of Celtic chants; none could cull from the gardens of the Gael what in the Greek anthology has been gathered out of time to be everlasting; perhaps only the love and passion of the stories of the Celtic mythology surpass the love and passion of the stories of the Hellenic mythology. The romance that of old flowered among the Gaelic hills flowered also in English meads, by Danish shores, along Teutonic Woods and plains. I think Catullus sang more excellently than Baile Honeymouth, and that Theocritus loved nature not less than Oisin, and that the ancient makers of the Kalevala were as much children of the wind and wave and the intimate natural world as were the makers of the ancient heroic chronicles of the Gael.

There is no law set upon beauty. It has no geography. It is the domain of the spirit. And if, of those who enter there, peradventure any comes again, he is welcome for what he brings; nor do we demand if he be dark or fair, Latin or Teuton or Celt, or say of him that his tidings are lovelier or the less lovely because he was born in the shadow of Gaelic hills or nurtured by Celtic shores.

It is well that each should learn the mother song of his land at the cradle-place of his birth. It is well that the people of the isles should love the isles above all else, and the people of the mountains love the mountains above all else, and the people of the plains love the plains above all else. But it is not well that because of the whistling of the wind in the heather one should imagine that nowhere else does the wind suddenly stir the reeds and the grasses in its incalculable hour.

When I hear that a new writer is of the Celtic school, I am left in some uncertainty, for I know of many Anglo-Celtic writers but of no "school," or what present elements would form a school. What is a Celtic writer? If the word has any exact acceptance, it must denote an Irish or a Scottish Gael, a Cymric or Breton Celt, who writes in the language of his race. It is obvious that if one would write English literature, one must write in English and in the English tradition.

When I hear, therefore, of this or that writer as a Celtic writer, I wonder if the term is not apt to be misleading. An English writer is meant, who in person happens to be an Irish Gael, or Highland, or Welsh.

I have already suggested what other misuse of the word obtains: Celtic emotion, Celtic love of nature, Celtic visionariness. That, as admitted, there is in the Celtic peoples an emotionalism peculiar in kind and certainly in intensity, is not to be denied; that a love of nature is characteristic is true, but differing only, if at all, in certain intimacies of approach; that visionariness is relatively so common as to be typical, is obvious. But there is English emotion, English love of nature, English visionariness, as there is Dutch, or French, or German, or Russian, or Hindu. There is no exclusive national heritage in these things, save in the accident of racial physiognomy, of the supreme felicity of contour and colour. At a hundred yards a forest is seen to consist of ash and lime, of elms, beeches, oaks, horn-beams; but a mile away it is, simply, a forest.

I do not know any Celtic visionary so rapt and absolute as the Londoner William Blake, or the Scandinavian Swedenborg, or the Flemish Ruysbroek; or any Celtic poet of nature to surpass the Englishman Keats; nor do I think even religious ecstasy is more seen in Ireland than in Italy. Nothing but harm is done by a protestation that cannot persuade deliberate acceptance.

When I hear that "only a Celt" could have written this or that passage of emotion or description, I am become impatient of these parrot-cries, for I remember that if all Celtic literature were to disappear, the world would not be so impoverished as by the loss of English literature, or French literature, or that of Rome or of Greece.

But above all else it is time that a prevalent pseudo-nationalism should be dissuaded. I am proud to be a Highlander, but I would not side with those who would "set the heather on fire." If I were Irish, I would be proud, but I would not lower my pride by marrying it to a ceaseless ill-will, an irreconcilable hate, for there can be a nobler pride in unvanquished acquiescence than in futile revolt. I would be proud if I were Welsh, but I would not refuse to learn English, or to mix with English as equals. And proud as I might be to be Highland, or Scottish, or Irish, or Welsh, or English, I would be more proud to be British — for, there at last, we have a bond to unite us all, and to give us space for every ideal, whether communal or individual, whether national or spiritual.

As for literature, there is, for us all, only English literature. All else is provincial or dialetic.

But gladly I, for one, am willing to be designated Celtic, if the word signify no more than that one is an English writer who by birth, inheritance, and temperament has an outlook not distinctively English, with some memories and traditions and ideals not shared in by one's countrymen of the South, with a racial instinct that informs what one writes, and, for the rest, a common heritage.

The Celtic element in our national life has a vital and great part to play. We have a most noble ideal if we will but accept it. And that is, not to perpetuate feuds, not to try to win back what is gone away upon the wind, not to repay ignorance with scorn, or dullness with contempt, or past wrongs with present hatred, but so to live, so to pray, so to hope, so to work, so to achieve, that we, what is left of the Celtic races, of the Celtic genius, may permeate the greater race of which we are a vital part, so that with this Celtic emotion, Celtic love of beauty, and Celtic spirituality a nation greater than any the world has seen may issue, a nation refined and strengthened by the wise relinquishings and steadfast ideal of Celt and Saxon, united in a common fatherland, and in singleness of pride and faith.

As I have said, I am not concerned here with what I think the Celtic genius has done for the world, and for English literature in particular, and, above all, for us of to-day and to-morrow; nor can I dwell upon what of beautiful and mysterious and wonderful it discloses, or upon its bitter-sweet charm. But of a truth, the inward sense and significance of the 'Celtic Movement' is, as has been well said by Mr. Yeats, in the opening of a fountain of legends, and, as scholars aver, a more abundant fountain than any in Europe, the great fountain of Gaelic legends. "None can measure of how great importance it may be to coming times, for every new fountain of legends is a new intoxication for the imagination of the world. It comes at a time when the imagination of the world is as ready, as it was at the coming of the tales of Arthur and of the Grail, for a new intoxication. The arts have become religious, and must, as religious thought has always done, utter themselves through legends; and the Gaelic legends have so much of a new beauty that they may well give the opening century its most memorable symbols."

Perhaps the most significant sentence in M. Renan's remarkable study of the Poetry of the Celtic Races is that where he speaks of the Celtic race as having worn itself out in mistaking dreams for realities. I am not certain that this is true, but it holds so great a part of the truth that it should make us think upon how we stand.

I think our people have most truly loved their land, and their country, and their songs, and their ancient traditions, and that the word of bitterest savour is that sad word exile. But it is also true that in that love we love vaguely another land, a rainbow-land, and that our most desired country is not the real Ireland, the real Scotland, the real Brittany, but the vague Land of Youth, the shadowy Land of Heart's Desire. And it is also true, that deep in the songs we love above all other songs is a lamentation for what is gone away from the world, rather than merely from us as a people, or a sighing of longing for what the heart desires but no mortal destiny requites.

And true, too, that no tradition from of old is so compelling as the compelling tradition that is from within; and that the long sorrow of our exile is in part because we ourselves have driven from us that company of hopes and dreams which were once realities, but are now among beautiful idle words.

In a word, we dwell overmuch among desired illusions: beautiful, when, like the rainbow, they are the spiritual reflection of certainties; but worthless as the rainbow-gold with which the Shee deceive the unwary, when what is the phantom of a spiritual desire is taken to be the reality of material fact.

And I think that we should be on guard against any abuse of, that we should consider this other side of, our dreams and ideals, wherein awaits weakness as well as abides strength. It is not ill to dream, in a day when there are too few who will withdraw from a continual business, a day when there are fewer dreams. But we shall not greatly gain if we dream only of beautiful abstractions, and not also of actual or imaginative realities and possibilities. In a Highland cottage I heard some time ago a man singing a lament for "Tearlach Og Aluinn," Bonnie Prince Charlie; and when he ceased tears were on the face of each that was there, and in his own throat a sob. I asked him, later, was his heart really so full of the Prionnsa Ban, but he told me that it was not him he was thinking of, but of all the dead men and women of Scotland who had died for his sake, and of Scotland itself, and of the old days that could not come again. I did not ask what old days, for I knew that in his heart he lamented his own dead hopes and dreams, and that the prince was but the image of his lost youth, and that the world was old and grey because of his own weariness and his own grief.

Sometimes I fear that we who as a people do so habitually companion ourselves with dreams may fall into that abyss where the realities are become shadows, and shadows alone live and move. And then I remember that dreamers and visionaries are few; that we are no such people; that no such people has ever been; and that of all idle weaving of sand and foam none is more idle than this, the strange instinctive dread of the multitude, that the few whose minds and imaginations dwell among noble memories and immortal desires shall supersede the many who are content with lesser memories and ignoble desires.

For the Beauty of an Idea

I: PRELUDE

THE short essay, entitled *Celtic*, which forms the second of the three parts of this study in the spiritual history of the Gael, appeared first in *The Contemporary Review*, and a few months later in the volume entitled *The Divine Adventure: Iona: and other Studies in Spiritual History*, and was a signal for divided comment. But for the moment I would recur only to the aspect it wore for many in that country for whose more eager spirits it was above all intended — Ireland being today not only the true home of lost causes, and a nursery of the heroic powers and influences that go out to conquer and die, but of the passionate and evil powers and influences which seek to conquer and are slow to die.

Although in Ireland, then, this essay towards a worthy peace, where peace may be and towards a compromise, in nothing ignoble, for the sake of union in a noble destiny, was welcomed by many — there were others, and among them one or two of those deservedly held in honour, who execrated the attempt. As it has been "authoritatively" stated that no Irish journal has endorsed these views, one out of six or seven of the leading Irish journals representative of all degrees of opinion, which have more or less "endorsed" the views here set forth, may be selected. In the reprinting of so personal a note the author trusts to be absolved of any other intent than to refute in what seems the simplest and most direct way a statement calculated to mislead:

> "It seems an unexpected utterance from Miss Macleod. Yet, in points of fact, it only shows the awakening of the same philosophic spirit which we have observed in other parts of this book and in other regions of her thought. Miss Macleod has noticed the narrow separatism of sentiment which has sometimes marked the Celtic literary revival, and sees that it can only keep the Celtic spirit in a hopeless and sterile conflict with fact and truth. ... In her own words: —
>
> "The Celtic element in our national life has a vital and great part to play. We have a most noble ideal if we will but accept it. And that is, not to perpetuate feuds, not to try to win back what has gone away upon the wind, not to repay ignorance with scorn, or dullness with contempt, or past wrongs with present hatred, but so to live, so to pray, so to hope, so to work, so to achieve that we, what is left of the Celtic races, of the Celtic genius, may permeate the greater race of which we

are a vital part, so that with this Celtic emotion, Celtic love of beauty, and Celtic spirituality a nation greater than any the world has seen may issue, a nation refined and strengthened by the wise relinquishings and steadfast ideals of Celt and Saxon, united in a common fatherland, and in singleness of pride and faith."

These are great, wise, and courageous words ... When the Irish Celt begins to heed them he will cease to be the type of self-torturing futility which, with all his gifts, he so largely is at the present day."
(From an article, "A Celtic Thinker," in the *Dublin Express*.)

I have no ill-will to those who, no doubt in part through a hurried habit of mind, sought by somewhat intemperate means to discredit the plea. I believe — would say I know, so sure am I — these had at heart the thought of Ireland, that passion which is indeed the foremost lamp of the Gael, the passion of nationality; and having this thought and this passion, considered little or for the time ignored the "sweet reasonableness," the courtesy cherished by minds less sick with hope deferred, less desperate with defeated dreams. But in controversy nothing else was revealed than that enthusiasm can sometimes lead to confused thought and hasty speech, and (it may well be) that the writer of "Celtic" had failed to be lucid or adequate on that fundamental factor in Gaelic union, that essential element in the continued life and development of the Gael — the proud preservation of nationality. I can imagine no worse thing for Ireland than that, in exchange for a dull peace and a poor prosperity, it should sink to the vassalage of a large English shire. In the wise words of Thoreau, the cost of a thing is the amount of what may be called life which is required to be exchanged for it, immediately or in the long run.

The aim of this essay was to help towards a workable reconciliation: not between "inveterate and irreconcilable foes" (which is but the rhetoric of those fevered with an epileptic nationalism), but a reconciliation such as may be persuaded between two persons, each with divergent individual aims and ideals, yet able to unite with decency and courtesy in a league for the common good, the commonweal. It seemed, and seems, to the writer that common sense (there is no Celtic word for it) makes clear that an absolute irreconcilability is simply a cul-de-sac, down which baffled dreams and hopes and faiths come at last upon a blank wall. Strength is built out of forfeiture as well as of steadfastness, and the man or woman, cause or race wins, which on occasion can relinquish or forbear. Merely to be irreconcilable is to prefer the blank wall to the open road.

But when that is said, it does not follow that there are no subjects, no ideals, no aims which stand apart from this debatable ground of reconciliation. On the contrary, I believed, and believe, that there are subjects, ideals, and aims whose continuity lies only in an unswerving steadfastness. Nay, further, with the author of *The Hearts of Men*, I would say with all my faith, "the people that cannot fight shall die." On any such people the shadow of the end is already come. All signs and portents will have borne testimony. Before a nation dies, the soul of that nation is dead; and before the death of the soul of the nation its gods perish: God perishes. For God, who is eternal in the Spirit, is, in the image and in the symbol, as in "omnipotence" as we conceive it, mortal. Unto every nation of man God dies when in the Soul of the nation the altars are cold. There are the altars of divine faith, and the altars of spiritual ideals, and the altars of the commonweal. Beware the waning of these fires.

The keynote of *Celtic* is in the sentence, "We have of late heard so much of Celtic beauty and Celtic emotion that we would do well to stand in more surety as to what we mean and what we do not mean."

But I generalised too vaguely, I find, in this, merely indicative, merely suggestive paper, when I wrote, "What is a Celtic Writer? ... It is obvious that if one would write English literature, one must write in English and in the English tradition."

Of course I meant nothing so narrow in claim, so foreign to my conviction, as that one must "be English." There is no "must," in the Academic sense, in literature: the most vivid and original literature has in truth ever been an ignoring or overriding of this strong word of the weak.

Only I can see how some — I am glad to know the few, not the many — misread this sentence. For that, I welcome this opportunity of the open word. There is no need here to recur to the literal meaning of the designation, a "Celtic writer." I would merely add a further word of warning as to the sometimes apt epithet and definitive but often ill-considered use of racial terms in speaking of what are individual qualities and idiosyncrasies rather than the habit of mind or general characteristic of a people. Swedenborg, Blake, and Maurice Maeterlinck do not stand for Scandinavian, and English, and Flemish mysticism, nor is any of these a mystic by virtue of being a Fleming, an Englishman, or a Scandinavian. I recall the considered judgment of an acute French critic, M. Angellier, in his essay on Burns: "The idea of race is fluctuating, ill-established, open to dispute ... you cannot obtain a conception of the soul of a portion of humanity by merely supplementing certain ethnological labels with a few vague adjectives."

To consider those only, then, who write in English, I would add to my statement that if one would write English literature one must write in English and in the English tradition, the rider that the English language is not the exclusive property of that section of our complex race which is distinctively English, the English nation — any more than it is the exclusive property of the Scots, who speak it, or of the Australians; or of the Canadians; or of the vast and numerically superior American nation. The language is common to all: all share in the heritage shaped by the genius, moulded by the life and thought, and transmitted by the living spirit of the common essential stock — now as likely to be revealed in Massachusetts as in Yorkshire, in Toronto as in Edinburgh, in Sydney or Melbourne or Washington, as in Dublin, Manchester, or London. An American writes in his native language when he writes in English: so does a Scot, now: so does a Canadian, an Australian, a New Zealander. Therefore the literature — of the Australians, the Scots, the Irish, the Americans, must be in English. It is the language that determines, but the thought behind the language may come from any of the several founts of nationality, to reveal, in that language, its signature of the colour and form of distinctive life. It is not the language that compels genius, but genius that compels the language.

Again, literature has laws as inevitable as the laws which mould and determine the destiny of nations. These can be evaded by decay and death; they cannot be overridden. Every literature has its tradition of excellence — that is, the sum of what within its own limits can be achieved in beauty and power and aptitude. This tradition of excellence is what we call the central stream. Of course, if one prefer the tributary, the backwater, the offshoot, there is no reason why one should not be well content with the chosen course. To many it seems, for many it is, the better way; as the backwater for the kingfisher, the offshoot or tributary for the solitary heron. But one must not choose the backwater and declare that it is the main stream, or have the little tributary say that though it travels on the great flow it is not part of the river.

That is what I meant when I said that if one would write English literature one must write in English and in the English tradition. To say that was not to bid the Gael cease to be Gaelic, any more than it would imply that the American should cease to be American. On the contrary, I do most strenuously believe that the sole life of value in literature is in the preservation of the distinct racial genius, temper, colour, and contour. If the poetry of two of the foremost Irish poets of to-day did not conform to the laws and traditions of English poetry — since Mr. Yeats and Mr.

George Russell write in their native language, English, the language to which they were born and in which alone they can express themselves — it might be very interesting "Celtic" or any other experimental verse, but it would not be English poetry. The beauty they breathe into their instrument is of themselves; is individual certainly, and, in one case at least, in spirit and atmosphere is more distinctively Gaelic than English. But the instrument is English: and to summon beauty through it, and to give the phantom a body and spirit of excellence, one must follow in the footsteps of the master-musicians, recognising the same essential limitations, observing the same fundamental needs, fulfilling the like rigorous obligations of mastery.

Since we have to write in English, we must accept the burthen and responsibility. If a Cretan write in the Cretan dialect, he can be estimated by those who know Cretan; but if he is ambitious to have his irregular measures and corrupt speech called Greek poetry, he must write in Greek and conform in what is essential to the Greek tradition, to the laws and limitations of the Greek genius. The Englishman, the Scot, the Irishman, the American, each, if he would write English literature, has of necessity to do likewise.

In a very true sense, therefore, there can be an Irish literature, a Scottish literature, an Anglo-Gaelic literature, as well as an English literature; but in the wider sense it is all English literature — with, as may be, an Irish spirit and Irish ideals and Irish colour, or with a Highland spirit and Highland ideals and Highland colour, or with a Welsh spirit and Welsh ideals and Welsh colour — as Mr. Thomas Hardy's writings are English literature, with an English spirit and English ideals and an English colour.

It is the desire and faith of the Irish nation to mould a new a literature as distinctively its own as the English nation has a literature that is distinctively its own: and to do this, in Ireland or the like in Scotland, is possible only by the cultivation, the persistent preservation of the national spirit, of the national idiosyncrasy, the national ideals. I would see our peoples reconciled, where reconciliation is just and therefore wise; believing that in such reconciliation lie the elements of strength and advance, of noble growth and conquering influence; but I would not have reconciliation at any price, and would rather we should dwell isolate and hostile than purchase peace at the cost of relinquishment of certain things more precious than all prosperities and triumphs. The law of love is the nobler way, but there is also a divine law of hate. I do not advocate, and have never advocated, a reconciliation on any terms. I am not English, and have not the English mind or the English temper, and in many things do not share the English ideals; and to possess these would mean to relinquish my own heritage. But why should I be irreconcilably hostile to that mind and that temper and those ideals? Why should I not do my utmost to understand, sympathise, fall into line with them so far as may be, since we have all a common bond and a common destiny?

To that mind and that temper and those ideals do we not owe some of the noblest achievements of the human race, some of the lordliest conquests over the instincts and forces, of barbarism, some of the loveliest and most deathless things of the spirit and the imagination?

Let us beware of kneading husks with Mâyâ's dew, and so — as in the ancient gnome attributed to Krishna — create but food for the black doves of decay and death.

As for the Gaelic remnant (and none can pretend that this means Scotland and Ireland, but only a portion of Scotland and only a divided Ireland) I am ever but the more convinced that the dream of an outward independence is a perilous illusion — not because it is impracticable, for that alone is a fascination to us, but because it does not, cannot alas, reveal those dominant elements which alone can control dreams become actualities. Another and greater independence is within our reach, is ours, to preserve and ennoble.

Strange reversals, strange fulfilments may lie on the lap of the gods, but we have no knowledge of these, and hear neither the high laughter nor the far voices. But we front a possible because a spiritual greater destiny than the height of imperial fortunes, and have that which may send our voices further than the trumpets of east and west. Through ages of slow westering, till now we face the sundown seas, we have learned in continual vicissitude that there are secret ways whereon armies cannot march. And this has been given to us, a more ardent longing, a more rapt passion in the things of outward beauty and in the things of spiritual beauty. Nor it seems to me is there any sadness, or only the serene sadness of a great day's end, that, to others, we reveal in our best the genius of a race whose farewell is in a tragic lighting of torches of beauty around its grave.

Notebook Jottings

THERE is the vain civilization in which new things grow old, are already old while they are yet new: it is that which is called the march of progress. And there is the fundamental civilization in which old things imperishably grow new, moving into continual life out of everlasting youth: it is called nothing in particular, though often by the adverse term, for it is of the inward direction and so beyond the common sight, or the discernment either of scorn or indifference.

I am hopeful that a new spirit is abroad. There are two flame-sworded servants of man, both of them at a discount just now — Pride and Enthusiasm. Let us not be afraid to enlist these great allies to our service. Enthusiasm — what is it but the flame and ardour of noble ideas on fire! Pride — what is it but the aurora of the spirit! Do not let us be ashamed to be aristocratically proud. Proud of what — aristocrats in what? Proud of our great traditions, our beautiful literature, our particular racial genius: proud of all these things, with pride unconquerable and elate. Aristocrats, in the high distinction of Spiritual Beauty, in the quest of Beauty, in the passion for Beauty.

I do believe that the Imagination is a living Spirit, and not merely the voice and apparition of that Spirit. Bacon, I think had something, however adumbrate, of this in mind when he wrote: 'Neither is the Imagination simply and only a messenger; but is invested with no small authority in itself, besides the duty of the message.'

Years ago, when writing went with drifting thought and not from thought rising from the depths, I wrote this: Without pain as a memory and without despair as a will o' the wisp, there would be no lyric poetry of enduring beauty. But now I do not think this, though up to a point its truth is obvious. For Joy can be and ought to be the supreme torch of the mind, and Hope can be and ought to be the inspiration of that grave ecstasy which is Art become religious, that is, Art expressing an august verity, with the emotion of life that is mortal deepened by the passion of the soul that is immortal. Nevertheless it is true that pain is a wind that goes deep into the obscure wood, and stirs many whispers and lamentations among the hidden leaves, and sends threnodies on long waves from the swaying green shores of oak and pine and beech. 'It is that which gives artists the strongest powers of expression,' wrote one who for himself knew the truth of what he said, the great Millet. But Despair, that is a quality of the mind, while pain is an elemental condition of life. It is in nature for all that lives to know pain: it is not natural for anything that lives to know despair. So while despair may have its beauty, as a desolate polar sea has, or a barren hillside where the dishevelled stony wilderness is without the green of grass or song of bird, or a marsh redeemed in the pale gold of the moon or the white mystery of starlight, it is the beauty of what is accidental and temporal, not of what is elemental and eternal. The clouds of man's hopes and dreams that drift through the human sky, and the wind of the spirit that shepherds them belong to the higher regions. And by some subtlety of association I recall with sudden pleasure those beautiful lines in Balaustion's Adventure: 'Why should despair be? Since distinct above Man's wickedness and folly, flies the wind and floats the cloud.'

Our thought, our consciousness, is but the scintillation of a wave; below us is a moving shadow, our brief forecast and receding way; beneath the shadow are depths sinking into depths, and then the unfathomable unknown.

As Art is the vision of life seen in beauty, and Poetry the dream of life remembered in beauty, and Music the echo of life heard in beauty, so dreams and illusions are the foam and phosphorescence on the ever changing yet changeless sea of Beauty.

I was born more than a thousand years ago, in the remote region of Gaeldom known as the Hills of Dream. There I have lived the better part of my life; my father's name was Romance, and that of my mother was Dream. I have no photograph of their abode, which is just under the quicken-arch immediately west of the sunset rainbow. You will easily find it. Nor can I send you a photograph of myself. My last fell among the dew-wet heather, and is now doubtless lining the cells of the wild bees. All this authentic information I gladly send you![98]

In a notebook from around the mid-1890s is the following entry:

I should like inscribed on my tomb
> *Farewell, then, to the known and exhausted:*
> *Welcome to the unknown and the unfathomed.*
The passage from Fiona Macleod ("The Distant Country")
> *Love is more great than we can conceive, and*
> *Death is the keeper of unknown redemptions.*[99]

---

98 This was a typical response Fiona would send to fans who requested photographs or personal information from her.

99 The epitaph on William Sharp's grave in Sicily reads slightly differently,

Farewell to the known and exhausted,
Welcome the unknown and illimitable.
Love is more great than we can conceive, and
Death is the keeper of unknown redemptions.

The first two lines are by William Sharp and the last two are taken from Fiona Macleod's piece *The Distant Country* in the collection *The Dominion of Dreams*. In a letter to a friend she said, "... there is nothing in *The Dominion of Dreams*, or elsewhere in these writings under my name to stand beside 'The Distant Country'... as the deepest and most searching utterance on the mystery of passion... It is indeed the core of all these writings ... and will outlast them all."

Bibliography

THE original titles and publication dates of Fiona Macleod's main works are given below, but it should be noted that most of them were reprinted several times in different combinations during William's life and for several years after his death. Several foreign publishers also published many editions and these are often different from their British originals. Not only were the collections of tales in each volume switched from one to another but the text of many of them was also edited and amended on subsequent editions, resulting in a confusing mixture of editions and versions.

- *Pharais: A Romance of the Isles* Frank Murray, Derby, 1894. Reprinted by T.N. Foulis, Edinburgh, 1907.
- *The Mountain Lovers* John Lane, London, 1895. Second edition John Lane, London & New York, 1906.
- *The Sin-Eater and Other Tales* Patrick Geddes & Colleagues, Edinburgh, 1895. Reprinted David Nutt, London, 1899.
- *The Washer of the Ford and other Legendary Moralities* Patrick Geddes & Colleagues, Edinburgh, 1896. Reprinted David Nutt, London, 1899.
- *Reissue of the Shorter Tales of Fiona Macleod* Patrick Geddes & Colleagues, Edinburgh, 1896. Reprinted David Nutt, London, 1899.
  Volume 1 - Spiritual Tales
  Volume 2 - Barbaric Tales
  Volume 3 - Tragic Romances
- *Green Fire: A Romance* Archibald, Constable & Co., Westminster, 1896.
- *From The Hills of Dream: Mountain Songs and Island Runes* Patrick Geddes & Colleagues, Edinburgh, 1896.
- *The Laughter of Peterkin: A Retelling of the Old Tales of the Celtic Wonderland* Archibald, Constable & Co., Westminster, 1897.
- *The Dominion of Dreams* Archibald, Constable & Co., Westminster, 1899. Reprinted Constable & Co., 1909.
- *The Divine Adventure: Iona: By Sundown Shores: Studies in Spiritual History* Chapman and Hall, Ltd., London, 1900.
- *Wind and Wave: Selected Tales* Bernhard Tauchnitz, Leipzig, 1902.
- *The Winged Destiny: Studies in the Spiritual History of the Gael* Chapman and Hall, Ltd., London, 1904.
- *The Sunset of Old Tales* Bernhard Tauchnitz, Leipzig, 1905.
- *Where the Forest Murmurs: Nature Essays* Georges Newnes, Ltd., New York, 1906.

- *From the Hills of Dream: Threnodies and Songs and Later Poems* William Heinemann, London, 1907.
- *The Immortal Hour: a Drama in Two Acts* T.N. Foulis, London, 1908.
- *A Little Book of Nature* T.N. Foulis, Edinburgh and London, 1909.
- *The Works of "Fiona Macleod"* Uniform Edition, London, Heinemann, 1910. Arranged by Mrs. William Sharp.
  Volume 1 - "Pharais" and "The Mountain Lovers"
  Volume 2 - "The Sin-Eater" and "The Washer of the Ford"
  Volume 3 - The Dominion of Dreams: Under the Dark Star
  Volume 4 - The Divine Adventure: Iona. Studies in Spiritual History
  Volume 5 - The Winged Destiny: Studies in the Spiritual History of the Gael
  Volume 6 - The Silence of Amor: Where the Forest Murmurs
  Volume 7 - Poems and Dramas

Readers interested in studying the complete texts of Fiona Macleod's output should take note of Elizabeth's comments in the Foreword to Volume One of this set: "*Into this collected edition are gathered all the writings of William Sharp published under his pseudonym "Fiona Macleod", which he cared to have preserved ... I have carefully followed the author's written and spoken instructions as to selection, deletion and arrangement. To the preliminary arrangement he gave much thought, especially to the revision of the text, and he made considerable changes in the later versions of certain of the poems and tales.*" In other words, it is necessary to go to the original printings of many of these works in order to read them in their entirety. For ease of reference here is a list of the contents of each volume:

Volume 1: ***Pharais - The Mountain Lovers*** contains a foreword by Elizabeth plus the first two novels *Pharais: A Romance of the Isles* and *The Mountain Lovers*. A bibliographical note follows these on the dates and publishers of the first editions. All of the following volumes in the set contain relevant bibliographical notes.

Volume 2: ***The Sin Eater - The Washer of the Ford*** contains *The Sin Eater* with its *Prologue - From Iona*, plus several short stories: *The Sin-Eater; The Ninth Wave; The Judgment o' God; The Harping of Cravetheen; Silk o' the Kine* plus *Ula and Urla* which was not in the original edition.

Alongside these are the tales originally published as *The Washer of the Ford* with the *Prologue* followed by *The Washer of the Ford; St. Bride of the Isles; The Fisher of Men; The Last Supper; The Dark Nameless One; The Three Marvels of Hy; The Woman with the Net; Cathal of the Woods* plus *The Song of the Sword; The Flight of the Culdees; Mircath; The Sad Queen* (not in the original edition); *The Laughter of Scathach the Queen; Ahez the Pale* (not in the original edition); *The King of Ys and Dahut the Red* (not in the original edition).

Volume 3: *The Dominion of Dreams - Under the Dark Star* contains the tales from *The Dominion of Dreams*: *Dalua; By the Yellow Moonrock; Lost; Morag of the Glen; The Sight; The Dark Hour of Fergus; The Hills of Ruel; The Archer; The Birdeen; The Book of the Opal; The Wells of Peace; In the Shadow of the Hills; The Distant Country; A Memory of Beauty; Enya of the Dark Eyes; The Crying of Wind; Honey of the Wild Bees; The Birds of Emar; Ulad of the Dreams; The Wind, The Shadow, and the Soul*. Also in this volume are the tales from *Under The Dark Star*: *The Anointed Man; The Dan-nan-Ron; Green Branches; Children of the Dark Star; Alasdair the Proud* and *The Amadan*.

Volume 4: *The Divine Adventure - Iona - Studies in Spiritual History* contains the whole of *The Divine Adventure* and the essay originally published simply as *Iona*. Alongside these two works are the tales originally published as *By Sundown Shores*, namely *By Sundown Shores; The Wind, Silence, and Love; Barabal: A Memory; The White Heron; The Smoothing of the Hand; The White Fever; The Sea-Madness; Earth, Fire, and Water*. These are joined by two extracts from *Green Fire* which are here called *The Herdsman* and *Fragments*. The volume concludes with the short essay *A Dream*.

Volume 5: *The Winged Destiny: Studies in the Spiritual History of the Gael* includes *The Sunset of Old Tales; The Treud Nan Ron; The Man on the Moor; The Woman at the Cross-Ways; The Lords of Wisdom; The Wayfarer; Queens of Beauty; Orpheus and Oisin; The Awakening of Angus Òg; Children of Water; Cuilidh Mhoire; Sea-Magic; Fara-a-Ghaol; Sorrow on the Wind; The Lynn of Dreams; Maya; Prelude; Celtic; The Gaelic Heart; The Gael and his Heritage; Seumas: A Memory; Aileen: A Memory; The Four Winds of Eirinn; Two Old Songs of May; "The Shadowy Waters"; A Triad; The Ancient Beauty* and *The Winged Destiny*.

Volume 6: *The Silence of Amor - Where the Forest Murmurs* contains the two pieces *The Silence of Amor* and *Tragic Landscapes* plus a collection of short pieces, here called *Where The Forest Murmurs* and individually as *Where the Forest Murmurs; The Mountain Charm; The Clans of the Grass; The Tides; The Hill-Tarn; At the Turn of the Year; The Sons of the North Wind; St. Briget of the Shores; The Heralds of March; The Tribe of the Plover; The Awakener of the Woods; The Wild-Apple; Running Waters; The Summer Heralds; The Sea-Spell; Summer Clouds; The Cuckoo's Silence; The Coming of Dusk; At the Rising of the Moon; The Gardens of the Sea; The Milky Way; September; The Children of*

Wind and the Clan of Peace; Still Waters; The Pleiad-Month; The Rainy Hyades; Winter Stars I; Winter Stars II; Beyond the Blue Septentrions. Two Legends of the Polar Stars; White Weather: A Mountain Reverie; Rosa Mystica (and Roses of Autumn); The Star of Rest: A Fragment and *An Almanac*.

Volume 7: *Poems and Dramas* contains twenty-eight poems collected under the title *Poems*; sixteen poems collected under the title *Closing Doors*; four poems collected under the title *From the Heart of a Woman*; thirty-eight poems collected under the title *Foam of the Past*; twenty poems collected under the title *Through the Ivory Gate*, five poems collected under the title *The Dirge of the Four Cities* and thirty-one poems collected under the title of *The Hour of Beauty*. The volume
concludes with a *Foreword* concerning the two plays *The Immortal Hour* and *The House of Usna;* both plays are then reproduced in full. Following Elizabeth Sharp's usual bibliographical note there is a sonnet called *Fiona Macleod* by Alfred Noyes.

Volume 8: *The Laughter of Peterkin* contains a *Prologue. The Laughter of Peterkin* is followed by *The Four White Swans; The Fate of the Sons of Turenn; Darthool and the Sons of Usna* and concludes with *Notes* on the sources used for these retellings of old Celtic tale plus a glossary of the Gaelic names and words contained therein.

William Sharp and Fiona Macleod both contributed essays, poems, criticisms and articles to many of the literary and art journals, anthologies and magazines of the day. Included in these are *The Canterbury Series, Camelot Classics, The Art Journal, The Academy, The Literary World, Literature, The Realm, The Young Folks' Paper, The Glasgow Herald, The Athenaeum, Modern Thought, Harper, The Fortnightly Review, Good Words, New York Independent, Atlantic Monthly, Nineteenth Century, Pall Mall Magazine, Century, Country Life, Theosophical Review, Dome, Contemporary Review* and *The North American Review*.

In the second volume of her two-volume biography of her late husband *William Sharp (Fiona Macleod) A Memoir* (William Heinemann, London, 1912) Elizabeth Sharp gives full details of all of these pieces, many of which were never reprinted anywhere else.

Lightning Source UK Ltd.
Milton Keynes UK
UKHW011138180121
377249UK00001B/103